BLEEDER

Christi J. Whitney

A Threshold Novel: Book One

For Doug –
You know me better than anyone,
and you love me still the same

Also by Christi J. Whitney

The Romany Outcasts Series
Grey
Shadow
Midnight

christijwhitney.com

Cover design: Cassidy Ibarra

"Tis said of love that it sometimes goes, sometimes flies;
runs with one, walks gravely with another; turns a third into ice,
and sets a fourth in a flame: It wounds one, another it kills: Like
lightning it begins and ends in the same moment."

—Miguel De Cervantes

Prologue

Selene couldn't see the light.

The hot, salty breeze caught her hair, whipping strands across her face, stinging her eyes and blocking her vision. She clawed at them angrily while everyone else stared wild-eyed up the path, pointing through the dead trees of the Georgia marsh.

Her cheeks burned and tears threatened. But she wouldn't cry. It was bad enough starting high school as a bottom-dwelling freshman, but doing it as the new kid in a small town was a twisted circle of hell.

"You see it, don't you, Selene?"

Ashlynn Sánchez, dressed too nicely for tromping through a marsh, crossed her arms, waiting for her response. She reeked of money, from her salon hair to her gold-glitter nails.

"Yeah, I see it," Selene replied.

She was a horrible liar.

The sugary aroma of Ashlynn's perfume made Selene want to puke all over those super-stylish sandals, but she mustered a neutral expression. She'd only known Ashlynn for two weeks, but Selene had heard plenty of stories from the other kids, including one about giving some girl a black eye. As Selene stared back at her, she believed it.

"Well, you know what they say about the light, right?"

Selene had lived in St. Mary's for a month, barely enough time to get moved in before school started; definitely not long enough to get familiar with the urban legends about the old coastal town. But she hated admitting she didn't know something. She took a breath, ignoring the stench of dead fish and stagnant water.

"It's ghost story stuff," she replied.

A lanky, red-haired kid with teeth like a groundhog's leaned down and scooped up a dead limb from the ground, swinging it like a baseball bat. "People say it's the ghost of some kid who drowed out there," he said, grinning broadly, "and he's still trying to find his way home."

Ashlynn yanked the limb out of his hands and whacked him across the leg. He yelped, turning a bright shade of pink.

"Shut up, Jamie! Nobody asked you."

The other kids snickered.

Selene didn't have time to feel sorry for him. He slipped to the rear of the group, nursing his pride and his shin at the same time.

"Okay, then what is it?" Selene asked. "I mean, if it's not a ghost."

Ashlynn jabbed the tree limb at her. "It's the spirit of an evil siren who attacked pirate ships and murdered their crews."

"So, the light's a psycho mermaid."

Selene inched backwards as Ashlynn leaned closer.

"The siren got trapped in the marsh centuries ago," Ashlynn continued. "And she waits, looking for victims to feed on. She pulls you into the water, but you don't die. You're cursed. Forced to serve her forever." Ashlynn jutted her pointed chin in the direction of the path. "As long as you can see the light, you're safe. But if you can't, then you're the one she's coming for next."

A smattering of dead leaves—fried by the blistering Southern heat—blew across the sickly, algae-soaked rocks at Selene's feet.

Anything could lurk in the marsh: alligators and water moccasins or even escaped convicts, intent on jumping a bunch of stupid high school kids and holding them for ransom. But she didn't see evidence of weird lights, fairies, or ghosts of any kind.

"There's nothing out there but fish and mud," she shot back.

"Are you calling me a liar?"

Selene felt the others' eager stares, like they were about to watch her walk barefoot over a bed of nails. No one crossed Ashlynn Sánchez. Selene swallowed, wondering how much a black eye would hurt.

But she couldn't back down now.

"Is this seriously what you do with your time? Taking people out here like it's some cheap entertainment?"

Ashlynn ran her fingers through her glossy brown hair, smoothing out the salon-bleached tips. "And you'd know all about cheap, wouldn't you, Little Miss Thrift Store?"

All attention went to her worn jeans and second-hand t-shirt, and Selene's temper flared at the base of her neck as she faced Ashlynn and her sequined tank top and cut-off shorts, with perfect rips and lacy edges—probably from one of those overpriced boutique shops in town.

Although the others weren't dressed as nicely as Ashlynn, it didn't matter. They stood there, giving judgmental looks and whispering to each other—anything to prove they were better than her, the grungy new girl who couldn't see their stupid little light. They belonged here. She didn't.

As she forced back tears, she kicked herself for accepting Ashlynn's text invite in the first place. A few friends would've been a nice refuge to have before the start of school, but she'd rather be alone than hang with a bunch of fake jerk-wads out of some pathetic desperation.

"I'm not going out there."

"I didn't think you had it in you," replied Ashlynn, winking at the others.

"So why don't you go first?" Selene demanded. "If there's really something, then show me."

But Ashlynn didn't take her bait. She only laughed.

"We've all seen it. But if you want to, then you've got to go into the marsh."

As Selene opened her mouth—unsure what would spew out, and too mad to care—thunder boomed overhead, vibrating the ground underneath her feet. The wind swept down the path, coaxing groans and creaks from the hollow trees.

"Too bad," said Ashlynn, glancing up. "You've missed your chance."

"Come on, guys," whined a girl in the back of the group. "I don't want to get wet."

The others agreed as more thunder crackled, and Selene felt the same. Jumping at their invitation had been a dumb idea, yet she'd done it anyway. Her cheeks burned hot again, but as she turned follow the others, Ashlynn grabbed her by the shirt and shoved her backwards. She landed hard in a patch of muddy moss.

Wet ooze seeped through her jeans, sticky and warm against

her thighs.

"Oops," said Ashlynn, sneering over her. "Hope you've got two dollars for a new outfit."

Selene lunged at her, but her shoe caught a root and she toppled forward, sending a fresh gush of sticky, dirty water across her face.

As she wiped mud spatter from her eyes, she glimpsed Ashlynn's perfect hair disappearing behind a hedge of cordgrass.

Picking herself out of the gunk, she ground her hands against her jeans. The thunder was louder now, mixed with flickers of lightning, and the wailing wind carried with it the threat of a summer storm.

Tears escaped the corners of her eyes, and she didn't bother to brush them away. She'd never appreciated having friends in her apartment complex back in Virginia, where at least she'd felt at home. All she had to show for trying here was bruised pride and mud stains that would probably never come out of her clothes.

The hair on her arms prickled, and she shivered despite the thick heat as a chilly sensation swept through her. Why was she so cold? Goosebumps rose on her arms, and she rubbed her hands against her skin.

And then, she saw it.

Something flickered to her right, just off the path. It wasn't lightning. It didn't flash or disappear. Instead, it grew more focused—as though someone were pointing a flashlight. As she watched the white-blue glow, the orb of light seemed to dance.

She stared at it. Her brain screamed at her to run, but she felt glued to the spot, rooted with a sudden realization.

It was real. The light was *real.*

She plunged her hand into her back pocket, grasping for her beat-up phone, all the evidence blinking in front of her. But as she aimed the camera at the orb, her heart sunk at the black screen. The stupid battery was dead. Again.

The light disappeared, then reappeared a few yards away. Adrenaline filled her blood, awakening a new thought. Camera or not, she was going to find the source of the light and show Ashlynn and the rest of them that she was just as good as they were. Then she'd prove the light wasn't some ghost or demon mermaid spirit.

She'd be the only one who knew the truth.

A bubbly excitement rolled through her stomach as she burst

through a wiry strip of undergrowth into a clearing. A carpet of cordgrass, an electric shade of green against the stormy sky, spread before her. The tangy, earthy scent of approaching rain filled her nostrils. And there, just above the blanket of vegetation, hovered the orb of light.

Diving ahead, she pushed her way toward it. Her shoes sank in the slush and muddy water, trapping her feet like giant, sucking hands; stealing her balance, pitching her forward, her knees squishing in the mud. She freed herself, her legs coated in nasty, smelly gunk.

But the orb taunted her like a vindictive mosquito. At times, it seemed close enough to touch; but in a flash, it darted out of reach, yards ahead, flitting over the grass. Gnats buzzed around her. She swatted at them as they invaded her eyes and mouth. Soaked and spattered with grime, she felt mad enough to spit. She wiped a sleeve across her cheek, dabbing her dripping nose. And she froze.

It was right in front of her.

Everything blurred. The pelting rain and ominous thunder faded as her eyes locked on the light hovering barely two feet ahead of her. The depths of it swirled like a cauldron of witch's brew. But it wasn't the orb that scared her.

It was the face looking back at her from within it.

A set of piercing eyes locked with hers. They were the color of caramel apples, smooth but hard. They sat deeply in a face defined by heavy brows, a prominent nose, and a slightly lopsided mouth. Thick, honey-colored hair framed the masculine features.

But was it a boy? A man?

Lightning brought her surroundings into sharp clarity again. She crossed her arms over her body like a shield, but she didn't want to move. The face hadn't moved either. His unfathomable gaze was fixed on her.

Although her heart crashed against her ribs, her curiosity propelled her closer to the piercing caramel eyes in the center of the shimmering light. The air around it flickered and then began to dim. As it faded, so did the mysterious face. A crazy panic went through her body. She stumbled, catching her foot in a deep pool of murky water.

"No!" she shouted. "Wait!"

The orb grew fainter until it vanished completely. Cupping her hand over her eyes, she peered through the curtain of rain. But nothing remained except the raging storm…and a cold, hollow feeling within.

***

Phoebus could see the light.

He'd stood before others just like it—a bluish-white orb, shimmering like a pearl in the midday light. A breeze rustled the trees of the Grove, and their fruit-laden branches creaked in protest. The wind scattered strands of hair across his eyes. He jerked his head to clear them away.

The light remained, emanating like a beacon.

Stepping forward, he flung the fabric of his green cloak behind him and raised his hands toward the light. The metal cuffs at his wrists began to vibrate as a familiar current flowed up his arms. His insides reacted to the surge as well; his entire body hummed with the fiery sensation.

Electricus.

He paused, allowing the energy to scorch through him like a pleasant burn. The back of his neck buzzed, enveloping him with a lightheaded aura—something that felt as natural to him as his own skin.

Reaching out, he traced the pattern of the glowing orb as it hung suspended in midair—its form not solid, yet distinct. Energy crackled as the light pulsed against his fingertips. It left a metallic taste on his tongue, and he savored the flavor, like a spoonful of rich honey.

His fingers stirred the energy, like water on the surface of a lake, as he checked for signs of instabilities or inconsistencies. The *Electricus* radiating from the orb felt…off. A nagging sensation was beginning to nip at the corner of his mind.

"What do you make of it, Fee?"

He ignored the voice behind him, his attention locked on the light, which pulsed like a beating heart. But there was an erratic skip in the rhythm. A slight flaw, easily missed by someone else.

But not him.

Narrowing his eyes to bring the orb into sharper focus, he waited for another glitch. But the pattern remained consistent. As he lowered his hands, the energy dissipated from his skin—a current, slightly disrupted. Nothing else seemed out of the ordinary, but the nagging in his gut remained.

"Well?" said the same voice.

He met eyes with Titus, who was leaning against a tree trunk, with his long tanned arms crossed over his chest and his longer legs crossed at the ankles. Titus was studying him through strands of untamed curls the wind had whipped across his forehead.

Phoebus felt a muscle jerk in his jaw. The light was nothing more than a Rift—a damaged section of the Barrier that protected their homeland. The *Electricus* powering the invisible shield had weakened and needed their attention.

But that wasn't the cause of his uneasiness.

"I'm thinking," Phoebus replied.

He ignored Titus' drawn-out sigh. He wasn't ready to share anything more. Not yet. The glitch could mean many things, and most of them were nothing to worry about.

Most of them.

"It's just a Rift," said another voice from his opposite side. Nyx brushed past them, tossing her dark braid over her shoulder. "No reason to keep thinking. Let's finish this and go home."

Pushing aside her cloak, Nyx withdrew her a gleaming *nadala*—the spear-like tool used to repair the Barrier. Like many Rover weapons, it was made of solid amber—a perfect conduit for *Electricus.*

"Better watch yourself," said Titus. "You don't want to end up like Yenna."

Nyx rounded on him. "You think I'd be so foolish as to sew my own hand into the Barrier, and give myself a trip to the infirmary?"

"I'm only saying—"

Her dark eyes glinted challengingly. "Or are you implying that I have the skills of a novice?"

Titus' hands rose in surrender. "Of course not."

"Good. Now, stand aside and let me work."

As Phoebus watched his Trinemates, he dismissed the wary feeling in his stomach. He was probably overthinking things.

Training the young novices over the last several weeks had mentally drained him—nothing a good night's rest couldn't cure.

"By all means, Nyx, go right ahead," Phoebus said, moving aside with a sweep of his arm. "After all, who am I to argue with a lady?"

She arched her brow. "No one of importance, obviously."

"That hurt."

"No, it didn't," she replied, looking him over. "Your skin's thicker than my boot soles."

Phoebus allowed himself a smile. Nyx always matched his wit—one of the things he liked about her. She moved with a confident stride and paused in front of the light. As she turned the *nadala* in her hands, he nodded his permission. She was well-trained in the process of mending the invisible membrane of the Barrier.

Better than anyone he knew.

A comfortable silence fell between them, resting in the knowledge that, despite the danger, this was standard procedure. They were Rovers. The Barrier was their responsibility.

Titus located Rifts. Nyx sewed them up. And he took care of everything else. Another task to complete. And then, it would be back to the Keep for dinner and a tall mug of Hythelberry cider. His stomach rumbled at the thought.

The spear glowed blue as the amber drew *Electricus* from Nyx's body, like a magnet attracting fragments of metal. She positioned it at the edge of the Rift, as though the light were simply a piece of fabric and not a deadly concentration of energy. As she pierced the shimmering border with the *nadala's* sharp point, the orb shuddered violently, like some living thing.

"In all seriousness, Fee," said Titus, lowering his voice as he glanced around the meadow, "there's something else going on here, isn't there?"

Phoebus kept his face carefully passive.

"What makes you say that?"

"I'm sensing an unusual level of weakness in the Barrier," Titus replied. "I don't know how, but it feels like it's happening on both sides at the same time." He frowned heavily. "So no evading the question this time, Fee. What's going on?"

Inhaling slowly, Phoebus surveyed the Grove. The area was vast, populated with trees in perfect rows. In one direction, they led to the front gates of the city. In the other, they extended to the rolling hills beyond. Bushes, ripe with fruit, hugged the stone paths.

All of it was safely nestled within the confines of the Barrier.

Without that shield, his world was vulnerable.

And it was his duty to make sure that never happened.

Rubbing the metal cuff on his wrist, he felt it vibrating with the orb's energy. The indigo sky flashed with lighting, and his chest rattled with an ominous sound. Thunder. The tops of the trees bent under a sudden gust of air. But this wasn't natural, and the rumbling had nothing to do with the wind.

His skin went cold.

The sensation pierced him, plunging deep into the marrow of his bones—a fierce, erratic concentration of *Electricus* in the air.

The discharge of energy hit him like a shock.

An unnerving awareness seized hold of him, crowding out the chill. He felt as though he were being…watched. Fighting against the electrical charge inside him, he peered into the light. There was someone was on the other side of the Rift.

She was staring straight back at him.

Phoebus was rooted to the spot, unable to look away. He saw fear in the eyes—a girl's eyes, a striking shade of hazel, too wide for her face. Every dark freckle spattering her cheeks, every poufy strand of windswept hair, every drop of rain on her brown skin—he saw the details as sharp as glass. Then a horrible, chilling realization struck him like whip.

She could see *him*.

The atmosphere crackled. Purple storm clouds swirled above him, but he couldn't take his eyes from the girl. The ground vibrated under his feet, and the trees wailed in the wind.

The Rift had to be closed. Now.

"Move faster!" he commanded, hearing the strain in his voice. "Move!"

"What is it?" demanded Titus.

Without question, Nyx jabbed the *nadala* in a blur of electrical stitches, shrinking the opening and closing the light. On the other side of the Rift, the strange girl's movements seemed desperate, almost pleading, as the orb began to fade, putting distance between them. And then he heard a voice—the girl's voice.

"No! Wait!"

The words shook him.

"Nyx, close it now!"

The orb's shape flattened as she drew the final stitch, and with one final buzz of energy, the light was gone.

But this wasn't over. Not for him.

"What happened?" said Nyx. "What did you see?"

Titus and Nyx didn't have his abilities. They couldn't see through the Rifts into the Otherside beyond. That was his burden. The girl's face flashed before him, and he blinked it away.

If he'd acted sooner, he could've avoided this. He could be on his way home, enjoying the end of another day. But he'd just seen a Viewer through the Rift.

And now, he had another job to do.

***

As thunder growled outside her window, Selene shuddered. With each flash of lightning, the mysterious face from the marsh light reappeared before her eyes. She couldn't shake it, like a bad dream that wouldn't go away. Maybe she should have been more scared, but she wasn't. The way he'd looked at her, the startled expression on his face.

It had felt forbidden.

Rubbing her arms against the chill, she surveyed her room, desperate for a distraction. Her gaze wandered to the haphazard arrangement of moving boxes her mom had been hounding her about for the last two weeks. She knelt at the nearest one and peeled away the tape.

Inside the box was a myriad of things she'd collected. Mostly junk. Except for one thing. She retrieved a small, hand-painted box and positioned the keepsake delicately in her arms. It was jewelry box, made by her grandmother, for Selene's eighth birthday; though there wasn't much jewelry inside. While some girls stayed indoors, playing dress-up, she'd been in the yard, climbing trees.

As she reached in, something cold brushed her skin. She held it to the light. It was an old-fashioned bracelet made of silver links, with a metal nameplate. On one side, her name was engraved in flowing script: *Selene Windell.* On the other side was a quote: *Travel not among the stars but through them.*

The bracelet was a gift from her grandmother for her ninth birthday. It had been the only real piece of jewelry she'd owned. At first, she'd worn it proudly; but over the years, she'd grown up, and the nameplate style felt childish. Eventually, she only put it on when she went to the assisted living home. Her mind conjured memories of her grandmother's wrinkled face and twinkling eyes—always eager to listen. Cancer was a selfish monster.

Her heart wrenched as she clasped the bracelet over her wrist.

Lightning crackled over the backyard, illuminating a rotting fence coated in blackberry brambles, a rusty swingset, and a dilapidated shed. It had probably been a nice yard once, before the previous owners moved out and the property sat vacant, but she doubted it would be nice anytime soon.

She missed the green space of their apartment complex. No mess. No responsibility. Living in a confined area—where you invaded each other's personal space every time you opened the front door—made it easy to feel like you were a part of things. But connecting with anyone in this new town seemed impossible. Her mother had been so convinced she'd make friends, but no one seemed to care about her. Ashlynn and her band of fawning puppies were proof of that.

Depositing the box on her nightstand with a heavy thump, she shuffled to her window and reached for the curtain. Then her insides flipped upside down.

The orb of light, alone in the darkness, danced just beyond the fence.

Like it had followed her.

Fear and adrenaline ignited her blood, and she ran—ran through the hallway and out onto the porch, grabbing her raincoat off the wall peg, before the rational side of her brain had time to kick in. She unlatched the hook on the screen door.

As soon as she hit the ground, her feet squished into the sodden grass. The air felt too cool for September, and the wind sent goosebumps up her neck. And the orb remained, as though waiting for her, at the edge of the marsh. She slushed through the yard toward the gate of their white picket fence.

Her nerves reactivated, swirling in the pit of her stomach. It didn't matter that she had no phone or any way to prove she saw the light. She wanted to know for herself. As she paused between the fence and the marsh, she squinted over her shoulder toward the house. It was the moment of truth. Do it, and get it over with.

She planted one foot in the mud and started through the gate.

Something changed in the air.

Her skin tingled.

Something wasn't right.

There was a flash of light, blinding. A deafening crack.

And then, darkness.

***

It was storming on the Otherside.

His leather boots sank in the mud beside the parking lot, and Phoebus slung water droplets from his hood, peering through the stinging rain at the three-story brick building in front of him. Tracking Viewers was a challenge he usually enjoyed, but this particular assignment gave him no pleasure. His neck and shoulders were stiff with nerves, and an uneasy feeling soured his stomach. The sooner he finished, the sooner he'd be home, with dry clothes and a hot meal as his reward.

His task wouldn't take long. One arrow. One shot.

But something wasn't right.

Electricus radiated all around him, like buzzing shockwaves, humming through his wrist cuffs and into his core. Something had happened here, not very long ago: a disruption. A vision crossed his mind—an image in gray-scale, like an afterthought:

Lying in a grassy field was a girl, her body twisted unnaturally—eyes closed tight, mouth gaped wide, brown skin splattered with mud.

The Viewer.

Phoebus faltered, as though he'd been slapped hard across the face. But he couldn't stop to figure out why she was here, in this place. He had to act now. Time moved differently on either side of the Barrier. Hours could be passing in Threshold as seconds passed here.

***

Phoebus hurried down the empty hospital hallway.

Wrinkling his nose against the stench of bleach and antiseptic, he huddled inside the protection of his *mantellum* cloak. He wasn't worried about being seen. *Mantellums* shielded a Rover's presence from most Othersiders. But it did little to shield him from the annoyance of the fluorescent lights.

Sifting through currents of energy, it took only moments to pinpoint the Viewer girl's signature. She was close. He doubled his pace. Although he didn't know why he'd seen the image of her sprawled in the marsh grass, it wasn't a coincidence. The unusual fluctuations in the atmosphere, the Rift, and now, this girl—they seemed somehow connected.

Two shadows appeared around the corner. He glanced at his hands—still visible, like ghosts from an Othersider story—and considered his options. Dulling memories of normal humans wasn't routine. The chances of killing them were high—and he preferred stealth when possible. But he didn't take chances either. He couldn't be seen.

Ducking behind a rolling bed, he hid—just as two nurses rounded the corner, passing casually by, heads bent in conversation. Once they were gone, Phoebus moved toward an intersection of hallways as he resumed his hunt for the girl.

The Viewer's *Electricus* pattern led him to a door labeled "Room 502".

He summoned the *Electricus* within his body to the surface, and the amber resin in his wrist cuffs flared to life, conducting the current, amplifying its power. A Rover with exceptional skill could manipulate that power. And he was one of the best.

As the energy surged over his skin, it felt like a river of needles, sending a painfully pleasant rush through his brain. His body flickered, turning transparent. Lightning flashed, and before he could draw another breath, he reappeared inside in the Viewer's hospital room.

He opened his hand, and the muscles in his fingers tightened as *Electricus* flowed through them. An arrow materialized in his palm. Its fletching, shaft, and arrowhead glowed like a streak of summer lightning.

One arrow. One shot.

The energy would act as poison in her brain, killing her memories of the Rift.

And of him.

He'd done it a hundred times before—one shot, at the base of her neck, and he'd be gone. The arrow would disintegrate on impact, the wound would heal, and the Viewer would spend the rest of her days thinking all mysterious lights were simply gaseous anomalies in the atmosphere.

But burning a hole in an adolescent's memories was tricky. Adult brains adapted easier to the Dulling process, and this young Viewer was still a few years removed from adulthood.

Do your job, his mind commanded.

He slipped behind the folds of the privacy curtain drawn across the entrance and heard the sound of a television and someone clicking through channels. Breathing out slowly—with the same steadying technique he used before shooting an arrow—he peered around the fabric.

No one was in the room, save the girl in the bed.

Although only an hour had passed in Threshold since he'd seen the Viewer's face through the Rift, it was obvious more time had passed on this Side. She was easily in her mid-teens, and her face was shapely, the spattering of freckles against her cheeks less pronounced, and maturity flickered in her hazel eyes.

She looked tired as she monotonously hit the button of the remote, and he watched with a strange fascination. What was so different about this girl that she'd been able to see him through the Rift? What set her apart from the hundreds of Viewers he'd Dulled across the years? His gaze shifted to the medical chart at the foot of her bed.

Lightning strike victim.

The words caused him to jerk. Lighting strike. His lungs pinched behind his ribs. That was the disturbance. This was more than a Viewer catching a glimpse of his world through a weak spot in the Barrier. This girl had broken *through* it.

He pushed the notion fiercely from his head. No, there was no way she could possess that kind of power. If she did, she wouldn't be lying in a hospital bed, wearing a hideous printed gown and sipping orange juice from a paper cup.

He had one duty, and he was going to see it through.

No more hesitation.

As he turned away, he opened his hand. A fresh arrow appeared, weighted in his palm, its amber head gleaming with blue light—the sharp point filled with the promise of the poison that would make the girl forget everything she'd ever witnessed about his world.

His fingers positioned the weapon with a hunter's care. He refused to make the same mistake twice.

He pulled the bowstring to his cheek.

As he stepped around the curtain, the girl's head turned in his direction. A frightened cry escaped her lips. Her eyes darted from the arrow to his body, and then to his face. Her gaze met his.

"Who are you?" she asked.

He took aim.

"No one you'll remember."

PART ONE

"The lofty pine is oftenest shaken by the winds;
High towers fall with a heavier crash;
And the lightning strikes the highest mountain."

—*Horace*

Chapter 1

She planted one foot in the mud and began to spin. One time around…then two…

Thunder boomed.

The air changed.

She jerked to a halt and stared at her arms. The hairs stood on end, like she'd rubbed them with a balloon. Her skin tingled uncomfortably.

Something wasn't right.

There was a flash of light, blinding. A deafening crack. Something fiery exploded through her, stealing her breath. Her body catapulted through the air like a rag doll. Then everything went dark. Her eyes were open, but she couldn't see. She tried to scream, but nothing came out. She couldn't feel her legs or her feet. Her heart ricocheted in her chest like a stray bullet in a metal room.

The world was a vacuum.

Then there were voices. Someone crying. Flashing red lights. Harsh noises that hurt her ears. She tried not to cry, but her cheeks were wet. The sky was blurry. Her lungs were on fire, her throat parched and burning. She was dizzy. Spinning. Someone held her hand. She closed her eyes. The darkness held her tight.

Flashing red lights.

A constant rhythm, beating in her unconscious. Dull and monotonous, it called to her. Telling her something she should have known. Rolling over, she yawned and cracked open her eyes. The blinking of her nightstand clock, its time stuck on 12:00, shocked the sleep from her eyes.

She grappled for her cell phone and stared at the cracked screen. It was black and lifeless.

"You've got to be kidding me!"

She couldn't afford another tardy. Detention cut into her afternoon, and her paycheck.

Untangling her feet from the sheets, Selene stumbled out of bed, grabbing her uniform polo shirt and khakis from the floor, rushing through her routine and beelining for the kitchen. She stuffed textbooks into her messenger bag and fumbled through enough lipstick and mascara to look alive as she eyed the empty coffeepot on the counter.

Her mother looked up from the stove, taking in her appearance. "I was wondering if you were going to get out of bed."

As Selene stuffed her feet into the nearest pair of loafers by the door, she grabbed her bagged lunch from the fridge. "The power went out last night, and my phone's fried. Why didn't you wake me up?"

"I tried. Three times."

"Seriously?"

"Hey, school's your job, *Senior*," her mom replied, emphasizing the grade level like it would magically speed up the process. "You'd think you'd have the hang of it by now and...wait, what do you mean, *fried*? Selene, I can't afford—"

"I know, and I'm sorry." She pulled the charred phone from her pocket and tossed it onto the table. "Must've been a bad power cable or something. Anyway, I've got to go."

Her mom sighed. "Need a ride?"

"Nope, I'm good."

"You sure?"

"Yeah." She gave her mom an obligatory peck on the cheek. "See you later."

Bolting out the door, she jogged to the sidewalk. School was only four-blocks away—one of the perks of living in a small town. After leaving Elm Street and taking a right onto Main, where the homes were larger and pricier near the oceanfront, she entered the historic district and the parking lot of St. Mary's Charter School.

The building looked like a swank prep school from a movie—all stone and ironwork, with massive oak trees lining the property. But inside, it was the same as every other school she'd attended—which meant it was out-of-date, smelled like lingering cafeteria food, and crawled with students who didn't want to be there.

As her feet touched the marble steps, she breathed a sigh of relief.

At least there wasn't a crowd of people to push through. Most kids attended the larger county high school twelve miles away, though having a smaller population did make it harder to blend in.

She reached for the railing when a sharp pain seared through her arm, snatching the air from her lungs. She jerked backwards like she'd touched a scalding pot and clutched her arm to her chest. The pain dissipated into a tingling rush up her arm and through her shoulders. As she rubbed at her wrist, a new, funny prickling on her neck seemed to draw her gaze toward the corner of the building—and her blood clogged with ice.

Someone was watching her from the shadows of the manicured shrubs.

Although she could only see the outline of a face and upper body in dark clothing, it wasn't a student—or anyone else she knew. The unsettling vibe radiating in her direction was beyond creepy. There was no doubt the person's attention was trained on her, with a laser-focused intensity that awakened her adrenaline.

The warning bell clanged from inside the school, echoing through the courtyard, unfreezing her veins. But before she could even take a breath, the person disappeared—and so did the weird sensation along her skin. Shaking out her arm, she glanced up at the antique clock over the entrance. Whoever the creep was, she didn't have time to dwell on it. She had ten minutes to make it before the tardy bell.

She grabbed the handrail and tackled the staircase, two steps at a time. But just as she reached the top, planting her foot on the verge of the step, she miscalculated.

Her foot slipped, sending her sprawling across the grimy marble entryway, knocking her breath from her lungs and catapulting her open bag. Books and papers scattered in all directions.

"And, she's safe!" yelled a kid near the front door, waving his arms like a baseball umpire.

Several students laughed.

And stepped right around her.

No one stopped to help, not that she was expecting it. Senior or not, high school was about survival of the fittest—Darwinism at its social peak. A pimple-faced freshman with a rolling backpack ran over her hand. Selene shook off her throbbing fingers and pushed herself to a kneeling position, her skin running hot and cold.

As she reached for her trampled bag, a biting laugh from above cut through the pain.

"How graceful," said Ashlynn Sánchez. "Do you work at that, or does it just come naturally?"

Her current set of followers giggled like it was Christmas morning.

Selene clutched her bag, throttling the strap between her fingers. Ashlynn flicked her sleek brown hair—filled with so many blonde highlights that it bordered on ridiculous—over her narrow shoulders and blinked with eyes from a makeup video tutorial.

"Like you even know what 'naturally' means," Selene fired back.

Ashlynn picked a piece of lint off her sleeve. She never complied with the school's dress code, and nobody seemed to care. Her skirt was too short, and her shirt wasn't the correct shade of blue—and probably cost more than most of Selene's wardrobe put together. Leaning in, Ashlynn smothered Selene's personal bubble with the smell of blatantly expensive shampoo.

"You only wish you could be me," she pretended to whisper, though loud enough for everyone to hear. "Too bad that will never happen." Her perfectly sculpted eyebrows rose daintily. "Oh, and nice lipstick. It's amazing what you can pull out of those clearance barrels at the dollar store."

Gliding past like she was walking a runway, Ashlynn disappeared inside the front doors with her pathetically slobbering entourage in tow.

Every hot retort on Selene's tongue went cold. Ashlynn just wasn't worth it.

Sighing, she gathered two of her folders from the marbled step. Never being able to get away from the same people was definitely *not* a perk of living in a small town.

"Hey, Selene."

Jamie Monahan swung under the stair rail and knelt next to her.

"Hey," she replied, stuffing the papers in her bag.

He retrieved a multitude of colored notecards—another casualty from her fall. "I'd give your landing a seven," he said, "but the overall performance was definitely a ten."

"You saw that, huh?"

"Saw what?"

He presented the notecards to her in a haphazard pile. Some things about Jamie never changed. While he still sported the same shaggy red hair, peachy-pink complexion, and green eyes, he'd grown a lot over the last two summers, shooting upward and filling out.

"Thanks," she said as Jamie helped her to her feet.

"Sorry you had to deal with that before I got here."

"You mean the steps or Ashlynn?" she replied, shouldering her bag. "Because I was handling both just fine, thank you."

"Yes, you were."

She made a face. "What did you ever see in her, anyway?"

He adjusted the collar of his shirt. "As I've said before, I have no defense for my past mistakes, other than the temporary insanity of a hormonal sophomore."

"But she asked you to homecoming *last* year."

"Okay, call it stupidity, then," he replied. "But it was only because Derek got a stomach bug, and you know she'd never show up without a date, even if said guy was a band-geek gamer-dude with questionable taste in fashion."

"And a charming personality," she added.

"Ouch," he replied, shaking his head. "You know that's code for 'yikes, he's hideous,' right?"

He grinned, and it was like a breath of fresh air from the ocean. She reached up and patted his cheek. His smiles always had a way of warming her from the inside out.

"Not true," she said. "And I must say, for the record, you're the only guy to ever turn Ashlynn down for anything. That's major points, in my book."

"Yeah, you can just mark that down in my extremely long column," he replied.

The sudden dinging of the tardy bell disrupted their conversation.

She rolled her eyes. "Well, crap."

So much for making homeroom. Or avoiding detention.

Why did she always do this to herself? It made her feel slightly better to put the blame on the shrubbery creeper. That's what had started this whole thing. Then that penetrating look from the shadows flashed through her memory again, and her stomach rolled in a queasy way.

"Well, I'll see you after class," she said, pushing the image aside.

As she headed for the Social Studies hall, Jamie fell into step beside her, his fingers tapping casually against his backpack strap as he strolled.

"As long as I'm late too, I guess I'll walk you to homeroom," he said pleasantly.

She looked him over suspiciously. Jamie was meticulously punctual to everything.

"Is this a pity walk?"

"No, it's more of a chance-to-talk-to-my-buddy-Selene walk." He shrugged at her. "Plus, unlike you, I don't already have three tardies to my name."

"Thanks for the reminder."

"Seriously, though," he continued. "I don't like not having classes together this semester. No one appreciates my humorous back-row commentary like you do."

She bumped her shoulder against his. Jamie was always her constant. Without him, she never would've survived St. Mary's. Stopping at her locker, she spun through the combination while he leaned against the wall, brushing a hand through his shock of red hair.

"Well, when you think of something funny during class, shoot me a text," she replied. "Oh wait, never mind. My phone's out of commission."

"Again?"

She snatched her history book. "Yep."

"Didn't you just get a new one?"

"Uh huh."

"Interesting." Jamie leaned in, peering into her eyes. "I'm starting to think you've got mutant powers you're not telling me about."

"Yes, destroying phones ranks high on the superpowers list. I'm sure they'll bring me in the next time there's a crisis." She slammed the door shut. "So, meanwhile, I continue to be the only person in a hundred-mile radius without modern communication."

He nudged her playfully. "Well, things could be worse."

"Oh yeah?" she countered. "How?"

"You could be the only person in a hundred-mile radius without a friend as awesome as me."

She laughed and shoved him into the lockers.

***

After detention, she headed downtown, grateful for some fresh air after a day surrounded by brick and concrete. The breeze rustled the oak and palm trees in the park, waving Spanish moss at her, and the sky was clear, though it was still too hot for the first official day of autumn.

On her left, the coastal waterway spread before her, lined with docks and small boats. On her right, rows of restored historic buildings glinted in the afternoon sun. Downtown was her favorite part, an eclectic combination of new and old things.

As she shifted her bag across her back, the sunlight reflected off her silver bracelet. She never took it off, not even to sleep. But although the sight of it always stirred up comforting memories of her grandmother, she didn't wear it just for sentiment.

It had another function as well.

She adjusted the nameplate, hiding the glaring burn mark on her freckled wrist. She'd worn the jewelry on the night of the lightning strike two years ago, and the surge of electricity through her body and the metal had left a permanent scar, like an unwanted gift, in the shape of the bracelet itself.

She didn't remember much about her accident—mostly what the doctors and her mom had told her—but sometimes she felt a painful buzzing in her skin, followed by a swirl of fractured images of things she couldn't place.

Her mind returned to the stranger watching her outside the school.

And the uncanny prickling she'd felt.

She glanced up, almost expecting to see the same dark figure lurking between the buildings that lined the street. But the sunlight kept any shadows at bay, and no one was there.

Briskly rubbing her arms to ease the sensation, she jogged across the painted intersection to the corner of Main. A building with a green storefront and a wooden sign that read *Far and Away: Gifts and Books* awaited her on the other side of the street. As she pushed open the door, a bell jingled, signaling Miss Claire's appearance, with her blonde hair piled atop her head.

"Hello, Selene. You're late today."

"Detention," she replied, offering an apologetic smile.

"Ah ha," said Miss Claire, peering over her red-rimmed glasses. "Well, there's a shipment in the back that needs to be inventoried and stocked. I've got to run out for a bit."

"No problem."

Slipping behind the counter, Selene deposited her things as silence echoed through the store. That was what she liked most about working in the little boutique. Afternoons were never busy, giving her plenty of time to finish her homework in peace.

After she tended to the shipment, of course.

Pushing away from old manual register, she headed to the back room to retrieve a freshly delivered box. Just as she returned, the bell jingled, and she caught sight of red hair bobbing like a cork behind one of the shelves. She dumped the box onto the counter.

"Excuse me," she said, using an overly serious voice. "You've got the wrong store. *Hot Dog Haven* is one street over."

Jamie popped around the corner shelf. "What's up?"

"Work, obviously."

"Is that what you call this?"

"What are you doing here?" she asked, rolling her eyes.

He shrugged. "I'm bored."

"Uh huh," she replied, slicing open the packing tape with a pair of scissors. The smell of newly printed books filtered through the cardboard flaps. "I thought you and Mudge were going to play *Rebels of Moron* today."

"It's *Rebels of* Maldron," said Jamie, looking offended. "And yes, we were. But my laptop has been crapping out since lunch."

"Whoops."

"How do you *do* that?" he said, brows raised. "I mean, you only used it for two minutes."

"Mutant power strikes again?"

"Maybe you could start wearing gloves. You know, like Rogue from the *X-Men*."

"No, thank you," she replied. "I refuse to level-up any more on the freak register." She focused on the collection of novels in the box. "But I'm really sorry about your computer. I just needed to double-check my work schedule. I didn't think a few clicks would hurt anything."

Hopping precariously onto the counter, Jamie examined a container of rock candy. "Eh, no biggie. Mudge was getting on my nerves today, anyway." He unscrewed the lid. "So I thought I'd come keep you company instead." Pulling out a piece of the wrapped candy, he scrutinized it with squinted eyes. "Does anybody actually *buy* these?"

"Not really." She plucked it from his fingers, relieved to focus on something other than her stupid electronics curse. "But trust me, Miss Claire would know if one was missing."

Jamie went slack-jawed and pressed a hand to his chest. "You don't think I would actually *steal* something, do you? I mean, how long have we known each other?"

She laughed. "Too long."

As she reached into the box, she found several thin paperback books. Most were history-related, written by local authors. But as she dumped them on the counter, one caught her attention. It was entitled *Georgia Legends*, and the cover was a blown-up photograph—a black-and-white image of an old country road in the woods, taken at night. The road was deserted, save for an object hovering in midair: an orb of white light, the edges blurred and fuzzy.

Her arms prickled.

"Found something interesting?" asked Jamie, leaning over the counter to catch a glimpse.

"I've seen this before," she replied.

"This?" He took the book and examined it. "You've seen it in the store?"

"No, not the book. The picture on the cover. I've seen it somewhere else." Her face felt flushed. "Or maybe not. The picture just looked familiar. Maybe I read the book or something, you know... before."

Flipping through the pages, Jamie frowned in contemplation. "Well, it looks like your typical old ghost story book, but the picture is definitely of a marsh light. We used to go out there and search for them sometimes, remember?"

As if catching himself too late, Jamie clamped his mouth shut.

It felt hard for her to swallow. "You know I don't remember a lot of stuff from before my accident."

"Yeah, I know—"

"And lots of what I do is all jumbled up."

"I didn't mean—"

"And I don't go to the marsh, Jamie. So no, I don't remember the light thing."

This time, he didn't try to interject. He handed the book over, and they sat in silence. She mentally kicked herself. Her problems weren't Jamie's fault. Memory loss was a common side effect in lightning strike victims. Sometimes people regained their memories, and sometimes they didn't.

"Jamie," she began softly. "I'm sorry. I didn't mean to go off like that. I just...you know how I feel about the marsh."

He glanced at her through his baby-fine eyelashes, his expression serious. "Look, I know it's a touchy subject for you," he replied. "I wasn't thinking when I said that."

"It's no big deal."

Guilt was plainly etched behind his eyes. "You sure you're okay?"

"Yeah." She discarded the book and put on one of her better smiles, one she knew would cut through his guilt. "I'm fine. Promise. And listen, I hate to kick you out, but I've really got a lot of work to do here today before Miss Claire returns. Maybe I can catch up with you later?"

"Hey, no problem," he replied. "I should stop procrastinating on my English paper anyway." He leapt off the counter with the resilience of a scolded and forgiven puppy. "You'll be online tonight?"

The tension between them disappeared, like a breeze shifting over the ocean.

"Definitely."

"Don't work too hard." He saluted playfully.

As Selene watched his lean form cross the street, the book weighed heavy in her hand. The light stared hauntingly back at her from the cover, sending a sharp, buzzing sensation up her neck and into her scalp.

"I've seen you before." The tips of her fingers brushed over the photograph. "But where?"

The light was silent.

Chapter 2

The Assembly bells were ringing.

Phoebus sprinted down the corridor as light flashed through the windows, brightening the rafters and creating shadows on the walls. But unlike storms on the Otherside, there was no wet, torrential downpour. Storms in Threshold were an impressive show of *Electricus*, nothing more.

Until now.

Water drummed strangely against the roof, spurred on by the increasing gusts of wind.

He hesitated outside the massive double doors. There had been no time to change into formal Assembly attire. His leather breeches and boots were stained with Othersider marsh, and his tunic sleeves were damp. But the low, dull clangs announced the start of the meeting, and his presence was mandatory.

The Assembly Chamber was a circular room, supported by columns and carved totem poles. Stained glass windows stretched to the domed ceiling, and their glass reflected the hearth fires, spattering a myriad of colors across the marbled floor.

Men and women filed into the benches, dressed in ornamental robes. On the right were the Regents, wearing floor-length *mantellums* of silver-gray. On the left, in midnight blue, were the Preceptors. At the far end of the room, nine chairs were arranged on a single platform, and on those chairs sat the Elders of Threshold in their elaborate russet-colored apparel, like royalty among a court of nobles.

Along the back wall, Rovers stood in a perfect line. Several tugged at their formal satin tabards and velvet vests with expressions that mirrored Phoebus' unease. He adjusted the cuffs of his tunic over his wristbands. He'd rather be outside, patrolling Threshold, keeping the Barrier intact and their people safe.

The Assembly was a place of tradition, not of action.

As the last of the milling crowd found their places, Phoebus slipped in next to Titus and Nyx, who'd saved him a vacant spot against the wall.

Titus eyed his muddy clothes. "What took you so long?"

Uncurling his fist, Phoebus adjusted his longbow. The weapon was something he could understand, unlike his careening thoughts and feelings. The girl's face crossed his vision—the way she'd looked at him, and the strange, spiking current he'd felt radiating from her was far more than unusual.

It was dangerous.

"Had to track down a Viewer," he said.

"But, I wasn't aware you were going—"

"There was no time."

Titus cut him a sharp look. "Fee, what aren't you telling me?"

"Nothing," he replied.

The final bell sounded throughout the chamber.

Every movement stilled as Elder Grimm rose from his chair, his russet-colored robes adorned with amber designs billowing around him. Although he appeared a man in the later prime of life, no one knew the Elder's true age. He'd looked the same as far back as Phoebus could remember. He stroked his finely shaped goatee, seeming to somehow catch each person's eyes before he spoke.

"Greetings to the Assembly," Grimm called out. All hands went to hearts. "As you are aware, we've been experiencing increased activity within our atmosphere over the last few hours. While fluctuations are not uncommon, these recent storms have raised some concern."

Across the chamber, heads dipped together in discussion.

Phoebus shifted on his feet, feeling restless. This was an issue between the Regents and Elders, one that delved into politics he didn't have the energy to endure. With the raging storm going on, the Rovers would be better off outside than stuck in this stuffy Assembly.

"Your attention, if I may," said Elder Grimm, his deep voice restoring order. "Before we proceed, I would like to ask if the Regents have any information that would enlighten us."

A milky-faced man with a slack jaw and thinning hair struggled to his feet: Regent Jareth, one of the most respected scholars in Threshold. A spark of curiosity flickered in Phoebus' chest.

"With respect, Elder Grimm," puffed Regent Jareth, as though speaking were an exertion. "A few storms escaped our notice, though I don't believe they pose a threat to the Barrier." His lips pursed together, causing his pasty cheeks to expand. "However, it would be helpful to know if anyone witnessed other unusual events today. Such information would greatly aid our research."

"I couldn't agree more," said Grimm.

Those dressed in green straightened attentively, and Phoebus felt a sinking feeling as Grimm's gaze moved over the Rovers, and then rested on him.

"There was an unusual signature of *Electricus* in the Grove today," said the Elder, his voice carrying throughout the room. "Phoebus, your Trine was patrolling that sector. Please, step forward and tell us what you witnessed."

Moving out of duty rather than desire, Phoebus approached the center of the marbled floor. His Trinemates followed, compelled by the same force of duty.

"Greetings to the Assembly," Phoebus said, placing his hand over his heart. "My Trine did locate a Rift earlier today, inside the Grove. As we set forth to mend it, there was an intense surge in power, as well as a weakness in the Barrier—a combination we'd never experienced."

A woman rose from the platform. Phoebus bowed his head. The lady was Elder Ania, and Grimm's sister. She was at least as old as brother, but her looks also had a quality that made one unsure of her age. Copper hair spilled down her back, and her smile sparked like fire.

"Did you mend the Rift?" she asked, her authoritative voice that of one accustomed to being heard.

"Yes, Elder Ania."

She fixed her look on Phoebus. "And this concludes your report?"

He was ready to move on, and to forget he'd ever seen the girl.

"It does," he replied.

Elder Ania's soft blue eyes shifted to his companions. "And

does your Trine have anything to add?"

"They may speak, if they wish."

He stepped aside, and Nyx took his place, her eyes respectfully downcast.

"No, Elder," she said. "I have nothing to add."

"Very well. And you, Titus?"

For the first time, Phoebus felt a twinge of uncertainty. It was only right that Titus should say something. Phoebus hadn't followed protocol, and even now, he was omitting his actions from his report. Withholding information from the Assembly was a serious crime, unbefitting the leader of a Trine.

Duty ranked above all relationships—friendship or otherwise.

It was their way.

Clenching his fist inside his cloak, Phoebus braced himself.

"I have nothing to add," said Titus.

Phoebus' muscles went lax, nearly tipping his balance, and he worked to maintain his formal posture as he stared into the grandstand. He took a quick breath and his poise returned.

"Is there anything else you require of us, Elders?" he asked.

Grimm descended the stairs. Phoebus didn't blink or break his gaze. The Elder couldn't read minds—no one had that ability—but sometimes, it seemed like Grimm came close.

The Elder looked him over. "Well then, if that concludes your—"

A flash streaked across the ceiling, and a violent tremor rocked the chamber's foundation. Phoebus lost his footing, hitting hard on his hands and knees, as benches overturned and artwork dislodged from the walls. Glass shattered. The floor cracked. He scrambled to his feet, shielding his eyes against the blast as another convulsion shook the room.

A stone column yanked free and toppled toward them. He dove for the Elder, bowling him out of the way as the pillar crashed to the floor. Phoebus shielded him from debris as it littered the chamber. Thunder rumbled through the room like an aftershock.

And then, everything went still.

After a few uncertain moments, people began to regain their composure. Some Elders huddled in conference, while Rovers moved among the Assembly, checking the injured.

As he helped Grimm to his feet, Phoebus dusted debris from his own cloak and surveyed the damage around him. The chamber was in shambles. A hand gripped his shoulder. Titus stood behind him, his eyes milky white and eerily out of focus. Phoebus knew the look.

"Titus, what do you sense?" he demanded.

"The Grove." His voice sounded strange and far away. "A Rift has opened in the Grove."

"Another one?"

Titus's eyes refocused. "No, Fee. It's the same one."

"That's impossible," he shot back.

"You must close it," coughed Grimm, clutching his arm. "Immediately."

Without hesitation, Phoebus bowed and spun on his heel, Titus beside him. Nyx hurried to catch up.

They tore through the corridors of the Hall and burst through the massive doors into the courtyard. It was evening, which meant shops were closed and the population of Threshold had retired to their homes, leaving the roads deserted.

As they passed through the gates, Phoebus allowed Titus to take the lead. The milky white of his Trinemate's eyes reflected the lamplights as he navigated the trio through the Grove.

Although Phoebus had been expecting it, his heart clenched as they found the orb of light—exactly as Titus had said—in the spot where it had been before. Beside him, Nyx was already pulling her *nadala* from her satchel. Dread curdled inside him as he peered into the light.

Would the Viewer be on the other side?

Before he could blink, the orb began to fade under the speed of Nyx's amber needle.

"No, wait!" he ordered. "I haven't told you—"

"You heard Elder Grimm," said Titus. "We have to close it."

What Phoebus could see of the Rift was gone.

"Then finish the job," he barked.

Chapter 3

"So, are you going on the camping trip next weekend?"

Selene didn't look up from her book. "Nope."

"Why not?"

"Cause everyone else is going."

The bench quivered as Jamie plopped beside her. "All the more reason to go, then. We could, I don't know, fling mud at them or something. Like baboons."

She grimaced at the page. "Baboons fling mud?"

"Well, yeah," said Jamie. He kicked at the gravel with his shoe. "But I think it's like a mating ritual or something. I don't remember."

"How romantic."

"Okay, how about this," he continued, undeterred. "Big open spaces and no technology to fry."

"I don't fry *everything*."

Although no one else directly connected her to technology problems when she was around, her reputation as the weird lightning strike survivor spoke volumes. She knew people thought it. The idea of being away from electronics for a little while was tempting.

She shot him a sideways glance. Jamie was grinning, making the freckles on his pink cheeks dance. At moments like this, he reminded her of an impish kid.

"I'll think about it," she replied.

He licked his thumb and held it out. "Swear?"

Sometimes Jamie also *acted* like a kid, too. But that was the best thing about him. He never pretended to be something he wasn't.

She licked her thumb and pressed it against his, like they'd jokingly done since freshman year. "Swear."

Leaning against the bench, she enjoyed the warmth of the metal as it seeped into shoulders. At least school allowed outdoor lunches.

The sapphire sky and cool breeze held the promise of autumn, and she turned her face to the sun, her eyes drifting closed.

"Whatcha reading?"

Without looking, she tucked her scrap paper bookmark into place before passing over the book. "I borrowed it from the store."

"Hey, didn't this book come in with that shipment? The one you were looking at?"

"Yup."

She heard him thumbing through the pages. "So, what's with the sudden interest?" he said. "You've lived here long enough to know pretty much every urban story we've got in this town."

"I know." She'd been sure that something in the book would jog her memory, but nothing had surfaced so far. She opened her eyes. "Okay, so I have a question."

Jamie kept reading. "I'm confident I have an answer."

She hated dwelling on her fractured memories, but she hadn't been able to shake one particular moment from the marsh since she'd seen the book cover. It hovered on the edges of her consciousness, taunting her.

"Remember that time, not long after I'd moved here, when Ashlynn took us out to the marsh?"

Jamie's gaze roamed her face, as though testing the waters. "Yeah?"

"I know what I said yesterday, about not wanting to talk about things. But I need to know. Because the truth is, I actually *do* remember some things about that day. Like, there was a bad storm brewing over the ocean, and Ashlynn hit you with a tree branch."

"Oh, yeah. I probably still have a bruise."

"I don't get it," she continued. "I mean, it's all part of the same memory, but there are chunks of it missing, and other things that are cloudy, like a dirty window."

Jamie nodded tentatively. And she couldn't blame him. She'd never said anything like this to him before. They hadn't been friends when it happened, anyway. He'd been just an acquaintance, someone she only knew because of Ashlynn.

"So, did we see a marsh light?" she asked.

There was a silence she hadn't expected.

Jamie shut the book, and his face colored up to the roots of his hair. "Well, we *pretended* to."

Her stomach twitched. "What do you mean?"

"It was Ashlynn's idea to mess with you," he replied. "Her own little hazing ceremony. She really hated you when you didn't go through with it."

She studied Ashlynn and her crew as they camped out in their usual spot under the front awning, flirting with the guys from the soccer team. "Well, it's good to know her feelings haven't changed."

"That's not true," said Jamie. "I'd say they've cooled to a mild disgust."

"There wasn't anything out there?" she replied, foregoing any therapeutic Ashlynn-bashing. "I mean, it was just a stupid prank?"

"As far as she was concerned, yeah. I just remember we left before the storm hit."

Disappointment pressed down on her. It wasn't the answer she wanted.

"So why do I keep feeling like I saw something that day?"

Jamie shrugged. "Maybe you did. Lots of people say they have. You know this town: it's full of supernatural stories. I even spent the night in the cemetery once, waiting for old Captain Brecker's ghost." He scrunched up his face. "Got the flu instead."

Looking for a ghost.

Something flickered in her brain. Then it was gone again.

"Hey, you okay?" Jamie blinked at her. "You look like *you're* the one who saw the ghost."

There was concern in his expression, the kind that made her feel comfortably warm. She reached out and tweaked a lock of his fiery strands. Jamie's hair had always been what he'd called "circus clown orange," and it hadn't changed much. But his other features had matured, tempering it out. The color suited him.

"I'm fine," she said, tugging playfully on his hair once more before letting it go. "I just wish I didn't have these gaps in my head. It sucks that I can remember some stuff so vividly, and other things are just black holes. I know the memories are there, but I just can't pick them out."

Jamie gave her hair a return tug. "Hey, any gaps you want filled regarding our golden Disney Channel years, you can ask me. I know it's not the same as actually remembering, but I'm a really good storyteller."

"A good storyteller, or a good liar?"

"Same thing," he replied. The bell rang, harsh and mocking, and he uncurled himself from the bench. "See you after school?"

She made a face. "Tutoring."

"Ouch."

"Tell me about it," she sighed as they left the freedom of the great outdoors. "But I'll call you later."

"Okay." He wrapped his arm around her shoulders, squeezing gently. "And don't forget about the camping trip."

He held up his thumb and wiggled it. She waved and shook her head as Jamie disappeared around the corner.

***

After struggling through an hour of tutoring, she was free to head to work. Miss Claire usually forgave her occasional tardiness due to school, but this was the second time in a week.

"If you'd apply yourself in class," she'd say, "there'd be no need for extra help."

Another joyous, long-term consequence of the lightning strike.

Some things didn't make it into her long-term memory, no matter how hard she studied. Maybe it would get better, maybe it wouldn't. But one thing that soured her stomach was being looked at like some kind of victim, someone who used her accident as an excuse to slack off. So she kept her mouth shut around people like Miss Claire.

Which wasn't easy.

As she hurried across the intersection of Elm and Main, her mood deteriorated into the realm of foul and irritable. She hoped the shop owner had errands to run. A few hours of quiet was what she needed. She studied the refurbished sidewalk as she walked, not paying much attention.

Until a shop door nearly smacked her in the face.

Selene jumped out of the way just in time. It hit the side of the building with a bang, rattling the glass in the windows. She pressed against the brick wall as two people shot through the door.

They were men, both wearing long leather jackets and dark

clothes. But they didn't look like any of the local bikers she normally saw riding around St. Mary's, and they didn't have any biker gear. Each wore a hat with a wide brim and dark sunglasses.

Then, just as the first man brushed by, she felt a sharp shock, like a build-up of static electricity, and she gasped. It was the same person from the school grounds. The man jerked to a halt and turned, his head dipping low. He peered over the top of his glasses.

His eyes were the bluest blue she'd ever seen, as if electricity lit the irises from behind. Veins streaked across his face and neck, surrounding his lips—lips tinted blue, as though his body were deprived of oxygen. Before she could even think to move, both strangers hurried down the sidewalk, their jackets flapping in the breeze. In a matter of moments, they were gone.

Trembling, Selene fell back against the building, her body tingling all over. Her blood burned inside her, but her fingers and toes were numb. She gasped for breath, shivering and terrified.

It was like being struck by lightning.

Again.

Chapter 4

"By the Grove, Fee!" hissed Nyx. "Shifting across the Barrier without permission is forbidden!"

Phoebus propped himself on his elbows in the soft grass and gazed across the fields beyond the Grove, which were coated in an early morning glow. The *Electricus* storms had ceased, giving way to a beautiful day. The trees smelled of spring, and the sky was a rich violet once again, touched with shades of mauve. Although there was neither sun nor moon in Threshold, or even stars, the brightness indicated the times of night and day.

Everything was back to normal.

"Thank you for the reminder," he replied.

"Well, someone needs to," Nyx huffed sharply. "The Elders could banish you for a stunt like that."

Leaning back in the grass, he turned his face to the sky, but the warmth-giving light couldn't penetrate the cold wariness gnawing at his insides. He'd erased the girl's memories, and with that, any chance she'd catch a glimpse of his world again. But despite the confidence he felt in completing his task, he was growing more certain by the minute that the girl was connected to what was happening.

A heavy thought tugged at his loyalties: He should tell Grimm about the Viewer.

He smiled lazily anyway. "I wasn't acting without permission. Taking care of Viewers is my job."

"There was a Viewer?" asked Nyx.

The girl's face permeated his vision. He'd thought that erasing the Viewer's memories would put his mind at ease, but it hadn't. Because the fact remained, the Viewer *had* seen him—not just in the hospital room, but here, in the Grove itself: *through* the Rift, straight into his world. He hadn't imagined it, any more than he'd imagined the *Electricus* surging through her.

He felt his Trinemates' critical stares, waiting for something he couldn't provide: The truth. But the pursuit of knowledge often came with consequences, and he wouldn't drag them down this path with him. Some things were worse than banishment.

"I Dulled her memories. End of discussion."

"No, it's more than that," said Titus. He plopped beside Phoebus in the grass. "Otherwise you wouldn't have lied to me about it at the Assembly, and you wouldn't have left the Viewer out of your report. I've known you too long, Fee. I can tell when something's eating at you."

"You're correct. It's a prying Trinemate that I'm finding quite annoying at the moment."

"See, that's exactly what I'm talking about. Every time you deal with Othersider situations, you get this same attitude."

"And what attitude would that be?"

"It's your trademark deflection when something major's going on inside your head," Titus replied. "Not to mention the fact that you look terrible."

Phoebus smoothed down the front of his fresh tunic. "You're just jealous because the uniform has always looked better on me."

"And you've just proven my point."

He felt a sudden heavy weariness steal his retort. "It doesn't matter," he said. "What's important is that we mended the Rift. Everything's settled."

Titus tilted his head. "Then why are you acting so *un*settled?"

The sound of footsteps on the pebbled path saved him from a reply. A lone figure approached, wrapped in midnight blue attire. The hood was drawn up, despite the warmth of the day. Although tight sleeves, leather gloves, and a loosely belted robe covered every inch of the approaching figure's skin, Phoebus was more than familiar with the commanding stride. All Rover novices and apprentices lived in the Preceptory, learning under the watchful eyes of their Preceptors.

And all Preceptors answered to *her*.

She halted in front of the trio, giving them a thorough looking-over. Or, at least, that was what she appeared to be doing. All the details Phoebus could ascertain were a shadowed outline and the unnerving glint of piercing, electric blue eyes.

"Preceptor Moth," said Phoebus, dipping his head.

"Rovers," she replied in low, smooth voice, laced with a touch of disdain that Phoebus recognized keenly. "Elder Grimm wishes to see you in his chambers."

Showing no inclination of waiting for a response, or even caring for one, the Preceptor walked back the way she had come. They waited until she had rounded a thick hedge of shrubbery—putting a fair amount of distance between them before following.

"This must be serious," observed Titus as they made their way to the Keep. "When has Grimm ever sent Preceptor Moth to fetch anyone, anywhere? I didn't think she did that sort of thing."

"I don't even remember seeing Moth outside," said Nyx.

As the Preceptor glided ahead, her long *mantellum* rippling over the cobblestones, Phoebus remembered his training days. He'd worked with Moth in the courtyard as he honed his *Electricus* abilities—which was technically outside. But Nyx was mostly right: he seldom recalled the Preceptor leaving the walls of the Keep.

Passing through the gates, they entered the bustling center of the Keep. All inhabitants of Threshold lived within the boundaries provided by its lofty walls and spired towers, which resembled many of the great ancient cities of Othersider history: blending eras and cultures into one.

Wood and stone structures loomed over busy streets, which wound through a multitude of districts, each with their own homes, markets, and shops. At the center stood the Hall, the palatial mansion where the Assembly met and where the Elders and Regents resided.

The citizens seemed occupied with normal activities—hurrying on business and errands—but he noted more dark green uniforms in the streets, doing sweeps of the Barrier. The hours after a fluctuation were always tense. It was the only time Thresholders felt vulnerable. And after what had happened in the Assembly Chamber, nerves were on edge.

He gave a salute to the two Rovers at the gates of the Hall. Grimm's quarters were located in the south wing of the mansion, and Phoebus knew the way by heart. He let his fingers roam the paneled walls as he walked, his mind wandering through memory. He'd grown up here. That is, if one could call it "growing up." Rovers didn't really have childhoods.

Moth paused at one door and stepped aside.

Phoebus rapped his knuckles on the wood.

As the door opened, he found himself staring into Elder Ania's soft blue eyes. Her countenance was still as tense as it had been in the Assembly Chamber.

"Greetings, Phoebus."

"Elder Ania." His hand moved to his heart. "Are we interrupting?"

"Of course not," she replied, smiling. "I was just leaving."

She moved from the doorway, greeting Nyx and Titus, and then she noticed Preceptor Moth. Although the Elder's expression didn't change, her smile stretched into a firm line.

"Elder Ania," said Moth, her voice reminding Phoebus of cracked glass.

"Preceptor Moth. It is good to see you again."

The Elder's words fell like glass against the stone floor, and Phoebus felt the air thicken around them. Ania dipped her head once more to the group, then gathered her russet gown and exited down the corridor.

Phoebus entered Elder Grimm's quarters. Titus and Nyx trailed behind him, keeping a more respectful distance. Their relationship with Grimm wasn't as comfortable as his.

The Elder was sitting in his favorite leather chair near an enormous hearth. A glass of wine dangled from his fingers. He was no longer wearing his ceremonial robes, but he had changed into a tailored frockcoat and cravat. Phoebus almost smiled. The Elders were fond of modeling their clothes after various time periods from the Otherside, and Grimm had a fondness for the Regency period.

"Please, do take a seat," he said, gesturing to a long wooden table.

The table was loaded with books, scrolls, and maps of all types. The Elders kept close tabs on the Otherside with such devices—along with their collection of amber mirrors, which allowed them to see through the Barrier to varying degrees.

Phoebus shrugged off his quiver and bow, setting them atop a sprawling map of ancient Gaul. Nyx held her satchel in her lap, as though unwilling to risk disturbing the chaos, while Titus arranged his long legs underneath the table.

"Thank you for meeting with me here," said Grimm as he strolled to the table. The Elder stroked his goatee. "I trust you had no difficulty mending the Rift?"

"None at all," Phoebus replied.

"Good, good," said Grimm, almost to himself. "And you're certain this weakness in the Barrier is the same one that you repaired earlier today?"

"Yes, it was."

"I was afraid of such," the Elder replied. The lines in his face deepened, aging his appearance. "This Rift is evidence of a larger problem, but we will tackle that matter in a moment. First, I would like to discuss what happened in the Assembly Chamber."

Phoebus nodded. "The lighting strike."

Grimm's brows rose. "An interesting description, Phoebus. But I'm afraid it was something more serious than even that. The Elders believe it was an attack."

"An attack," he repeated, keeping his tone neutral.

"Yes." The Elder's eyes seemed distant as he maneuvered around the table, as though he were collecting his thoughts from far away. "You see, a few months ago, we lost contact with the Mocama Coil Outpost."

"Lost contact? How?"

"I suppose I should start further back," said Grimm pointedly at Titus and Nyx, "for those not as familiar with these matters. As you know, Coils are areas of powerful electromagnetic fields. They are found in every known dimension, including the Otherside. They once functioned as gateways, allowing travel through the Barrier. But they were sealed after the Rebellion for the safety of the Otherside."

"Sealed," Phoebus interjected, "but not destroyed."

"No," said the Elder. "The fields are too strong to be eradicated. So the Elders created Outposts at every Coil, and manned them with a contingent of Rovers to protect them."

"Manned by Rogues, you mean," Phoebus said tightly.

Working in an Outpost was a task reserved for apprentices or by those serving penance—such as Rogues. Occasionally, some volunteered for service, but Phoebus couldn't imagine willingly exchanging his homeland to live in such a flawed world as the Otherside—adopting the mannerisms of another dimension and running the risk of permanently losing his home in Threshold.

"Where is this Mocama Coil, Elder Grimm?" questioned Titus. "I apologize for my ignorance, but I've never heard of it before."

"Nor would you have," said Grimm. "Rovers are not privy to such information, as your duties mainly pertain to the Barrier. Certain Trine leaders being the exception, of course." The Elder indicated Phoebus with a nod, and then his gaze roamed over the parchments. "The Mocama Coil is quite old, and very small. Only a single Trine is assigned to the Outpost." The Elder rotated the map, then shoved it across the table. "It's located here."

Leaning forward, Phoebus focused on the parchment. It was a drawing of the southern portion of the Otherside country known as the United States. Grimm's knotted finger slid down the eastern coast to a point on the map. Phoebus jerked involuntarily.

Grimm glanced up. "Do you know this place?"

"The Rift opened into this Otherside location," he replied quickly. He pointed to a stretch of marshland. "Somewhere in this vicinity."

"Ah yes. Wetlands are notorious for *Electricus* fluctuations," said Grimm. "We've seen them in Europe and Asia as well. With such strong currents in a place such as this, Viewers would be quite common."

Phoebus studied the area—the same marsh he'd plodded through on his way to the Viewer's home. Warning needles jabbed his spine. These were pieces of the same puzzle, surely, but he didn't know the picture. The connection seemed too much for coincidence. And if that were the case, had Dulling her been enough?

"What does this Outpost have to do with the incident in the Assembly?" he asked instead.

Grimm straightened his wiry form. "Outposts not only protect the Coils, but they also monitor unauthorized activity from other dimensions—including creatures that would seek to do harm."

A chill prickled Phoebus' scalp like the atmospheric tension before a storm. He exchanged a sideways glance with his Trinemates, but it was Nyx who voiced their shared question.

"Do you mean Leeches?" she asked.

"I do," replied the Elder.

A vile taste filled Phoebus' mouth, and he resisted the urge to spit. Leeches had once been inhabitants of Threshold, exiled for treachery—an act that had caused a bitter war: the Rebellion. Eventually, the traitors were driven from Threshold and banished, where they continued to live a twisted existence that was only spoken of in hushed tales around Rover campfires. They were found in places where the *Electricus* was strong. They fed off the energy like starving dogs, unable to live without it.

"Not that I'd ever stoop so low as to become a Rogue," said Phoebus, not bothering to contain the sneer in his voice, "but I do see the appeal of being assigned to an Outpost. Charring a few Leech hides would certainly put me in a pleasant mood."

"I'm quite sure that it would," said a voice from the corner.

Everyone turned.

Preceptor Moth was seated in a tall-backed chair to the right of the fireplace. Phoebus hadn't realized she'd entered the chamber. He was either more distracted than he wanted to admit, or Moth was stealthier than he remembered. From her shadowy corner, she stared unblinkingly, and her eerie eyes pinned him like darts.

"All of this," said Grimm, commanding attention, "brings us back to the Mocama Coil Outpost."

The Preceptor leaned back in her chair, disappearing into the shadows once more.

"Leeches usually keep to themselves," continued Grimm. "However, they'd like nothing more than to find a way back through the Barrier, which would endanger both worlds. The Elders believe the incident in the Assembly was an attempt to breech the Barrier and gain access to Threshold. And it may have originated with this Coil. But since we've lost communication with the Outpost, we have no way of knowing."

Phoebus rose to his feet. Nyx and Titus did the same.

"If you have a task for us, Elder Grimm," he said, "my Trine is ready."

The Elder looked down the length of his thin nose. "You must travel to the Mocama Outpost."

Taking a breath to buy some time, Phoebus pondered the order. Checking on the Outpost wouldn't be that bad—a quick assignment, even if he didn't care for Rogues. But it would also provide him the opportunity to check on the girl without raising suspicions. He prayed that he was wrong about her, but his mind wouldn't rest until he knew for certain.

"Consider it done," he replied. "If you'll excuse us, we shall go and—"

"Wait," said Grimm. "I haven't finished. This will not be a quick assignment, such as repairing a Rift or Dulling a Viewer. This task will require more time."

"Time," repeated Phoebus.

His stomach cramped, like he'd eaten a bad piece of meat.

"Yes. You must Merge."

Phoebus felt his lip curl into a grimace. He hated Merging. It was one thing to cross through the Barrier to Dull the occasional Viewer. As long as there was no extended interaction with Othersiders, the Rovers could pass seamlessly back into Threshold, experiencing only a minor time difference between the two worlds.

But Merging meant that a Rover lost his transient status—his ability to Shift across the Barrier at will. He was no longer a ghost, moving invisibly through the Otherside. Once Merged, he would become a part of life there, subject to that world's laws of time and environment.

Just like the Rogues who manned the Outposts.

"Why *my* Trine?" he demanded, barely controlling his rising anger. "Surely there are other Rovers who would relish an assignment such as this." He tamed his snarling lip into a quirked smile. "Besides, I'm rather out of practice."

"I would think the reasons for my choice are obvious," Grimm replied. "Your Trine is one of our best. And you, Phoebus—your skills are more advanced than any Rover I've ever known."

A soft sound—very like a snort—came from the shadowy corner.

Phoebus bristled at Moth's interruption, but forced himself to relax, uncurling his fingers from his palms.

Grimm placed a hand on his shoulder. "Phoebus, you have an incredible sensitivity to *Electricus* as it exists on the Otherside. That will be a great asset, and it will aid you well in this assignment."

"Which is what, exactly, Elder Grimm?" asked Nyx carefully.

Grimm kept his eyes on Phoebus. "You will Merge," he said briskly. "You will make contact with the Outpost. Should you find Rifts, repair them. Should you encounter Viewers, Dull them."

Grimm's gaze shifted to include the others. "But most importantly, find out what is happening on the Otherside that is putting our world at risk."

"Of course." Although his voice was steady, Phoebus' heart skittered erratically beneath his tunic. He didn't like the way this was going. "And the Leeches?"

"If you find a Leech attempting harm to either world, I expect you to deal with it." Grimm's face darkened like a stormcloud. "In any way you see fit."

Phoebus felt Moth's stare with the same intensity as if she'd thrown a shard of ice into the back of his skull.

"We are at your service," he said, forcing the words from his lips.

Grimm rolled the map between his deft fingers. Strolling across the room as if he'd asked them to join him for tea, the Elder slid the scroll into an empty spot on his long bookcase and adjusted his waistcoat.

"The Weavers will gather suitable attire and documents," he continued, "as well as provide you with any information you require about the area."

Phoebus caught Nyx beaming. She'd always been intrigued with Othersider fashion. Even Titus looked as though Grimm were giving them dessert before dinner. But Phoebus had to work to control own his frustration. It was eating at the back of his throat, bubbling like acid.

He knew exactly what this assimilation would mean: He would be stuck there—cut off from his home, from the constant connection of *Electricus* that felt like his second skin. He would be forced to live in open secrecy among people with whom he shared nothing in common. Forced to hide who he was for the sake of Threshold's secrecy.

But orders were orders, and he'd carry them out.

"We'll make preparations now," he said.

"Also," said Grimm, raising his hand. "I've asked Preceptor Moth to assist you."

As Phoebus shouldered his bow, Moth rose from her seat. She hovered like a midnight shadow, darkening the room in more ways than just her physical presence, and his skin crawled. He cut his gaze from the Preceptor to the Elder.

"And why, exactly?" he asked.

"Preceptor Moth is our most respected authority on Leeches," said Grimm, his tone reprimanding. "Her knowledge is a valuable tool. But you will also need a liaison. Since you can't physically report back to Threshold once you've Merged, Preceptor Moth will be your point of communication."

"With your permission," she said, and her cloak shifted, as though she were nodding in the Elder's direction. "I will make the arrangements for their journey."

Preceptor Moth glided through the doorway and was gone.

"You'd better hurry," said Grimm, sounding amused. "She waits for no one."

Phoebus felt the sudden urge to shoot something. Or, possibly, some*one*.

"Courtesy has always been her trademark, obviously," he said.

Grimm caught his arm as he passed. The Elder's humor had vacated, leaving his face a visage of solemnity. "This mission is of uttermost importance, Phoebus." His dark eyes flickered dangerously in the light. "Whatever happens, do not forget that."

***

"Why do we need her?" asked Titus as they walked along the passageway.

Moth was a good thirty feet ahead of them, her floor-trailing *mantellum* swirling like a tempest as she led them through the Preceptory to the Weavers' Room.

"You know the rumors," said Nyx in a hushed tone. "She's a Leech."

Phoebus caught sight of the milky-faced Regent Jareth, heading in their direction. His eyes darted toward Preceptor Moth, and the Regent gave a curt nod as he retreated to the opposite side of the hall to pass. If Moth was aware of the man's avoidance, she didn't react to it. Her stride continued, unbroken.

"Moth isn't a Leech," said Phoebus.

"Then explain why she looks like that," said Nyx pointedly.

He shrugged. "Preceptors are supposed to dress like that."

"You know what I mean."

"You grew up hearing the same stories I have," he replied. "*Electricus* damage from a training accident."

"Yes, but...you have to admit—"

"I admit this conversation is as irritating as following Moth, like I'm some first-year novice." Phoebus' annoyance returned, rubbing like sharp gravel on his skin. "I'm capable of handling this assignment without her breathing down my neck."

"I just feel we have the right to know the truth," Nyx said. "If we're going to be working with her."

"I'm afraid," said a low voice, causing all three to halt abruptly, "you do not have a right to know things that don't concern you."

Preceptor Moth was only a few feet away, and Phoebus got the impression she was smiling, in a smug but unseen way, from underneath her hood. His neck grew prickly hot. It was the second time she'd caught him off-guard today.

With her gloved hands, she tugged her hood lower, as though warding off a chill.

"You still question my loyalties," she mused, her stare directed only at him. "After all the years we spent together, as trainer and apprentice."

Phoebus didn't respond.

"I have taken on this task at the request of the Elders," said Moth, emphasizing each word in a low, cool tone. "And I do not intend to disappoint them. So, let's put any of your irrelevant concerns aside—" the Preceptor inclined her head toward Nyx "—and complete our assignment, for the good of Threshold."

She led them into an octagonal room—jammed full of tables, chairs, books, and chests. There were no windows, but the walls were lined with amber mirrors, which hung from the vaulted ceiling. The Weavers' job was to keep up with the culture of other dimensions—an occupation that proved difficult more often than not. Like the Elders, they used the mirrors to catch glimpses of the Otherside.

But there were no Weavers in the room.

"Did you forget to tell them we were coming, Preceptor?"

She gave him a look, something tight and ugly he couldn't see. "I dismissed them. Since the Elders wish to keep this assignment secret, I thought it best that only I handle the details." She indicated three duffle bags. "Your things have been packed."

He gestured to a pile of folded garments. "And these?"

"Articles of clothing," Moth replied, sounding bored and irritated, all at once. "I trust you know what to do with them. Now, as a reminder to those not overly familiar with Merging—" Although she didn't look toward Titus or Nyx, her intent was obvious. "Your weapons will appear invisible to Othersiders, so long as they are not in use. But exercise caution, as there is a risk of Viewers seeing them, just as they can glimpse Rifts in the Barrier." She turned to Phoebus. "It would do some of you well to remember that."

"I know the drill," he replied.

"Finally, you must communicate directly with me, and only me," said Moth, her piercing gleam from her shadowed eyes unwavering. "I will be your anchor while you are in the Otherside. Without me, you will lose your footing in Threshold and be unable to return."

Phoebus tensed. He didn't like that at all.

"Light on your journey," said Moth smoothly.

He sucked down a breath. "And on yours."

Chapter 5

It was overcast the next day.

By the time school ended, leaden clouds had obliterated the sun, turning everything gray. And it hadn't improved by the time Selene had reached the *Far and Away* for her afternoon shift. The dreariness had kept the shop pretty empty, and she hadn't seen a single customer in over an hour.

"Miss Claire, do you mind if I head out a little early?" Selene eyed the sky outside the store's front window.

Miss Claire peered over the cash register. "What's the hurry?" she asked, licking her fingers as she counted a stack of bills.

"I think it's going to storm."

Even inside, Selene smelled rain in the air, an earthy scent that tickled her nose. The top of her head throbbed with the dull headache that only happened when the barometric pressure changed.

"If you feel you must." Miss Claire sighed. "But one day, you'll have to outgrow this little fear of yours. You can't live your life jumping at every rumble of thunder."

Managing a smile, Selene pushed herself to her feet and dusted off her jeans.

"Thanks. I'll finish shelving the rest of the books tomorrow. Is there anything you need before I go?"

Miss Claire waved her hand dismissively, caught up in her counting again, and Selene took her opportunity to hustle out the door.

So far, there was nothing outwardly ominous about the thick clouds, but she'd learned to trust her instincts where storms were concerned. Since her accident, she felt changes in the weather deep underneath her skin—like an annoying, post-traumatic sixth sense.

As she reached the corner, her arms prickled. Some weird

phantom sensation tripped up her feet and made her stumble. She grabbed hold of the brick wall storefront to keep from biting it on the pavement. Two buildings down, under the cover of a faded blue awning, she saw them: the two strange men.

And they saw her.

Shouldering her bag, she took off in the opposite direction, moving at a casually fast gait, her heart thudding in her ears. Most of the stores had already closed for the weekday evening. She ducked into a short alley and around an old picket fence, taking the back road toward home, checking over her shoulder every few seconds, her rising panic making it hard to breathe.

Selene made it home in double time.

When she hit the front sidewalk, she took a ragged breath and turned fully around. Relief washed through her.

They hadn't followed.

Pushing open the front door, she was met with the tangy smell of pasta from the living room. Her mother was sitting on the couch, the TV was on, and a microwaved meal, freshly opened and steaming, rested on the coffee table.

Her mother raised a fork to her mouth. "I didn't expect you home for dinner."

Warding off a shudder, Selene regained her breathing and pushed the image of the two strangers from her mind. She didn't need her mom thinking she was any more paranoid. Things had been tense enough between them since her accident.

"It's fine. I got off early." She locked the deadbolt. "I think a storm's rolling in."

Her mother flipped the channel to the news. The weather segment was already in progress, announcing a thunderstorm watch. She shot up and collected the flashlights and portable radio from the kitchen.

"Your father always loved a good thunderstorm," she said as she returned.

"He's not dead, Mom."

Her mother turned the volume up on the television. "Yeah, I know."

As much as she missed her father, she didn't really know him anymore. Weekend visits, as his Naval job allowed, didn't constitute a relationship. Her mother had adjusted to his absence better than she had, and Selene felt irritation and jealousy roll together in her stomach. But a sharp crack of thunder kept her from pushing the subject further.

"I'll be right back," she said, darting up the stairs to her bedroom.

She grabbed her old beat-up laptop—which she kept in a thick silicone case—and a picture of her family in Disney World when she was a child, and an early edition copy of *The Silver Chair* that Jamie had given her last summer—her most prized possessions. As she bounded down the stairs, thunder rumbled. Flinging open the basement door, she took her armful of items to the bottom of the steps and ran back up.

"You know," said her mother, handing her the flashlights. "We don't really have to do this every time."

"I know."

"And we have the tornado siren down the block." Her mom settled back into the chair with her dinner. "You know it'll go off if the weather turns bad."

"Yep. I know that, too."

They had the same conversation before every storm. Her mother insisted there was a time when she'd loved the flashes of lightning across the marsh and the way the thunder made the house shake. But she didn't remember that. She only knew how storms made her feel now—and the freak she was because of them. Now, she huddled in the safety of their small basement and prayed it would pass as quickly as possible.

"I thought you were finally getting over this, Selene." Her mother's words were gently biting. "You said the counseling was helping. The last year or so, you've been so much better."

"I am. And, it is. I was. It's just..."

She faltered as she hovered near the basement door. She *had* been better, especially the last six months. But after seeing the cover of that book in the shop, something had awakened inside her, crawling slowly like a spider along the back of her brain—something she could almost grasp, but then it flitted away, as unobtainable as the ghost lights.

And then, there were those strange men in town.

The sensation when they'd touched was frighteningly similar

to those terrible seconds before the lightning hit. She wondered why she never had any trouble remembering *that* moment when so many of her other memories were a screwed-up mess.

"I don't know," she continued, keeping her voice steadier than she felt. "There's just something about this storm that's freaking me out more than usual. And I've had a lot of work at school. Just one of those weeks, I guess."

"Okay, honey," said her mother, turning back to the TV. "Whatever you need to do."

***

Thirty minutes later, the storm hit St. Mary's in full force. It was an impressive display of lightning, followed by hail the size of nickels. While her mother watched the news, Selene huddled at the bottom of the stairs, listening to the cracks of thunder and feeling each one like a slap to the face. She gritted her teeth against the sharp hatred that bubbled under her ribs—hatred for having to be this way, paralyzed by one moment in her life and unable to get past it.

She felt weak, and she despised that.

Her dinosaur of a laptop computer pinged. It was the one piece of technology she owned that still worked—even if it only had a short battery life and she typed with a stylus to make sure it didn't fall victim to her stupid electronics curse.

She read the message from Jamie, thankful that the power had stayed on so far.

I need this storm to end. Mudge has been stuck here so long that he's depleted my supply of microwavable burritos. And we all know what happens in the aftermath of a burrito-fest.

Jamie: her faithful and constant distraction, as always.

She typed out her reply.

Stay strong. And stay far away. Sounds like it's going to be bad.

As she sent the message, her eyes drifted to her bracelet. Flashes of her grandmother lit up her memory—visions of her sweet smile, the too-pink lipstick she always wore. Thank God, those memories—like pretty much everything *before* St. Mary's—were still intact. Taking the metal plate between her thumb and forefinger, she squeezed it gently.

She wished she could still talk to her grandmother about everything.

Her fingers prickled, like tiny needles being pushed into her skin. The metal bracelet vibrated. She jerked her hand away as the bracelet changed from dull pewter to a glowing, incandescent blue. An odd sort of panic gripped her as she remembered the inhuman blue eyes of the men in town.

Leaping up, she fumbled with the clasp, fear stealing the air from her lungs. But before she could rip off the bracelet, the brilliant metal suddenly dulled. Her fingers froze over the nameplate. One moment it was glowing, and the next, it was ordinary. Taking a shaky breath, she blinked at her wrist. Had she imagined it?

"Selene?"

She jumped. "Yeah, Mom?"

"The storm's passed, honey. You can come back upstairs."

She placed her finger against the nameplate, feeling cool metal against her skin. No prickling shock or buzzing vibration.

She wrapped her laptop and valuables in a blanket and flicked off the light.

Chapter 6

The *Seaside Inn* was an old building wedged between a pub and an antique shop, right in the historic district. Large curtained windows peered warily from the brick-faced front, and the door hung precariously on its hinges. It didn't look like the kind of place one might wish to stay on a romantic holiday, despite the painted signs stating otherwise.

But they weren't here for pleasure.

Phoebus rapped on the door. Almost instantaneously, floorboards creaked on the other side, followed by the light tread of footsteps. There was a dull clank and the sliding sound of several locks being turned. The door cracked open, revealing an eye and half a face.

"Can I help you?" asked a woman.

"Yes," he said in his casual voice. "We need to book a room."

The door didn't budge. "I'm sorry, but we're full."

Phoebus sighed. He didn't have time for this. He was in a bad enough mood already. "Well, then I suggest you go and get your manager. Because, I can assure you, we're not leaving until we have a room."

The eye blinked several times. "Wait right there."

The door closed, and the locks were fastened back into place. Footsteps echoed again and faded away.

"No appreciation for manners in this town." Phoebus strolled to the edge of the porch and leaned against the white support column. "It's very disappointing."

Titus glanced up at him from the bottom step. "Are you sure we're in the right place?"

"I can feel the *Electricus*," he replied, studying the building. "If there aren't Rovers or Rogues inside, then I guess we'd better be prepared for a fight with something ugly."

"That makes me feel a lot better, thanks."

He smirked at Titus. "Nervous?"

"Of course," said Nyx from her seated position on the top railing. "You'd be foolish not to be."

Hearing footsteps, Phoebus struck a casual stance as he waited. Metallic swishing and clicking of the locks sounded, and the half-face reappeared.

Phoebus waved. "Hello again."

The woman's one visible eye blinked. "We have one room, if you're still interested. But it's around back." The crack in the door narrowed. "The alley's to your right."

The door shut.

"Charming," he said, shaking his head. "You see what I mean, Titus? Not polite at all."

"Well, what were you expecting?" asked Nyx, leaving her railing perch and gliding down the wide stairs. "We're not exactly locals. St. Mary's is a small town, and I'm sure they know everybody around here."

"My point exactly," he said, following her. "How are you supposed to run a business and procure more customers if you aren't friendly? Remind me to have a word with the staff, when we actually meet someone."

Between the inn and the pub, an iron gate opened into an alley. A metal sign with an arrow boasted of additional parking in the back, although Phoebus failed to see the point, since the alley was too narrow for a car to pass through. The rear exterior of the inn was quaint, with a meticulously landscaped yard, a tall privacy fence, and an assortment of outdoor furniture. He paused.

Perhaps he'd been mistaken after all.

A door was propped open at the back of the inn. He adjusted his traveling bags and stepped inside. The hallway was dark and confining, with no windows or lights. He squinted into the shadows. Nerve endings prickled across his shoulder blades. Something didn't feel right. But just as he opened his mouth to give warning, a large weight slammed into him.

He hit the wooden floor with a grunt, scrambling to grab

hold of the person on top of him. Cold metal grazed his neck. He wrenched his body, twisting to get his legs under the assailant. Then he pushed off with a yell. The attacker careened backwards into the wall. Pictures rattled in their frames. Phoebus was on his feet with lightning speed, his body tensed to spring.

"Hold!" cried the attacker.

He jerked, then froze, peering through the dark. "Who are you?"

"I'm Marcelo," said the attacker, breathing heavily. "Welcome to the Mocama Outpost."

***

The interior of the *Seaside Inn* was nicer than its exterior, though the décor left something to be desired. Most of the furniture was worn and the pictures on the wall had faded with time. Still, it had a comfortable feel, like the libraries Phoebus haunted in the Preceptory back home. Leaning into the couch cushions, he kicked his feet up onto the worn coffee table.

"Forgive our lack of hospitality," said Marcelo, offering a cup of coffee and a disapproving glance at Phoebus' boots. "But we weren't sure if you were Rovers at first, and we can't be too careful."

Phoebus took the coffee. It was black, just the way he liked it, and his first sip of the hot liquid did wonders for his mood. He clutched the mug, letting it warm his fingers. "No apology needed. We're not exactly in uniform."

Marcelo dipped his head. He was a small-framed man, who looked several years out of his teens, with olive skin and warm brown eyes. He handed mugs to Nyx and Titus, who'd found two high-backed chairs opposite the coffee table.

"In our defense," Marcelo continued, "the *Electricus* currents are muddled here, being so near the Coil. At times, it makes it difficult to differentiate individual signatures."

"Not to mention," interjected another voice, "it's been a long time with since any Rovers have paid us a visit."

The woman from the front door sauntered into the room, the edges of her long skirt flicking around her ankles, and placed a tray of tea sandwiches on the table. She was also slight, with features remarkably similar to Marcelo's. Ringlets of black hair framed her neck as she arranged the food.

"Well," said Phoebus. "We don't usually make house calls."

"That much is obvious," she replied coolly.

"This is Paloma," said Marcelo, smiling. "My sister."

Phoebus took another swig of coffee, and it suddenly tasted bitter in the back of his throat.

"So, you're the Rogues," he said flatly, though a hint of the disdain bubbling in his chest leaked into his voice. Even using their title felt like a curse on his tongue. He swept his gaze with purposeful laziness over the room. "And this grand facility is the Mocama Outpost."

He noticed Marcelo flinch, but recover. "Yes, we are, and yes, it is. You must understand: St. Mary's is a small town, and not many things go unnoticed. We must keep our presence in sync with the inhabitants. It's not like the Outposts in the bigger cities. It's more difficult to hide. Using the inn as a cover works nicely for us."

Nyx straightened in her chair. "And you're in charge of this entire area?"

"Yes," answered Paloma. "We've been here for ten years, by Othersider time."

Phoebus tried calculating in his head, but there were too many variables. Ten years in this dimension could easily equal a few years or only several months in Threshold. Without the aid of a Preceptor to ascertain the time difference, he wouldn't chance a guess.

"Forgive me, but I don't usually keep up with Merged Trines." He studied the Rogues, memorizing details with instinctive care. "Which of you is the leader?"

"Neither," replied Marcelo curtly. "But he'll return soon. It's his night to close up the shop."

Titus nodded, seemingly both impressed and confused. "You run a shop as well?"

At this, Paloma beamed, her pride evidenced by her firm, upright posture and the angle of her shoulders. "One of the town's best," she replied. "Of course, we do well enough with this inn to meet our monetary needs, but the antiques shop gives provides a bit extra, and it gives us something to do."

Marcelo shot his sister a look.

"Well, it sounds like you're all quite content," said Phoebus.

The disgust in his voice was evident now, and he didn't bother leaving it out. "All happily settled and living your life here, in this suffocating...*place*."

"It's not so bad, Rover," said Marcelo. "Once you get used to it."

Taking another sip of coffee, he shrugged. "I have no intention of getting used to it. But whatever suits you, I suppose."

Marcelo regarded him with narrow eyes. "Well, it sounds as though the pleasantries are done. So then, if I may ask, why exactly are you here?"

Phoebus shifted to the edge of his seat. He appreciated the Rogue's dismissal of time-consuming social customs. Although he didn't mind the coffee, he wanted to get through this with as little useless conversation as possible.

"We've been ordered to check in on you," he said simply. "The Elders have lost communication with this Outpost, and they've grown concerned."

He wasn't quite sure what he was expecting in response, but the expression on Marcelo's face certainly wasn't it. The Rogue turned his head toward the fireplace. Hanging above the marble mantel was a large rectangular amber mirror, polished to a gleaming shine.

"I don't understand," Marcelo replied, his forehead tight with furrowed brows. "Cruz speaks with the Elders every month."

It was as though some unseen fist punched Phoebus in the gut. The edges of his vision darkened, and the muscles in his neck stretched tight, like a braided rope.

"Is that the name of your Trine leader?"

Marcelo stepped back. "Yes."

Phoebus clenched his cup until his knuckles bulged and the ceramic strained against his grip.

"I see," he spat out. He worked his mouth into a smile, though his lips were numb. "Well, I look forward to speaking with him then, when he returns."

An awkward silence enveloped the room as he kept his gaze fixed on the mirror. He felt Nyx and Titus' collective stare, their unspoken questions like barbs, but he knew they wouldn't dare voice them. He wouldn't have answered anyway.

Instead, he downed the rest of his coffee, relishing the burn in his esophagus. It was a good distraction from the nagging at the back of his skull. He wasn't ready to think.

After a moment, Paloma dropped a few napkins on the coffee table and cleared her throat.

"Shall I go and make up your rooms?" she asked, glancing at their bags.

It was Nyx who replied, offering up a polite—and apologetic—smile. "Yes, thank you."

Marcelo pulled a jacket from a coat rack in the corner. "And I've got to step out for a bit. It's my turn to patrol."

Phoebus jerked his attention from the mirror. "Patrol?"

"Of course," said Marcelo. "You Rovers don't do all the work for Threshold, you know." He shrugged on the jacket. "I'll be back later tonight."

Without another word, he left, and the front door thudded behind him. His sister placed her hand over her heart—the gesture somewhat stilted. Phoebus doubted the traditional Rover salute got much use in an Outpost like this.

"I'll let you know when everything's ready for you upstairs," she said.

She exited with the same speed as her brother.

Phoebus unpeeled his fingers from the mug handle.

"What was that all about, Fee?" asked Titus, munching on a sandwich filled with a bright orange substance. "You were in a foul enough mood *before* we left Threshold."

"You noticed," he replied. "I'm touched."

Nyx set her plate aside with more force than necessary. "We are not going down this path again. Stop sulking like a shriveled-up Preceptor and talk to us. Have you got something against those two?" she asked, gesturing toward the front door. "Or is this still about that Viewer that—"

He silenced her with a searing look.

To her credit, Nyx barely reacted. Beside her, Titus noisily finished off his sandwich and grabbed another, not missing a beat. Phoebus shifted his gaze toward the fireplace and up to the mantel. The reflection of the amber mirror took in nearly the entire room.

As Nyx leaned forward to take a napkin, wiping her hands daintily, Titus continued to plough through the items on the tea tray. Phoebus let out the breath he'd held tightly in his chest. His

Trinemates had understood his warning clearly.

It wasn't safe to talk here.

"I don't care for this assignment," he said, keeping his voice at a casual volume. He scratched at the cuff of his jeans, irritated at the feeling of stiff denim against his leg. Then he uncurled himself from the couch, surveying his own reflection in the mirror. Although his new clothing blended perfectly with common Otherside attire, Phoebus missed his Rover greens. "But we have our orders, and I will see them carried out."

He frowned at the mirror. In the amber, his face looked sallow. Joining him, Nyx took in her reflection with a more pleased eye. She looked older in her silk blouse, dark jeans, and leather boots. She still wore her long hair in a braid, but the style was loose and casual.

"So, what now?" she asked.

"For now, we wait," he answered.

Titus held out the tray. "Sandwich?"

***

Evening was long past when the front door rattled, then swung open. Phoebus looked up from the book of poetry he'd occupied himself with. A large man appeared in the hall. His skin was such a rich brown that he nearly blended with the shadows until he stepped into the room.

Phoebus' feet hit the floor, his legs feeling stiff as metal bars. The man flicked his gaze immediately in his direction. Surprise registered on his face, quickly followed by powerful recognition. Then his expression settled into an easy smile.

"Well, well, if it isn't Phoebus Peregrine himself," he said in a booming voice. "Have you come to join the rabble of the Otherside?"

A sensation of ice and fire collided between Phoebus' shoulder blades. He drew himself up to his full height, glaring so hard that his eye sockets burned.

"Cruz," he said tightly. "It is you."

"You seem surprised, Rover." Cruz chuckled, but it was a harsh, bitter sound. "Or have you forgotten that time passes differently here?"

"I know how it works," he said crisply. "I just wasn't expecting—"

"That time had taken its toll on me as well?" Cruz finished. "That's what happens when you Merge, Fee. Remember? You become subject to this world's time. And when you're forbidden from passing back through the Barrier, then you start aging just like the Othersiders."

Phoebus gritted his teeth. Of course, time existed in Threshold. People grew old and died there, just like any other dimension. But for those inside the protection of the Barrier, the effects of time were slower and didn't always follow as consistent a pattern.

He'd seen decades come and go on the Otherside, but for all appearances, he was nineteen at most. He and Cruz were close to the same age, back in their training days, and had both looked as much when they'd first took on their duties as Rovers. But the man standing before him now looked many years Phoebus' senior.

"How old?" he asked bluntly.

"Thirty." Cruz lifted his chin. "As Othersiders would chart it."

The declaration hit him like an arrow in the chest. It had been two years since he'd last seen Cruz. But that was Threshold time. Ten years had gone by here on the Otherside. For someone like him, it made little difference. For a Rogue like Cruz, it was another matter.

But it wasn't time that bothered Phoebus.

"You know I tried—"

"Save it, Rover," said Cruz. "It wasn't your fault."

Phoebus grimaced. No matter how many times he heard that, it was something he'd never believe. A dark weight sank into his stomach. Cruz had been his Trinemate once.

He'd been *his* responsibility.

Cruz stomped across the room, chucking the bag he'd been carrying into a corner. "You'll forgive me if I don't hug you," he said. "I'm not a fan of Rovers."

"And you'll forgive me if I don't care," Phoebus replied. "I'm not a fan of Rogues."

They stared at each other, unmoving. The other Rovers in the room watched in silence. It was Cruz who finally broke the standoff.

"As much as I'm enjoying our little reunion, Fee, something tells me you're not paying me a visit to hash up the past."

"Very perceptive," he shot back. The exchange brought him back to his senses. "We're here on orders from the Elders."

Cruz crossed his arms, his upper lip twitching as he surveyed the trio in his living room. "And what would those orders be, exactly?"

All eyes fell on Phoebus expectantly. Moving carefully past Cruz with a casual grace, he walked toward the fireplace, his fingers thumbing through the book in his hand. As he slid a pen from his pocket, he paused just under the amber mirror. He wrote with a quick flourish and turned to the others, shielding the book from the mirror with his body. On the inside cover he'd written one word:

Viewers.

Chapter 7

A boom of thunder startled her awake.

Selene jolted in bed, heart racing underneath her t-shirt. Rain spattered the windowpane and thrummed on the roof. She checked the clock on her nightstand. 4:15 AM. Lightning streaked on the other side of the curtain and she flinched as the flash brightened the room.

Fumbling for the bag containing her laptop, she grabbed the rest of her take-cover items—wide awake, but feeling like a zombie. She was sick of these autumn thunderstorms, especially when they hit in the middle of night. Which they usually did. She heard her mom's snoring down the hall. The way her mom could sleep through bad weather made her want to scream.

She paused, her hand on the doorknob.

"Stay in the basement if it makes you feel safe," her mom had said last spring, after she'd burst into her room in the dead of night and scared her mom so bad she peed herself. "And don't wake me up unless there's a warning issued."

Selene hurried to the living room to check the weather report instead. A strong band of storms passed the coast on their way to the ocean. There were a few thunderstorm watches in the neighboring county, but nothing in St. Mary's. She left the TV on and went to the kitchen to grab some water. She wasn't ready to endure the musty basement yet. But she wasn't going back to her room, either.

As she filled her glass over the sink, she peered through the curtains. Lightning gave substance to the darkened marsh, stretching out into the black waterways beyond. Cordgrass twisted with the wind. A series of dim white lights skittered atop the surface of the grass, pulsing slowly in the rain.

The orbs flickered with a life of their own, morphing in and out of view—just like the stories in the book. A tendril of ice wound its way through her insides and settled around her heart, squeezing with uncomfortable pressure.

Her blood pumped in her ears, filling her brain with steady drumming; then the sensation crept down her arm and around her wrist. Her bracelet pulsed an incandescent blue in the same rhythm as her heart—in the same rhythm as the strange ghost lights in the marsh.

"Stop it...stop it...stop it..."

Her voice sounded as though it were underwater. A streak of lightning lit up the window, and her breath caught. There was something moving at the edge of the marsh. Frozen over the kitchen sink, she stared outside—unable to rip her gaze away, trying desperately to imagine it wasn't there.

But she wasn't seeing things. Something *was* crawling through the grass. Its form was as black as the night—man-sized, but moving like some giant, creeping spider. Her wrist throbbed underneath her bracelet. She clutched the metal, and her skin burned, like she was holding a hot plate.

Was it the men from town?

The image of their creepy eyes stared back at her from inside her brain.

Or was it something even worse?

"Go away," she croaked. Her throat was like sandpaper.

"Please, just go away."

The entire marshland was illuminated with an eerie white-blue light. And then the light dissipated, like leaves scattering on the wind. Unfreezing, she pressed her palms against the glass panes, staring—not wanting to see, but needing to see. Beyond the yard, the vast line of cordgrass stood erect and still, like thin green sentinels. But the figure and the orbs were gone.

Chapter 8

Phoebus studied his lodgings. It was a decent room and the décor was simple, orderly.

Thunder rumbled and lightning flashed behind the curtains. Rovers crossing the Barrier often caused storms to manifest on the Otherside. It wasn't intentional, but manipulating the *Electricus* produced an electrical chain reaction in this world's atmosphere.

His wristbands reflected the lightning, highlighting the designs, which were as familiar to him as his own face. Rovers could harness electrical energy, but the amber resin allowed them to conduct it.

Which made them the equivalent of living lightning rods.

Draping his *mantellum* across the foot of the bed, he rummaged through his supplies: clothing and toiletries, an electronic device native to the Otherside, and a manila folder. He opened the paperwork. Standard documents: birth certificate, driver's license. And something else. He yanked it out with a groan.

St. Mary's Charter School Enrollment Form.

"Perfect," he muttered.

It was bad enough that he had to *dress* like an Othersider youth. Now he was going to be *smothered* by them. Although he could've passed for an older age than his documents declared, playing the boring "new student" role was one of the quickest ways to acclimate. Even he had to admit that. It gave him access to the inner workings of the town, and it allowed him to observe, to single out Viewers...

And that would make it easier to locate the girl.

His head weighed heavily with the effects of Merging. The sensation would ease, but it put him in a disagreeable mood nonetheless.

A loud hum reverberated through the room. The papers dropped from his fingers as his muscles tensed, and he turned his eyes to the room's entrance. It was then that he noticed the long rectangular mirror hanging on the back of the door. Like the one downstairs, it was also made of amber.

The resin shimmered brightly within the frame, then swirled like a whirlpool. A familiar polished voice drifted toward him from the depths of the mirror.

"Greetings, Phoebus."

He pressed his hand reluctantly to his chest. "Greetings, Preceptor Moth."

The woman's dark blue hooded *mantellum* swirled into view as the ripples in the mirror stilled, like a quiet lake. He glimpsed the outline of a face and the hint of electric blue eyes from within the mirror, but her crisp demeanor chilled, as though they were in the same room—or someone had opened a window to winter. He clenched his hands behind his back. Why couldn't Grimm be his anchor? Why did it have to be *Moth*?

"What have you to report?" she asked silkily.

"Oh, not too much," he replied, not bothering to hide his curt tone. "We've managed to settle in nicely at the Outpost. You'll be happy to know that the Trine assigned here is doing quite well."

Moth's hood shifted. "Indeed?"

"Oh yes. Absolutely perfect."

"That is...surprising."

"Yes, I suppose it would be, after everything I'd been told." His words burned hot against his tongue as his irritation flared. "But would you like to know something even more surprising?" He squared his shoulders. "This Trine claims they've been communicating with the Elders every month."

Moth's eerie eyes stared back at him. "That's true."

Phoebus worked his mouth open, then closed again, only half-believing what he'd just heard. His irritation cooled, but now something else burned inside him: the sting of confused betrayal.

"Then why did Grimm tell me the Elders had lost communication with this Outpost?"

Moth made a slight motion with her head—an action that seemed like a sigh, though he heard nothing. When she spoke again, her voice was level but, as always, with a draft of cool air seeping through it.

"Grimm doesn't believe the reports."

He paused. "Why didn't he just say that in our meeting?"

"Because there is something amiss, Rover. Grimm feels there is a traitor among us, and the details of this assignment must be kept as secret as possible."

"And the rest of the Elders…"

"The less people we have in this inner circle, the better our chance of success. Grimm has informed his sister, Elder Ania, but that is all. The remaining Elders believe you have gone to check on the Outpost, nothing more. As for the others, this is not a matter that concerns either the Regents or the Preceptors. "

"You being the exception, of course."

"I am the most qualified for this position," said Moth, the temperature of her voice dropping several more degrees. "Much like you."

There's no comparison, Phoebus wanted to say.

But he bit back his response.

Although he'd never feared Moth, as many did, he'd always regarded her from arm's length—like a stray dog that could turn at a moment's notice.

The Preceptor appeared to take his silence as disapproval. She drew closer, and he could clearly see the near-glow of her icy blue eyes.

"And unless you've forgotten your place," she said lowly, "my involvement in this assignment is not up to you."

"I never said it was," he replied.

Several beats of silence passed between both sides of the amber mirror.

"Something else is troubling you," said Moth finally. Her intonation morphed to a mild curiosity. "What is it, Rover?"

He didn't feel the need to lie. "You didn't tell me Cruz was head of this Outpost."

"Ah," said Moth, a hint of a smile in the word. "That is because you would have been more disagreeable about this assignment than you already were."

"That's very perceptive."

"Grimm is not the only one who knows you, Phoebus," she replied. "I know how you think, and I know your weaknesses. But you must put those aside. We have more important matters to contend with than an Outpost of Rogues or your stubborn attitude toward any of them."

Phoebus pressed his lips together until the blood drained out of them. *Just stay focused on the task,* he repeated several times to himself. "Is there anything else Elder Grimm requires of me?"

"There is one more thing." Preceptor Moth's shadowed face hovered ominously in the amber light. "Consider it a personal request of mine."

A dark wariness crept over his skin.

"And that is?"

She leaned into the swirling mirror. "Search for Bleeders."

He kept his gaze carefully blank. "Bleeders?"

"Yes, Rover. I trust you know what they are."

"Of course," he replied, feeling like he was eating rusty nails. "But there hasn't been evidence of one for nearly a century, Preceptor. What makes you think there would be one here?"

"With the attempted attack on the Chamber, we must consider all possibilities." Moth moved a few paces from the mirror. "A Bleeder would place the balance of both dimensions in jeopardy."

"How do you wish for me to proceed?"

"Continue with Elder Grimm's original orders," she replied. "Deal with disturbances and investigate the area. But your primary focus will be to search for Bleeders. You can sense Viewers on the Otherside better than anyone I've ever trained, which means you have the best chance of finding a Bleeder, should there be one near the Mocama Coil."

"I'll inform the others immediately."

"No." Moth's voice was like a whip. "This stays between us, especially if there is treachery within our ranks."

"If you think either Titus or Nyx could possibly be—"

"I doubt either of them would have the ingenuity for such deception. However, that does not change the facts. No one at the Outpost, including your own Trine, can know your new orders."

PART TWO

"Where shall we three meet again?
In thunder, lightning, or in rain?
When the hurlyburly's done,
When the battle's lost and won.
That will be ere the set of sun."

—MacBeth

Chapter 9

Selene slammed her locker shut. "Can we just skip school today?"

"Bad morning?" Jamie inquired, leaning against the metal door.

"It's just the fact that it *is* morning."

"Ah," he replied. "Somebody needs another cup of coffee."

"Not even a latte could help right now."

She couldn't shake the creeped-out feeling from last night's storm, but she hadn't said anything to her mother—about her bracelet or what she thought she'd seen in the marsh—and she wasn't sure she wanted to tell Jamie, either. The freaky men, the lighting storms—it all sounded *like* she was having some relapse from her past trauma. Her nerves felt like raw bacon, popping and sizzling in a pan.

"Well, if it's beyond the aid of the magical coffee bean, then it must be serious," said Jamie, his eyes roaming her face. "You want to talk about it?"

Guilt nudged at her. Jamie was her best friend. She'd cried on his shoulder more times than she wanted to admit, and their late-night conversations online had gotten her through bad dreams and loneliness when she missed her dad.

"Maybe later," she replied.

Jamie knew not to push, but he stared at her a moment longer, playing absently with the strap of his bag. Then he shifted his gaze over the heads of passing students in the hall and cleared his throat. "So, have you thought about the camping trip?"

"Yeah, I've thought about it."

"And?"

The hopeful look on his face made her cringe.

"I don't know, Jamie. I mean, it's not as though I actually like camping, especially not in the marsh—"

"*Near* the marsh."

"Can't we just hang at your house?" She offered a peace-treaty kind of smile. "I promise I'll stay away from your gaming system. You can even invite Mudge and the guys over, and I won't complain... too much."

"Man, you're really going to be stubborn about this, aren't you?"

"Look." She hesitated, hating what she was about to say. "I'm just not okay with spending the night outside, in the open, you know, what with my being nearly electrocuted and all."

The stench of hypocrisy filled her nose, nearly making her gag. She was actually using her accident as an excuse—the one thing she promised herself she wouldn't do. And what made it worse was that it was immediately effective.

Jamie's countenance clouded over. "I'm not trying to push you or anything, Selene. I just thought that maybe it would do you some good, you know?" He looked down at his Converse, and his voice softened. "You can't live in fear forever."

"I'll think about it. "She reached for his arm with the same gentleness as his tone. "Promise."

They looked at each other, both knowing exactly what that meant.

But it was better than hearing the "no" out loud.

Someone yelled Jamie's name from down the hall. A sloppily dressed boy with a mop of frizzed-out hair waved his arms in their direction.

"Mudge," said Jamie, shaking his head. "That idiot devastated my fridge last night. Excuse me while I go and say something crude and inappropriate to him." He winked at her. "I'll be right back."

She watched Jamie dodge several couples and a group of chattering freshman. She'd never understood what he saw in Mudge, other than their mutual love of gaming. The guy always leered at her, and he smelled like a pair of old gym shoes.

Rolling her eyes, she opened her messenger bag and dug for her lunch. Maybe a few bites would help the caffeine headache already threatening just inside her temples. As her fingers closed around her snack, a sharp electric tingle raced up her arms.

Someone tapped her on the shoulder. She jumped and spun

around.

A guy stood in front of her—so close she'd nearly hit him. She froze, staring, with her protein bar positioned like a foil-wrapped weapon between them. She had no idea where he'd come from, but she was positive she'd never seen him before now.

There was *no way* she could've forgotten a face like that.

"I didn't mean to scare you," he said.

He had a prominent nose and a set of full lips that were crooked at one corner, almost lopsided in shape. It was deadly attractive. His skin was a golden brown, like he'd spent his life on a tropical island, and his eyes were the color of warm caramel. Smooth hair, almost the same shade as his eyes, was tied against the nape of his neck in a low ponytail. A few strands had escaped, and they fluttered against his jaw as he spoke.

"Oh, you're fine," she replied, cringing immediately at her word choice. "Like, I mean, yeah…it's all good, no problem." She stuffed the bar inside her bag. "You didn't scare me."

He didn't seem to notice her fumbling response. His attention was on the slip of paper he held in his hands—hands with really long fingers, clean nails, and lots of callouses, she noticed. Maybe he played guitar?

"Could you help me find my class?" he asked. His voice sounded refined, with a hint of some kind of accent she didn't recognize. "I appear to be lost."

Although he was only a few inches taller than her, she couldn't help noting the broad span of his shoulders and his athletic build. Maybe he was a sports guy, not a music guy. Or maybe both. Whatever he did, it looked like he hit the gym regularly.

She blinked back to focus as she realized she'd completely forgotten his question.

"Um, what?"

As he glanced at her, his lips wrinkled in a crooked smile. "My next class," he said. "I'm new here, and I don't understand the schedule."

"Oh, right," she laughed, feeling warm. "Sure, I can help."

Reaching for the paper, her fingers brushed against his. A buzz surged through her skin, and she froze again. The sensation mimicked the shock she'd gotten from the strangers in town. Not as intense, and not painful, but definitely similar—a lingering static electricity.

Like when she'd fried her phone or touched her computer without a stylus.

The new guy was staring at her with a curious expression, and she pulled herself together. This wasn't the time to look like an absolute freak. She took the schedule out of his hands and scanned the document. His homeroom was the same as Jamie's, and his next class was chemistry. She read his student details at the top of the paper.

"Oh, you're a senior, too."

"A senior what?" he replied.

His question made her pause. "Um, you're in 12th grade, according to this. Did they get that wrong in the front office?"

She saw something flicker behind his caramel eyes, like he was registering and processing information.

"Yes, of course," he said, shaking his head, causing a wisp of honey hair to flutter against his jaw again. "Sorry, I don't think I've had enough coffee this morning to be thinking clearly."

"I hear you," she replied, handing him the paper. He took it, but he made no move to leave, and she tried to ignore the weird buzzing current moving up her arm as the temperature in her cheeks kicked up several degrees. "Would you like me to show you the way?"

"That would be great."

Gesturing toward the vicinity of the science classrooms, she started in that direction. The new guy fell into step beside her, moving with a light, confident grace. His khakis fit as though they'd been tailored, as did his blue collared shirt, though it didn't have the school crest embroidered on the left chest. She noticed he wasn't carrying any books or bags.

"So, what's your name?" she asked.

At her question, she sensed him tense, and she could even see a muscle jerk along his jaw. They weaved around a few milling students before he finally answered.

"Fee."

"That's unusual," she replied.

"It's a nickname."

"Irish?"

He looked momentarily impressed. "Greek, actually."

As they turned the corner to head into the science hall, she chanced another quick sideways glance, pretending to look at a group of kids crowded around one of the lockers. The new guy carried himself with a kind of sauntering ease, almost like he was bored; but although his face looked relaxed, the tension radiating off him seemed to say otherwise.

"So, don't you want to know my name?" she ventured.

The expression on the boy's face told her instantly that he didn't.

But he smiled, nonetheless. "Of course. What's your name?"

"Selene."

"Greek as well, if I'm not mistaken."

"I'm not sure," she replied, feeling suddenly confused. "Maybe."

The flush in her face cooled, as though she'd just stepped into a gust of winter air. Although his response sounded friendly, his attitude had a strange, frozen quality; but she couldn't put her finger on it. There was something off about the guy, despite his easy good looks and casual demeanor. Or maybe even *because* of those things.

She circled her fingers around her bracelet, playing absently with the metal, until she stopped in front of Mr. Parker's classroom.

"Well, this is it."

He surveyed the room, and his intense caramel eyes took in the rows of desks and chattering teenagers, as though he were memorizing details of a crime scene. Then his expression shifted, and he looked slightly irritated—though his lopsided smile was fully visible again as he turned to her.

"Thanks for the escort," he said.

She smiled back at him. "No problem."

As he crossed the threshold of the classroom, he looked over his shoulder. "Maybe I'll see you later?"

"Oh, sure." She gripped her wrist tighter. "Maybe later."

He made his way down the aisle and slid into a seat in the back of the room, ignoring the chaos of students around him as he proceeded to examine his nails and tend to a button on the cuff of his sleeve. With his tied-back hair, perfect outfit, and aloof behavior, he looked totally out of place.

She studied the arrogant tilt of his chin as he leaned back, as though he were far too superior to be sitting in a high school chemistry class. But he was still way different than the typical snobby crowd of "old money" kids that ruled St. Mary's Charter. Maybe he was a Navy kid—although he didn't fit that description, either.

Just as she started to turn away—not about to be caught staring—she detected a faint aura around his body. As she blinked, it seemed to grow brighter, hovering along his arms. But just as quickly as it appeared, it dimmed, and then faded away. But none of the other students had reacted to it. She rubbed her eyes. A trick of the fluorescent lights, maybe.

The warning bell jolted her to reality. She backpedaled, nearly slamming into Jamie. Her messenger bag slipped down her arm, scraping painfully against her bracelet.

"I thought you were going to wait on me," he said.

"Oh, hey," she stammered, trying to move away from the door.

Jamie looked past her into the classroom. "Who was that?"

"New kid," she answered. "He was lost."

He arched an eyebrow. "Uh huh. I bet he was."

Chapter 10

Phoebus slouched in his chair, but his thoughts ran wild. The levels of *Electricus* radiating from the girl were unlike anything he'd registered from a Viewer before—even stronger than when he'd last encountered her in the Othersider hospital. The energy pulsed with a life of its own, almost like the Barrier itself.

"Schedule, please?"

A balding man stood over him, hand outstretched.

Phoebus held out the paper. "It's my first day."

Looking thoroughly unimpressed, the teacher studied the schedule. "Nice to meet you, Ph—"

"Just Fee, thank you."

The teacher scrunched his pudgy face. "Well, *Fee*, make sure you pick up your textbook from the supply room. You've got a lot of catching up to do."

He returned the schedule and waddled to the front of the room.

Fee glanced at the paper, frowning at his typed name: *Phoebus Peregrine*. It had been so long since he'd used his surname. Everything about this—his new clothing, his new identity—it all felt wrong. A hot, uncomfortable feeling prickled against the back of his neck underneath his shirt collar. How had it come to this? He'd gone from moving invisibly through this world to being stuck in the middle of it.

Although Titus and Nyx had insisted on coming along, he'd refused. One Rover at St. Mary's Charter School was enough. After all, according to Moth's orders, he was supposed to be searching for Bleeders on his own, without anyone else's knowledge—and that included his Trine. So he'd sent them with the Rogues to get acquainted with the town.

With each tick of the analog clock hanging precariously above the door, he felt himself adjusting to the passage of Othersider time. When he was simply a transient in this world, his body was able to resist its clutches. But now, with every moment that passed, his body reflected the change.

He studied his hands. They had lost the blue gleam he was accustomed to when he passed through the Barrier, coated with remnants of the membrane's *Electricus*. The act of Merging had solidified his body. His skin looked as normal here as it did in Threshold.

Calloused. Veins under flesh. Ordinary.

He'd forgotten how quickly his mind assimilated everything about the world he Merged with—knowledge, social patterns, nuances of language, even cultural tastes and behaviors. It was an adaptation Thresholders had perfected over the centuries. Camouflage, at its best.

"Alright, class," said the teacher, projecting his voice over the final ringing of the bell. "Let's start by going over your vocabulary from last night's homework."

And with that, he tuned out. He wasn't here to learn about Othersider science. His mind was occupied with more important matters, like what to do about the girl.

Selene.

Although she'd changed some since he'd Dulled her in the hospital room—taller in height and with a lengthier style to her hair—her marshland eyes held the same bright intelligence. Gauging what he knew, it seemed two or three additional years had passed.

His mind replayed the events, which had only been a day's worth for him. He'd done his job in the hospital; he'd erased her memories, which should have severed any future interference she might've had with the Barrier. Yet here he was on the Otherside again, tasked with investigating Viewers—and the girl still seemed to be in the center of it all.

Dulling Viewers was typically a one-time operation. The fact that this was now the third time he'd come face-to-face with the same one left an uncomfortable weight in the center of his gut. Had the girl endured hardships as the result of his actions? Or had his arrow cleanly hit its mark, eradicating all traces of anything related to Threshold, including himself?

It was clear the girl had more connection to the *Electricus* than he'd first thought. But just how much?

Was she even aware of it?

A flash of irritation surged through him, and he reprimanded himself for letting sentiment worm its way into his head. He knew Moth would be keeping close tabs on him from across the Barrier, and he had to be careful. Everything Moth discovered would be reported to Grimm. Phoebus had kept the girl a secret from Grimm when he thought she was just a harmless, innocent Viewer. Now, the safety of Threshold was in question.

He had his orders. Nothing else mattered.

His leg began to vibrate, and he tensed—probing the atmosphere around him for the source of the disturbance, but sensing nothing. The vibration continued, centered near his hip. A few students looked in his direction as he clamped his hand over his pocket. Then, he remembered. He pulled out the piece of technology and stared at its rectangular screen.

"Mr. Peregrine," the teacher called out. "I don't know how things worked at your old school, but we don't allow students to use their phones during the class period."

Ignoring him, Phoebus put the Othersider communicator to his ear. "I told you not to contact me here."

"Why not?" asked Titus' voice in the receiver.

"Mr. Peregrine," barked the teacher. "Put the phone away."

He sighed. "Because the use of cellular devices is prohibited on school grounds, Titus, and the reigning authority figure doesn't appear happy with me at the moment."

The teacher forced his wide body down the aisle. "Mr. Peregrine!"

"How are things going on your end?" asked Titus.

"We'll talk later. Do not contact me again. Is that understood?"

"Understood," Titus replied on the other end.

He ended the call and shoved the phone into his pocket before looking up at the teacher, who was standing over him, puffing so hard that it looked as though his pudgy face might explode. The class had gone silent with expectation, all eyes on them. Phoebus leaned back and smiled his most pleasant smile.

"Forgive the interruption. You may continue with your class."

***

Explaining his infraction to the office staff was tedious, but he succeeded in getting released with only a warning. Using the new student charm had its uses. Unfortunately, by the time he returned to the teeming adolescent population, science class was over, and the early lunch period was getting underway.

He selected an empty bench along the outskirts of the cafeteria where he could think in peace. He didn't see the girl, but he picked up the traces of other Viewers all around him. Grimm had been right. The marshlands surrounding the town were dripping with *Electricus*, and human populations around such places usually contained more Viewers.

Although all Othersiders possessed *Electricus*, only ones with above-average levels were considered Viewers—because they could see traces of the Barrier where it had weakened, which manifested as faint glimmers of light. Othersiders had even come up with their own explanations over the centuries: ghost lights, swamp gas, concentrations of methane, even fairy tales. Rovers were only required to Dull those who were deemed a hazard to the secrecy of Threshold.

Bleeders, however, were a different story.

Closing his eyes, he blocked out the undesirable cafeteria sights and smells and allowed his body to meld with the *Electricus* around him. His wrist cuffs hummed against his skin, hidden under his shirt, as he focused his concentration. There were no Viewers here who even came close to threat levels, which meant that the girl couldn't be in the cafeteria.

"Hey there."

Phoebus opened his eyes. A pretty girl with olive skin and long silky hair was blinking down at him, her brown eyes twinkling under layers of makeup and false eyelashes.

"Hello," he replied.

"You're new here, aren't you?" the girl asked, looking him up and down as she twirled a strand of her hair between her glittery fingernails "My name's Ashlynn."

"Fee."

She giggled. "Just Fee?"

"Just Fee."

She perched herself on the bench next to him, adjusting her khaki skirt and crossing her legs in a manner intended to catch his attention. "Well, it's nice to meet you, Fee."

"And you," he replied, keeping his smile carefully placed, despite the assault of heavy perfume in his nostrils.

"So, what's your next class?" she asked, leaning closer.

"History, I believe."

Her glossed-over lips puckered. "Well, that's no good. I was hoping it was English. I wanted to introduce you to my friends. We don't get many new people here, unless they're with the Navy." The girl's eyes roamed over him again. "And you don't look like Navy brat material to me." The bell pealed throughout the cafeteria, and she sighed dramatically. "I swear, there's never enough social time in this school."

"Probably because it's meant to be an institute of learning," said Phoebus, standing. He didn't have the patience for pointless flirtation. "It was a pleasure to meet you, Ashlynn. I'm sure we'll see each other again."

She laughed, reminding him of a chattering squirrel.

"Oh, most definitely," she said. "Catch you later…Fee."

***

It was a monotonous routine, moving from one class to the other; avoiding the more irritating students, pretending to care about the work he was given by well-meaning teachers, and learning his way through the school with ease. But he didn't see the Viewer. Not until the end of the day.

He leaned against a tree in the front courtyard, watching students exit the school. Although he kept his expression apathetic, his senses were on alert. It didn't take him long to spot her. She was with her friend—the lanky red-haired one she'd been talking to earlier that morning. They were heading away from the school, in the direction of the town.

She laughed at something Red-Hair said, and the sight of them bothered Phoebus, like an annoying insect buzzing around his head. He closed his hand into a fist, dimly aware of the currents swirling to the surface from deep inside him. That didn't matter. His only concern was setting his mind at ease—to prove that he'd done his job, and she posed no threat.

He needed to find an opportunity that would allow him to concentrate on her *Electricus* without weaker Viewers clouding his senses. But the thought of being near the girl both angered and unnerved him. The emotions caught him off-guard, and his chest tightened, pressing against his ribcage.

As he observed Red-Hair, who was fawning around her like some simpering puppy, his palm twitched, and he glanced down. A streak of blue light wrapped around his hand and then materialized into an arrow in his palm, its amber tip pulsing. If he'd been anywhere else, his course of action would be easy: fire a quick shot and knock the chattering boy unconscious for a few hours. Then he'd be able to focus on her alone. The weapon seemed to call to him, demanding it be used to fulfill that precise purpose.

He needed more *Electricus* to draw from, to harness. But where would be a feasible location for the energy he required?

Where could he take her?

"Hi again."

He flexed his fingers, and the arrow dissolved. The electrical energy dissipated into his skin as he slowly turned around. The heavily made-up girl from the cafeteria was at his shoulder, her smile nearly as bright as the sunlight radiating off her large gold earrings.

"We meet again," he said evenly. "Ashlynn, isn't it?"

"You remembered," she replied with too much excitement in her voice for his taste. "Well, I wasn't about to let you get away." Her fingers brushed the sleeve of his shirt. "Listen, there's a bunch of us going camping next weekend. Me and the girls thought you might want to come. You know, get to know some people, since you're new to school and everything."

She tossed her head, flinging her hair off her shoulders, and jutted her chin toward the front steps. The girls she'd mentioned all waved at them from the railing. Phoebus let his gaze roam over them for a moment while he thought.

"Camping," he replied. "Where?"

"In the marsh," she said, making a face. "And yeah, I know it sounds completely gross, but there's actually some really nice spots that aren't that marsh-like, and the best thing is, it's totally adult-free, if you know what I mean." She winked. "It's going to be a lot of fun."

Movement caught his eye, and he glanced over her shoulder as the Viewer and Red-Hair disappeared around the corner of the building. But as he watched them leave, his mind regurgitated a conversation he'd overheard between them earlier that day, just before he'd approached. They had been talking about a camping trip. In the marsh—a place where Barrier energies were unstable and the *Electricus* was high.

Exactly what he needed.

"Alright," he said, turning his attention on Ashlynn. "Count me in."

Her mouth dropped open in surprise, but she quickly recovered, taking hold of his arm and blinking her lashes rapidly. "Oh, that's awesome," she cooed. "I'm totally going to need someone to help me with my tent." She grinned up at him. "Think you're up for it, Fee?"

"Absolutely."

Chapter 11

"You want to go camping," her mom said, with a laugh. "In the marsh."

"Yeah," she replied. "Just overnight. With a bunch of people from school."

Although Jamie was convinced that he'd worn her down, in truth, her change of heart didn't have anything to do with his persistence.

Pulling out a cutting board, her mom began slicing apples. Her mom had no problem cooking for weekend parties at the homes of other Navy wives, but Selene couldn't remember the last meal they'd had together that wasn't microwavable. It would've been nice to sit down to a real dinner every once in a while, like they'd done when her father used to be home.

Her mom dumped a pile of red slivers down the garbage disposal. "You've always hated the marsh."

"Not always."

"Okay, well, you have since your accident, then. You've barely even set foot in our backyard, let alone the marsh, in two years. What's changed?"

As she tugged on her ponytail, Selene's gaze drifted to the kitchen window. The marsh beyond their backyard was already turning brown with the autumn season, and the gray sky only added to the almost poetic dreariness of the scene.

What had changed had a lot to do with Mr. New Guy from school. She couldn't stop thinking about the weird aura that she'd seen clinging to his body. It reminded her of an image she'd seen before, but couldn't place—no matter how much she wracked her brain. She'd avoided the marsh for so long. But now, some long-dead curiosity sparked inside her. What was out there among the cordgrass and gnarled trees?

She thought about the men in town and the weird buzzing that lingered along her arms, just under her skin. The sensation sizzled with familiarity, too, in ways that made her head hurt. Slowly, the need for answers, for closure...for *something*...replaced her gnawing trepidation.

"Selene?"

"Yeah?"

"You didn't answer my question."

"I don't know what's changed, Mom," she replied, letting the half-lie slip past her lips with ease. "I guess I just want to hang out with people and do something different, for once."

"Well, I'm glad you're finally—" Her mother frowned. "What exactly do you mean by 'different'?"

The screen door creaked and Jamie burst into the kitchen. His hair was obscured by a hoodie, but his face beamed like sunlight on water.

"Hey, Mrs. Windell." His gaze darted to the counter. "Apples!" He snatched one and bit into it, crunching loudly.

"I just peeled that." Her mother raised the knife.

Jamie backed away, hands up in surrender and grinning through a mouthful of fruit that dribbled down his chin. "Sorry!" He wiped his face with the back of his sleeve. "You ready to go, Selene?"

"Yeah." She grabbed her jacket from the chair. "I was just talking to Mom about the camping trip next weekend."

"Ah ha," said her mom. "Now I see why she's begging to go. You've put her up to this, haven't you?"

"It was the power of my thumb-swear," he replied, holding his hand in hitchhiker position for effect. "She can't resist."

"Oh, yeah," said Selene. "Because a thumb soaked with your spit is just so convincing."

"I'm just doing my part to get you out of your social rut," he said, giving her a light shove. "I'll look after her, Mrs. Windell, don't worry."

Selene smacked his arm. "No, I'll be looking after you."

"I'm all for you hanging out with people, Selene." Her mom's smiled faded. "But I don't know that I'm comfortable with you being out there all night."

"Mom, you've told me a million times that I need to put my accident behind me. Now I'm finally trying to, and you're giving me a hard time about it?"

"Blake's parents really need a headcount by tomorrow," added Jamie. "They're going to reserve the campsites for us."

Her mother flicked the switch for the garbage disposal, her expression wavering. When the apple peels were sufficiently disposed of, she looked back at them sternly.

"Okay." She held up her hand before either of them could speak. "But I expect you to be careful. You can use Jamie's phone to check in with me. And no drinking. Do you hear me?"

"Mom, you know I don't drink."

"Then no other illegal activities."

"Unless Jamie annoys me into committing murder, I think I can stay out of trouble for one night."

Jamie pulled an offended face. "Man, with friends like this..."

Opening the screen door, she pushed Jamie in front of her, and he hopped down the steps like a kid going to the circus.

"Hey," said her mother, hurrying to the door. "Where are you going? I bought a new brand of frozen pizza. I thought you might like it."

Ducking inside, Selene kissed her on the cheek. "Mom, not to be rude or anything, but that sounds gross. Jamie and I are going to grab some food at the festival, anyway."

Her mother rolled her eyes to the ceiling. "What is it with this town and festivals?"

"Tourists," called Jamie from several yards down the front walk. "The locals gotta make money somehow."

"Fine. Just don't be too late," said her mom, closing the screen.

Selene ignored her mother's frown as she hurried to catch up.

Chapter 12

Phoebus paced the room like a caged tiger.

"Where've you been?" he snarled.

Nyx shot him an incredulous look from across the room. "Doing what you ordered. Getting acquainted with the town."

He flung himself into a chair. "It's nearly nightfall. I was getting worried."

Nyx shifted her gaze to Titus, who shrugged as he closed the front door of the *Seaside Inn* and walked into the sitting room. Unlike the living room on the opposite side of the foyer, the only mirror in the smaller room was one made of common glass, which meant no Elder—and no Preceptor Moth—would be able to listen in. It was something Phoebus made sure of before choosing the location.

"Well," Titus asked. "Did you locate any Viewers?"

He glared out the window. "One."

"And?"

"Her educational records indicate that she is in her last year of required schooling, making her slightly older than when I Dulled her, of course." He forced her face from his mind, determined to concentrate only on facts. "But *Electricus* doesn't lie. It is, without a doubt, the same Viewer."

"You located the same Viewer?" said Titus. "Well, that was easy." He perched on the edge of a patterned chaise, reminding Phoebus of a large scavenger bird. "What else did you find out?"

"She has fifth-period English and her locker combination is 10-27-10."

"That's it?"

"What sort of answer were you expecting? It's a *school*, Titus. Social interaction is somewhat limited." He glowered at the crumpled piece of paper beside him. "Especially when the schedule you were given by the Weavers doesn't include a single class with the object of your investigation."

"I'm sure you could get the schedule changed," said Nyx. She sat in the chair opposite him. "Otherwise it's going to be difficult getting to know her."

"I don't need to know her," he snapped.

He refused to admit weakness concerning his assignment, but it had been eating at him like a disease. He rubbed his fingers against the metal cuff hidden beneath his tailored sleeve. His skin still prickled with a trace of the girl's unusual signature.

He'd never felt anything like it before.

"Why are you acting so defensive?" Nyx demanded. "We need to collect as much information about the anomalies surrounding this Coil as we can. Elder Grimm told you to investigate Viewers you came across, and since you've already had contact with her, it only makes sense to—"

"I know my orders," he replied firmly. "And I will carry them out."

Nyx's eyes remained calm, like deep pools of dark water. "Surely there are more Viewers in this town to investigate."

"Do you require help?" asked Titus, his brow furrowing in a way that Phoebus had seen many times when he sensed things lurking beneath the surface. "Is there more to this than what you're sharing?"

Bleeder.

Although Phoebus hadn't said the word out loud, it echoed in the recesses of his mind.

No one at the Outpost, including your own Trine, can know your new orders.

Moth's words joined the silent cacophony inside his head. This wasn't the first time he'd kept things from his Trine, but it had always been his choice, and for his own reasons—to protect them, or to protect himself.

Although he strained to tell Titus and Nyx the truth—and relay Moth's information—his orders screamed louder, setting him back on the path of duty. A smile slid carefully across his face, as smooth as butter and as sharp as broken glass.

"I can handle my own assignment, thank you. Now, let's talk

about yours."

Titus gave him a strange look, but obliged. "Well, Cruz and his Trine showed us around St. Mary's while you were gone." He plucked a handful of candy out of a crystal bowl on the table. "It's not a bad sort of town. Quaint and a bit backwards, perhaps, but pleasant."

"I'm pleased you enjoyed your little outing with the Rogues." He didn't hide the venom in his voice. "But your orders were to investigate the Barrier and the Coil, not to take a tour with a Trine of renegades."

A rare flash of anger ignited behind Titus' eyes. "What have you got against these Rogues, Fee? You're acting as though they're worse than Leeches."

"Outpost Trines aren't like us," he replied, lacing his fingers under his chin and squeezing them until his knuckles burned. "They've permanently Merged with this world. They aren't Thresh-olders anymore."

Titus popped a piece of candy in his mouth. "That viewpoint's a little extreme, don't you think? What about us? We were required to serve in an Outpost as part of our first-year apprentice training."

"These aren't apprentices, in case you haven't noticed," he replied. "They're about ten years too old for that."

"Alright," said Titus. "So that means they either volunteered for service at this Coil, or they were…" He dropped off as his eyes sharpened with understanding. "Or they were sentenced here."

"Correct." He snatched the candies from Titus' open palm and examined them. They appeared to be some kind of chocolate, covered with hard multicolored shells. He ate a few, satisfied at the way the sugar melted against his tongue. "These are quite good."

"Don't change the subject," said Nyx. She smoothed her dark braid and glanced around the room, as if she were expecting the Rogues to materialize from the walls. "What did this Trine do?"

The chocolate turned bitter in the back of his throat. "How should I know?"

"You seem to know something, at least with regard to Cruz."

Phoebus studied the remaining candy in his hand. The outer shells had already begun to melt with the heat of his skin, leaving streaks of blue, green, and red food coloring against his palm. He blinked once as his mind folded inward with memory.

Blue Electricus *streaked back and forth across the courtyard of the Keep as the Preceptor and her apprentice faced off. Despite the quick movements of their sparring, Moth's hood remained fixed in place, as always, with only a few wisps of black hair coming loose from the shadowy depths. Phoebus never understood how the Preceptor managed it. His own hood had long since fallen about his shoulders during their session.*

"Your guard is pathetic," hissed Moth.

He sidestepped a flash of Electricus. *"So is your aim."*

Aiming rapidly, he fired a shot from his bow.

Moth slammed her gloved hands together, catching the energy-infused arrow between her palms. It disintegrated between her fingers in an impressive, shimmering display. She brushed her gloves off against the sides of her mantellum *and nodded.*

Phoebus sensed her smirk within the hood.

"That would've struck the heart of one who was not prepared," she commented, "But you must always assume your enemy will be prepared."

He had nearly completed his training, and he'd already been assigned his first Trine. He was eager to begin his first mission. But Moth hadn't given her approval yet. There was always one more training session with her. One more lesson to learn.

And he was growing impatient.

"Preceptor, surely I've proven my capabilities by now."

Moth approached the large fountain in the center of the courtyard. She sat on the edge of the stone wall. The tilt of her hooded head indicated that he should join her. Although he obediently approached, he did not sit. Apart from sparring, he didn't feel comfortable being too close to the Preceptor.

It was like a rat venturing too close to a snake.

"You are capable, Phoebus," she replied. "Of that, I must admit."

"Then why all these extra sessions?"

"Your new Trine is young, but eager. Cruz, in particular, is headstrong."

"Not always his best quality," he replied, allowing a smirk. "But it's what I like about him."

Moth tilted her head to one side. "A quality you may come to regret."

"I haven't so far, and I've known him as long as anyone here." Phoebus shrugged. "I trust him completely."

Several uncomfortable moments passed, and he desperately wished someone would come and interrupt them—even an annoying young novice would be preferable to the Preceptor. Any time he was with her, it felt as though she were analyzing his thoughts. Out of the corner of his eye, he watched Moth's gloved hands clenching and unclenching in her lap. Finally, she drew in a deep breath.

"I understand you and Cruz are close," she said in a low tone, "but I am concerned that your friendship has clouded your judgment. Although he is skilled and ready for duty, he does not always listen to reason." Moth paused and glanced into the pool of indigo water. "I believe Cruz glories more in the actions of his position than in the purpose behind it. He will need someone equally as strong to bend his will in the proper way and keep him on the right path."

"And you believe that's me."

Moth glanced up at him, and Phoebus could see the gleam in her electric blue eyes.

"I do not," she replied coldly. "But Elder Grimm thinks so. Therefore, so must I."

Phoebus' mind lifted from the memory, and his eyes refocused on the melted chocolate in his palm. He took a tissue from the table and wiped off the mess.

"Cruz chose this life over his duty," he said. "And I won't waste my breath on any conversation that involves him. So let's talk about something more pleasant, shall we?" He took another piece of candy from the crystal bowl and rolled it between his fingers. "Like these delicacies."

With an irritated sigh, Nyx stood and moved to the entryway. "Well, regardless of why this Trine is here, they've been entrusted with protecting the Barrier and the Coil. No matter what we might think about them, we need them."

"Doesn't mean I have to be happy about it," he replied.

"Maybe not," said Titus in his firm voice, "but you should give them a chance. Like it or not, Fee, we've got to work with them. We have to become a part of this Otherside."

"I'll do what needs to be done here, Titus. But I'll never be a part of this."

"You were once, though."

Slowly, Phoebus wrapped his fingers around the arms of the chair. There was a roar in his ears—a dull sound at first, but rising quickly, like surging floodwaters, until it was so loud that the edges of his vision went black. His entire body was shaking, and in his hazy tunnel-vision sight, he could see Titus stand quickly, the color draining from his face.

Closing his eyes and squeezing them shut, Phoebus shoved memories deep down before he could access them, forcing his body to relax while clamping down on his control. Like pressure being released from a steamer, his anger cooled.

"Never mention that again."

Titus regarded him like a dangerous wild animal he'd just encountered in the woods.

"Forgive me, Phoebus."

The air was stifling, and he pushed past Titus to the front window, raising the sash. Rows of streetlights were flickering on, warding off the approaching night. As the fresh air entered the room, he was able to structure his thoughts until a familiar calm settled over him, like a comfortable suit of armor.

He was tired of being cooped up at the Outpost. Idle time wreaked havoc on his resolve, and the longer he remained boxed in like some stuffy Regent, the easier it was to forget who he was and what he was meant to do. He took a cleansing breath. He was a Rover again—a Rover with a mission to complete.

And there was only one way to do that.

He faced his Trine. "This morning, I heard Paloma mention something about an event being held in town tonight. Do either of you know anything about this?"

"It's a festival," said Nyx, her expression indicating that she was trying to figure out his sudden change in mood. "Apparently, St. Mary's is famous for them. Traders, music, food—that sort of thing."

"Sounds like fun," he said. "Perhaps we should go."

"What?" said Titus and Nyx, together.

The unison of their reply caused a genuine smile to tug at the corner of his mouth. There was no reason to burden his Trine with his secrets, even if he did have liberty to share. Sentiment never achieved anything when it came to being a Trine leader. But maintaining unity and mutual respect was crucial.

"You were right, Titus," he said.

Titus crossed his arms. "About what?"

"About being a part of the Otherside," he replied lightly, though the words made his stomach roll. He clasped his Trinemate's shoulder. "We can't track and monitor Viewers if we don't mingle with the crowds. And since we're supposed to be townsfolk now, I suppose it's time we started acting like it."

"By attending the festival," said Nyx, her face like a sunrise.

"Yes," said Phoebus, feeling a little nauseous. "Just don't make me regret it."

Chapter 13

The pavement glistened like jewels under the glow of St. Mary's streetlights. Carpets of golden leaves plastered the curb, their sodden bodies clogging the gutters. Although the brief evening shower had done little more than wet the ground, it had cooled the air, leaving the night pleasant and breezy.

"You're being quiet," said Jamie. He pressed his sneaker into a pile of leaves until they oozed water. "You gonna tell me what's up?"

"Just enjoying the walk," Selene replied.

That much was true. It was nice being outside, enjoying the aftereffects of the rain—especially since there hadn't been any thunder or lightning accompanying it. It was a reminder that she hadn't *always* been freaked out by storms.

"Okay, changing gears," said Jamie. "So what really made you decide to go on the camping trip?" He looked at her quickly. "I mean, not that I'm complaining or anything. Just curious."

She hesitated. It wasn't as though she had an easy, solid answer—at least, not one that he would understand. "Maybe I've just been thinking about stuff lately."

"Stuff?"

"Yeah," she replied, keeping her eyes on the street. "Like how I need to finally get past my accident and looking over my shoulder every time I see a gray cloud, and well, just…everything, really. Maybe it's time for me to start taking some chances. Get out and do some things."

Jamie adjusted the collar of his jacket. "Well, if you need any help with the doing of said *things*," he grinned, "let it be known that I'm here to help."

She bumped her shoulder against his bicep, since she couldn't quite reach his shoulder. He'd really shot up over the summer. "Yeah,

I think I'm going to pass on that offer. But thanks."

"Okay. Your loss. Remember that."

"Oh, I will."

Turning onto Main Street, they weaved through several orange barriers that had been arranged to close off the road to incoming traffic. Rows of booths and tables lined the streets, each crowded with people. Vendors hawked their wares under strings of colored lights and lanterns. Festival-goers milled about, tasting samples and examining the arts and crafts.

Everything smelled of boiled peanuts and barbeque, of autumn spices and apple pies. She took a deep breath, letting the aromas hug her insides. This was when she liked St. Mary's best: comfortable, filled with history and tradition.

As they passed the darkened windows of one of the vacant buildings, uneasiness slithered its way into her mood. She glanced over her shoulder, half-expecting to see someone watching her from behind. But no one was following her. Why would they?

She had to get a grip on her paranoia.

Jamie took the lead, and her pace slowed as she tried to take in the sights. A few people waved at her—mostly moms from Navy families. But Jamie, who was homegrown and proud of it, returned numerous greetings as he navigated through the festival coterie.

"Hey, pit stop," he called over his shoulder.

"You're supposed to take care of that before you leave the house."

Before she could make another smart comment, he grabbed her elbow and steered her across the street. She knew where he was heading: *The Reading Room*. It was the only other bookshop in town, but it boasted a large comic book and science fiction section.

"Okay," she said, laughing as he maneuvered her through the front door. "But just a quick look, okay? I'm starving."

"Yeah, yeah. Ten minutes, tops."

His mop of red hair disappeared around a bookshelf.

Hovering near the counter, she thumbed through a collection of bookmarks, antsy to be back in the open. For the first time in years, she felt better being outside. Even if there were weird creeps following her, the festival was well-lit and there were people everywhere. Nothing could happen.

She stared through the windows, listening to the dull strains of music coming from the waterfront. Even the air seemed differently charged tonight. But maybe this was turning over a new leaf. She was taking charge of her life, beginning with crushing her old fears.

A display had been set up near the front door, advertising horror books for Halloween. Red and black streamers hung from the ceiling. A couple of covers with zombies on them caught her eye. As she plucked one from the shelf, she noticed someone in the aisle. He stood with a casual posture and a thick hardback book in his hand, his attention on what he was reading.

Fee.

She held her book closer and peered over the top. The new guy's profile was unmistakable, with his prominent nose and jaw. The way his hair was tied at the nape of his neck contrasted the tailored look of his shirt and jeans.

His stance shifted, injecting her with the panic of nearly being caught staring. The words on her page swirled, making it useless to concentrate, so after a few seconds, she allowed herself to watch him again. His lips moved slightly as he read, and the lopsided crook of his mouth was visible, even from the side.

There was no aura around him; no faint glow like she'd seen in the classroom—if she hadn't imagined it, which was still a *big* "if".

Should she speak to him? It would be the friendly thing to do. But his behavior yesterday had been odd. One minute, he'd been pleasant. The next, he was standoffish. Plus, she'd seen him talking to Ashlynn after school, and he'd been all charm and smiles. If she approached him now, what version of the new guy—of *Fee*—would she be talking to?

As she took another guarded peek in his direction, Jamie rounded the corner of the same aisle, almost running into Fee. Jamie jerked back on his heels as Fee's head snapped around, and he drew up, like he was ready to fight. His free hand curled into a fist, and she could've sworn there was a glimmer of blue shimmering between his fingers.

"Sorry, man," Jamie said, seemingly oblivious to his reaction. Then his face flickered with recognition. "Hey, you're the new guy, aren't you? I remember seeing you in class."

Fee's face relaxed into a cool mask. "Yes, that would be me."

As she hesitated, feeling weird to intrude, she focused on his voice. It was deep, rich, and carried that slight hint of an accent she didn't recognize.

"Good to meet you." Jamie held out his hand. "I'm Jamie."

She could see the new guy physically hesitate before returning the handshake.

"I'm Fee."

"So where'd you move from?" asked Jamie, ever the conversationalist.

Fee closed his book. "Up north."

"Cool. Is your family with the Navy, too?"

Something dark passed over the new guy's face, and his brows lowered, as though he were calculating something in his head. Then his expression smoothed into that same cool mask again.

"Ah, no. I'm actually staying with some family here for a few months."

Jamie shifted a stack of comics under his arm. "I thought you might be a Navy import, like Selene."

He gestured in her direction. She clutched the book in a death grip, heat prickling behind her ears, as Fee slowly turned. By the look on his face, he'd had no idea she'd been standing there. His skin turned an odd shade, and his lips tightened into a firm line.

"Hi," she said, waving awkwardly as she approached.

At their last meeting, she'd been struck by the gorgeous caramel color of his eyes. Now, observing closer, she noticed the hint of dark circles discoloring the skin underneath. He looked at her in a preoccupied sort of way, like he had more important things to do than make small talk with a couple of locals. His vibe was impossible to read, unlike Jamie's—who displayed his thoughts like a flashing neon sign.

"Glad to see you survived your first day," she continued.

He seemed almost pained, caught between speaking and not speaking. Returning his book to the shelf, his long fingers graced the spine as he released it. She noted the author: Edgar Allen Poe.

"It wasn't too difficult," he said after a long pause.

"O-kay," said Jamie. "Well, it was nice to meet you. I'm going to part with my hard-earned money now." He gestured to his armload of comics. "And then we've gotta get going. Right, Selene?"

"Yeah." She shelved the book she'd been strangling, nowhere near where it was supposed to go. She looked at Fee, then blurted, "Why don't you hang with us? We can show you around the festival, if you want."

A comic slipped from Jamie's hand, fluttering to the floor.

"Yeah," he said, sounding less than enthusiastic as he bent to retrieve it.

Fee's eyes met hers. Under the store lights, they appeared flecked with copper. He shoved his hands into the pockets of his jeans, his arms tense under the form-fitting sleeves of his shirt. But his smile was easy, carefree.

"I'd like that."

"Perfect," said Jamie. He shot her a hidden look as he shuffled to the counter.

After leaving, she insisted they get something to eat—partially because she *was* truly hungry, but also because she couldn't find anything else to say. What the heck had she been thinking, inviting him along? Was it curiosity about the aura light, or wanting to figure out his chameleon personality—or was it just his good looks that caused her brain to come up blank?

Jamie, who thankfully remained pleasantly talkative—even with Fee in tow—agreed to the eating plans, then began suggesting different food booths as they neared the waterfront. As for Fee, he maintained a fairly consistent distance between them since joining their company.

"Got a food preference?" she asked over her shoulder.

Fee's eyes snapped to hers, and there was a glaze in them, as though he'd been deep in thought.

"Whatever you two would like to eat is fine with me," he replied.

Jamie raised a brow at her, which she could read like a news statement: *Why are we putting up with this guy?*

Reaching over, she squeezed Jamie's hand and returned his silent question with her own look. *Just trying to be friendly.*

It was enough to return him to the topic of food options, and it gave her another chance to steal a glance at Fee, who was staring into the distance, jaw as tight as a rubber band. His fingers were constantly twitching at his sides, like someone might do if they were sifting through sand at the beach, looking for shells.

"Ah, barbeque, how I love thee," sighed Jamie.

He pointed to a striped pavilion framed with strings of decorative lights. A rusty barbeque smoker billowed scents into the night air, and the smell of the cooking meat made Selene's mouth water. Jamie skirted around a few people and secured a place in line as she followed, and Fee eased in behind them.

"Is this okay with you?" she asked.

Fee's gaze swept over the crowd.

"It's fine," he replied, clearly not interested in food.

She crossed her arms—feeling a little stupid, but also a twinge of irritation. "Hey, if you don't want to hang with us, it's okay. I'm sure you can find your way around easily enough."

As he looked at her again, her arms tingled, and she shuddered. Above their heads, the lights flickered with a sharp buzzing sound. Suddenly Fee's expression hardened, and he glared over her shoulder. Instinctively, she followed his line of sight. A boy and a girl stood at the corner of the opposite street. Fee seemed bothered by their presence.

"Friends of yours?"

"Cousins, actually," Fee replied.

Selene squinted through the haze of streetlights. The girl had gorgeous skin and black hair that spilled down her back in a loose braid. The boy was tall, with floppy brown curls and hawkish features. Although the girl stood with a casual, confident air, and the boy leaned lazily against the lamppost—just like Fee—they seemed out of place.

"I didn't see them at school," she said.

"They're just visiting," he replied.

People nudged past them, and she realized that she and Fee had dropped out of the food line. Jamie was up front, being served his dish.

Although the street was crowded, Selene couldn't shake the jittery feeling that someone's eyes were on her. The tips of her fingers prickled, like tiny insects stinging beneath her skin. Shaking out her hands, she stared through the dim glow, mingled with shadows. In every shadow, she kept seeing images of looming figures, even though her logic told her it was all in her head.

"So," she said, turning to Fee for distraction, "do your cousins want to join us?"

For a moment, he seemed caught off-guard. His brow was deeply furrowed, increasing the lines around his eyes.

"I have to go," he said tightly.

"What?"

He didn't reply—didn't even look at her.

He just left.

She was too stunned to call after him as he crossed the street toward his cousins. And then, she saw it: the same apparitional glow, clinging faintly to their outlines as well. An eerie sensation fluttered in her stomach. She couldn't be imagining it. Not this time. The three hurried away from the festival, vanishing behind a building.

"Weird," she breathed.

Jamie appeared, bearing a heaping plate of barbeque. "You've called me that too many times. I'm afraid it's no longer an insult."

"Yeah," she said, only half-listening.

He took a bite of barbeque. "So, where'd the new guy go?"

She shrugged on her jacket. That's exactly what she wanted to know.

"Hey, I'll be right back, okay?"

She darted across the street, leaving Jamie behind her.

Chapter 14

"I told you to keep your distance."

Phoebus ushered his Trine behind a storefront and checking to make sure he hadn't been followed. He'd felt the Viewer girl's eyes bearing down on him the entire way across the street.

"We did," said Titus, falling into step beside him.

"Keeping your distance requires subtlety, in case you two have forgotten."

"We were easily forty feet away," said Nyx, sounding defensive.

"Yes, and staring me down so hard I think you left a mark on my forehead," he replied. "I had to make up some ridiculous story about you being my cousins."

"Did she believe you?" asked Titus.

"Would you?" he replied. Nothing about the assignment was going well. "I was trying to glean some information from her before your untimely appearance."

Nyx's thin brows rose to her hairline. "Really? Because it looked as though you were trying your best to avoid her. And since when do you back away from a pretty girl, especially one who seems so drawn to your charms, as pompous and egocentric as they may be?"

Phoebus' chest tightened, even as he shot Nyx one of his best smiles. "There's no need to overwhelm the poor girl. My charms have been known to cause permanent injury."

Titus huffed. "Yeah, like brain damage."

"Ah, jealousy rears its ugly head," he replied.

"I'm not jealous."

"Of course you are. It's completely understandable." He ducked as Titus took a swing at his head; the reaction improved his mood. "But back to the matter at hand," he continued. "What *are* you doing here? I specifically told you to do an inspection of the Barrier while

I talked to the girl. Something about the *Electricus* hasn't felt right since we arrived at this festival."

Titus shoved his hands into his pockets with an uncharacteristic sneer. "That's what we've been doing, Fee. While you've been flirting-not-flirting with Viewers, Nyx and I explored the waterfront and the cemetery. But I'm having difficulty getting clear readings tonight. My senses are clouded, for some reason."

"Paloma said that St. Mary's is sitting on top of what used to be the active Mocama Coil," said Nyx, studying the sky above the waterfront. "Maybe it's the concentration of energy."

"It's possible," Phoebus replied, though he didn't believe his own words. He'd been around enough Coils in his life. Their unstable energies set his senses firing, like a spinning compass near a magnetic field. But what he was feeling now was different, and he didn't have an explanation. Not yet. "Perhaps we should—"

"Wait," said Titus abruptly.

As Phoebus jerked to a halt, he saw Titus sway unsteadily on his feet, the color draining from his face. His eyes shifted out of focus and filmed over until they looked like two white marbles—signs that Titus was keyed in to a change in the Barrier—a draining ability Phoebus was thankful he didn't share.

"What is it?" he demanded. "What do you sense?"

"There's something wrong," Titus murmured, rocking forward.

Nyx sucked in a breath. "A Rift?"

Phoebus scanned the area around them, searching for the telltale white light that meant a tear had opened in the protective membrane. Although everything appeared normal, his skin felt hot with warning, and hairs lifted along the nape of his neck.

Titus crumpled forward, as though someone had kicked him in the gut. Phoebus reached out to steady him, but his Trinemate shook him off and took a gulp of air. His eyes were normal again, but his face remained contorted, like he was trying to breathe and choking on foul air.

"Not a Rift," said Titus, shaking as he came back to himself. "It's something else."

"What are you talkin—"

Then he felt it, too. There was a presence nearby.

And it wasn't native to this world.

Moving with brisk strides, he began a search down the rows of old buildings just off the main roadway. The breeze had picked up, and the bloated clouds above their heads felt ripe with energy. The air around the three of them hummed, and Phoebus felt his wristbands vibrate in response.

"Behind me," he ordered.

The Trine moved as one unit, gliding behind storefronts, away from the pleasant sounds of the festival. Phoebus' Othersider shoes sank into dirty gravel, and he scowled, wishing for his sturdy Rover boots. The air smelled damp, with a hint of sewage that made his nose burn.

"Down this alley," Titus whispered, pointing to a narrow opening between two buildings.

Phoebus nodded grimly. The presence was unmistakable now, and he knew one thing for certain: *it wasn't a Rover or a Rogue.* With a flick of his wrist, he summoned his longbow, and the weapon materialized in swirl of blue light. The bow's amber designs flickered like streams of lava along the stave. He didn't like the idea of entering an enclosed space.

It made it harder to fight.

"Ready?" he whispered.

Nyx positioned her *nadala* in front of her like a rapier.

"Ready."

Titus' twin knives appeared in his hands, metallic and blazing. "Right behind you."

Phoebus led his Trine into the alley.

He slid along the wall, which was dripping with ooze and grime. It seeped through his thin shirt and chilled his skin. As he moved behind a stack of rotting crates, he glanced at his Trine and tapped his ear, and both nodded in response. They could all hear it: a low, buzzing hum. It was a noise that common Othersiders might associate with high-voltage power stations or transformers.

With a jut of his chin, he motioned his Trine into the corner formed by the wall and the crates. Then he approached the edge of their hiding place and peered around the wood.

A dark figure hovered near a collection of trash bins. Its body was hunched over some object he couldn't see. Blue sparks pinged off the metal dumpsters, producing an unnerving, static-charged reverberation as it moved closer to the object with desperate jerking movements.

As if sensing their presence, the thing's head snapped up. Eyes blazed like blue fire from under its hood, illuminating hollowed features, with bones protruding under deadened skin that was stretched far too thin. Although a thick cloak shrouded its body, its spidery limbs and grotesquely twisted frame were visible enough.

"Leech," hissed Phoebus.

The creature shrieked and clutched the object to its chest. The object, he realized with horror, was an old man—thin and shabby, his head rolling lifelessly as currents of *Electricus* streaked over his body. Phoebus rushed forward, and an arc of electricity spewed from the Leech's hand, slamming him in the chest. He went airborne and crashed into the wall.

The impact rattled Phoebus' teeth and his weapons skittered over mucky concrete. Titus sprang into action, wielding his knives. Another arc spewed from the Leech's hand, but Titus rolled under the stream, flinging one knife. The weapon ripped through the creature's cloak, pinning him to a piece of discarded paneling. The Leech dropped the old man and clutched the knife hilt with a hideous scream.

"Nyx!" shouted Phoebus, scrambling up. "Open the Barrier!"

Without hesitation, she slashed the air with her *nadala*. The atmosphere rippled, but no opening appeared. She yelled in desperation, slicing madly around her.

"I can't find it!" she cried. "Titus! I can't find it!"

Titus turned and opened his mouth, but the Leech was suddenly free. It grabbed him by the shirt, hoisting him into the air. As Titus grasped the creature's discolored arm, he turned his whited-out eyes to Nyx and waved his free hand toward a space near the garbage bin.

"There," he sputtered.

Nyx pierced the empty air in the exact spot Titus directed. The air shuddered and shimmered brightly, and a Rift opened in the space like a yawning beast. With a furious screech, the Leech heaved Titus aside. It leapt for Nyx, lips pulled back from blackened teeth.

But Phoebus intercepted it.

"I don't think so," he snarled, taking aim. The Leech blasted another current, but he sidestepped the arc. "You've worn out your welcome."

With a sizzling zing, his arrow sank deep into the Leech's cloaked chest. The creature gagged, and its luminous eyes flooded with pain. *Electricus* built too rapidly in its body to contain. It clawed at the arrow, trying desperately to pull it out.

The Leech exploded in a nova of blue electricity.

The Rift spun like a whirlpool and sucked the light debris into its shining maw, absorbing the remnants of the Leech's energy. Nyx drove the *nadala* into the orb, sewing with such speed that Phoebus couldn't see her hands. As the light evaporated, then fizzled to nothing, the alley went still and dark. The creature was gone, its life energy swallowed by the Barrier itself.

Titus picked himself up as Nyx hurried to the old man's side. She knelt, feeling for a pulse. After a moment, her dark eyes flooded with relief.

"He's alive," she said. "Just unconscious."

They propped the man's body against the dumpster. He groaned, eyes still closed. Titus studied the man's tattered shirt. The fabric had been ripped open, exposing his chest. The skin was an ugly shade of red, just below the collarbone, and there was a fist-size wound in the middle of his sternum that looked like a bad burn.

Titus glanced up, his face grim. "Extraction."

"A Viewer, then," said Phoebus.

He didn't have to read the man's energy levels. He could see the evidence for himself. It was obvious that the Leech had been siphoning the extra *Electricus* from the Viewer's body and absorbing it into his own.

A dangerous process. And illegal.

Phoebus flexed his fingers, allowing his weapons to dissipate into thin air.

"Come on," he said.

Nyx stood, looking apprehensive. "But what about him?"

He glanced at the old man. "You know the Viewer won't remember anything when he wakes. Best to just leave him here. Now, let's go."

Brushing himself off, he sloshed through the narrow alley toward the street. He could hear the others scurrying to catch up behind him, and he picked up his pace, trying to cool off the sliver of molten fury that was lacing its way around his chest.

"Where are we going?" asked Titus as they reached him.

Phoebus growled darkly. "To have a little chat with Cruz."

Chapter 15

The monster exploded.

Knocked off her feet, Selene choked back a cry as gravel bit her hands and scraped her shoulder. A strange noise filled the alleyway, and then everything around her went silent. She laid perfectly still in her hiding place, heart racing, too afraid to move.

She heard Fee's voice—firm, commanding, and furious. Footsteps echoed against the brick walls. They grew faint and disappeared. After another few moments of quiet, she forced her body to move again. Sitting up, she sucked in gulps of cool, but sour, garbage-tinged air.

The alley was deserted. There was nothing but trash bins, cardboard boxes, and rotting wooden pallets—and an old man, leaning against one of the dumpsters, wrapping his ratty clothes around his thin frame.

Pushing back her fear, she brushed dirt off her knees and approached, moving with slow, cautious steps.

"Sir?"

The old man stared at her, blank-faced.

"Are you alright?" she asked.

He made a grumbling sound, staggered to his feet, and headed for the nearest garbage can, ignoring her completely. The metal lid creaked as he opened it and began rifling through the trash.

She hesitated. "What are you doing?"

With a glare over his shoulder, he huffed at her. "What does it look like I'm doing? I'm going through the garbage, lady. It ain't a crime."

"There were some people here, just a second ago. Did you see where they went?"

"Ain't been nobody back here but me," he growled, returning

to the trash. "Now leave me alone."

***

Selene grabbed Jamie's arm so hard that his bag of peanuts went flying, like the explosion of a circus canon. The container hit the ground and little brown bodies spilled over the pavement.

"Oh, man!" he cried, dismayed. "That cost me six bucks!"

"Let's go." She was practically pulling him down the street.

"What's your deal?" He scooped up the bag and followed her obediently, but with a massive scowl on his face as he studied the pitiful handful of peanuts that remained at the bottom of the container.

"We just need to go home," she replied. "I need to get out of here."

Every shadow looked like a monster now.

She pressed against the edge of the buildings, looking so hard into the darkness that her eye sockets burned. No Fee. No creature. But panic had its fingers around her throat. She heard every buzz of electricity in every streetlight they passed under, and visions of the creature played over and over in her head.

Jamie was at her side. "Selene—"

"No," she snapped. "Not yet."

Everything buzzed in the same rhythm. Her wrist throbbed underneath her bracelet.

She needed it to stop before she lost it.

The quickest retreat was Jamie's house, two blocks away. Without waiting for him, she shoved open the front gate and hurried up the walk. The door to the house was locked, and he pushed past her, thrusting the paper bag into her hands as he fumbled for his keys.

"My parents are at the festival, running their pottery booth," he said, opening the door.

She collapsed on the sectional couch, not bothering with the lamp. Jamie walked in behind her, switching on the lights himself. He eased cautiously into the cushions beside her, and from the corner of her vision, she saw him studying her, his green eyes wide and confused.

Shivering, she fought against the urge to blink...because the instant she closed her eyes, she saw the lights in the alley, the monster disintegrating, and the fierce expression on Fee's face.

Jamie remained silent. Waiting for her to speak.

After a moment, he reached for her hand. The buzzing in her body abruptly ceased. She curled her fingers around his, relishing in their familiar comfort and warmth. Everything slowed. Whatever was wrong with her, it didn't faze Jamie in the least. He cupped his free hand over hers, and it felt like a soothing blanket.

"Can we watch TV?" she asked, knowing she needed to give him something—even if she couldn't talk about it. "Just for a bit?"

Her voice trembled, and Jamie heard it, too. But, true to form, he didn't question her request. With a grateful sigh, she curled her legs underneath her, as he flipped through several channels before settling on the science fiction station. They were playing *Star Wars: A New Hope.* He positioned the remote on the arm of the couch and settled in next to her.

Selene leaned against him, concentrating on her breathing until the tightness in her throat eased. As she pressed her cheek into Jamie's warm shoulder, she sighed. This was normal. This, she understood.

They watched the movie in mutual silence for a while. Jamie still held her hand, and the action radiated comfort and friendship and security. But there was also expectation. It was time for her to tell him what was going on. She kept her eyes on the young form of Harrison Ford running across the screen.

"Okay," she began. She felt Jamie straighten attentively beside her, and she worked the words around in her head before continuing. "It's that new guy, Fee. There's something wrong with him."

"Are you referring to his choice of hairstyle or his stellar attitude? Because frankly, I'd say it's a toss-up."

"I'm serious," she replied. "After I left you, I followed him into an alley. He was there with these other people." She looked down, refusing to blink. "And they *killed* something."

"What?"

Muting the television, Jamie repositioned himself to face her. She felt a wave of nausea wash over her, but she forced her mouth to keep forming words.

"There was something in the alley, Jamie. Something not...

human."

His lips pressed together for a thoughtful moment. "Okay, so I'm going to make the assumption that your phrase 'not human' isn't referring to anything in the animal category."

She shook her head, the image of the creature still fresh behind her eyes.

"So not a possum, dog, or rodent of an unusual size?"

"Did you not just hear the part about me being serious?"

He raised his hands in surrender. "Okay, okay. Just trying to be helpful here." His expression turned studious, almost clinical, but not unbelieving. "So, describe the whole thing to me."

"I can't, really." She hugged her arms, feeling icky inside, like she'd swallowed sludge. "It happened so fast. But the thing...what they killed...there was a kind of energy with it. And a blue light. I mean really blue. Like the flames in the burner when you turn on the stove."

"Okay. A gas monster. Sounds very Scooby Doo."

"Minus the bad '70s animation."

He moved closer. "And the new guy killed it?"

"Yeah," she replied, trying not to shudder. "I mean, I saw him fighting it."

"Fighting it how?"

Staring out the darkened window, she felt another smack of stupidity. Her explanation was sounding more ridiculous by the second. "I don't know," she snapped, suddenly irritated. "Like all Robin Hood and stuff, with a bow and arrow."

"Okay," said Jamie, drumming his fingers against his thigh. "We have a gas monster and the Prince of Thieves engaged in an energy battle in a back alley of town. It makes for a pretty crazy story, but I guess we should report it."

"Yeah, to *who*?"

"The police, of course," he answered, looking at her strangely. "That is, unless you've got the names of some paranormal investigators in town. Or, come to think of it, maybe the power company would be the best way to go."

"Oh, you're hilarious."

"I'm trying not to be. It's just my default setting."

"Well, there's nothing *to* report," she replied. "The thing I saw exploded, like into-thin-air exploded. Fee's gone, and the only person left in the alley was some old guy who didn't see a thing." She paused, running her thumb underneath her bracelet and feeling the raised skin of her scar. "The thing is, I think I've seen something else, before tonight. Maybe not exactly a monster...but the last few days, I don't know...I feel like someone's been following me."

Jamie frowned sharply. "Wait, following you? Why didn't you say something before now?"

"Because I'd just end up sounding like I was smoking something," she shot back, shuddering all over. "And honestly, now that I've said it out loud, it sounds even worse, and maybe I did imagine the whole thing, which would just be one more glorious thing to add to my growing list of freakiness. Besides, no one would believe me, anyway."

She glared at the television. Han Solo was in the middle of a fight, his gun blasting sharp bullets of light. What she'd seen in the alley was so much more real than the special effects she was watching on the screen. But it didn't make nearly the same amount of sense.

"I believe you, Selene."

She jerked her attention back to Jamie. "Seriously?"

"I thought we'd already established this whole serious thing. But yeah, seriously." He shrugged. "I don't know what you saw, exactly, but I do know there has to be something going on with that Fee guy. I mean, nobody wears their hair like that. Unless they work at the Renaissance Faire."

She almost smiled. "You're probably right."

"And besides," he continued, settling back into the cushions. "I'm required to believe you. It's part of that unspoken friendship bond thing. Like that time you told me you ate a whole pan of fried worms in middle school."

"Because I did."

"Yeah, but I didn't know you then, so there's no proof."

"Well, I couldn't exactly regurgitate them and take a picture for posterity."

"Tragic," Jamie mused. "That would've made a great scrapbook entry."

Although she wasn't sure if he totally believed her, she had to appreciate his effort. She didn't know if she really believed it either.

But her arms still prickled, and she was convinced, deep down inside her, that she hadn't imagined the creature in the alley. Or the way Fee and his companions had fought it. The way Fee looked.

Like some warrior from another time and place.

"There's something else, isn't there?" Jamie asked.

As he studied her, the humor drained from his expression. But she couldn't look at him this time. She focused on the movie, trying to purge her thoughts of Fee. She needed time to process things, on her own.

"Let's just watch the movie, okay?" she said, leaning against his shoulder.

His fingers slipped through her hair, tucking a strand of it behind her ear, and he pressed a kiss on the top of her head. "Don't you need to call your mom? She'll wonder what's happened to you."

"Mmm." She closed her eyes, suddenly exhausted. "Call her in a minute."

Jamie squeezed her shoulder. Then he turned off the mute, and the familiar sounds of intergalactic battle filled Selene's ears. She relaxed, allowing it all to take her far away.

Chapter 16

Cruz was making tea when Phoebus burst into the kitchen. Paloma and Marcelo looked up sharply from a plate of scones.

"We need to talk," said Phoebus, his voice crackling with ice.

Nyx and Titus stepped into the room behind him, taking positions near the door.

Cruz took the kettle from the stove. "Care for some tea?"

"That would be lovely," he shot back. "We'll have crumpets, too. And those little sandwiches. Then we'll discuss how you've been lying to the Elders and how pretty your neck's going to look on those shoulders once your head's been lopped off."

"I don't know what you're talking about, Rover."

"Oh really?" He circled the kitchen, his eyes fixed on Cruz. "So you're telling me that you're oblivious to the fact that there are Leeches running free around your little town, right in the middle of the population, extracting *Electricus* from people?"

"I didn't say that."

"Then what *are* you saying, Cruz? Because you haven't been honest with me from the moment we arrived here."

The heat in his chest was threatening to set fire, and though he kept still, inwardly he was pacing like a madman. He waited as Cruz sat down and leaned back in his chair, looking steadily into his face, his chin thrust out.

"Like you're one to talk about honesty, Fee."

"Talk."

Marcelo and Paloma exchanged hooded glances. He sensed their hesitation, but they deferred to Cruz with their shaded eyes. Rogues or not, they shared the same authority structure of any Trine. Since Cruz was their leader, he'd be the one to speak.

Wrapping his thick fingers around his drink, Cruz peered

into the liquid, as if pulling the answer from its steaming depths. "While Leeches were once content living out their banishment in the marshlands, they grew tired of being confined. Over time, many began moving into more populated areas." He took a sip of his tea before continuing. "We patrol the town as best we can, and we keep the peace by only dealing with Leeches that directly pose a threat to Othersiders."

"Leeches are mandated to stay clear of Othersiders," said Phoebus lowly. "If you've been having trouble keeping things under control at this Outpost, you should've said something to the Elders. They would have sent additional Trines to assist you."

Cruz laughed—a sharp, mocking sound. "The Elders *know*, Fee. And they don't care. If it doesn't directly affect Threshold, they look the other way." He took another long swig of tea as his features twisted into a sly smile. "But I see by your reaction that the Elders didn't share this information with you."

Phoebus kept his voice deadly calm. "We were told what was needed in order to complete our mission. That's not the issue, Cruz. I want to know why you didn't mention this kind of Leech activity to me when we arrived."

He shrugged. "I assumed you knew. Besides, I didn't think that was part of your task here. You're looking for Viewers, not Leeches, correct?"

The heat inside him now stung, like tiny insect bites. He was not accustomed to being out of the loop, not when it came to important matters. Grimm had only given him permission to deal with Leeches that posed a threat to his mission. Did that mean the Elder had already known what was going on here? Even Moth admitted that the Elders had been receiving reports from the Outpost every month.

"Yes," he replied, making certain that his face remained blank. "Elder Grimm thinks that there may be some who possess unusual concentrations of energy, posing a threat to the security of the Barrier."

"And have you located any of these *unusual* Viewers?"

"Not yet."

Cruz's dark eyes glittered. "Now who's not being honest?"

Phoebus paused, trying to force the ever-present image of the girl from his mind's eye; collecting himself as he clung to the kitchen counter with stiff fingers. "You're charged with keeping things safe on this Side."

"Things are safe," Marcelo answered quietly.

"How can you say that?" he demanded, shifting his glare around the table. "There was a Leech in town tonight, extracting from some defenseless old man. If we hadn't come along, that Viewer would very likely be dead. Grimm gave orders to deal with any Leech that was causing harm. That order extends to all of us, but especially your Trine!"

"Grimm doesn't understand!" Cruz exploded. He slammed his mug on the table. "Look, Rover, you may be the Elder's darling, jumping through the Barrier whenever you want like it's some kind of circus trick, but you don't know how things work here. You're not a part of this world." He leveled his gaze. "We are."

"So forget the Tenets and the Elders. Just let the Leeches roam free, no questions asked. Is that it?"

"If they keep out of trouble, yes." Cruz added sugar to his tea. "They aren't that different from us, Fee. They're banished, cut off from Threshold, just like we are. This is their home now." Setting the spoon aside, he took a deep breath. "They want to survive, and extracting from the odd human here and there isn't causing harm. The victims remember nothing; their wounds heal. Life goes on. As long as the Leeches don't do anything to jeopardize this world, I say live and let live."

"Until they kill an Othersider."

"And if that happens, they will be dealt with."

Phoebus quaked with the effort of controlling his rage. "They are the *enemy*, Cruz. Or have you been away from Threshold so long that you've forgotten why the Leeches were banished here in the first place?" He dug his fingers into his palms. Everything in him wanted to lunge at Cruz. "Leeches are dangerous. And in a place like this, with so many weaknesses in the *Electricus*, what's to prevent them from attempting to breech the Barrier?"

"Us," said Cruz.

"You just said 'live and let live,' and now you're telling me you fight them off?"

"Not exactly," Marcelo said quietly, from the table. "We have... an arrangement."

"We assist them with supplies," said Paloma, adding to her brother's words. "With things they need to survive here."

It was as though Phoebus was hearing them speak from deep underwater. He shook his head several times. "You *help* them?"

Paloma nodded. "It pays well."

"Curse you to the Wastelands," he hissed.

Cruz leapt from the table. "Oh, come down from your pious tower, Fee. Rogues have done this for ages. There were too many Leeches trapped here after the war to control. So we manage things. We keep the real troublemakers in line. And we leave the rest alone."

Phoebus sprang, grabbing Cruz by the collar. He slammed him over the counter and held him in place with an iron grip.

"Give me one good reason why I shouldn't kill you right now."

Cruz gave a pained smirk. "Because you need us, Phoebus. The Elders need us. Who else keeps peace on this Side? You Rovers pass through, mending the Barrier and taking care of Viewers, but everything you do is for the benefit of Threshold—for keeping your precious paradise safe. But what about this Side, Phoebus? What about these people? Have you forgotten what it was like to be among them? To be *one* of them? Have you forgotten the beauties of this place? Or has your heart grown cold, shrouded under duties as thick as a Regent's robes?"

Everything went still. No one spoke or moved. All eyes were on him as he held Cruz against the table. His head whirling, his heart pounding like a hammer, Phoebus could barely see straight anymore. Everything was crumbling, including his control. He released Cruz and stumbled back, feeling half-wild and dangerously close to losing it. Without another word, he turned and stormed from the room.

***

The bedroom ceiling pressed down on him, crushing him with its weight, squeezing air from his lungs. He breathed sharply through his nose and out his mouth, forcing calm with each movement of oxygen. Cruz had made him lose control—a moment of weakness. He couldn't let himself crack like that again. He rubbed his eyes until his head hurt. What was happening to him?

It had all started with the Viewer girl.

There was a knock at the door.

"Fee?" It was Nyx.

"I'm sleeping," he answered. "Go away."

The lock jiggled, and the door swung open. Nyx stood there, her *nadala* in her hand. He rolled over, cursing her skills under his breath. The floorboards creaked as she approached.

"You're not sleeping," she said. "So let's talk."

He squinted over his shoulder.

"Any particular topic?" he said. "There are so many to choose from. What about how Cruz is living in blatant disregard for our laws, despite the leniency the Elders granted him? Or perhaps we can talk about how Leeches are running wild, with no one to keep them in line but a trio of useless Rogues?"

Nyx rolled him over to face her.

"Let's start with how this Viewer of yours fits into all this," she said. "Because only you seem to know."

"That's not the issue."

"Yes, it is. You left the old man tonight without trying to get any information from him. And you've barely mentioned any other Viewers you've encountered. So what's really going on? And don't talk to me like my Trine leader, for once. Talk to me like Fee...the boy who used to hide my satchel in the Grove trees and taught me how to fight behind the walls of the Keep. Talk to me like that, Fee. Talk to me like your friend."

"You are my friend, Nyx," he said, propping his head atop his hands.

"You say that, but Titus and I are the ones you're pushing out. Deny it, if you want, but you haven't been yourself since the Rift in the Grove." She studied him for a moment, her dark eyes searching his face. "Don't tell me you're going *light-mad*."

"Fine," he replied. "I won't tell you."

Her fierce expression said she wanted to hit him with excessive force, but instead, she only sighed. "You know, Phoebus...one day, the madness will actually take you, and no one will be there to help, because we won't believe you."

"I suppose that will simply be my burden to bear then, won't it?"

"I won't come and visit you."

"What a relief."

"By the Grove," she muttered, pressing her hand on his chest. "Maybe I'll run you through with my *nadala* now and save us the trouble of dealing with you later."

A smirk tugged at his upper lip. "*Light-madness* only affects Rovers who are careless. And I am never careless."

"You do know that being delusional is one of the first signs, right?"

"Is it?" He blinked slowly. "I had no idea."

She cuffed him on the arm. He rubbed his shoulder, keeping his smile intact, though Nyx had struck upon a fear that always lurked in his mind: *light-madness.*

All Trine leaders had been told tales of sailors who'd gone mad from too much time spent on the ocean. Maybe one day, he'd suffer a similar fate because of his duties.

Perhaps he already was.

"You've been focused on this one girl since we've arrived," Nyx continued, taking his silence as an invitation. "Yet you avoid her, and you evade any questions we ask about her. I'm not a novice, Fee. And it doesn't take Preceptor skills to know that you have more interest in her than our mission requires."

He glanced around her toward the open door of his room. But it wasn't the potential of eavesdroppers in the hallway that concerned him. It was the amber mirror hanging on the other side of the door, out of sight. He swallowed, his jaw working.

"The Viewer saw me through the Rift in the Grove."

The words slipped out before he could catch them.

Nyx sat back as if she'd been struck. "She *saw* you? But that's not—"

"Possible," he finished, his voice laced with anger. "I know. But she did. That's why I Shifted without informing Grimm. I had to Dull her memories, and I sensed something more was at work. But I wasn't certain until I saw her at the school."

"Do you think she remembers you?"

"No." He shoved his hands through his hair. "Of course not."

Nyx watched him, and he could see her trying to piece his words together.

"You think she's more than a Viewer, don't you?"

Phoebus cursed himself under his breath. What was wrong with him? A moment of uncontained emotion, and he was blabbering like a novice. He fell back against the pillow. He was a pathetic excuse for a Rover. Inexcusable.

"I don't yet have proof," he replied. "But I see no other explanation."

"Then we must tell—"

"No."

"Why?"

Phoebus closed his eyes, feeling as though his head were weighted down with rocks.

"I have orders, Nyx," he said quietly. "Given only to me."

"Orders," she repeated.

Pressing him to say more.

But he couldn't.

"There's nothing more to talk about, Nyx. I know what I have to do."

"I know that tone," said Nyx, leaning closer to him. "You're conflicted."

The words pricked at his inner denial. He'd thought his hesitation to act was because she was young, or because she was unusual, and her energy was a curious abnormality. He'd almost convinced himself it was wrong, no matter how much Threshold's safety depended on his actions.

It was for all these reasons that he struggled. His morality and the very fibers of his Rover being wrestled with them. But it was also against something else he struggled. Something far deeper. Something that terrified him to the core.

He *felt* something for this girl.

For Selene.

"I'll see my orders carried out," he replied, hoisting himself onto his elbow. "And then, we're going home. Task accomplished. Mission complete."

"But maybe there's a way around it," said Nyx, "maybe you don't have to—"

"Preceptor Moth was very clear," he replied.

Her eyes turned to stone. "You've spoken with Moth?"

Phoebus felt the amber mirror pulsing on the other side. The

Preceptor could make contact him at any time, with little warning, and that was more unsettling than anything else. He dipped his head in a way that neither confirmed nor denied Nyx's question, but he sensed her doubt.

"Alright then, what about the Leeches?" she asked. "Do you believe what Cruz said tonight? Do you think the Elders already knew about the activity surrounding this Coil?"

"I'll inform Preceptor Moth of the situation," he said quickly. "Whatever the case, the Elders will deal with this however they see fit." His words hardened in his throat. "Just like they always do."

"Fee?" Her voice dropped suddenly to a whisper. "Do you... trust...the Elders?"

Phoebus paused, then suddenly pulled Nyx into bed next to him, pressing his lips to her ear, shielding his face.

"I believe there's a lot we don't know," he whispered. "Grimm's convinced there's treachery going on somewhere, but he's ordered me to be quiet about it, even to you and Titus. I can only assume he thinks I'm going to find the traitor here."

By the Grove, there really was something wrong with him.

Why couldn't he shut his mouth as easily as he could shut a Rift? He clenched his teeth so hard his vision swirled, and he looked quickly at the open door.

Nyx pressed her lips against his cheek, her voice faint. "You think it's Cruz."

He swept Nyx's braid out of his eyes but kept his mouth against her temple as he spoke. "Seems the obvious choice."

"But you're not convinced?"

He felt the sensation of Nyx swallowing against his neck. She smelled like wildflowers, despite having just fought a Leech in a grimy alley. Her hand pressed against his chest in a way that made his skin warm underneath his shirt.

A warning tingling of *Electricus* skittered through his body. Was the mirror activating? With all the muddled energy in this place, he couldn't tell. The fact that the door hid the amber mirror from view made little difference if the Preceptor decided to appear.

Moth didn't need to see them to hear them.

He smiled into Nyx's hair. "I'm afraid I'm not at liberty to say at the moment."

Her voice was breathy. "So this is why you've been keeping so many secrets?"

"Maybe," he replied, purposely raising his voice to normal volume. He pulled back and tilted his head to the side, quirking his lips upward. "Or maybe I just like being mysterious."

Nyx glared at him for a moment, then pinched his arm.

"Ow," he said, smiling wider.

"That's not mysterious, Fee. That's annoying." Nyx pushed away from him and stood from the bed, straightening her hair. Her breathing sounded shallow in the quiet room.

He spread his fingers behind his head and leaned against the headboard. "Annoying," he mused. "Not exactly what I was going for."

"Well, it's fortunate that I'm not the object of your affections." She flicked her braid over her shoulder and walked to the door. "Because you'd be failing miserably."

She shut the door firmly behind her, and he let his smile drop after she was gone. He'd spilled more details to Nyx than he'd wanted, but he'd at least kept enough to himself to live with—for now. He kicked off his muddied shoes and socks and rolled out of bed, shivering as his bare feet touched the wooden floor.

The night had grown cold. He strolled to the window. The clouds had cleared, and an enormous orange moon hung heavily over the horizon, staring balefully back at him. He rested his head on the windowpane, letting the coolness of the glass seep into his skin. The longer he stayed here, the more it felt as though his world were turning upside down. And he couldn't do anything to stop it.

His shoulders slumped under the weight of what he was going to do. What he'd been *ordered* to do. But what choice did he have? He couldn't go against the Elders. Or the Tenets. He couldn't allow Threshold to be put at risk. But doubt continued to creep into his conscious thoughts.

The object of your affections.

Nyx's words rang inside his head like the clang of a church bell in an ancient belfry. The ominous peal shook the cobwebs free from the rafters of his mind. Is that what Selene was?

"Ridiculous," he said, louder than he'd intended.

Stripping off his dirty shirt, he balled it fiercely between his fists and flung it across the room. Then he leaned against the windowsill. Each breath he took felt painful as it mixed with the emotions attempting to seep out. He pressed his fingers fiercely against his sternum, refusing to let them free.

"Just do your job," he snarled out loud. "And then we can leave."

Suddenly, light flickered across the room.

It was coming from the mirror, which was now visible—hanging on the back of the closed door. His stomach twisted as he approached the frame. The mirror's reflection shimmered, then swirled. When it cleared, instead of seeing his own reflection, he was staring into the face of Regent Jareth. The man's pasty face was twisted up, as if he were straining to see.

As the glass smoothed, his gaze fell on Phoebus. "Ah, there you are," he said stiffly. "Elder Ania has had me checking in every few minutes until you returned."

Not only did the pale, sickly Regent look like a cross between a jackal and a skeleton, he was known for sniveling around those with influence and trying to gain favor with the Elders.

"Forgive me," Phoebus said cautiously. "I was expecting someone else."

"It's alright," said another voice, just out of view.

As he watched, the figure of Elder Ania took the man's place. She was dressed in her Elder's russet robes, which highlighted the coppery color of her hair.

"Greetings, Phoebus."

He bowed. "Elder Ania."

"I asked Regent Jareth to keep watch for me while I finished up some business with my brother," she said lightly. "With Elder Grimm, I should more properly say."

He paused. Had something happened with Moth?

"It is a pleasure, as always," he replied, putting his hand to his heart.

"How are things faring on that Side?" she asked.

He maintained his expression, unsure of how to continue the conversation. Moth had said that Grimm was keeping his sister informed, so Ania could be trusted, but this didn't fit Moth's typical protocol. And where was the Preceptor?

"There are Leeches here, Elder Ania," he said. "My Trine

encountered one tonight. Apparently there are quite a few of them living around this Coil, according to the Rogues. But I was not made aware of this fact before we Merged."

"Elder Grimm mentioned the possibility of Leeches to you, Phoebus," she replied, nodding in a way that said she understood his concern. "And you know our policy. As long as they do not directly pose a threat, the Elders don't worry about them."

"Yes," said Phoebus carefully. "But this Leech was in the town, extracting openly from an Othersider. And it seems this is not an isolated incident."

Elder Ania's reflection hovered in the glass, making it impossible to read her expression. "But you vanquished the Leech, yes? Disbursed its energy into the Barrier?"

"Of course," he replied.

"Then all is well, Rover," said another voice—a cold, smooth voice.

Preceptor Moth appeared beside Jareth in a swirl of midnight blue *mantellum*. Although she wasn't quite the Regent's height, she still seemed to tower over him. He looked at her with wary surprise.

"Preceptor—"

"Back away," said Moth. "This does not concern you."

Jareth turned his pasty face questioningly to Elder Ania. But her attention was on Moth. In the mirror, the Elder's soft blue eyes took on a darker gleam.

"I see that your meeting is over, Preceptor," said Ania. Her voice held none of the coldness of Moth's but every bit of the same authority. "I will take my leave and allow you return to your duties."

Moth's hooded head dipped sharply. "Thank you, Elder. I shall."

Ania's gaze returned to the mirror. "It was good to see you, Phoebus, and I look forward to hearing the rest of your report when the Preceptor brings it to us."

The Elder and the Regent moved out of view, and Phoebus watched as Moth's unseen eyes followed them out. After a few silent, tensely thick moments, she faced him. When she didn't offer a greeting, he decided to speak first.

"Preceptor Moth."

"Rover," she replied. Her tone was neutral.

"I wasn't expecting to speak to anyone else in Threshold," he said, studying her hooded reflection critically through the mirror. "I thought I was only communicating with you."

Moth clasped her gloved hands in a casual gesture, but her fingers were so stiff, Phoebus wondered how they didn't snap in two. "There are certain Elders who do not place much faith in me."

"She doesn't trust you," said Phoebus flatly.

Moth looked at him, and he caught the gleam of blue eyes. "No."

He couldn't say he really blamed anyone. As an apprentice, he'd trusted Preceptor Moth to show him how to control *Electricus* or to teach him how to fight a Leech, but he wasn't sure his own trust extended much further than that.

"And what about Jareth?" Phoebus questioned. "Why was he here?"

As she turned over her shoulder, Phoebus got the sense that she was glaring heavily at the door.

"Elder Ania felt that we should have one representation from the Regents involved," said Moth. Her voice sounded uncharacteristically pained. "It was...in her words...only *fair*. Since Regent Jareth is the head of their order, and I am already here as a Preceptor, Elder Grimm agreed."

"So Jareth knows everything, then."

"Not everything," Moth replied, her tone laced with honey and venom, all at once. "There are certain issues which, as of now, are only between us. Which brings me back to our report." She drew closer to the mirror. "Have you located any Bleeders?"

"I'm not certain at this point, Preceptor. I need more time to determine."

The image in the mirror swirled. "Rover, do you think I'm unaware of your actions? I have seen and sensed enough, even on this side of the Barrier. I believe you have found a Bleeder. Why have you not completed your task?"

"I have made preparations, Preceptor."

Moth reached up as if to slide back the hood of her *mantellum*. But she seemed to change her mind, and leaned forward instead. He felt the crackling energy keenly on his side of the amber mirror, almost as though she were going to step through it at any moment.

"I hope so, Phoebus, for your sake," she said. "I don't have to tell you that disobedience in these matters would be cause for trial before the Assembly. You know the law."

"I know the law," he replied curtly. "Elder Grimm taught me well."

Moth drew in a hissing breath. "Grimm thinks of you as family," she said, sounding as though she were chewing on something unpleasant. "And he is always concerned for your safety. But I trained you. Duty ranks above all else. And your orders have not changed."

An icy feeling skittered up Phoebus' spine. "Understood."

What Moth was asking of him would require more than a simple wound with an amber arrow. His jaw clenched so tightly that it hurt. The Preceptor's cool voice cut into his thoughts.

"Rover."

His eyes flicked to the mirror. "Preceptor?"

"Surely I don't have to remind you of your responsibilities," she said airily. "Not to mention the Tenets that you know by heart." Moth's hooded head rose, as if she were peering into his soul. "What must you do if you discover any Bleeders on the Otherside?"

Phoebus didn't hesitate. "I kill them."

Chapter 17

As Selene packed her duffel bag, she debated whether to stuff her raincoat into it. The idea of being outside in the damp and cold wasn't particularly thrilling. Although it was only October, the southern coastal weather had turned unusually crisp.

"And you're absolutely sure you want to do this?" her mother asked from the door.

She'd been watching her like a hawk the last few days—since she'd gotten back from the festival. Selene knew she'd been acting a little off, but she wasn't about to tell her mom why. She'd think her daughter was having some post-traumatic relapse or something.

And she wasn't going to let anything keep her from going.

"Mom, it's going to be fine."

She'd decided to face her fears, and she wasn't about to back down now. She swiped her bracelet from the dresser, clasping it onto her wrist, hiding her scar. The cold metal sent goosebumps up her arms.

Worry lurked in her mom's eyes. "Okay, then."

"Well, I've gotta go," she said, shouldering her bag. "Jamie's waiting on me."

"Please be careful," her mother replied, giving her a quick hug. "And keep in touch."

"I will."

Outside, the air felt as though it were humming, and she felt a sudden, nervous jitter.

Although there were no storms in the forecast, the sky had turned an ugly shade of gray.

A shade she'd grown to hate.

Rubbing her arms to ease the sensation, she tried to shake off the images that kept plaguing her: the monster and the blue lights.

And Fee. Although she'd searched for him the next day at school, she hadn't seen him anywhere. He'd become a ghost. If it hadn't been for her talks with Jamie, she could've almost convinced herself she'd imagined him, too.

Jamie's small brown pickup truck was waiting for her at the end of the front walk. Leaning across the seat, he opened the heavy passenger door, and she climbed inside, clicking on the seatbelt and hugging the duffle bag against her chest. He shot a sideways look at her.

"You don't look so good."

"The clouds have me a little spooked, that's all."

"You're going to be fine, Selene. There's nothing on the radar for tonight. But listen, if we hear even the tiniest bit of thunder, then I'll take us both right home." He placed his hand on her knee and squeezed. "Promise."

"Oh no, I'm staying, no matter what. I can handle this."

Jamie shrugged. "Okay, then. You're the boss."

"And don't forget it," she said, winking back at him.

Pulling onto the street, Jamie pointed his truck toward town. The drive to the park only took a few minutes, but it felt like hours as Selene kept drumming her fingers against the dashboard and glancing occasionally at Jamie. He was whistling to himself, completely content. For some reason, his good mood only made her feel worse.

"So, is Lindsay coming tonight?" she asked, ready for a diversion.

Jamie's face turned an odd shade. "I don't know," he said quickly. "Why?"

"Oh, I'm not sure. Maybe it's just that she's liked you since, what, sophomore year?"

"Huh."

As she laughed, she tugged a strand of his hair. "What's that supposed to mean?"

He slowed the truck to a stop underneath a traffic light. "That was a sound of noncommittal acknowledgement. Did I do it wrong?"

She smirked. "Huh."

After paying the entrance fee at the campground, Jamie found a spot near the back of the parking lot, right next to a Jeep full of soccer players and a car with some girls from the cheerleading squad.

More people had showed up than she'd expected.

"Fantastic," she said, pushing open the door. "Yeah, this is going to be *so* much fun."

Jamie retrieved his bag from the trunk. "Your positive vibe is overwhelming." His voice muffled as he bent over, searching through his backpack. "Oh man, don't tell me I forgot my snacks."

While he continued his desperate food search, she leaned against the car. A flash of color caught her eye. Ashlynn was strolling across the parking lot in their direction, decked out in a cute fuchsia shirt and paper-thin leggings, with her hair pulled together in a ponytail of a level Selene could never achieve. She groaned and turned the other way.

"Hey," chirped Ashlynn as she approached.

"Hey," she replied between tight lips.

"I knew Jamie was coming," she said, tilting her head to look Selene in the eyes, "but I didn't expect to see you here."

"Why? Am I suddenly un-invited?"

Ashlynn's gaze dropped to Jamie, but he seemed completely engrossed with the contents of his bag. "Of course not," she said, turning up her nose. "I just didn't think you'd have the guts to come. Hope you have a good time tonight, if you can."

She flounced off with her salon-styled ponytail bouncing behind her.

"I hope she freezes to death in those leggings."

Jamie looked up innocently. "Who?"

"You jerk." She kicked him in the hindquarters. "What did you tell her?"

"I'm sorry," he replied quickly. "I may have mentioned something about your accident still freaking you out, but that was before you finally agreed to come."

"I think you'd better find your junk food," she replied. "Cause I'm eating all of it."

As though presenting a peace offering, Jamie held up a bag of chocolate-covered pretzels. She ripped open the bag while Ashlynn leaned into the passenger window of her silver sports car. A tingle raced up Selene's neck, and as the car door opened, her chest froze.

A guy stepped out of Ashlynn's car. His long honey-colored hair caught the fading sunlight as a few strands escaped his ponytail and stuck to his jaw in the breeze.

"Unbelievable," she murmured.

Jamie stood and shouldered his bag. "I know," he said morosely. "I was sure I packed everything, but I'm missing my Pringles."

She pointed across the lot. "I was referring to that."

Fee was smiling at Ashlynn as she beamed up at him, jabbering nonstop. But he didn't look thrilled. In fact, he looked almost sick. His face seemed more sallow than when she'd last seen him—when he'd been fighting that monster in the alley.

"Where's he been hiding all week?" asked Jamie.

"Obviously, he's been hanging out with Ashlynn."

She was surprised at the sarcastic tone of her own voice.

Jamie caught it, too. "So, Renaissance Faire dude kills some freaky creature at the festival and then goes off the radar, but he catches a ride with Ashlynn tonight, and *that's* what bothering you?"

"No," she said, probably too quickly. "And I told you I'd probably just imagined all that alley stuff, anyway."

She felt Jamie's hard stare. It wasn't like her to care about Ashlynn's social life—or anything related to her. Ever. But seeing her with Fee bothered Selene in ways she couldn't explain, and didn't really want to think about either. She turned her attention to a small group of upperclassmen on the opposite side of the lot.

"Come on," she said. "I see Lindsay. Let's go say hi."

***

While most of the guys occupied themselves with setting up the campsite, Selene stuck with the girls, chattering and observing the chaotic insanity.

Hanging next to Lindsay, Selene couldn't help laughing as they watched Jamie fight a losing battle with an old aluminum lawn chair. For all the maturity he'd gained the last few years, he was an uncoordinated mess when it came to anything outside of video games and musical instruments.

"Should we help?" Lindsay asked, her nose scrunching. "I think that chair's going to kill him."

"I think he'll survive," Selene replied. "But maiming is a possibility."

Lindsay tossed her short hair and giggled. She was totally adorable, like a little pixie. Selene never got why Jamie hadn't asked her out. But then again, he'd always been picky when it came to girls.

"I can't handle it anymore," said Lindsay. "I'll be right back."

Allowing her attention to drift over the rest of the campsite, Selene spotted Fee only a few yards away, leaning against a tree, not seeming the least bit concerned with the setup. He wore a bored expression, his jacket draped over his arm, but she could see a tense set to his shoulders.

He didn't have any bags with him—which she didn't get, being that it was a camping trip. But he hadn't carried anything with him at school that first day, either. It was like he was a drifter, just passing through. She remembered how he'd looked in that alley—like he was from some faraway place—as he'd stretched the bowstring to his cheek and released the arrow.

Just then, his eyes flicked in her direction. It happened too quickly for her to look away, to pretend she hadn't been staring. The damage was done. She either had to go talk to him now, or risk feeling awkward for the rest of the evening.

Putting on what she hoped looked like a friendly smile, she headed for the tree Fee had claimed. She was almost afraid that he would turn and walk away, like he'd done at the festival, but as she approached, he simply watched her, unmoving; his expression frozen, like a mask.

"Hey," she said lightly.

As she stared through the dim light, meeting the glint of his caramel irises, she also noticed that the dark circles under his eyes were more pronounced and, despite his carved-stone countenance, she could easily read the emotion radiating off of him—the desire to be anywhere else but with her.

"Hello," he answered smoothly.

She kept smiling, though her insides were turning. "I wasn't expecting to see you here."

"Your friend Ashlynn invited me."

"She's *not* my friend."

Fee raised a brow. "Oh, really?"

The look was something Jamie often did, too. On him, it was comical. On Fee, it was strangely intimate, almost knowing—an elegant lift of his left brow in a way she'd only seen done by characters in movies.

"It's a long story," she replied. "And really, no big deal."

"I see."

"So, is everything okay?" she asked. Hesitating for a second, she decided to press ahead. "I haven't seen you since you left the festival the other night."

"Family emergency," he answered, without blinking. "All taken care of now."

Although she knew he was lying, there wasn't anything she could call him out on—not without admitting what she'd thought she seen and accusing him, point-blank, of being involved. "Okay, well, that's good." She shrugged. "Anyway, I'm glad you're here."

His brow did the movie-guy lift again, more pronounced this time—like he was genuinely puzzled. "I thought it rude to refuse the invitation."

Refusing an invite from Ashlynn would've been social suicide, but Selene got the feeling that Fee wouldn't have cared.

"Well, it's a good way to get to know people," she said.

Fee's countenance shifted, like water rippling on a pond. "Yes, that's what I was hoping."

Stuffing her hands in her pockets, Selene watched Blake and Graham hammering pegs into the ground. Her curiosity was unbearable. It wasn't just that Fee was aloof, like some pained Jane Austen hero. Or smooth. Or even out of place. There was something... *familiar* about him, something that kept prickling at the corners of her memory. And the way he looked at her...was she being overly sensitive, or did he sense it, too?

"I suppose I should make myself useful," he said, suddenly. He gestured to three boys who were struggling with a tent. Then he dipped his head—an odd gesture. "Catch you later."

"Okay," she replied, somewhat stunned.

She tried not to stare as he maneuvered gracefully through the trees.

***

After the campsite was established, everyone broke into groups.

Ashlynn and her posse held Fee captive for much of the evening. They were disgustingly pushy, which almost activated Selene's gag reflex. Fee seemed to take it in stride, but she couldn't help noticing the occasional glances he snuck her way, his eyes dark behind his stray locks of hair.

Hovering as close to the fire as the heat allowed, she toasted a marshmallow with a metal coat hanger. Jamie had gone to talk to Mudge and some nerdy guys on the other end of the campsite. Lindsay and a few girls sat across the fire, making s'mores.

Selene talked to them, but she kept getting distracted, and she was trying not to glance at Fee. Turning the full force of her mental capacity onto her marshmallow, she propped her chin in one hand as she held the straightened hanger over the fire.

"You're about to burn that," said a voice from behind.

She nearly dropped the hanger. Fee stood over her, his gaze on the marshmallow. The firelight caught in his eyes, turning them a brilliant shade of copper.

She gripped the metal tighter. "Excuse me?"

"The flames," he said.

She stared at her marshmallow, which she'd let droop way too low, and pulled it toward the cooler embers on the outskirts of the fire.

"Crisis averted," she said.

"May I sit here?" he asked, his voice soft and deep.

As she nodded, Fee placed something on the ground and then sat next to her. His movements were easy, yet hesitant, and he stretched his legs toward the fire. He looked completely natural sitting around the campfire, as though it were something he did it all the time.

Images of Fee in the alley sparked in her brain again, like the flames of the fire in front of her, fueling her need for answers. She bit her lip, torn between curiosity and doubt. But she *had* to know more.

"So," she began, "how are your cousins?"

"My cousins," Fee repeated slowly.

"I mean, you took off at the festival, and I haven't seen you since. I thought you were avoiding me."

"I haven't been avoiding you," he replied, and she felt his defenses locking down.

"So everything's okay with your family?"

"They are quite well," he replied. "Thank you for inquiring." Grabbing a stick, he twirled it between his fingers. "It's a nice night."

"Yeah," she replied to his obvious subject change.

She plucked the gooey marshmallow from the metal, tested it for heat, and popped it in her mouth, enjoying the momentary respite of warm sugariness. Being away from technology and imaginary strangers wasn't bad either. She rubbed her sticky fingers on her jeans and focused on the bits of dark sky visible through the pine trees.

"I was afraid it was going to rain," she said.

Fee jabbed the stick into the fire, releasing a light spray of embers into the night.

"Not a fan of getting wet, I take it?" His eyes remained on the fire.

"I don't mind rain, as long as it doesn't storm." She set the coat hanger aside. "Storms freak me out."

She felt him tense again—a sharp, coiled sensation—and that same muscle worked in his jaw. It was evident that he was having some kind of internal debate. Intrigue tickled the back of her neck. The unusual vibe that she'd felt on the night of the festival was there, too, crackling like static.

Following the direction of his gaze, she realized that the thing he'd set on the ground beside him was a small mound of dark green fabric, rolled into a tight ball—larger than the jacket he was wearing, and too small for a sleeping bag. But where had it come from?

"What?" he said, his smooth voice marred with a defensive edge.

Cheeks burning, she met his look solidly. Although he seemed to keep his face purposefully blank—like a skill he'd perfected with great care—his eyes weren't as unreadable. They changed, like currents of wind. One moment, they were so warm that she felt dangerously close to melting, and the next, they were hard, brittle; scorching her with their metallic glint.

"You keep acting like you want to ask me something," she said, trying to appear casual; but her insides were rolling in a funny way, and the vision of Fee fighting in the alley was now playing on constant repeat in her mind. "So, what is it?"

"You were struck by lightning."

It felt as though she'd lost her breath. "That's not a question."

"I never said I had one."

She blinked, feeling off-balance. "How did you know?"

"People talk," he said with a shrug.

"And by *people*, I'm sure you're referring to Ashlynn."

"Perhaps."

"Of course," she replied, bitterness creeping into her tone. "And I'm sure she told you the lighting fried my head, so I'm brain-damaged, too."

Fee's lopsided smile appeared. "No. Well, not in those exact words." He tilted his head to look at the fire. "For the record, though, I don't believe her report."

"About the lightning?"

"No, the brain damage."

She felt her body relax a little. "Thanks. I appreciate it," she replied. "Sometimes I think I've got some stupid curse. I've been known to fry a few phones and computers, and my mom has gotten sick of replacing the light bulbs in my room."

Fee paused to poke at the fire again. "And you believe it's because of the strike."

Leaning forward, Selene watched the stick as it brightened each coal it touched, giving the black, charred pieces new life as Fee maneuvered the burning wood around the firepit. There was something disarming in the pointed questions Fee asked. Or maybe, it just felt nice to talk to someone about her accident instead of pushing it off like it was no big deal.

"I don't know. It happened a couple of years ago, near the marsh behind my house. But I don't remember much about the whole thing, other than scattered images," she confessed. "One of the side-effects is memory loss." She stared hard into the dying flames. "Actually, a lot of stuff before the lightning strike is a blur."

"You have amnesia?"

"No, it's not like that," she replied. "I knew who I was and my parents and other people. I can remember a lot from before I moved to St. Mary's. I have certain memories, and I get bits and pieces of others, but there doesn't seem to be a reason for what I can remember and what I can't." She swallowed, and her throat felt dry. "But I get these certain…images sometimes, like flashes of things I know I should remember."

Fee stared into the trees. There was something in his features, an emotion Selene couldn't quite place. It almost looked like regret.

"That must be difficult," he said quietly.

His face and his eyes were both solid now. Unreadable.

"At times." She rubbed her forehead, feeling beads of sweat along her hairline. "Sometimes I see things that seem familiar to me, but I don't know if it's because of my screwed-up memory or just pure coincidence." She took a deep breath and plunged ahead. "Like you."

Fee glanced away. "I'm no one you should remember."

The words echoed in her brain, said in the same mellow timbre of Fee's voice, with the same, slight accent. She blinked her eyes once, twice. There was a hospital room and someone stepping around the curtain. Something glowed in his hand.

"Are you sure we haven't met?" she asked. Her heart jolted strangely.

"Of course not."

"Are you *sure*?"

She leaned closer, coaxed by some compelling force, every fiber of her being straining to recall something. Things were flashing through her head, more powerful than any previous sensation of memory she'd had before. Almost without realizing it, she reached out, and her hand brushed his. Fee jerked, as if he'd been stung. A shock raced up her arm.

Fee stood, his face hidden in shadows.

"I'm sorry about your accident," he said.

He grabbed his bundle, retreated from the fire, and darted through the darkened trees. But she refused to let him go this time. Springing up, she followed him into the brush. Fee moved quickly with a strange—almost practiced—grace, and she had to run to keep up. He flitted in and out of shadows, away from the campsite, away from the noise and light, his form drifting like a predator on the hunt.

As he walked, he took the bundle he'd been carrying and unfurled it with a snap, his pace never faltering. It was some kind of heavy cloak, like the kind people wore for costumes at fantasy conventions. He flung it over his shoulders in one fluid movement, and something...changed.

His body shimmered with a bluish light, and her breath wedged in her throat as she watched Fee morph from a normal flesh-and-blood person to something like a half-visible ghost—his body bathed in an apparitional glow as he maneuvered through the brush.

Her legs felt like jelly, and she wiped her hand across her face as unnamed memories raged inside her like wolves. As she closed the distance between them, moving faster, her head pounded. The trees gave way to thickets, and then to grass and brush, and suddenly, she burst into the open marshland.

With her shoes sinking into the mud, she waded through the vegetation, each slosh threatening to send the wet slop through her the canvas and into her socks. The sky had grown heavy with clouds, and flashes of light illuminated them from behind. Her heart thumped behind her ribs. Everything felt too familiar here—the earthy scent of promised rain, the static charge in her skin, the cold, unpleasant breeze.

She heard an echo of a voice in her head. A younger voice. *Her* voice.

No! Wait!

"No!" she shouted. "Wait!"

Several yards ahead, Fee froze in a carpet of cordgrass. She stumbled to a halt, breathing heavily, as he turned around to face her. The apparitional glow of his body seemed to fade, and she saw him more clearly. He'd pulled up the hood of his cloak, and underneath its shadows, his face was flushed, his copper eyes wild. His gaze locked with hers.

"Have you ever had a moment," he said, "when everything you've ever known and trusted crumbled at your feet?"

She stared at him. The honesty in his tone changed his voice, making it softer—vulnerable, even with the distance between them. She heard him speak again—but this time, it was inside her memory, like a wave surging toward the shore.

I'm no one you should remember.

The words crashed into her brain again, and with them, the image of the hospital room. She saw the person stepping around the curtain, draped in a dark green cloak. He carried something in his hand.

An arrow.

The memory hit her so hard that she staggered backwards. She remembered the orb of light, and from within it, the strange boy with the prominent nose, hardened jaw, and caramel eyes—the face she'd promised herself she would never forget.

It was *Fee's* face.

"You," she whispered. "You're *him.*"

As though her words were a slap, Fee's head snapped back.

Choking on the damp air, she tried to move, but she was frozen. Memories and reality collided. The lightning. The boy.

She felt a buzz of current, tingling through her blood.

Fee held out his hands in an imploring gesture, and the air swirled around him as blue light gathered in his palms, stretching forth like bolts of lightning. A bow and arrow materialized from the electric glow. He notched the arrow, and she heard the hum of the string as he pulled it taut against his cheek.

"Selene." His voice was as tight as the bowstring. "I'm so sorry."

Fee aimed the arrow at her chest.

Chapter 18

Phoebus' shoulders pinched so tight that he wanted to scream. His palms itched. His skin burned with anticipation. The *Electricus* was pricking at his fingertips, ready to do his bidding. Above, the sky loomed, dark and foreboding. The stars flickered out behind rolling clouds.

A cold chill flooded his spine. Dulling an Othersider was one thing.

Killing an Othersider was another.

He flung his *mantellum* around his shoulders and fastened the clasp with one hand. The Thresholder fabric would hide his presence from any wandering youth that might stray from the campgrounds.

Unfortunately, it wouldn't hide him from her.

He felt her signature as she followed him. A few moments more and the *Electricus* he summoned would produce a storm in the atmosphere. A few steps more and he would have her far enough away from the campgrounds. There'd be no witnesses. Their authorities would rule it a fatal lightning strike.

Phoebus moved with a steady gait, but in his gut, he felt sickened by what he was about to do.

What he *had* to do.

Why had he bothered to talk to her at all? Why had he nurtured the stirrings of feelings he'd been experiencing? He'd only made things harder, and his will was already too close to faltering. From several yards back, he heard her pleading for him to stop. If he didn't act now, he wouldn't act at all.

But then, she spoke.

"You," she whispered. He saw the recognition in her eyes. His chest ached with a pain he hadn't imagined possible. "You're *him*."

Across the marshlands, thunder rumbled.

His palms flooded with current, and it scorched through his

skin, exploding into blue light. His bow and arrow formed, familiar and true. On these he could count. His weapons were old friends. They'd never steered him wrong.

There was no turning back now. He lifted his bow, drawing the string. She stared back at him, too stunned to move. He'd fell her like a deer. The shot would be painless; death, instantaneous.

"Selene." His voice cracked, betraying his emotions. "I'm so sorry."

It was a pathetic plea for forgiveness, he knew. As her eyes held him, the moment froze in time. He smelled the marsh, full of rot and heady moss and saltwater. He felt the first drops of rain on his cheeks. But he'd remember the details in her horrified expression forever.

The air rippled, currents shifting like wind.

Something caught his eye—a current, pulsing around her, emanating from her arm, coated in a blue aura. He hesitated, the arrow shaft buzzing between his fingers.

A screech ripped through the marsh.

A dark form hit Selene in the back, and she sprawled. Phoebus aimed and fired. His arrow pierced the Leech's shoulder, crackling sparks as it burst through skin. The creature fell back, splaying in the mud. Phoebus rushed forward, a new arrow already forming in his palm.

Thunder cracked. He spun, going down in the grass as a second Leech pinned him to the ground, nearly cracking his ribs. He cried out in fury as he stared up into its face. The Leech was male, with a more humanoid face than the creature in the alley. Corpse-blue lips peeled back, exposing dripping, blackened teeth. Electric currents slithered like snakes under its corrupted skin.

Hands the color of bruised flesh reached for him, but Phoebus dug his heels into the ground and pushed off, flipping the Leech onto his back. Then he was atop him, straddling the creature's bony chest, gagging on the creature's sulfuric breath. He pressed his arrow's tip to the Leech's throat.

"Why are you here?" Phoebus snarled.

"For...the girl," hissed the Leech, eyes glittering with blue fire.

The other Leech—a vile deformity with gangly arms and a hollowed face—was skittering toward Selene. It moved on its spindly legs with the speed of some terrible, half-human spider. Its elongated neck strained with bulging muscles as it reached for her.

Tightening his grip, Phoebus rammed the arrow through his attacker's pasty throat. The Leech gurgled, its body convulsing as *Electricus* poured from the wound like blood. Jumping off the creature, he rolled away and bolted through the grass toward the other creature as fast as he could.

"Selene!" he yelled. "Run!"

She clawed through the weeds as Phoebus sank an arrow into the creature's side. The thing stumbled but didn't fall. He cursed and formed another arrow. But before he could fire, the Leech had Selene around the waist, dragging her backward through the mud. She yelled and struggled, kicking out with her feet, making impressive contact, but the creature was too strong and too fast.

"Drop her, parasite!" Phoebus yelled. "Or this arrow's going straight through your skull!"

The Leech turned, pointed teeth spilling over deadened lips. Phoebus growled in frustration. He needed a clear shot at the creature's vulnerable chest, but Selene's body was blocking the target.

But that wasn't Phoebus' only problem.

Rover weapons could kill Leeches, but he needed a Rift to absorb the *Electricus* expelled upon their deaths. Even if he had clean shot, Selene would be too close. The Leech's exploding body could destroy her as well. Without Nyx and her *nadala*, opening the Barrier would be too dangerous. He'd never close it fast enough.

As if sensing his thoughts, the wounded Leech behind him clutched at the arrow in its neck and forced out a sickening, gurgling laugh.

"You...are alone, Rover...and she is...ours..."

Selene's frantic eyes fixed on her captor, and she rammed her elbow into the Leech's side. It screeched, loosening its hold. Scrambling free, she bolted away from the Leech as Phoebus directed his arrow toward its exposed chest.

A bolt of lightning pierced the night. The Barrier ripped open in a whirlpool of light. Phoebus jerked, barely keeping the arrow against the string. Selene was crouched beneath the Rift, her face drained of color, her arms thrown over her head. Her bracelet glowed a brilliant blue, humming against her skin.

And suddenly, he knew.

She could do it.

"Party's over," he shouted.

His arrow pierced the Leech's ribcage. The creature screamed, enveloped in voltage. Its body grew brighter as Phoebus dove for Selene. He shielded her as the Leech exploded.

The other Leech flailed in fury. Phoebus rolled into a crouch, coming up with an arrow and firing off another shot. The creature's body became a fireball of electricity, caught in the gravitational pull of the Rift. The gaping maw sucked the remains of their energies through.

Phoebus whirled on Selene. "Close it!"

The wind from the vortex whipped her hair across her face, and the bracelet glowed like an electric band across her skin.

"I don't know how," she cried.

Phoebus notched another arrow to his bowstring, preparing for the worst. If the Rift wasn't closed immediately, there was no telling what might come pouring out.

"I think you do, Selene," he snapped. "Just *concentrate*!"

She looked ready to bolt; her grim, panicked gaze shifted to the swirling opening of light. Her eyes closed. A bolt of lightning streaked across the sky, followed by the crack of thunder.

The Rift shimmered, faltered, and then faded to nothing.

The marsh went calm. Above them, clouds rolled back; stars shone in the velvet night. Letting out a cry, Selene slumped forward, but he was there to catch her. He lifted her into his arms, and his head tingled with remnants of energy. He watched tiny sparks from her bracelet buzz around her arm before dissipating into the air.

He stared down at her, hardly daring to breathe. He'd been right all along. The girl *was* special.

And that changed…everything.

Selene's eyelids fluttered, and she stared into his face. In that moment, she looked very much like the image he'd first seen of her through the Rift. But this time, there was no fear in her eyes. As his fingers brushed against her skin, he felt power radiating around her—a power she wasn't even aware of yet. She'd opened a Rift and closed it again. Phoebus took a steadying breath as his mission sharpened into new, crystalline clarity.

He wasn't supposed to kill the girl. He was supposed to save her.

Chapter 19

Selene sat on the couch, her brain feeling like a blender on maximum speed. Although she'd never been inside the *Seaside Inn*, she passed it on her way to work. The old two-story house looked quaint from the outside, but it had always given her a weird vibe.

Now she understood why.

The room buzzed with energy. It prickled her arms and the back of her neck, similar to the sensation she kept getting around Fee. It pressed in on her like invisible gas in a closed container, and something inside her felt ready to ignite.

"Would you care for some tea?" asked a voice that nearly caused her to jump off the couch. The short, olive-skinned woman who'd spoken smiled apologetically. Her face was kind, though her eyes were guarded. "I understand you've had a difficult night."

"Tea," she repeated. Her toes felt numb and her hands shook.

Dressed in a belted tunic, trousers, and a tan cloak, the woman embodied the same grace as Fee, though without his commanding air. She poured steaming liquid from a kettle into antique teacup.

"It's Earl Grey," said the woman.

"Thanks."

"I'm Paloma, by the way. I've seen you in town, but I don't think we've ever spoken."

Selene studied her over the rim of the teacup. St. Mary's was a small town, but not small enough to know everyone. "No, I don't think we have."

"My brother Marcelo and I own this hotel," Paloma continued.

Selene held the cup handle in an iron grip. Maybe she wasn't as okay as she thought. Her skin felt clammy and cold.

"What's going on?" she asked quietly.

"I'm not at liberty to say. Phoebus is speaking with the others now."

She frowned at the strange name. He'd told her the first day that his name was a nickname, but she'd never stopped to think about it.

Phoebus.

"What others?" she asked. "You mean his cousins?"

"I forgot to slice the cake. I'll be right back."

Paloma quickly exited the room. As soon as she was gone, Selene stood and crept into the foyer, peering around the staircase into the adjoining room: a larger parlor, crammed with antique furniture and a fireplace with an ornate mirror hanging over it. Backing up, she edged closer to the front door, feeling her heart kick up a notch. If she left now, no one would know.

Just as her hand touched the brass doorknob, she heard muffled voices coming from down the hallway. The buzzing along her arms increased in intensity. Letting her hand drop, she eased forward, stepping gingerly over the creaking floor.

At the end of the narrow passage was a door, cracked open. The voices were wafting from below. Selene's throat felt like dried leaves. She couldn't leave—not after everything that had just happened. With careful fingers, she opened the door enough to pass through and padded down the wooden stairs. The musty scent of old basement filled her nostrils.

Reaching the last step, she drew in a breath and peeked around the paneled wall. The basement was a single room with concrete walls, littered with outdated dining furniture. The only light came from a tiny bulb dangling from the ceiling and a dull brass lamp.

Two guys stood opposite a heavy-looking china cabinet. The first shared Paloma's looks. The other was one of Fee's supposed cousins—with the unruly, curled hair. The second cousin sat in a wooden chair, her posture still and formal. All wore cloaks—the brother in tan, like his sister, and the others in dark green.

A well-built man loomed in the corner, arms crossed. She remembered seeing him before. He ran an antiques repair shop, just around the corner. He was, by the looks of him, the oldest member of the group, and he was oozing defiance as he glared at last occupant, who was poised in the center.

Fee.

And he was glaring back, eyes glinting like those of a bronzed statue.

"You aren't listening." His words snapped like a whip. "They *attacked* her."

"You said she's a Viewer," the man shot back. "Obviously, their intent was to extract. If you hadn't interfered, they'd have taken what they needed and left. The girl would've been none the wiser."

The tall companion looked stunned. "How can you *allow* them to do this?"

"It's part of our agreement," the man answered with a scowl. "And don't you dare look at me like that, Titus. You know extraction doesn't hurt Viewers. The *Electricus* is absorbed through physical contact, and the only evidence is a mild burn that fades away. The Viewers don't remember a thing."

"That doesn't make it right," said the tall boy—Titus—through clenched teeth.

The large man laughed. "Are you going to tell me that what Rovers do is any different? You seek out Viewers and poison them. You flood them with *Electricus* to wipe out their memories. Don't lecture me about right and wrong on this side of the Barrier."

"What we do is for our protection," said Titus.

"And what the Leeches do is for their survival," said the man. "Both are acts of necessity."

"Enough!" All eyes turned to Fee. "Now is not the time to debate ethics," he said firmly. "We have larger concerns. This wasn't some random extraction. The Leeches *wanted* this girl."

Selene felt a frigid lump settle in her stomach.

"But why?" asked the brother, shaking his head. "They only use Viewers for *Electricus*."

"Which is still against the Tenets," growled Titus.

Fee's jawline worked, as though he were struggling with words he didn't want to say. As Selene watched, the air seemed to press in from all sides. They were talking about her, and she had no clue what it was about. As though searching for something, Fee scanned the walls. When he finally spoke, his voice dropped so low that she strained to hear.

"This girl is more than a Viewer," he said. "Tonight, in the marsh, she opened a Rift...and then, she closed it again."

The room went silent.

"You were sent to kill her, weren't you, Phoebus?" said the large man. "That's what your little mission's really been about. But you failed."

Kill her?

The stairs seemed to be rocking underneath her and her stomach churned.

"I didn't fail, Cruz," said Fee, with a deadly smile. "I merely changed tactics."

"So you brought her here," he replied. "A pretty bold move, even for you."

Fee glanced around, then shrugged. "I see no mirrors in this room."

Cruz smirked. "For a Rover, you seem to break your fair share of laws. If you ask me, you'd make a much better Rogue."

They locked gazes.

"Let's get back to this business with the girl," said Titus.

Her nausea evaporated, replaced with anger of her own. She was done eavesdropping like a helpless child outside her parents' bedroom door. She was scared, but with her fear came adrenaline. It surged through her, twisting her emotions into a fury that propelled her forward.

The light overhead flickered violently.

"Okay," she said, rounding the corner. "No talking about me when I'm not in the room."

All heads jerked, almost comically, in her direction. Only Fee seemed unaffected. His gaze flicked up to the light and then back at her, smiling in such a way that Selene believed he'd known she was there the entire time, and something in his expression tempered her emotions.

"Hello," he said in his casual voice. "Please, come in."

"Already have," she fired back.

At that moment, Paloma skittered down the stairs, a plate of cake in her hand. "I'm sorry. I only left her a moment."

The idea that Fee had assigned her a babysitter ignited her anger again. The lights buzzed as she stood there, but her anger faded. Fee's expression shifted into the carefully constructed mask she was growing accustomed to.

"I suppose introductions are in order," he said, gesturing to the others. “You’ve already met Paloma. And I’m sure you’ve guessed the man with the sullen face over there is her brother Marcelo.”

“Good evening,” said Marcelo, dipping his head.

“The tall one is Titus, and our lovely Trinemate here is Nyx.” Fee jutted his chin toward the corner. “Oh, and the large, irritating one is Cruz.”

“And you’re already acquainted with His Majesty, Phoebus the Pisshead,” replied Cruz, nodding at Fee.

Fee’s lips quirked in a smile, but the movement made him appear like an animal about to strike. Ignoring Cruz completely, he motioned her to sit, and she hesitantly complied. As he crouched in front of her, she felt the uncomfortable heat spread down her neck.

“You’ll forgive our lack of manners,” he said. “Things are a bit tense, as you might have noticed. But we need to talk.”

Shoving aside her trepidation, she held his gaze. “Okay, so talk.”

He glanced over his shoulder. “Cruz, can I trust your Trine to patrol the marsh tonight? There are students camping there, and there could be more parasites lurking around. I don’t think it would be in your best interest to have reports of Leech sightings circulating in your little town.”

“Yes, Your Majesty,” said Cruz, with a sneer.

Yanking up the hood of his cloak, he stomped up the stairs with Paloma and Marcelo at his heels. Fee continued smiling, but his hands were curled so tightly his whitened knuckles popped.

“As I said before,” he sighed. “Large and irritating. Now, come on. We’ll continue our conversation outside.”

“Why outside?” She tensed, her fear surging back. “That can’t be safe.”

“Rovers function better in open spaces,” he replied.

“But those things—”

“Can’t track us while we’re wearing our *mantellum.*” Fee gestured to his green cloak. “I’d lend you mine, but they don’t work for Othersiders. But we can mask your signature, so long as we find a place where the Barrier is strong. And for that, I must call upon our talented Trinemate, Titus.”

As he stepped forward, Selene jolted at the sight of his eyes, which had turned completely white and strangely unfocused. “The city park,” Titus said. “No weaknesses. Strong currents.”

"Perfect," said Fee, heading for the stairs.

Rovers...mantellum...barriers...

None of what he was saying made sense, but Fee had the answers she needed. He'd been there in the hospital room with her. He... knew about her. There was no way she was going to pass this up. She leapt for the front door after him, before a wave of panic hit her—almost worse than her fear.

"Wait," she called out. "I need to call my friend first."

"Oh yes," said Fee, and she heard the sigh in his voice. "The boy."

The boy? Selene stared incredulously at him, nearly laughing out loud. Fee didn't look much older than Jamie. Two or three years, at most. Hardly old enough to be calling him a boy, like he was some old geezer yelling at kids from his front porch.

"Uh, yeah. That's him. But I don't have a phone."

He held out a cell phone. "Use mine."

"Thanks."

Wrapping her fingers protectively in her sleeve, she quickly punched Jamie's number, praying her curse wouldn't act up in the next few seconds.

The phone barely rang before Jamie picked up.

"Hello?"

"Hey, Jamie."

"Selene!" His voice was strained. "I was two seconds from calling your mom. Are you okay? Where are you? What happened? Please don't tell me this is about to turn into an episode of CSI."

"Why would you say that?"

"Why? Oh, I don't know. Maybe because Lindsay said she saw you and the new guy talking at the campfire, and now you've both freaking disappeared."

The would-be laugh died in her throat, replaced with the acrid taste of guilt. With everything that had happened, she hadn't even considered how much time had passed. She swallowed. "Yeah, I'm with him."

There was a long pause on the other end of the line. "Fantastic."

"Well, I mean, not really. I...I had a little issue."

"An issue," Jamie repeated after another pause. She could almost hear his brain gears turning as he worked to decipher her words. "Look, just tell me where you are," he said. "I'll come and get you."

She looked at Fee. He shook his head.

"It's okay, Jamie, really," she replied, holding the phone like she was strangling it. "It was nothing serious. He's going to take me home in a few minutes. I'm just drying off."

Jamie made a weird sound in the back of his throat. "What?"

"I fell in the marsh. Ruined my jeans." She bit her lip, tasting blood. She didn't like where this conversation was going. She'd never lied to Jamie before. "I think I'm all camped-out for the night. But look, you wanna come over later? We can watch a movie or something. I mean, unless you want to stay there, which is totally fine, too."

"Okay." He sounded way more than doubtful. "Guess you want me to bring your stuff?"

"That would be great. Thanks, Jamie. I'll call you when I get home." She pressed the button to end the call and handed the phone back to Fee. "This had better be worth it. I'm not big into lying to my friends."

"That wasn't lying," he replied, pocketing the phone.

"Yeah? What world are you living in?"

An odd look crossed his face, but he didn't answer. Instead, he turned to the remaining group members, wearing his smile once more. "Alright, children," he said, clapping once. "Gather all your belongings and follow me. It's time for a play date at the park."

Chapter 20

"So, I assume you know what you're doing," said Titus.

He studied Phoebus as they strolled down the sidewalk, heading into town.

"My dear Titus, surely you don't doubt my leadership abilities."

"Your abilities, no." He shook his head. "But your sanity? Quite possibly."

Phoebus cast a guarded look to ensure that Selene was still behind him, several yards back, keeping pace with Nyx. He hadn't given her the option of walking with him.

He needed space to think.

The aura cast by the *Electricus* within her was visible, even away from the potent grounds of the marsh. It shimmered like a bluish apparition. He wondered why he hadn't noticed it so keenly before tonight. Were her powers growing? Although he doubted any Leech would be able to sense her with so many Rovers so close, she still felt uncomfortably like a beacon.

Before leaving the inn, he and his Trine had donned their Rover uniforms. If they ran into another Leech, he preferred fighting in more suitable gear. Nyx had loaned Selene some Othersider clothing, and the dark jeans and V-neck shirt didn't fit her quite right. But to him, she looked just as captivating in ill-fitting clothes as she did in her own. He stared daggers at the concrete walk, feeling Titus' gaze boring into the side of his skull.

"Why do you keep looking at me like that?" Phoebus snapped.

"Because I'm waiting on the fantastic explanation you're about to give me."

He scowled. "Then you'll be waiting a while."

"Why the sudden lack of trust?" asked Titus, a sliver of hurt in his voice. "We've been friends for decades. You don't have to keep up this pretense."

"Actually, I do, thank you very much," he said, gritting his teeth. "If I don't, then I'll..." He shook his head, almost violently. He didn't like how close he was coming to the edge of his emotions. "Come on. We're almost there."

Titus peered down at him. "Fee—"

"Let's *go*."

Ahead, the dark shapes of docks and boats loomed against the darker shadows of water and sky just beyond. Phoebus cut a sharp right, checking the street signs almost as frequently as his *Electricus* senses. St. Mary's City Park was a few blocks away. He increased his gait until the rest of them were jogging in order to keep up.

Titus remained annoyingly at his shoulder.

"At least tell me why you brought the girl to the inn," he pressed. "It seemed like a risk."

"Curiosity," said Phoebus. "I wanted to see how Cruz would react."

"Why?"

"I have my reasons," he replied. "Let's just keep it at that for now."

"Fair enough," sighed Titus. "For now. But what about Grimm?"

Keeping his eyes ahead, Phoebus rubbed the bridge of his nose with enough force to make it burn. It was bad enough that he was about to reveal forbidden secrets to the girl. But to *purposefully* keep secrets from an Elder? And worse, Preceptor Moth had the ability to read him better than most. He couldn't be sure what she might tell Grimm, regardless of his reports. An unsettled wave rolled through his stomach.

"I'm working on that."

Titus nodded slowly. "But you *are* going to say something to him."

As they passed through the front gate of the park, he slowed his pace. "When the time is right."

"You've known this girl was a Bleeder the whole time, haven't you?"

He cut his eyes to Titus. "Nyx told you."

"About your conversation?" He smirked. "Of course she did."

Phoebus had expected as much. He looked steadily at his Trinemate. "Then you understand: the less you and Nyx knew about all this, the better." He paused. "Especially if I get dragged before the Assembly for my actions."

"It's not your job to protect us, Fee."

"Yes, it is."

"Alright, but not like this," said Titus. "I've never known you to shirk the law in this way. I've got to admit, it's scaring me."

"Trust me, you're not the only one."

Titus sighed again, but this time, the sound was resigned.

Oak trees, heavy with Spanish moss, filled the center of the park. Phoebus stretched out his hand, searching for unusual energy signatures. Titus had said the Barrier felt strong here—which meant the chances of a Leech appearing were slim, though that knowledge gave him little security. More was happening in St. Mary's than he or his Trine had been led to believe.

Beside him, Titus walked with his eyes now closed.

"Anything?" Phoebus asked.

"Nothing," he replied. "Everything feels stable."

"I'll talk with the girl here. I want both of you to patrol the area. If anything changes, report back at once. Otherwise, stay out of sight. I don't want to risk being out in the open too long, especially after what happened tonight."

"Understood."

Gesturing to Nyx, Titus melted into the shadows of the park and Nyx, without a word, followed after, leaving Selene alone, looking confused. Phoebus took another gander around the park, mostly to buy a few extra seconds of time.

Dread was building inside him, like water flooding into the bulkhead of a ship. Not only had he disobeyed his orders, he'd broken the laws of his Rover creed. He'd crossed the line, and there was no going back now.

"Alright," he said, smiling slightly. "Let's talk."

PART THREE

"And as for fate, I'm sure no man escapes it,
Neither a good nor bad man, once he's born."

—*The Illiad*

Chapter 21

They'd stopped inside the city park. Selene felt like a little kid wearing her older sister's hand-me-downs, while the others—with their leather boots, slim-fitting outfits, and flowing cloaks—looked like medieval huntsmen out of a fairy tale.

Every nerve in her body felt charged with adrenaline. If something bad happened to her out here, Jamie would have no idea where she was. Uncertainty churned in her chest. Why had she been so quick to trust these people? Rubbing her fingers against her bracelet, she felt the now-familiar tingle of energy—almost as though the jewelry and her skin were connected. Did Fee really have the answers to what was wrong with her? And if he did, why had she lied to Jamie? After all, he'd believed her story about the electrical monster in the alley.

Titus beckoned to Nyx, and she disappeared into the shadows created by the scattered lamplights. Fee approached with the slow, graceful movements that seemed to be another of his trademarks. With his dark green uniform, he was easily twice as intimidating, especially as he swept his cloak aside and smiled at her.

Waiting expectantly, she noted how his lips remained fixed in their attractively crooked but unnerving expression. His eyes, dulled bronze under the streetlamps, held a glimmer of conflict and doubt, and she was afraid to even blink—afraid he would just disappear into the night like his companions.

With a flick of his head, he indicated for her to follow, and he took off with measured strides, passing a gazebo and several picnic tables. She kept his pace, hovering weirdly between reality and a storybook. Stopping in front of a metal swing set, Fee leaned against the frame and crossed his arms. The chain rope swings clinked gently in the breeze.

"Alright," he said—more to himself, it seemed, than to her.

Moving to the nearest swing, she wiped a patch of grime from the plastic seat.

"Alright," she replied as she sat.

He shifted his arms, his long fingers working against something on his wrists—cuffs, made of metal, with intricate designs covering the bands. Like the rest of his uniform, the jewelry was definitely more Renaissance Faire than preppy chic.

"I'll keep this brief," he said. "My people think you're dangerous."

Her jaw dropped open. "You were aiming an arrow at my heart less than an hour ago. I think that makes *you* the dangerous one. You and those things that tried to eat me tonight."

"They weren't trying to eat you."

She twisted the chain cables and rocked forward. "But you guys were talking about them extracting from people."

"That's different than eating," he said, his eyes following her swinging movement. "And to clarify, those things are called Leeches. They require energy to survive; something we call *Electricus*. They can't produce it on their own, so they pull it from other sources. Extracting from living things keeps them alive, but—as I'm sure you noticed—it hasn't done wonders for their looks, because their bodies can't metabolize the *Electricus* properly. The higher the concentration of *Electricus* from which they extract, the more humanoid a Leech might appear, but they'll never be what they once were."

"Okay, stop right there," she demanded. "You just started in the middle of everything, and you can't do that. I feel like my head's about to explode. Start at the beginning."

"The beginning of what?"

"Everything!" she snapped, kicking off higher on the swing. The motion calmed her nerves. "Like, for instance, *who are you*, exactly?"

"We don't have time—"

"Make time."

Fee looked amused. "Feisty. No wonder that boy is so smitten with you. Very well. But let's just tackle the main points. My cousins—who, as you've guessed, are not my cousins—and I are not from this world. We live in a different dimension—more like a liminal plane."

"Liminal...plane?"

"It's a space between worlds," he continued. "If your worlds are rooms in a house, then my homeland is the doorway between them. Does that make sense?"

"Is it supposed to?"

Fee looked to the heavens with a pained expression. "I'm a Rover," he said. "We're a special class of our people, charged with protecting the invisible Barrier that separates this world—which we call the Otherside—from ours. The creatures you encountered tonight are our enemies. They were banished here after a war in my world, a long time ago. Otherside is their prison, and they cannot return."

"Wait a minute. You *put* those things here?" She felt hot, then cold. "And then you just let them run around attacking people?"

"The decision wasn't mine," Fee replied. "Leeches have been in your world for centuries, hiding among you. They don't generally attack people. Not only is it against our laws, it attracts too much attention. Besides, most humans don't possess enough *Electricus* to justify the labor." His brows lowered in thought. "Like an oyster. Your people consider the meat a delicacy, but it takes a good deal of effort to obtain a meager amount of sustenance. Leeches view most humans that way. The *Electricus* you possess is a delicacy, however not often worth the trouble."

"But it happens."

"To Viewers," said Fee, his eyes narrowing. "Some humans are born with abnormal levels of *Electricus*. It allows them to see aspects of our world that other people can't. It also makes them appealing to Leeches. Take you, for example. Your levels are very high. To a Leech, you'd be the equivalent of a protein bar—a ton of nutrients packed into one small, convenient package."

"What's with all the food analogies?"

"I skipped dinner. I'm a little hungry."

"Oh, you're funny."

He shrugged. "It's a gift. Anyway, as I said, Leeches need this energy to survive. They seek out places with high concentrations of *Electricus*, like swamps or wetlands, or low-lying areas."

"Okay, but what *are* they, exactly?" She gripped the chains tighter. The eerie blue eyes of her attacker blazed through her memory. "And where did they come from?"

Pushing himself from the metal frame, Fee brushed his palms across his thighs. "They used to be like us, a long time ago. But they're cursed now." His face twitched into a snarl. "It's too long of a story for now, and it's not important. What is important, however, is preventing them from getting to you. And that starts with me helping you manage your excess *Electricus*."

"I don't understand."

He reached into his cloak and pulled out his cell phone. "Your habit of damaging Otherworld technology. Does it happen every time you touch something, or is it sporadic?"

She clenched the chains tighter. "Sporadic, I guess. I never know, for sure."

"Well, you used my phone without destroying it, which suggests you already have some form of focused conduction. I've noticed lights flickering in your presence as well, which suggests a connection to your emotions. What else have you experienced?"

As Fee's words loomed over her, Selene's heart beat hard in her throat. "I can...I don't know...see something around you, and the others. Like an aura. Not always, just sometimes. I saw it the first time I met you, when you were sitting in the classroom."

"Then subconsciously, you've already begun to channel it—at least on some level."

Her mouth felt suddenly dry, and her tongue tasted like ash. "Back at the inn, you said something about a Rift, and there was that light in the marsh tonight. You told the others that I caused it. That I opened and closed it."

His coppery eyes bored into her. "You did."

"How?"

"You're the one with the answer to that," he replied.

She jerked the swing to a halt. "But I don't know what you're talking about!" Flames of anger, rooted in fear, set her skin on fire. "You were about to shoot me, and then this Leech thing appears out of nowhere and tries to drag me into a wall of light. I don't know what happened after that!"

"Try to remember," Fee replied. His voice was as smooth as glass. "Just like you remembered me." His brows pinched together. "Somehow, your mind was able to reconstruct the memories that I Dulled in you, memories of my presence, and of the light you saw when you were younger. That light was a Rift, a tear in the membrane of the Barrier. You opened those Rifts, and the knowledge of how you did it is here."

Fee tapped his temple, then pointed to hers.

Giving in to a gnawing desire for her lost memories, she squeezed her eyes shut—blocking out the park, the swings, and him. For a moment, she saw only the darkness. Then, as if from some murky pool, something surfaced in her mind, twirling, until the images ceased moving and slid into focus.

She saw the ghost light from her past.

She saw the mysterious face with the caramel eyes when she was fourteen. She felt the hum of electricity; heard the sharp crack as she was struck by lightning. She saw Fee, in the light, looking back at her from a beautiful purple garden. She felt his presence in the hospital room. She saw the carved designs of his longbow and his glowing arrow flying toward her.

There was a blast of white.

Her eyes flew open. She gasped and bolted out of the swing, nearly pitching forward. Fee reached out, but she jerked away, staring at him wildly.

"These last three years," she panted, "those blanks in all my memories, living with all those missing pieces and the crap I've dealt with because of my accident—" She clutched her wrist, rubbing frantically at the scar underneath her bracelet with her thumb. "It was all because of you."

Fee flinched, and for a moment, she saw a crack in his armor.

"I will protect my world at all cost. You are not the first Other-sider I have Dulled, nor will you be the last. It is for the protection of both our worlds." His eyes softened, as did his voice. "I erased your memories, but I did not cause that lightning strike, Selene. I believe you did."

She gaped at him. "What?"

"I believe you tapped into something inside you three years ago that you didn't know how to control," he continued. "Just as you did tonight, in the marsh. Think back to that moment the Leech attacked you. Try and remember what you did."

Her insides burned as she thought about the Leech. Something had jolted in her brain—she'd felt it, though she didn't understand it. She remembered the way Fee's face had looked when he shouted the order for her to close the Rift. She felt her bracelet, glowing hot against her wrist. And she remembered power—welling up from inside her, somewhere she hadn't known existed before.

"I do remember," she said, her voice shaking. "But I don't know how I did it. When you yelled at me to close the light, I just...*knew* what to do at that moment."

"Because you're a Bleeder."

She stopped the swing.

"That sounds completely gross."

"The term has nothing to do with blood," he replied. "It refers to your abilities."

"My abilities?"

Geez, she sounded like a freaking parrot.

Fee's gaze swept toward the sailboats at the docks, with their masts like black spires reaching for the sky. His fingers toyed with the metal cuffs at his wrists, and she found herself enthralled by his hands.

He noticed her look and crossed his arms. "You're a Bleeder, and that's why my people say you're dangerous. You have something the Leeches want. But you obviously don't know how to control it, so we're going to need to work on that."

She felt herself shrink. "What do they want?"

"Access to Threshold." Fee's features faded into a sallow, haunted expression. "My home."

Understanding crept through her consciousness, and with it, a frigid realization.

"Is that why you were ordered to kill me?"

"You're considered a threat," he replied.

"But I didn't know I was a threat."

"Doesn't matter."

She nodded, letting the weight of the conversation sink in, but the compartments in her brain felt as though they were reaching capacity. She tugged at the bottom of her shirt and looked at her shoes.

"Fee, I want to know something."

"What is that?"

"If that Leech hadn't attacked me, would you have gone through with it? Would you have..." She couldn't bring herself to complete the sentence. "You know..."

There was a long, hard silence.

Gathering her courage, she glanced up. She needed to see his face, to read the emotions behind his coppery eyes. But his posture was like a statue, and his expression had turned void.

"I don't know," he said finally.

She didn't know what unnerved her more: the magnitude of his confession or his raw honesty. But as his words shot through her, they filled her with the power only anger and fear could summon, and she launched toward him.

"Well, I *need* you to know, Fee," she said, right in his face. "Because if I'm going to have anything to do with you, or with any of this, I need to know that you're not going to be pointing another arrow at me the next time something changes."

As Fee stared at her, a smile crept over his face, quirking the corner of his crooked lips. He stepped closer, and Selene found herself back in the swing, her skin buzzing. Despite his easy look, he felt coiled tight, like something wild and untamed.

"After all I've told you, you're not running away," he said. "You have a stronger constitution than most. I promise that if I decide to try and kill you again, I'll give you advance notice. Is that good enough?"

"Not even close."

"Then let's say that you've brought up questions about my world that I need to figure out, and I can't very well do that if you're dead." His eyes crinkled slyly at the corner. "Besides, the fact that we're standing here talking about all this should be proof enough that I've changed my mind. How's that?"

Although his smile was far from serious, the sincerity in his gaze was genuine. Of that, at least, she felt certain. It was insane. It was all completely insane. But something inside her had finally unlocked, and she couldn't help feeling weirdly free as she pushed against the ground with her feet.

"Not exactly reassuring," she replied. "But okay."

Fee placed his hands on the chains, stopping her forward progress, and his eyes roamed over her face, taking in every detail. She swallowed, realizing she was breathing a little shallow. He was so close she could see the coppery flecks in his irises. A few wisps of hair drifted across his face, and her fingers suddenly itched to touch the strands. They looked so silky against jaw. Fee smelled good, all wild and unearthly.

What was she doing?

His eyes were soft once more, the same warm caramel she'd wanted to melt into the first time she'd seen him. Was it just her imagination, or was he breathing a little harder, too? He leaned down, and his hair brushed against her cheek.

"We need to go," he said in her ear.

She jerked, blinking up at him. "What?"

He pulled back and flashed his lopsided smile. "I'm glad we had this little talk," he said, his tone casual, as though they'd been discussing the weather. "Now, I suppose I'd better take you home before your Jamie thinks I've been less than gentlemanly with you."

As he turned away, she suddenly wanted to punch him—punch him so hard he'd double over and puke. Her heart was pounding, and she was pissed. Why did she keep letting him so close? She barely knew him, and she wasn't sure she even trusted him.

"He's not *my* Jamie, thank you." She brushed by him. "But, you're right. I should go."

"Wait a moment," said Fee. "It's not wise to walk back."

"Well, unless your Rover powers can poof a car out of thin air, I don't think I have much choice."

"Who said anything about driving?"

He took her hand with a familiarity she hadn't expected, and her heart flipped from irritation to excitement, totally against her will.

"What are you doing?" She pulled away, but kept her hand in his.

"I'm about to manipulate the Barrier, of course."

All his explanations made her head feel thick, like someone had stuffed it full of cotton. She felt stupid for asking, but after everything she'd witnessed tonight, she had to know.

"You *are* human, right?"

"Of course I'm human," he replied. "I'm just not human like you are."

"What does that even mean?"

"Rovers are born with the ability to produce and conduct electricity." He spread his hands and blue sparks crackled along his fingertips. "The closest comparison in your world would be marine creatures. Electric eels use electroreception. And hammerhead sharks are sensitive to electrical signals from other animals. Shall I go on with the science lesson, or can we just skip to the fun stuff?"

"At no point in this conversation have I heard anything that sounds like fun."

The corners of Fee's eyes crinkled again. "Rovers can also access the Barrier that separates our worlds. We use our power to travel through it."

"What, like teleporting?"

"In a manner of speaking," he replied, looking impressed. "It's a difficult skill, developed over time." He adjusted the tight sleeves of tunic. "Some are better at it than others."

"Like you, I suppose."

"Oh, I'm one of the best, no doubt about it."

As she watched him, her anticipation shifted to wariness. "And Leeches have the same power."

"They can move about in the Otherside, but that's as far as they can travel. But our leaders fear the Leeches' powers are growing, which is precisely why I can't let you fall into their hands."

She pulled back, her doubt growing. "You really should've killed me, then, huh? It would have saved you a lot of trouble."

"Personally, I think you're worth far more alive than dead."

Fee moved ahead of her with a feline grace. But instead of following him, like everyone else around him seemed to do, she planted her feet.

"So that's why you're doing this?" she snapped. "I'm just some pawn caught in the middle of your jacked-up interdimensional conflict?"

He froze in mid-stride. Although his body remained rigid, there was a droop in his shoulders and, for the first time since she'd met him, he seemed truly unguarded.

"That's not what I meant," he said quietly.

Her anger faded. "So what *did* you mean?"

"You're not a pawn."

"Wow," she said. "Glad you straightened that one out for me."

Fee whirled on her, his defensive walls shooting up, his eyes flashing. "I'm trying to help you. This is not a game. These parasites are dangerous, and my people are your world's only line of defense. If they invade my homeland, then it's over, for all of us."

The silence between them was fierce, louder than the sounds of crickets and distant ocean waves. When Fee spoke again, his voice was deep, rich, and amazingly calm.

"Don't worry about the Leeches. I'll keep you safe."

"So says my would-be murderer."

"Point taken," he said. "Alright then, *we'll* keep you safe. My Trinemates and the Rogues, I mean. I was the one ordered to kill you, not them."

"But Nyx and Titus, they're with you. So I can't trust them anymore than I trust you."

"They wouldn't lay a hand on you unless I ordered it," Fee replied. "And I'm giving you my word."

"How comforting."

"Do you require a handshake or something?"

"Wouldn't help," she replied.

Instead of replying, Fee closed his eyes. Selene felt the hair on the back of her neck rise, and the air between them seemed to change. The cuffs on Fee's wrists glowed as currents of blue-white electricity sparked along his arms.

"This is *Electricus*," he said without opening his eyes. "This is power in its purest and most natural form, and it's the lifeblood of my world."

As the sparks passed through the cuffs, they seemed to act like conductors, harnessing the energy and shooting it into the air. Selene felt something warm at her wrist, and she was startled to see her own bracelet glowing. The air around them shimmered, rippling like water in a pool.

"The ghost light," she whispered.

Opening his eyes, Fee offered his hand. "An opening in the Barrier," he corrected. "Think of it as a door." Without hesitation, she put her hand in his, and electricity sparked through her palm with prickling shocks. "Now," he said, "don't let go."

Although it didn't seem possible, Fee stepped inside the whiteness, guiding her after him. Her insides twisted. There was no air, no oxygen. Her lungs screamed for release. And then, air rushed into her again. She gulped and staggered forward. But Fee had her around the waist. She blinked, trying to focus, and the dizziness subsided.

She was standing in her own backyard.

"Wow," she breathed. "That was…wow."

Fee's eyes were uncharacteristically wide. "You passed through. Impressive."

"Wait," she said, heart stopping. "You weren't sure I could?"

"No."

She hauled off and hit him, square in the chest. "You're a freaking jerk! What if I'd been killed?"

"If you're going to be killed, I'm going to be the one to do it," he said calmly, rubbing his chest with the heel of his hand. "Not Leeches, and definitely not the Barrier. Me. I thought we had an understanding about that."

"You could've warned me first!"

Fee adjusted his cuffs. "Where's the fun in that?"

Balling up her fist, she glared, pissed enough to take another swing. But a flicker across Fee's amused expression cooled her temper—like water over a fire. She studied him as he absently traced the designs on his metal band, looking back at her.

Each time his eyes met hers, it was getting easier to spot—the undercurrent of emotion, visible just beneath his sculpted exterior. There was something he kept fiercely locked down inside him, and his flippant attitude was his way of hiding it.

It was another mystery added to the pile, and it was a mystery she was going to solve. But for now, the fact that she'd just walked through a wall of light and ended up across town was more pressing. Her stomach fluttered like butterflies.

"Fun would be slapping that smile off your face," she said. "But I'm going to let it go, because I'm the bigger person between the two of us." She rubbed her arms. "And, honestly, because that was an amazing ride."

"Of course it was," he replied with a shrug. But he looked pleased.

"So what now?"

"Tell no one what happened tonight," he stated. "And that includes your little friend. Some Leeches can look remarkably human. You may not know who is listening. Keep a low profile. Don't go out at night. Leeches prefer to attack when the air is coolest."

"But you said they can track me."

His lips tightened into a firm line. "Viewers who emit higher *Electricus* patterns are easier to detect, so I would recommend staying away from places where the Barrier is weak, such as the marsh."

"You do realize these instructions are pretty vague, right?"

Instead of answering, Fee took hold of her wrist. The unexpected touch made her feel warm, and she tried to ignore the sensation—as well as the way her heart kicked up a notch. He ran his thumb over the smooth metal of her bracelet.

"I noticed this at the campground," he said. "Where did you get it?"

"It was a present from my grandmother."

"Does she live with you?"

Slivers of memories—ones that had remained intact, even after the strike—pinched at her: disastrous attempts at baking, her grandmother laughing and mopping eggs and flour off the floor, sleep-overs and watching old movies while snuggled under homemade quilts.

"No," she replied, swallowing a hard lump of emotion. "She died when I was a kid."

A crease appeared along Fee's forehead. "This bracelet contains properties similar to my cuffs. I don't know how it came into your grandmother's hands, but it is valuable. Keep it on at all times."

"Alright, fine," she replied, feeling as though a heavy weight had dropped on her shoulders. Maybe the shock of the evening was catching up with her. "Anything else?"

"Yes."

Fee's long fingers traveled away from the bracelet; her heart skittered again.

"What?"

"Come by the *Seaside Inn* tomorrow at noon," he replied.

Once again, like the flip of a switch, his voice changed from one used to being in charge to something gentle—if that word could be applied to Fee, she mused. Compelling, maybe. Carefully controlled? Definitely. As his lips pressed together, as though he wanted to say something else, lights suddenly flashed in the driveway, and Selene heard the sound of a car engine.

Fee's body shifted into a defensive posture, but just as quickly as he'd moved, he relaxed into his carefree stance, flashing his crooked smile toward the brown pickup truck rolling to a stop in the drive.

"It seems the boy has arrived to make sure you're safe," he said. "So I'll take my leave now." His lopsided grin twinkled in the darkness. "Do give him my fondest regards, would you?"

The engine turned off, and Jamie's shadowy form emerged from the driver's side. She waved at him, opening her mouth to reply, but as she turned back, there was only darkness and empty space.

Fee was gone.

Chapter 22

Selene banged the cordless phone against the kitchen table and flopped in the chair, pulling her pajama pant-clad legs against her chest.

"Something wrong?" asked her mom, closing up a package of coffee. Her gaze slid to the phone. "Please don't tell me you broke our landline."

"It's Jamie," she almost spat back. "I've been trying to get hold of him all morning, and he won't answer anything." She toyed with the frayed edge of a placemat. Jamie had dropped off her stuff last night and left without so much as a goodbye. "I think he's mad at me."

"I didn't think you guys ever fought."

"It wasn't a fight, exactly," she said, watching her mom pull two mugs from an overhead cabinet. "It's just...I was talking to this new guy last night at the campground. When it started thundering, I got nervous, and he offered to take me home. Jamie wasn't too happy about it."

"I take it you didn't tell him you were leaving."

"I just didn't think about it," she replied. It was true; she hadn't even stopped to consider him, even though things had been pretty insane out in the marsh. Guilt wrenched her insides. "I guess I was just too freaked out about the storm."

Leaning against the counter, her mom frowned. "I didn't hear it storm last night. Then again, I didn't hear you come in, either, so I must have been really out."

"It blew over," she replied. "Anyway, I asked him to stay and watch a movie, but he just took off. Now he's ignoring me."

Her mom poured the coffee. "He could just be busy, or hanging out with that Mooch guy."

"His name's Mudge."

"Okay, whatever." Handing Selene one of the mugs, she sat across from her. "My point is, there's probably a reason he hasn't called you back."

"I guess so." She took a sip of coffee. "Ugh, needs creamer."

As she pulled the bottle out of the fridge, she caught sight of her bracelet and thought of Fee's instructions. And the way he'd held her wrist. Feeling another punch of guilt, she closed the door. Jamie had every right to be ticked with her, but she had no way to explain herself if he refused to talk to her.

"I need to get ready for work," she said. "I told Miss Claire I'd be there after lunch."

Although she wasn't really needed at the store until two, she didn't want to tell her mom that she'd made plans to stop by the *Seaside Inn*. There would be questions, and after everything from last night, she was tired of questions. There were too many things whirling around in her head as it was.

Her mom stirred her coffee with her finger. "How long are you working?"

"I don't know. Probably until close."

"Okay, well I'll be next door at Amy's house tonight, hanging with the girls."

She nodded. She was used to her mother's late nights with the other Navy wives in the neighborhood. Sipping down her sweetened coffee, she looked at the wall calendar. "Dad's coming home at the end of the month, right?"

"Yeah, that's the plan," her mom replied, looking down. "Unless something changes."

"Okay."

She felt an icky pang in her stomach—the same one she got every time her dad came home. She missed the way their family used to be. When they actually *were* a family. Having her father home felt more like a disruption in their lives, rather than a part of it, these days.

"Well, I'll see you later," she said. "Gotta get ready."

Hurrying down the hallway, she was determined to try Jamie one last time. She sprawled on the bed, holding the phone gingerly between her fingers. Her stupid curse hadn't acted up since last night, but she wasn't sure how long that would last. Using a pencil to press the keys, she tapped the speaker button and waited, listening to the ring. At this point, she expected his voicemail. But instead, she got his voice.

"Hey," he said flatly.

"Jamie, I've called you a million times this morning!"

"Funny. My call history says five. Guess I need to get this thing looked at."

"Seriously," she said, her voice rising. "What's wrong? Are you still miffed about me leaving without telling you? I told you, I'm sorry. It was a stupid thing to do. I wasn't thinking straight."

"Yeah, no, I get it," he replied. "And I told you last night that it's fine. No big deal, really."

"Then why are you being all standoff-guy?"

"Just a busy morning, okay?" His voice sounded more strained than she was used to. "I've been at the mall with Mudge, getting a new game. We're going back to his place to check it out."

"Can you stop by the store after my shift?"

There was a long, discomforting pause. "Yeah, sure. I'll be there."

"Great," she breathed, flooding with relief. "I'll see you in a few hours."

Tossing the phone aside, she yanked open her dresser drawers, selecting a decent pair of jeans and a peasant top, and slipped into a pair of flats. As she opened her makeup bag, she contemplated doing something different with her hair—especially after the rain-drenched look she'd sported last night.

She set her lipstick down and twisted her hair into a quick ponytail. Why should she care what Fee thought? Comfort-before-style had always been her motto, and she wasn't changing now, not for some guy. She rushed down the stairs, dumped the remnants of her coffee down the sink, and headed out the door.

Wrapping her arms around her torso, her thoughts drifted to Jamie. It wasn't like him to hold a grudge—not that she blamed him. She needed to clear the air, but she couldn't tell him the real reason she was with Fee—not because he'd told her to stay quiet, but because the last thing she wanted to do was to drag her best friend into danger.

She approached the two-story front of the *Seaside Inn*. Although she didn't know how she felt about any of this, somehow she found herself standing on the front porch, just as Fee had asked, despite every reservation flashing in her head. She knocked on the door. Several seconds passed before it opened a crack, revealing a female face.

"Hi," she said. "Remember me? It's Paloma, right?"

"Of course." The door opened wider. "Hello, Selene."

"Fee asked me to stop by," she replied, feeling awkward saying the words out loud. "If that's okay?"

"He's not here, but he said that you would be coming by, and he gave instructions that you were to wait for him in the living room until he returned."

"When will he be back?"

"He didn't say," Paloma replied, her tone apologetic. "You're just supposed to wait."

"*Wait* for him?" Her chest suddenly burned with irritation. Fee told her come, and then he didn't bother to show up? "Well, you can tell His Highness that I don't have time to wait. I have a job. If he wants to see me, he can come and find me."

Bounding down the steps, she stormed across the street. She didn't care what world he said he was from, it was no excuse to be a self-centered pig. Maybe the others had to follow his orders, but she wasn't one of them. Why did she keep allowing Fee to get under her skin?

The sun was bright, and thoughts of monsters in the marsh seemed like fairy tales now. She'd probably imagined most if of it, anyway. It seemed like something her lightning-damaged brain would do. She'd likely wake up tomorrow and not remember any of it. She refused to even look over her shoulder. By the time she reached the *Far and Away*, she was over the whole stupid thing.

She'd work her shift, and then she and Jamie would go hang, and then everything would go back to the way it had been. But when she pushed on the front door, she was surprised to find it locked. It wasn't like Miss Claire to run errands before she arrived to watch the store. Pulling out her key, she unlocked the door and stepped inside.

It was dark.

"Miss Claire?" she called out. No response.

She maneuvered through the shelves. The light switches were located in the back room. Her arms tingled, causing every hair to rise on her skin. Slowing her pace, she moved with cautious steps, barely breathing. Something didn't feel right. The door to the back room was cracked ajar.

Miss Claire lay on the floor, eyes staring blankly.

Hovering over her was a dark form, its body hidden by a ragged cloak. Selene stifled a gasp with her hands, and her bracelet flashed in the corner of her eye, as though telling her do something. Her stomach churned with nausea. In the marsh, her actions had come naturally. But what could she do here?

"Hey!" she shouted. "Leave her alone!"

Cloak splaying, the figure whipped around to face her. Terrifyingly blue eyes fixed on her, glowing like pilot lights in the darkness of its hood. She stumbled back, feeling the crackle of electricity in the air. Her fingers reached for the broom behind the door, and she swung it wildly by the handle.

Momentarily surprised, the figure retreated. She raised the broom again, but a crackle of electricity flashed over her head. Something buzzed by her like a bolt of lightning, and the hooded figure wailed, clutching its shoulder. A gleaming arrow struck the wall behind it.

With a wild screech, the figure leapt for the window. Glass shattered as it crashed through, spraying debris, and Selene ducked and threw her arms over her face.

"That was a perfectly good window," said a familiar voice. Fee was beside her, a glowing bow in his hand. "How inconsiderate."

"Aren't you going after it?" she panted, bracing against the wall.

Fee looked hurt. "Of course I am. What kind of Rover do you think I am?" An arrow formed in his free palm. "But first things first." He turned, aimed, and fired. The arrow tore through the air, straight into Miss Claire's shoulder at the base of her neck. She went limp against the floor as the arrow sparked and fizzed, and then disintegrated to nothing.

"No!" She jerked Fee's arm. "You killed her!"

"I didn't," he replied, in a judgmental voice. "I'm fairly certain I've explained this already. I Dulled her. When your boss wakes up, she'll have no memory of this, and her brain will fashion a logical explanation. She slipped and fell. Hit her head. Something like that. She'll be fine."

Biting back angry words, she knelt beside Miss Claire, feeling her pulse. Her breathing seemed normal, and her skin was warm. As Selene watched, morbidly fascinated, the wound at the base of Miss Claire's neck crawled with little blue electric sparks. They swirled over the skin, like tiny veins, and then faded into nothing.

"There's no mark."

"That would be evidence," Fee replied. "I'm too good for that."

"And she won't remember this?"

"No."

She glanced at Fee, who looked so normal in his jeans and shirt. Yet the way he stared at her, eyes brimming with intensity, brought another image of him to the surface of her mind. Her stomach rolled uncomfortably, and her throat felt prickly, like she'd swallowed a cactus.

"Is this what you did to me, in the hospital?"

"Yes." His coppery eyes were guarded now.

"So why didn't it work on me? Why did I remember you?"

As Fee held out his weapon, the entire longbow dissipated into the air as though it had never existed. He flexed his fingers, looking aggravated once more.

"Because you're a Bleeder, Selene. Haven't you been listening? It worked on you for a while, but Bleeders are extremely resistant to our poison. The *Electricus* within you eventually repaired the Dulling process, ending with you remembering me."

"Another reason you people think I'm dangerous, I suppose?"

"Bingo."

She brushed aside a wisp of Miss Claire's blonde hair. "How long will she be out like this?"

"A few minutes."

She looked at the window. "Was that Leech after me?"

Kneeling on the other side of Miss Claire's body, Fee passed one hand over her chest, a few inches above her dressy jacket. "I don't think so. I can feel this woman's *Electricus*. She's a Viewer. The Leech must have been trying to extract from her."

"What do you mean…feel?"

"It's a skill," he replied. "If the *Electricus* isn't too muddied with interference, I see the energy, similar to how you saw my aura. But mostly, I feel the currents." He sat back and wiggled his fingers.

"It's difficult to explain."

As though struck with some terrible thought, a fierce expression—like a stormcloud—raced across Fee's face. His lip curled from his bared teeth, and Selene was reminded once again of a wild animal. He clutched at his left cuff, and she heard the soft click of an unseen lock.

"Here." He took it off and fastened it to her wrist. "Wear this."

Before she could protest, the lock clicked into place, somehow small enough to fit around her narrow wrist. She expected the metal to be cold, but it felt warm against her skin.

"Why are you giving me your jewelry?"

"It's not jewelry," he said, standing slowly. "It's a tool."

"And?"

"There was a Leech in your store just now."

Reaching down, her offered his hand, and though she didn't need the help, couldn't resist taking it. She tried to pretend she didn't notice his strong grip and the tender, confident way he pulled her to her feet.

"Wait a minute," she said. "You told me Leeches mostly came out at night."

"Glad to know you *were* actually listening."

"Trust me," she replied, irritation flickering. "It wasn't easy. You talk way too much."

"I like the sound of my voice."

"Somebody has to, I suppose."

As Fee's brows shot up, she caught the impressed look in his eyes again, followed by a genuine smile on his crooked lips. "Touché."

"So, back to your pretty little man-jewelry," she continued. "Why do I have to wear it?"

Reaching into his backpack, Fee pulled out his green cloak and fastened it around his shoulders. The cloak—he had called it a *mantellum*—was thick and draped in beautiful folds across his back. Selene itched to touch the fabric. Fee held up his right arm, the one that still had a cuff around it.

"I'm operating on the assumption that your bracelet has similar properties to mine," he said, "but I don't know exactly *what* properties. You see, every Rover possesses a talisman, fashioned with our unique signature embedded within it." He traced the designs along the metal. "Our talismans help shield our presence from Leeches by—well, to use an Othersider phrase—by 'jamming our frequency' so they can't pinpoint us. I'm not sure if your bracelet works that way, so I want you to wear one of mine, just in case."

"I really don't understand."

An amused expression flitted over his features. "You're not expected to. Just wear it, okay? I've got to go kill that window-smashing parasite, and I don't want you left defenseless while I'm gone."

"I'm not defenseless," she snapped. She didn't like being told what to do, like she was a child. Even if Fee was probably right. "I've got a broom."

Fee perched on the windowsill like a cat. "And one more thing. Wait for me at the inn."

"No can do. I've got to work today."

He glanced at the body of Miss Claire. "Somehow, I doubt your employer is going to care if you don't show."

"But—"

"Selene!" He closed his eyes, and she could actually see the effort it took for him to rein in his emotions. Once his face had gone neutral, he fixed his gaze calmly on her again. "I'm not trying to order you. I'm asking you nicely. Please, wait for me at the *Seaside Inn*. I won't be long."

She swallowed her pride, leaving a bitter taste in her mouth. "Fine."

Fee leapt from the window, leaving only the image of his Cheshire Cat grin behind.

Chapter 23

As Phoebus darted through the alley, he sent out *Electricus* charges at random, searching for signs of the Leech. But every volt that came back provided no information. It was as if the creature had simply disappeared. He shouldn't have talked to Selene so long. But then, he'd always been an expert tracker. It was only a matter of time before—

The sound of labored breathing reached his ears. He paused, muscles tensing, senses straining. It was coming from behind a pile of wooden crates. He glided forward,, feet soft against the ground; his *mantellum* flowing behind him, protecting him from Othersider eyes. He pressed his shoulder against the side of one crate, preparing; his body coiled to spring.

A figure huddled against the greasy wall. Without hesitating, he lunged and yanked it hard by the shirt, shoving its body against the bricks. The ragged hood fell from its head, and Phoebus' froze. The thing in his grasp wasn't a Leech, but a teenaged boy. His wild, frizzy hair hung over his face as he ducked low, trying to hide against the wall.

"Who are you?" he demanded.

"Please, don't hurt me," the boy whined, averting his head. "I know what you are."

"Then you know you'd better answer my questions."

The boy nodded pitifully.

"Let's start again," said Phoebus. "Who are you?" The boy didn't answer, but his body shook, and his head rolled, as though he were having a fit. He gripped the boy's neck. "Well?"

"I don't remember," the boy sniffed.

"Don't lie to me," he growled. "You tried to extract from that Viewer in the shop." He leaned closer, trying to peer into the boy's face. Something was extremely off, but he couldn't place the sensation. "You feel like a Leech, but that's not possible. So I'm going to ask you one last time. Who are you?"

The boy trembled, then looked up.

His eyes were electric blue, set deep in a face with skin as thin as parchment, revealing a tangled web of streaky vein-like lines just beneath the surface, running from his forehead down to his neck. Corpse-blue lips and the teeth behind them were a sickening shade of gray. Phoebus could see the evidence of his arrow wound where it had sliced through his shoulder; the skin oozed with something that wasn't quite blood.

He'd never seen a Leech look so human before.

He shook him hard. "What manner of creature are you?"

"I don't know," the boy gasped. He was shaking violently now, and the vein-like cords spread deeper down his neck, bulging under the skin. He clutched at the wall, his face drawn in agony. "I... escaped," he gagged. "Was so weak. Needed...to feed. Had to try. The V-Viewer called to me. Couldn't...stop...myself."

"Escaped from where?"

"The p-place he holds us."

"Who holds you?" Phoebus yelled, his patience gone. "Who is *he*?"

The boy slid to his knees, wailing and clawing at his throat like a choking man, gasping out one word before collapsing into a pile at his feet.

"His name's...Cruz."

***

After wrestling with Fee's order-request for several minutes, Selene scribbled a note to Miss Claire, saying she'd gone home sick. Making sure the door locked behind her, she left, praying that what Fee had told her was the truth, and her boss wouldn't remember a thing.

Although she tried to keep her emotions in check, by the time she arrived at the inn, she was fuming. Her mood worsened after nearly five minutes of pounding on the front door with no answer, and she was dangerously temped to throw a brick through the window.

Then she heard voices from around the back.

Looking past the porch, she noticed a pathway that ran between the inn and the adjoining lot. She followed the path, which led to a well-kept backyard, surrounded by a privacy fence and decorated with several birdbaths and antique tables and chairs.

Titus and Nyx were squaring off in the middle of a thick patch of grass.

The Rovers circled each other, eyes locked. Like Fee, they were wearing regular clothes—not the huntsmen look from the night before—which made their actions seem even more out of place, as if she'd stumbled upon a couple of medieval knights jousting with lightsabers.

As Titus made one full circuit, he flung his arms out to his sides. Two amber-colored knives, each as long as his forearm, appeared in a swirl of blue light. The blades crackled with electricity.

"Your move," he said, smirking through gritted teeth.

Nyx flicked her wrist, and a smooth object—nearly the size of a sword—materialized in her left hand. Whirling it over her head, she swung the weapon in a wide arc, spewing a streak of lightning through the air—right at Titus' chest.

He deflected the blow with both knives.

"Not good enough," he laughed.

But before he could maneuver his weapons, Nyx sent another volt, causing him to dive out of the way, narrowly avoiding the electricity. He rolled and came up on one knee.

Nyx smiled. "How about that one?"

"Cheap shot," he said, brushing off his jeans.

"You're too slow."

As Titus opened his mouth to respond, his body stiffened, like Selene had seen Fee react, and he faced in her direction. At the same moment, Nyx also spun, her weapon in front of her, poised to strike.

"Hey!" Selene called out, backpedaling. "Hey, it's just me."

A full three seconds passed before Titus lowered his knives. The blades disappeared as rapidly as they'd formed. Nyx, her weapon also gone, stepped forward.

"What are you doing here?" she asked.

"Fee told me to meet him at the inn."

Nyx's elegant brows pinched together. "He is not with you?"

"He's off killing some nasty in an alley."

"A Leech," said Titus, doubt tainting his voice. "In the heat of the day?"

"Yeah," she said, rubbing her arms. "I understand that's not normal."

The two Rovers exchanged looks, as though an entire conversation passed between them. Nyx pointed at Selene's arm.

"Why are you wearing Phoebus' talisman?"

"He said something about interference and masking my signature, whatever that means," she replied, twisting the heavy cuff. "He thought it might help keep me hidden from those creatures."

"And compromise his own location in the process," said Nyx. She placed both hands on her hips. "You must be quite important to him."

A self-conscious burn radiated along Selene's shoulders, and she searched the backyard, desperately needing another topic of conversation.

"So, what were you guys doing?"

"Sparring," said Titus. His teeth flashed white in the sunlight. "It keeps our reflexes sharp on this Side. The *Electricus* in your world is constantly changing. We have to stay in tune with how it flows."

"So your job is fighting Leeches, like I saw you do in that alley."

"You saw that, did you?" he replied, scratching his curly head. "Yes, fighting does come with the territory, but we have other duties as well. Some of us can detect the weaknesses in the Barrier. That would be me. And some, like Nyx, can repair Rifts."

"Our weapons are made with amber," Nyx explained. "It helps to focus and conduct our powers."

As Selene traced the cuff's designs, she could see that the grooves were filled with yellow-orange resin. It was the amber that glowed blue in Fee's weapons when he was fighting, she realized. Her skin prickled at the contact, as though the band were an electrical outlet.

"Do you have wrist cuffs, too?" she asked.

"No," Nyx replied. "Those are reserved for Trine leaders."

"Preceptors align us to one particular area of service, based on our relationship to the *Electricus*," added Titus, gesturing to himself and Nyx. "Trine leaders, like Phoebus, are chosen for their acute sensitivity to the Barrier currents that shift and change with it, which makes them best suited for tracking Viewers."

"So you're tell me that, deep down, he's a really sensitive guy."

Titus gave a huffing chuckle. "In a manner of speaking. Unfortunately, that kind of connection puts Rovers like Phoebus at higher risk for light-madness, so the Preceptors created those talismans to help guard against it."

Before Selene could voice the question, Nyx answered.

"Light-madness is a condition that affects those who spend a great deal of time moving through the Barrier. It develops slowly and is incurable. It's one of the reasons we must continue to work with the *Electricus* here in your world, to keep up our resistance to its effects."

A weird shiver went down Selene's spine as she pressed her fingers to Fee's wrist cuff. He'd willingly given her one of his protections, yet he'd admitted, from his own mouth, that he'd been planning on killing her just the night before. The thought made her heart throb.

"Fee said he could feel the *Electricus* inside Viewers?"

"Well, we all can, to varying degrees," said Nyx.

As Selene continued to study the metal, she felt the power emanating from it. "So how is this *Electricus* different than, you know, just regular electricity?"

"You Othersiders have learned how to harness it to power your machinery and technology," said Nyx. "But for Thresholders, the *Electricus* is the essence of who we are."

Titus sifted his fingers through the air in the same manner Fee had done, as though he were testing the water in a pool. Tiny blue volts crackled along his palms. "*Electricus* exists within every living thing," he said. "In our world, it's as essential as breathing air."

Enthralled, she couldn't wrench her eyes from the blue arcs. They reminded her of the plasma globes that science teachers sometimes used to teach about electricity. The tips of her fingers tingled, almost as though urging her to copy Titus' movements.

"So Electricus does more than just power your lights, I take it."

"It keeps Threshold alive," replied Nyx. "But more than that, it keeps us alive. Without the constant flow of Electricus through our bodies, we'd be—"

"Like the Leeches?" she finished.

Nyx looked at her with an appreciative expression. "Exactly."

Taking a hesitant breath, Selene extended her index finger toward the blue arcs as the hair on her arms rose in response. A tiny stream, like a miniature lighting bolt, jittered in her direction. Her breath caught, and she jerked away reflexively. The arc shifted back to Titus, and with a flick of his hand, the electricity vanished.

"By the Grove," whispered Nyx. "You summoned it to you."

Selene shook out her hand. "I didn't do anything."

"*Phoebus* was right about you," said Titus, holding his hand toward her, palm outward. "Your energy signature is unusual." His eyes turned eerily white, blocking out his pupils and the blue of his irises. "I can't always read your pattern," he continued. "It's almost as if you merge with the Barrier at times, and then you disappear altogether."

Shivering at the freaky zombie-like quality of his eyes, she also felt exposed, as though he'd looked into her private life.

"Is that a good thing, or a bad thing?"

As Titus blinked, his eyes returned to their normal color. "Are you kidding? It's amazing. I can see why you're considered a threat. I didn't think anyone except the Elders had that kind of power."

Something twisted inside her chest. Fee had talked about her power, too. But she didn't have powers. All she had was a stupid curse, from a lightning strike that she'd apparently caused herself. With a frustrated breath, she stepped around Titus and slumped into one of the lawn chairs that littered the backyard. The Rovers followed her and took up residence in two nearby chairs.

"Okay, so who exactly are the Elders?" she asked, deflecting the conversation.

"They oversee Threshold," replied Titus. "Along with the Regents and Preceptors. They are what you might call our ruling body."

"And how do you fit into all this?"

"Well," he replied, using his sleeve to wipe sweat from his forehead. "Rovers are trained from a young age in the Preceptory. It's an academy, where we receive lessons on the other worlds surrounding Threshold. We can Shift through the Barrier, but it's an ability that diminishes with age. Once that happens, we go into service as Regents or Preceptors."

"Huh," she replied, feeling overloaded to the point of numbness.

"But I'm sure Phoebus has gone over this with you already."

"Phoebus seems to leave out a lot of details," she replied crisply.

"Well, that sounds typical," said Nyx. As she perched on the edge of her seat, she began unbraiding her damp hair with her fingers. "I've never known him to be otherwise, always quick to keep his guard up around everyone."

"That's no excuse for sucking at explanations."

Titus smirked. "No, it's not."

"But, seriously," she pressed, the blistering urge to vent overtaking her numbness. "What's with his attitude and ordering everybody around like the Commander-in-Chief? I get that he's in charge of you people, but I know he's only telling me whatever he thinks I need to hear."

The Rovers exchanged another round of looks.

"If he's guarded with what he says, he has his reasons," said Nyx. Her voice had taken on a different tone. "We don't often question them."

"Because you trust him."

"To a fault, perhaps," said Titus, looking out over the fence. "He's my oldest friend, and he's saved my life more times than I can count. There are things he doesn't even tell us, when he must place the Tenets above his friendships." He placed a hand on her arm. "Phoebus has his flaws, as we all do, but he's worth your trust, Selene. If you have the abilities he believes you to possess, then it would be wise to listen to him."

"Did you know about me?"

"No," replied Titus. "At least, not everything."

Leaning her back against the metal chain, she shook her head. "Look, I'm sorry if your speech doesn't inspire me, Titus. But when a guy tries to kill you, it takes a while to get over. Besides, Cruz doesn't seem to trust him, either."

"Well, that's a whole different thing," said Titus. "He and Phoebus have issues, going back to a time before I was a Rover."

Curiosity raced up her spine. "What happened?"

"He's never spoken about it," Titus replied. His expression seemed resigned. "All we know is that Phoebus was in charge of training a new Trine. Cruz was a part of the group. Something happened on this Side, and Cruz never returned to Threshold. Phoebus hadn't seen or spoken to him since, until we arrived here."

Beside her, Nyx was occupied with tying the laces of one of her sleek-looking boots. She reminded Selene of a heroine from a comic book: confident and naturally beautiful, in that effortless way, and totally capable of kicking butt at a moment's notice.

"So, how long have you known Fee?" Selene asked.

Nyx smoothed a wrinkle in her shirt. "Ever since I entered the Preceptory and was assigned to Phoebus' training squad. Quite a while, in other words."

"So you two are his closest friends, and he still keeps stuff from you? It's a wonder he has any friends at all. You guys must be martyrs or something."

Her thoughts went suddenly to Jamie, and her cheeks burned with hypocrisy.

"Law and Threshold are what matter to him," said Nyx, with a clouded expression. "Those are the things that hold his heart. Sometimes he lets us in, and sometimes he doesn't. Just know that he's not likely to change, even if you do manage to break through all his charming defenses."

And just what was Fee defending himself from, Selene wondered.

"Trust me, I'm not trying to break through anything. I'm just trying to figure him out."

"I hope you do," said Nyx, and her smile felt sincere. "It would be a first."

Selene felt a solidarity with the two Rovers that caught her by surprise—something honest and genuine that made her feel as though she had a place here, in the middle of all this insanity.

But her feelings toward Fee were another matter. She didn't know how to take him, and it gnawed at her insides like a stomachache. If all this was real—and she'd seen enough to be pretty convinced so far—then she had to decide if she could truly place her safety in Fee's hands. And, if she did, what would she tell Jamie?

Jamie.

Realization struck her like a blow to the face. She should've been at work. Jamie was supposed to stop by, and she wasn't there. She'd done it again. With a sickening feeling, she bolted from the chair.

"Crap! I have to go."

But Nyx was also on her feet. "You can't, Selene. Phoebus told you to wait here."

"Yeah, well, you guys may have to listen to him, but I don't." She checked her watch. "I'll come back, I promise. I just have to see a friend of mine. I need to make something right that I screwed up."

Nyx stepped in front of her. "You have to stay."

"I don't think Phoebus meant for us to forcibly keep her here," said Titus. "Selene's right. It's her decision."

The two Rovers locked eyes.

"So we're just going to let her go?" asked Nyx.

"Yes," Titus replied, looking sideways at her. "But we're tagging along."

Chapter 24

As Phoebus half-pulled, half-dragged the strange boy out of the alley, he kept to the back streets, avoiding the main parts of town. *His mantellum* couldn't shield both of them from view.

The boy was like dead weight in his arms.

"What is wrong with you?" he snarled in frustration.

The boy gurgled. "Feel sick..."

"Well, that's too bad," he growled at him, lips tight. "You're not extracting from any more Viewers. I don't care what kind of agreement you've got going on with Cruz. And you're going to show me this place from where you escaped."

The boy shook with such violence that it was difficult to keep a quick pace. He'd never seen a Leech like this before, and certainly not one in such bad shape. Leeches could pull enough *Electricus* from plants or smaller living things to survive. But this Leech seemed incapable of doing anything. The veins in his neck and face bulged and sparked under his skin, and his eyes were desperate, as though whatever energy he had left was trying to burn through his body.

"Past the docks," said the boy. "The...woods."

As he moved to the outskirts of the town, the buildings gave way to undeveloped land. The marsh stretched out before him, vast and ominous, and just beyond it, the coastal waterway. With his discolored hand, the Leech boy pointed to a thick gathering of trees. Deep in the shadowy copse, Phoebus saw the outline of a cabin, barely standing, in a small clearing. He grabbed the boy around the waist with one arm and formed an arrow in his free hand.

Flinging the boy aside, he glared down at him. "Don't move."

The Leech boy didn't answer; he curled up in the dead grass, quivering. Phoebus almost felt sorry for him. Almost. He was a Leech, a cold-hearted killer and a member of the race that threatened to destroy his homeland. Turning up his lip in disgust, Phoebus ducked under a window and peered through one of the broken panes.

Huddled on the rotting floor were the bodies of several men and women with dazed eyes, staring blankly. He read their signatures immediately. They were all Viewers. Swirls of *Electricus* flooded his senses, and the hairs on the back of his neck rose as he braced himself against the cabin wall and turned his attention to three figures standing in corner of the room.

Two of their signatures he registered as Leeches, but what he saw made his guts twist behind his ribcage. They weren't the grotesque, twisted-up monsters he was accustomed to fighting. These Leeches appeared far too humanoid, which could only mean one thing.

They'd been extracting from Othersiders for a very long time.

Both were male, clad in dark leather and wearing coats that were inky black. Long spindles of white hair framed their faces—human-looking faces—though they appeared more like corpses than living things, with gray skin and sunken features. But their eyes were clearly Leech eyes—near-glowing, electric blue—and they shone like beacons as they talked to their companion.

Cruz.

A surge of rage welled over Phoebus, and it took every bit of strength to push it back. There would be time for emotions later. Crouching near the broken window, he leaned closer to hear the conversation.

"What progress have you made?" the first Leech was asking. His voice was inhuman—metallic and cold.

"Not much," said Cruz, looking over the clustered bodies. "I don't believe these Viewers are strong enough to sustain the effects of the hosting."

Phoebus' brow wrinkled at the unfamiliar term. *Hosting*?

The first Leech hissed, a sound like nails against glass. "You try our patience."

"I don't take well to threats, Ka'nar," said Cruz, a dangerous glare in his eyes. "I'm not doing this for your benefit. You know my terms."

The Leech named Ka'nar moved away, his legs carrying him with unearthly grace. He tilted his head at the grouping of Viewers, studying them as one might study insects in a lab. "You are one less."

"A boy," said Cruz, leaning against the wall. "He escaped, but I doubt he got far. He was already half-dead, thanks to your experiments. One of yours is searching for him now."

Phoebus stole a quick glance at the frizzy-haired boy, who was sprawled pathetically on the ground behind him, clawing at the grass and whimpering.

Ka'nar paused in front of a young woman.

"This one seems promising," he said.

"I can't afford another dead body," said Cruz, stepping forward.

But Ka'nar ignored him, keeping his attention on the woman. He raised his hand, extending fingers the color of charred flesh toward her neck. The woman moaned in protest as their blackened tips touched her skin and spread over her collarbone.

The Leech's cold, metallic voice echoed through the room. "This will only hurt a moment."

Sparks of electricity burst from his hand, spreading over the woman's chest like wildfire. Her body jolted, a gasping scream wrenched from her throat. From outside the window, Phoebus watched in horrified fascination. He'd seen Leeches extract before, but this was different.

The woman didn't slip into unconsciousness as the *Electricus* was sucked from her body. Instead, she continued convulsing, fighting against the Leech's grip. Blue electricity spread over her entire body, and then…her flesh below her neck began to burn.

As the stench of it reached Phoebus' nostrils, his Rover instinct kicked in. He sprang up, his longbow forming in his hands, and he aimed an arrow through the cracked glass, toward the Leech's own neck. But suddenly, the Leech released the woman and she fell back to the floor, gasping for breath.

With the amber fletching of his arrow still at his cheek, Phoebus watched as Ka'nar rolled the shuddering body of the woman over, and her face came into view. His bow went slack in his fingers as Phoebus stared, hardly daring to believe what he saw.

The woman's eyes had turned the same inhuman blue as the Leech hovering over her. Her skin, clear and tanned just moments before, was drawn and pale, revealing a myriad of bright blue veins—seeping with electricity, bulging grotesquely underneath the flesh.

The color had drained from her lips, tainting them blue, as though she'd been exposed to extreme cold, and her fingers were darkened, like frostbitten skin.

"She received my energy well," said Ka'nar. He rose and turned to his Leech companion, and as he smiled, he revealed blackened teeth. "You see, Tur'lon? I think the experiments are coming along nicely."

Using the wall to steady himself, Phoebus drew in a ragged breath, his head pounding as he tried to process what he'd witnessed. As ludicrous as it was, he couldn't deny it. The Leech hadn't taken *Electricus* out of the Viewer. He'd somehow placed it *inside* her.

But why?

"Perhaps," said Tur'lon, the second Leech, surveying the woman with a dubious expression. "But can she extract?"

Cold spread through Phoebus' spine. Othersider humans couldn't take *Electricus* from other living beings. Not even Rovers could do that. Only Leeches had developed that kind of power.

Only Leeches could extract…

Cruz, who'd silently watched the proceedings, knelt beside the woman, his dark face unreadable. He unbuttoned his shirt, exposing his bare chest.

"There's only one way to find out," he said stiffly.

As the woman's gaze slid to Cruz's skin, a desperate hunger burned in her eerie blue eyes. She spread her discolored fingers against his chest, just along his collarbone. The two Leeches looked on, their own eyes ablaze with anticipation. Tiny sparks spouted from the woman's fingers.

"It's working," said Ka'nar. "She's extracting his *Electricus*."

But Tur'lon held up his hand. "Just a moment."

Suddenly the woman wailed and jerked, as though she'd been shot. Collapsing to the floor, she shook with violent tremors, curling up in a fetal position as spasms overtook her thin frame. Phoebus looked at the Leech boy in the grass behind him, and everything clicked together. That was why he looked so human.

He wasn't a Leech. He was *human*.

Cruz stood and buttoned his shirt, turning away from the writhing woman on the floor.

"I told you, these Viewers aren't strong enough to handle your extraction process. Now I'm going to have another dead Othersider to deal with."

"That is your problem," said Tur'lon, shaking back his tendrils of white hair. "But you will keep trying. Ji'roth has grown tired of waiting."

"Let these others go," said Cruz. "They are of no use to you at this point."

"Of course," said Ka'nar. "After we've taken our fill."

Clenching his jaw, Phoebus remained still as the Leeches moved among the Viewers and siphoned *Electricus* from their bodies. As disturbing as the process appeared, he knew the Viewers would be okay. They'd wake up with burns, but no memory of the event.

Once Ka'nar and Tur'lon had satisfied their needs and their infused veins pulsed like electrical currents under their skin, the Leeches joined Cruz, who stood over the body of the whimpering woman. The Rogue's clinical expression hadn't changed, and Phoebus itched to bury an arrow right between his eyes. But he had to find out the reasons for these experiments first.

"Are you certain a Viewer is even capable of hosting?" asked Cruz.

"It will work," said Ka'nar. "We must find the right one."

Around the cabin, the Viewers began to stir as they wakened from the effects of the Leeches' extraction, and Tur'lon gestured to Cruz.

"You may let them go. They'll remember nothing by the time they arrive at their warm little homes."

The Rogue slipped a knife from his belt and cut their bonds. They staggered to the door and stumbled out, like a pack of drunkards, and Phoebus pressed himself against the wall, watching as the dazed humans waded through the grasses, heading back to town.

"And what about this one?" said Cruz, pointing at the woman.

Ka'nar hoisted the woman over his spindly shoulder. She quivered uncontrollably.

"Ji'roth will be expecting you tonight," said the Leech. "I trust you will have stronger specimens to show him than what you've brought us so far."

At his remark, Cruz suddenly sneered. "Well, if your associates had done a better job of apprehending the girl last night in the marsh, your job would be finished. But no, you just let her slip right through your blackened little fingers."

Tur'lon lunged forward, hissing. "She had the Rover with her."

Cruz didn't budge. "That's *your* problem."

Phoebus' bow threatened to snap between his tense fingers. Rage boiled inside his gut, and he ground his teeth together.

"No matter," said Ka'nar. "You will bring the girl to Ji'roth at midnight, along with any other Viewers you deem fit to serve our purpose."

Cruz glowered. "And where does Ji'roth want to meet?"

Tur'lon pointed toward the window. "Just beyond the harbor. There is a pier—"

"Yeah, I know the place."

"Very well. We shall be waiting for you there." A putrid smile appeared on the Leech's corpselike lips. "Farewell, Cruz. Until our next meeting."

The air shimmered, and the Leeches vanished. Phoebus crouched in the grass as the cabin door flung open and Cruz stormed out. The Rogue plodded through the thick brush toward town, his large body finally disappearing around a tree

Phoebus's throat felt thick and coated in disgust. What he'd just stumbled upon chilled him to the core. Preceptor Moth had to be told. But as soon as that thought crossed his mind, his instincts rebelled against it. If Moth discovered what was happening here, she'd also know that he hadn't killed the Bleeder.

What would happen then?

He'd be stripped of his rank, at the very least. Banished, most likely.

No, he couldn't tell Moth. The Council had been lying about Bleeders for centuries, and he'd already helped one.

But what was happening here was more important than his fate. And it went far deeper than Leeches illegally extracting *Electricus* from Viewers. As revolting as that was, at least Viewers who were used as an energy substance weren't permanently damaged. But this Ka'nar and Tur'lon were doing something else to these innocent humans, and though he didn't understand why, the process was killing them.

And now, they wanted Selene.

His heart slammed against his sternum. He couldn't afford to leave her alone anymore, not even at the inn. There were far too many dangerous questions. Who was Ji'roth, and what sort of deal had Cruz made with him? He needed answers, and he needed them now. Remembering his captive, he reached down to snatch him up from the grass.

But the boy was gone.

***

Jamie agreed to meet Selene at one of their favorite haunts: a tiny sushi bar near the St. Mary's docks. It was never crowded. Most of the residents of the coastal town preferred their seafood cooked. As she opened the door, she spotted him, waiting for her in their usual window booth.

"Thanks for meeting me," she said, sliding into the seat across from him.

As he looked up from his soda, she grimaced at his appearance. His eyes were red-rimmed, and his fiery hair was unkempt, like he'd been up all night.

"Yeah," he said quietly.

She tugged her sleeve down over Fee's bracelet, and then folded her hands in her lap. Maybe she was being a little hypocritical, but she also refused to be like Fee—only telling people half-truths. Maybe it was justified in his mind, but it wasn't who she was.

"I want to say I'm sorry," she began. "I haven't been totally honest with you, and I want to make things right." She glanced at her best friend and swallowed hard. "That is, if you'll let me."

He blinked at her. Then, a slow smile graced his lips. "Want some dinner?" He took a menu and held it out. "I don't know about you, but I'm starving."

By the time their platter of sushi arrived, she'd told him the whole story—starting from her recollection of Fee in the hospital room from three years ago, up until the Leech's attack on Miss Claire. Jamie said very little while she recounted the events. He swirled his chopsticks through his soup.

"So, there you have it," she finished, suddenly nervous. "What do you think?"

Jamie nestled into the booth, uncommonly serious, his forehead lined in thought. As she waited, she chewed on her lower lip. She wasn't sure she'd done the right thing by telling him, but he was her best friend, and she owed him honesty.

"So that's everything," he said, eyeing her.

"Pretty much."

"And you really do have mutant powers."

"Not mutant powers. Still just my useless curse. But yeah, that's why."

"Fair enough," he replied. "But now, tell me again: why are *they* here?"

Jamie pointed with his chopstick toward a corner booth occupied by a dark-haired girl with large eyes and a tall boy with curly hair—both of whom were pretending to look over their menus.

"They wouldn't let me come alone," she replied. "They said Fee wouldn't approve."

"So you've got your own bodyguards." His expression turned strange for a split-second before his eyes shifted back to her. "Well, if all this is true, and I'm bound by friendship code to believe you, then I agree with them. You probably shouldn't be out this late."

"They aren't my guards," she replied, feeling the heat of indignation. "And they have to listen to him, but I don't. I'm not going to let him tell me what I can and can't do."

Jamie's lips tightened into a thin line.

"I still don't like him," he said evenly. "But I think you should trust him."

She couldn't keep the shock off her face. "What?"

He looked away with a shrug. "You said he had the answers you've been looking for. And whatever these things are that are roaming around, well, it sounds like these people—" he jerked his head in the direction of Nyx and Titus "—may be the ones who can help."

"Why the sudden change of heart?"

At her question, his face turned an odd shade. He ran a hand through his hair and looked at his plate.

"Jamie?" she pressed, feeling alarmed. "What is it?"

"Since we're being honest, I need to tell you something, too." The same guilt she'd felt minutes before was in his eyes as well. "I'm sorry, Selene, but I never told you the whole truth about the ghost light, like the one we saw in the marsh."

"You mean the one you *pretended* to see."

"I saw it."

"But you said—"

"That one was a joke," he said, cutting her off. "Or, at least, it was supposed to be."

"Okay..."

He propped his elbow on the table and jabbed his chopsticks into a green blob of wasabi. "I've actually seen a few of them. The lights, I mean. I've lived here my whole life, and you know St. Mary's is full of ghost stories. I've tried tracking them down lots of times." His shoulders rose in a half-apologetic shrug. "I even saw one last summer, when my family vacationed out on Cumberland Island."

"Why haven't you ever told me this?" Heat prickled the base of her skull. "Why lie to me, Jamie? I thought we were friends."

"We *are* friends, Selene," he replied, sighing heavily. "That's exactly why I've never said anything. I mean, we weren't close before your accident, and then after it, you used to have nightmares all the time. You always talked about weird lights and flashes. You were sensitive about your memory and scared of even the tiniest glow of heat lightning. I didn't want to freak you out by talking about glowing orbs in the marsh. So I just kept my mouth shut."

"What about Ashlynn and the others?"

"I don't know. Like I said, it was all one big joke, as far as they were concerned, and it was a long time ago." He cringed, his eyes wide with guilt. "But one day, back during the beginning of freshman year, Mudge and I were talking about stuff, and the topic came up. He said he'd seen some lights too, in the marsh and down by the river. So sometimes on weekends, we'd go out looking for them."

She choked down her hurt feelings. "And?"

"We didn't have much luck," he replied. "Mudge lost interest in the whole thing, and I started hanging out with you a lot more." His eyes flicked to hers, and he smiled softly. "And you were a lot more interesting than a bunch of ghost stories. So I just sort of forgot about it. Sometimes, I'm half-convinced that I imagined the lights I saw before. But with all the stuff that's been happening to you lately, I guess I need to rethink things."

"I understand," she replied, still nursing her feelings.

His eyes were large and serious. "I'm sorry, Selene. I wasn't trying to keep anything from you. I was just trying to…I don't know…make things easier on you. You've come so far since the lightning strike, and I never wanted to do anything to set you back."

"I know. Thanks."

Jamie reached across the table, taking her hand. "But that's why I believe everything you just told me. And that's why, as much as it pains me to say it, I think you're right to trust this guy."

"His name's Fee."

"Yeah," he said, releasing her hand. "I know his name. I just choose not to use it."

"Well, that's not very nice," said a voice. "The embodiment of one's self is wrapped up in one's name, and I'm rather fond of mine." They both looked up to find Fee standing over them, a bright smile on his face. "May I join you?"

"Yes," said Selene.

"No," said Jamie at the same time.

Sliding in next to her, Fee was all confidence and swagger, but she noted the ever-darkening circles under his eyes.

"Such hospitality," said Fee.

"I wasn't being hospitable," said Jamie.

Selene rolled her eyes. "I thought you told me to trust him."

"I did," Jamie replied. "But nowhere in our conversation did I say I had to be happy about it." He smiled coldly across the table at Fee. "No offense."

"None taken."

Fee propped his arm across the back of the booth. His close proximity and his smooth voice weren't things Selene could ignore. But his cockiness made her want to jab him in the ribs with her elbow. How could someone be so interesting and annoying, all at once?

"So, what's on the menu for this evening?" he asked. "Taking care of Leeches is hungry work." He studied their plates. "On second thought, I believe I'll wait. Your food smells horrible."

"What are you doing here?" she asked.

He dipped his head toward Titus and Nyx, who were perched on the edge of their seats as though waiting for a signal from their leader. At his movement, they returned to their menus. Jamie stuffed a large piece of sushi in his mouth and huffed under his breath.

"Well, first of all," said Fee. "I'm hurt that you didn't stay at the inn, as I instructed."

"I'd apologize," she replied hotly. "But I really don't care how you feel."

"Such manners."

"Are you going to answer her question or not?"

At Jamie's interjection, Fee placed his elbows on the table, turning his full attention on him. Selene watched as his gaze roamed over her best friend's features, and his scrutiny felt intense—even probing.

"You know," he said, "there's something intriguing about you, boy."

Jamie didn't blink. "My good looks, I assume."

"No, that's not it," he replied smoothly. "Your physical traits are too lacking to qualify as intriguing. I was referring to your energy signature. I've had my suspicions, but I've never really felt it before now. I suppose it's because every time I see you, you're always tagging along with our Selene here. Her energy tends to be a bit overwhelming. It does a number on my senses."

Feeling her cheeks glowing hot, she averted her gaze, choosing to look at Jamie instead; but that didn't help matters. He sat rigidly in the booth, his face twitching with the effort to remain casual.

"I have no idea what you're talking about," said Jamie.

"Don't try and pretend Selene hasn't told you everything," said Fee.

Jamie didn't look at her. "Do you have a point?"

"I never leave home without a point," said Fee, picking up a piece of raw fish and examining it. "Since you're aware that Selene is in danger, your tendency will be to want to protect her. I respect that. But your presence is not going to help matters." He set the fish aside, and his eyes gleamed like bronze under the light. "So I need you to stay away from her."

Jamie's face went red. "What?"

"You heard me," Fee replied. "Stay home, stay out of our way, and I give you my word: Selene will be fine. But if you interfere," he continued, his face hard and his tone deadly. "I promise, you'll regret it."

Chapter 25

"Jamie didn't deserve that," Selene snapped as she left the restaurant with Fee, going against every grain of good judgment she had left. "He's just looking out for me."

"He's incapable of protecting you," Fee replied, taking up a quick pace along the sidewalk.

She met his stride. "Why are you such a jerk?"

"I prefer to think of myself as practically blunt. Besides, it's better for him this way. Let him nurse his bruised feelings in the safety of that foul-smelling fish establishment you call a restaurant. He'll only get hurt if he stays with us."

She stopped abruptly. "If you dare lay a hand on him—"

"Me?" He looked honestly taken aback. "I don't want to hurt him. Sure, he's highly annoying, but that hardly warrants doing him physical harm."

"Then what are you talking about?"

"Your friend is also a Viewer, if you haven't put the pieces together yet. That makes him a liability. Leeches hone into Viewer energies, just as we do. Your signature may be masked by my talisman." He pointed to the wrist cuff. "Your friend's is not."

"His name is Jamie."

"Yes, I know," he said, smiling. "But I prefer not to use it."

She rolled her eyes. "I hate testosterone."

He resumed walking. "Oh, now you're just being unpleasant. Humor helps us deal with difficult situations."

"First of all, you're not funny—"

"Many people would disagree."

"—and secondly, is that what you think this is? A *difficult situation*?"

He glanced sideways at her. "How else would you define it?"

"Oh, I don't know," she huffed, hurrying to catch up with him. "Failing my senior year. Moving to an island with no internet. Those might be difficult situations. Not suddenly finding out my town is full of energy-sucking monsters who possibly want to kill me."

"More probable than possible, actually."

She nearly smacked him. "A week ago, I was doing my own thing, happily oblivious to this insanity."

"Happily oblivious," Fee mused. "Somehow, you don't seem like the kind of person who wants to live her life that way."

"Well, you don't know me."

As he looked away, she saw that haunted look she'd caught a few times before. The arrogance had vanished, and it was as though she were peering into something much more palatable below the surface. For some reason, it chilled her to the bone.

"Believe me," he said, after a pause, "when I say that I wish I could."

"Could what?" she ventured. "Know me better?"

Fee's personality really *was* his defense. But, just as she'd catch the chinks in the armor, they'd seal shut again. He increased his speed, but she stayed by his side. She'd gotten used to his pace.

"It doesn't matter," he said flatly. "This conversation is irrelevant."

"So what now?" she pressed. "You're honestly asking me to stay away from my best friend?"

"It wasn't a request."

"How dare—"

"Look," he growled, "you're the one who chose to involve your little red-headed puppy by telling him everything, and that puts him in even more danger. Don't you understand? This is far bigger than your Othersider relationships."

He took her hand as they crossed the street, and she was too shocked by the action to stop him. Once on the other side, he released his grip. She could tell he didn't want to stop moving, but he took a breath and stood perfectly still.

"Selene." The way he said her name sent a buzz of electricity up her arms. "There's more going on here than I was led to believe, and Cruz is involved. He's working with the Leeches, running some kind of experiments, and they're targeting Viewers."

"But you just said that Jamie's a—"

"Exactly."

"Are you sure?" she protested, feeling a surge of panic worse than when she'd been in the marsh. The crosswalk sign buzzed and flickered out. "I mean, he said he's seen ghost lights before, but not since last summer. And he'd practically convinced himself they weren't real."

"I'm not surprised," he replied, his brow lined with thoughts. "His *Electricus* levels are very weak. Almost unreadable. And what he's seen of the Barrier is minimal, at best." Fee's lip quirked upward. "What I said earlier to him is true. I hadn't picked up on his signature because he was always in close proximity to you. And Rovers don't concern themselves with such low-level Viewers because they aren't a threat."

Yanking up her sleeve, she clasped the metal cuff. "Okay, so what if we give Jamie your talisman, and I just keep my bracelet on? You said it helped hide my energy signature, right?"

"I said I wasn't sure what properties your bracelet contained," he replied, a hint of irritation creeping into his voice. "It may work like our talismans, but the Leeches still found you in the campgrounds, so I can't be certain. You need to keep wearing my cuff until we know more."

"Then what about another talisman for Jamie?"

Fee shook his head. "Talismans only work if you have a high enough concentration of *Electricus* in your body for the amber to conduct. It creates a kind of forcefield around the wearer that disrupts the signature. You're a Bleeder. You have plenty of energy to work with. Your friend does not."

"Okay, then your cloak—"

"Won't work on him. He's an Othersider."

The acidic taste of frustration stung her throat. "So, what do we do?"

The evening had deepened around them, the darkness held at bay by the bright windows of diners and shops on either side of the street. The shadows cast by the soft glow made Fee's features sharper and more pronounced as he paused under a streetlight.

"Don't worry about your friend," he said. "I left instructions with my Trine to make sure he arrives home unscathed tonight.

As long as he stays away from you and keeps out of our business, he'll be safe. From what I overheard, the Leeches are only looking for strong Viewers."

"Strong enough for what?"

Reaching out, Fee wrapped his hand around the lamppost. Muscles rippled along the back of his hands, and faint sparks ricocheted between his skin and the metal. The pause between them felt weighty and ominous, pressing on her shoulders.

"Fee?"

"Look," he growled as his head snapped back. "It's quite a lot to process, and you'll forgive me if I don't have all the answers yet." Pushing off the lamppost, he made a fierce sound in the back of his throat and passed a hand across his eyes. "My world is not what I thought it was. I'm not sure who or what to trust anymore."

Despite his sharp tone, he'd just been honest with her—more so than he'd been since they'd met. As if compelled by some unseen force, Selene laid her hand on his upper arm. His muscles quivered and tightened under her touch.

"Trust seems to be an issue with everyone right now," she replied.

As he faced her, the yellow light cast a soft halo around his honey-colored hair. He looked tired. Shadows lined his face, hovering in the hollows under his eyes and along his cheeks.

"I know I've given you little reason to trust me, Selene." His voice was soft, like rumbling thunder. "But I want you to know one thing." He stepped so close that their bodies almost touched. "You're much more than a pawn in this."

"Good," she replied, looking up at him. "I hate pawns."

"In fact, I would go so far as to say you have the ability to control the entire board, once you know how to move."

"And just how do you know that?"

The quirk returned to his crooked lips. "I can sense it."

For a moment, Selene thought about his wrist cuff and what Nyx had said about Fee at the inn. But then, he raised his hand to her face with an agonizingly slow movement, and she couldn't think or breathe. The electricity between them hummed in her ears as his fingers traced the outline of her jaw. She felt every callous, every crease in his skin.

"I can't get you out of my head," he rumbled in that gentle tone. "And since I arrived here, not a moment has gone by that I haven't wanted to be near you."

She felt herself lean into him. His eyes were far too bright, and the air felt heightened between them. As she stared up at him, her head spun. She imagined her fingers sifting through his thick honeyed hair. A pleasant buzz filled her ears.

"Okay." She struggled to catch her breath as she stepped back, breaking the charge and putting space between them. She needed her brain to kick back on again. Shoving her hands into her jacket, she curled her fingers into the fabric, drawing on the warmth. "I think, maybe, this isn't such a good idea."

Fee's bowed head nodded, and his eyes closed, though he didn't move from his spot.

"I agree," he said softly.

Then, suddenly, his eyes snapped open, and their depths solidified like hardened caramel. He sidestepped around her, hurrying down the sidewalk.

"Whoa now," she said, catching up to him. "I said it wasn't a good idea. I didn't say it was okay to bail."

As he glanced over, Fee's crooked smile reappeared. "That's not what's happening. You and I are going to the Outpost." His eyes softened a bit. "That is, if you don't mind, of course."

Although he was back in control and his confident swagger had returned, Selene felt a shift in the atmosphere. His shoulder pressed lightly into hers as they walked side by side. There was something different between them now, a connection far too new for her to comprehend. Studying his profile, she wished for the thousandth time that she could read his mind.

"So, does this mean you're not going to try and kill me in the future?"

Fee's lips quirked upward, but this time, the smile didn't reach his eyes.

"Never," he said, looking away from her. "I'd sooner kill myself."

***

As they hit the steps of the *Seaside Inn's* front porch, Selene felt

Fee's body go rigid. Wrapping his arm around her waist, he pulled her close and pressed his lips to her ear.

"Go straight upstairs," he whispered. "Quickly, but quietly. Wait in the hallway for me."

She was acutely aware of how his fingers pressed into her hip. "Why?"

"Could you just do as I ask, for once?" Although his breath was warm, she shivered. "Cruz is inside, and I don't want him to know you're here."

Putting her hand on his chest, she pushed away. "Fine."

As he approached the door, she heard him mutter, "Infuriating." Taking the lead, he stepped into the foyer, jerking his head in the direction of the stairs that led to the upstairs bedrooms. He waited until she had taken several steps before he left the entryway and strolled into the living room.

But Selene paused as soon as he was out of the foyer, and she eased back down the steps. With a steady grip on the railing, she leaned forward and peeked carefully around the wall, feeling a weird jitter of *déjà vu* from her last eavesdropping escapade—a moment that seemed like a lifetime ago.

Fee had crossed the parlor in a few lazy strides and was stretched out on the sofa, feet propped on the coffee table. Cruz was also in the room, peering over the magazine he'd been reading from his chair near the fireplace. With a flick of his wrist, Fee summoned an arrow, which materialized in his palm with a blue, electrical twang.

"Bleeders are quite annoying," he said, twirling the arrow between his fingers. "It's no wonder we kill them off."

Cruz's brows rose slightly. "The girl's dead?"

"It took longer than I would've liked," said Fee, lifting his eyes toward the ceiling. "But she insisted on stopping for ice cream first, and then there was a mundane walk through the park and lots of mindless conversation. Othersiders are utterly boring, Cruz. I don't know how you stand being around them."

It was as though Selene were watching an entirely different person than the one who'd spoken softly to her under the streetlights. His cold, casual demeanor was locked firmly in place. Fee was like a switch—one instant light, the next, dark.

"What happened to changing tactics?" asked Cruz, his voice

laced with an almost bitter sound. "What you said earlier—"

"As I recall, *you* were the one who suggested I'd failed."

Cruz opened his mouth, and then shut it again. His expression, like his tone, was difficult for Selene to read—much like Fee's—but she felt the tug of some strange power play going on between them—one that she didn't understand.

"I never said I wasn't going to complete my mission," answered Fee. "Just how I went about it."

"Where'd you do it?" asked Cruz, holding fiercely to the arms of his chair, as though he were about to crush them between his fingers.

"Just past the cemetery," Fee replied. "It wasn't the most ideal location, but I couldn't very well take her back to the marsh. She would've gotten suspicious. A date strolling through town was much less obvious."

Cruz rose slowly. "You were seen in town with her? That was a foolish move, Fee. When they find her body, the police will be knocking on our door, looking for you!"

"And I won't be here." Fee smiled, a flash of white teeth. "My mission's complete, which means my Trine and I will be leaving shortly."

"I don't believe you," said Cruz, his lip curling. "Now that you know there are Leeches here, you won't leave. You'd be turning your back on the precious safety of Threshold. And you'd never pass up the chance to try and put me in my place. Admit it."

"The Leeches aren't my business," said Fee. "And I couldn't care less about your place."

"That's a lie!"

Fee stood and flicked his wrist again. The arrow vanished. "You can do what you want here, Cruz. This is your Outpost. Like you said, the Elders know, and they don't care. So why should I? I made the mistake of getting involved in your business before. I won't do it again. We're leaving tonight."

"Phoebus—"

"Don't you have to patrol?" he said, cutting him off. "Or do you just send your Trine to take care of the details while you sit here and sip tea?"

A furious expression spread over Cruz's face. He took his tan-colored cloak from the back of the chair, shrugging it on. He rubbed his hands together. A spark crackled between Cruz's fingers and lengthened into a wicked looking mace, and each amber spike gleamed electric blue.

"I've already had my tea," he said. "But you're right. I've got to go and relieve Marcelo down by the school. We're expecting another round of storms tonight, and you know what a number that does on the *Electricus* around here."

"Well, have fun with that," said Fee. "I'll be here, packing my things."

Cruz pushed past him. "Good riddance."

Holding her breath, Selene backpedaled up the steps as Cruz stomped through the foyer. She eased into the long hallway at the top of the stairs and into the first room, shutting the door silently behind her before she released the air from her burning lungs.

The bedroom was decently sized and fitted with antique furniture. A few shirts were strewn over the corner of the bedpost, but everything else was pristine. Just as she leaned against the door, it opened hard against her, and she stumbled, covering her mouth with one hand as Fee entered.

Closing the door, he focused his attention on a long, rectangular mirror attached to the back of the wood. The frame made of dull brass, but where there should've been glass, a yellowish-orange surface swirled like a slow-moving current.

"What's that?" she whispered.

He cut his eyes to her with a look like jagged glass and pressed one finger to his lips. With a swift and fluid movement, he lifted the mirror from its hook, gesturing for the patchwork quilt on the edge of the bed. Handing it to him, Selene backed away as Fee wrapped up the mirror, opened the door and set it outside in the hall.

Shutting the door, Fee leaned against the wood frame.

"I told you to wait in the hall, not in here," he snarled.

"So you told Cruz I'm dead?" she replied, ignoring him.

"You're not, in case you were wondering."

Although she wanted to know more—and possibly slap the sass out of him at the same time—her curiosity was sidetracked by what he'd just done. "What's with the magic mirror you just banished?"

At her question, his expression softened. "It's not magic," he replied. "But it's our link between here and Threshold."

The way he smiled gave new life to his caramel eyes and smoothed the stressed lines from his forehead, and Selene suddenly wished he'd look that way more often.

"Can you step through it and get to your world, like a magic wardrobe or something?"

"I just said it wasn't magical." Fee's crooked smile grew. "But no, I can't. Amber mirrors are for seeing and speaking through only, similar to the way you video chat in this world—though more connected. I don't receive much warning before someone contacts me, which is why it's safer to leave the mirror outside for now."

"Then how do you get back to your world?"

"Rovers can travel through the Barrier, remember?"

"So you could open up the air right here, just like that, and go back to your world."

"I could," he replied, "but it wouldn't be wise."

"Why not?"

"Because the moment I step through a Rift, I lose my grounding in your world," he replied. "I could be in Threshold for only minutes, but two years might pass here." Fee's face darkened, like clouds passing over the sun. "The chances of my being able to return to this exact point in time are slim." He lifted a small quilt from the bed and approached the mirror. "But my current assignment is different. My Trine and I have Merged with your world. To return home, we require help from a skilled Thresholder on the other side of the Barrier."

"Like who?"

"Trust me, you don't want to know."

Perching on the edge of the bed, Selene watched as Fee glanced toward the door. Judging by the fierce expression on his face, whoever he was referring to definitely didn't seem like someone she wanted to meet. Silence built between them, followed by an acute awareness that they were alone in his bedroom. She pretended to study the details of a fringed lamp in the corner.

"So what was all that about downstairs?" she asked, breaking the quiet.

"Are you referring to my impeccable use of language or my acting skills? Both were equally impressive, I'm sure."

Selene bit back a surge of irritation. Not even Jamie could tick her off so quickly. Then guilt swelled in her chest as she remembered the crumbled look on Jamie's face when she'd left with Fee. Although she kept trying to protect her best friend by keeping him out of this, all she'd seemed to do was hurt him. He'd probably never speak to her again.

"You know what I mean," she said, focusing on the present. "Why did you tell Cruz you'd killed me?"

The moon shone through the windowpanes, casting Fee's silhouette in silver. His hair had come loose from his leather tie and, combined with his angular profile, it made him look eerily like a Greek statue.

"He has to believe you're dead. It's the only way this is going to work."

"The only way what's going to work?"

Fee shoved the curtain closed. "My plan."

Chapter 26

Someone was banging on the door of the inn.

Phoebus ordered Selene to stay put, and he eased down the stairs, his back against the wall. Fashioning an arrow, he wielded it like a spear and approached the door as the harsh knocking continued. He fixed his eye against the peephole, then released a heavy sigh. He dissipated the arrow, unbolted the lock, and swung open the door, glaring at Selene's annoying redheaded tag-a-long.

"Trick or treat," said the boy.

"What are you doing here?"

"Oh, I don't know. It's a small town, my parents aren't home—"

Snatching him by the collar, Phoebus yanked him into the foyer. "I told you to go home. I swear, does no one *listen* in this world?"

"Of course not," said Red-Hair, knocking his hand away. "Oh, and I thought you should know, I gave your buddies the slip back at the corner of Elm and Magnolia."

Phoebus crossed his arms with a mockingly pained expression. "Either you're slightly more intelligent than I've previously given you credit for—which is unlikely—or my Trine's tracking abilities have sunk to deplorable levels."

"The benefits of being a native. I know all the shortcuts around this town."

"Well," he replied coolly, checking his nails, "I suppose you should get on with whatever you've come here to say. I'm kind of busy at the moment."

Red-Hair stepped forward. "I don't know what you're up to, *Fee*. But you're not dragging Selene into all this. Not without me."

"Your concern is admirable, boy," said Phoebus. "But don't flatter yourself. We've got everything under control."

"You see, that's just the problem. I don't trust you."

"That's not what you told Selene."

Red-Hair huffed. "Yeah, well, what was I supposed to say? I was trying to be supportive. Besides, if I'd told her to say away from you, she wouldn't have listened to me."

"True." He rubbed his chin. "It's a terrible habit of hers, isn't it?"

"Pretty much her only fault."

"That's sweet," he replied, curling his lip. "Your loyalty is admirable, at least."

"You're not dragging her into this," Red-Hair shot back.

"No, I'm not. She's doing everything willingly, I must point out."

"Yeah? And why is that?"

He shrugged. "Because I'm irresistible."

"You really are an a—"

"I'm wounded by the insult you were about to sling at me," said Phoebus, using his most sardonic tone. "But I'll manage to pick up the pieces and move on. Right now, I have larger problems to deal with than your opinion of me."

Red-Hair pushed past him to the stairs. "Where is she?"

He flashed an easy smile. "My bedroom."

The boy whirled around, his face going as red as his hair. "If you—"

"Relax," he said, leaning against the doorframe. "My intentions are honorable, I assure you." His kept his smile in place. "I'm keeping Selene out of sight for her own safety. There are some people who are very eager to get their hands on her."

"The creepy guys with blue eyes and zombie complexions she told me about. They go around eating people."

Phoebus sighed. "For the last time, Leeches don't *eat* people."

"Whatever. All I care about is Selene. I'm not sure what kind of hold you have over her—"

"I told you," he replied casually. "I'm irresistible."

Lunging forward, Red-Hair tried to shove him. But Phoebus was faster, sweeping the boy's legs out from under him, causing him to hit the ground with a thud. An arrow charged in Phoebus's hand and he pointed the tip at Red-Hair's chest as though it were a sword.

"Your issue isn't with me, boy."

"It is when you're putting Selene in danger," Red-Hair replied, breathing hard as he glared up at him from the floor. "And stop calling me *boy*, you idiot. It's Jamie."

As Phoebus paused, he couldn't help feeling a twinge of respect for the boy's courage. He sucked down a measure of his pride, at least for Selene's sake. "Very well, Jamie of the Unfortunate Hair and Useless Combat Skills, I will grant you that much." He flexed his fingers and the arrow vanished. "But know this: I would never put Selene in danger. I am trying to protect her."

Jamie scrambled to his feet, beet-faced and fuming. "Yeah, well so am I."

"Ah, but there's the difference between us. I can actually do it. You would simply get in the way."

"What do you know about me?"

"Enough," he replied, looking the boy up and down. "You want to coddle her, to be her little safe space; but the reality is, she'll be hunted her entire life. I can protect her by teaching her what she needs to survive in her new reality."

"No, that's not fair to her. This isn't her burden. You can't force her into this."

"I'm not forcing her," he replied. "I'm preparing her."

Movement beyond the door caught Phoebus' eye, and he looked past Jamie to the sidewalk beyond, his jaw clenching at the sight of his Trinemates appearing out of the evening shadows.

"I'm so glad you two could join us," he said as they ascended the stairs.

"Forgive me, Phoebus," said Titus, his eyes darting to Jamie. "You said to give him some space. I suppose we gave him a bit too much."

"Clearly," he replied. "Remind me to schedule extra training sessions at the Preceptory when we get home. Merging has made you lazy." He stepped onto the porch and checked the nearly empty street before easing back into the foyer. "Just make sure he gets home this time."

Red-Hair seemed caught between running up the stairs and running out the door.

"And what's to keep me from coming right back?" he demanded.

Phoebus studied him for a moment. "I don't believe I heard Selene invite you here, which was a wise decision on her part. We have business to take care of, and the less of you I have in my way, the better." He opened the door wide. "I don't intend to remain on the Otherside longer than I have to, and I can assure you, once we've taken care of these Leeches, we'll be gone."

His own words slapped him in the face. Leaving the Otherside. Returning home. It was everything he'd wanted at the start of this assignment. And now, it was the last thing he desired. And probably impossible, anyway, since he was, for all intents and purposes, a traitor himself. Phoebus growled and backed away from the opening.

"Please, ensure that our guest arrives at his destination."

"Do you want us to stay with him?" asked Nyx.

"You can tuck him into bed for all I care," he replied, starting up the stairs. "Make him hot cocoa. Read him a bedtime story." He paused and turned around. "Just take him home."

***

Huddling into his jacket, Jamie dodged the irritating wind sweeping autumn leaves across his face. How had the temperature dropped so much since sunset? But though he clenched his fists inside his pockets, it wasn't really because of the cold. On either side of him, Fee's friends walked with silent steps, keeping his pace with weird, unnerving ease.

He cleared his throat with louder-than-needed purpose, and the girl regarded him with her large chocolaty eyes. She was definitely pretty, and had it not been for the fact that she was digging some kind of pointy weapon into his back, he'd even have thought she was pleasant.

"So," he said. "Nyx, is it?"

"It is," she replied.

"What happens next? I mean, am I supposed to invite you two inside for milk and cookies when we get to my house? Because I wasn't really prepared for company. The place is a wreck."

"We're escorting you home, that's all."

Her reply was neutral, but he noticed her slight smile in the semi-darkness. His other escort, the tall guy walking on his right side, cast a frowning look in his direction.

"I hope you understand," he said.

"That you're taking me home by force? Well, yeah, but understanding it and being okay with it are two different things, you know." He twisted his back. "And I'd really appreciate it if you could put away the whatever-it-is you're prodding me with. It's pretty uncomfortable."

"If you promise not to run away," said the guy.

"Okay, dude…"

"Titus."

"I'm sure you both topped the baby names list this year. Ow!" He leapt as Nyx poked him with her weapon. "My apologies. They're *lovely*. I'll be sure to name my children after you. But as I was going to say, this chaperoning thing is pointless. I'll figure out a way back there. Wherever Selene goes, I go."

"Not this time, I'm afraid," replied Nyx, and her eyes were serious. "We are sorry it has to be this way."

"We know this is difficult to understand," said Titus.

"You guys are from another dimension, sent here to kill my best friend because she poses a threat to your homeworld. But now you've changed your minds, and you're going to use her to help fight some other guys from this same dimension who are your enemies and are living illegally in my world. CliffsNotes version."

Nyx looked impressed. "Basically."

"Chalk it up to watching too many movies, but I don't find any of that difficult to comprehend," he replied. "What I don't get is this: why does it matter if I'm involved or not? I mean, why do you guys care?"

"We don't drag Othersiders into our affairs," Titus answered. "The fact that we're even speaking to you so freely is an abnormality. People like you shouldn't know we exist."

"Okay, then aren't you supposed to kill me because I know all your deep dark secrets?"

Nyx laughed, which caused the weapon in his back to dig a little digger.

"We don't hurt the inhabitants from the worlds we protect," she replied. "Only Leeches and the occasional Farsider, when they refuse to obey the Tenets."

"The…*what*?"

"Our code of laws," she explained. "We prefer to prevent harm, rather than causing it."

"But we do wipe out memories," said Titus. "And after this is over, we'll do the same to you."

Jamie felt his blood run cold. But keeping a conversation going was his defense, his way of working out what to do next in a situation.

"Why not now?" he replied, attempting to keep his voice light. "Why the wait?"

"Phoebus is the only one of our Trine with that ability," said Nyx. "But I'm sure he feels there is no need to erase your memory until our business here is complete. Too much repeat-tampering with a Viewer's memory can cause permanent damage."

Damage?

For the first time in his life, Jamie felt at a loss for words.

His house was the third on the right, and the only one without lights on. He pushed ahead, yanking up the hood of his jacket against the wind. He'd been pissed when he'd gotten to the *Seaside Inn*. But now, he simply felt helpless. It would've been one thing if Selene had insisted that he go along with her.

But she hadn't. She'd just left him.

And now he was being escorted home by a couple of cronies from another world, who acted like they were the cops, taking him home because he hadn't obeyed the curfew rules. As he paused at his front stoop, Nyx disengaged her weapon from his back. The glowing needle disappeared, leaving fragments of electricity that dissipated into the night.

As he studied them both from the corner of his vision, he had to admit that they looked a lot more intimidating—not to mention capable—than he felt, standing there in his ripped jeans and beat-up kicks, fumbling in his pockets for his elusive house key like a moron.

No wonder she'd left him at the restaurant.

"Just promise me that Selene will be okay," he said softly.

To his surprise, Nyx placed a hand on his arm, and her touch was like a tiny static shock through his skin. "I tell you the truth, Othersider. Although I do not know all of Phoebus' plans, you can rest assured he will protect her."

"After all," said Titus with a shrug. "In whose hands do you really want to commit her safety? Yours, or ours?"

Although he didn't like the answer, it didn't change the truth. "Yours."

"Don't worry," said Nix. "Soon, this will all be over."

"Yeah," he replied. "That's kind of what I'm afraid of."

He watched as the Rovers disappeared into the darkness. Then he jammed his key into the lock and turned it. The deadbolt slid back, and he opened the door and stepped inside. Immediately the hairs rose on his arms. There was a light coming from the living room. Then he heard the sound of the television. He breathed a sigh of relief. His parents must have gotten back early from their trip. Locking the door behind him, he tossed his key and his cell phone onto the kitchen counter.

"Mom? I thought you guys were staying with Aunt Caroline until Monday."

Everything was dark, save for the glare of the television. Someone was sitting on his couch, back toward him, but it wasn't either of his parents. Fear crept up his spine, awakening his adrenaline. He took a few steps forward, and then he recognized the frizzy brown hair.

"Mudge?"

"Hey, man. I was wondering when you'd get home."

He peered through the dim light. Something about Mudge's voice didn't sound right.

"How'd you get in?" he asked.

"The window," Mudge replied. His breathing sounded weirdly labored, as though speaking were taking as much effort as rock climbing. "Hope you don't mind. I was bored. Thought we could hang."

"Okay," he replied, trying to sound normal, but the cold feeling slithering through his stomach wouldn't let him. "Of course, you could have called first, you know. I was out with Selene."

"Of course you were. You're always with her."

"Well, she *is* hotter than you, Mudge."

As the boy on the couch turned, Jamie stopped dead in his tracks. Mudge's eyes flashed an eerie electric blue. His pudgy face was ashen, and his expression twisted, as though he were in pain, as he stood and clutched the edge of the couch. His skin, drawn tight over his cheeks, was a strange hue, like he'd been out in the cold too long, and veins bulged beneath the flesh, winding like iridescent blue cords.

Jamie retreated slowly. "What's wrong with you, man?"

Mudge began to pant, now looking and sounding like a rabid dog. His lips pulled back in a grotesque smile, full of blackened teeth, and he reached out with trembling arms.

"I'm…hungry…"

"Okay, well, we've got frozen pizzas."

"Not…for…that."

Jamie choked. Mudge lunged for him.

Chapter 27

"Listen, I need to call my mom," said Selene, pacing in front of the drawn curtain. "It's getting late, and she worries. I'll tell her I'm spending the night at Lindsay's house or something."

They'd been hiding out in Fee's room for a half-hour—and it was bothering her a lot more than it was him. At least, as far as she could tell. But he'd insisted it was the safest thing to do while waiting for Nyx and Titus to return. He didn't want to take a chance on her being spotted.

Especially when she was supposed to be dead.

Fee glanced up from his coffee. "So I'm not good enough to mention to your mother. I'm hurt."

"What? No. Don't flatter yourself," she shot back. "But I have to tell her something. And I doubt she would go for an explanation that included me spending the night in a hotel with a strange guy."

"It's an inn, not a hotel," said Fee propping his feet on the dresser. "And I'm not strange, merely eccentric. But as for spending the night with me—"

"Save it," she replied, pulling up a chair. "You are ridiculously unbelievable."

Shrugging innocently, he handed her his phone. The conversation went easier than she thought it would. But her mom was too busy with her Navy-wives group to catch any dishonesty in her voice—something she was normally good at doing. Feeling another block of guilt on her already impressive stack, she returned the phone and stared at her coffee.

"Well," said Fee. "I suppose I won't be using this again."

He held out his phone, grasping it by the upper corner. The screen was blank and the edges were charred black.

Selene's mouth dropped open. "I did that?"

"Obviously," he replied, and his brow quirked. "Why do you seem so surprised now?"

"But I thought…I mean, I'd hoped…that I was getting a handle on it." Everything felt heavy again inside her. She slumped in the chair. "But nothing's changed. I've still got the bad luck mojo."

"It has nothing to do with luck," he replied. "Just a lack of control."

"How encouraging."

"I try."

Feeling resigned, she raised the mug to her lips. The coffee had grown lukewarm, and there wasn't enough sugar. Butterflies warred with the irritable anger swirling in her stomach. As she set the cup down, she looked sideways at Fee. His confident, easygoing mask was set firmly in place. He looked back at her in a way that sent heat rushing up her arms.

"I'm going to assume that deadly look on your face is meant for me," he said.

"Of course it is," she replied, keeping her tone as cool as his expression. That was one thing she could control. "It's the best I can do, since I can't magically produce weapons like some people around here."

"Not magic," he said, sounding painfully dignified. "*Electricus.* Like this."

He opened his palm, and his longbow appeared—nearly as long as she was tall, gleaming like metal and glowing with blue light. The amber designs crafted into it seemed to pulse like beacons of orange flame.

Fee held it out. "Here."

A surprised feeling of excitement took hold of her. "I can't touch it…can I?"

"It won't feel that pleasant," he replied. "But if you want to learn, then you have to be willing to take that risk."

As she wrapped her fingers around the bow, nerves fired in her skin, registering as hundreds of tiny shocks skittered up her arm. Gritting her teeth, she resisted the urge to cry out. The energy seemed to flow through her like hot liquid, pouring even into her bracelet, which hummed against her wrist. And then, almost instantly, the pain ceased, and she held the bow with a firm grip, using her other hand to touch the string.

"That wasn't so bad," she said.

"You're adjusting to the *Electricus*," said Fee. His voice sounded unusually low, deep, and thick. "That's actually very impressive."

"High praise from His Highness, himself," she replied.

She felt, rather than saw, his smirk—like heat from the sun on the back of her neck. But when he didn't reply, she raised her eyes to his. The look on his face had returned, and this time, he didn't turn away. And neither did she. Swallowing hard, she was almost afraid to blink. The way he held her gaze with the same gentle power as he'd held her hand felt terrifying and wonderful.

As he placed his fingers over hers, his touch was soft, but brimming with heat and electricity that she could feel beneath the surface, filtering through her blood. Fee's eyes drifted closed, and blue sparks crackled between his fingers, radiating throughout the longbow. The weapon vanished, but somehow, her hand was still in his, tingling with energy.

The bedroom door swung open.

She bolted upright, knocking over her chair with a loud clatter that reverberated down the hall. Fee stood and righted it with a disapproving huff as Nyx and Titus stepped inside the room and shut the door.

"The boy's home, safe and sound?" Fee seemed to catch himself and executed a perfect eye roll. "I mean, Jamie, of course."

Titus shrugged out of his jacket. "Yes, and none too happy about it, either."

Fee returned to his coffee. "Well, that can't be helped."

Selene cringed. She'd handled everything wrong with Jamie, but she couldn't change it now.

"Was...was he okay?" she asked.

Nyx didn't blink. "Would you be, in his place?"

The question hung painfully in the air. In any other circumstance, Jamie would have been by her side. But she refused to put him in harm's way. Right or not, she'd made her choice; she'd just have to figure out how to make it up to him later.

When this was over.

"So, what are you doing up here?" asked Titus, sprawling on the bed.

"We needed some alone-time," Fee replied.

Titus shot him a look. "Ah. Well, we can come back later, if you want."

"That's not what he meant," said Selene hotly. Fee chuckled, and she kicked his feet off the dresser. "Are you going to explain, or do I need to do it? I know how difficult forming complete sentences is for someone with your IQ."

Fee didn't fire back a response. Instead, he looked pleased. "Titus, the reason we are in my room is because I didn't want Cruz knowing Selene was here, in case he or his Trine came back to the inn."

"Well, the inn's empty," said Nyx. "We searched every room when we returned."

Pushing to his feet, Fee went to the window and peered through the curtain, as though assuring himself that no one was nearby. His previous amused expression had vanished, and Selene felt the entire atmosphere of the room shift under his commanding look.

"This Outpost has been compromised," he said. Gone was the sarcasm. He was all business. "The agreement Cruz has with the Leeches is more serious than I first thought. I witnessed a meeting tonight between him and two of the parasites. Cruz was holding a group of Viewers in a cabin not too far from here. He's been allowing Leeches to extract from Viewers for quite some time. In fact, he's been assisting them."

Titus made a fierce choking sound. "That traitor."

Fee crossed the room and placed his ear against the door. When he seemed satisfied, he continued. "Yes, Titus. What he's done is vile enough, but that's not the worst of it."

"Then what is?" asked Nyx.

"One of the Leeches chose a Viewer from the group," he replied. "A woman. He placed his hand on her, as though he were going to extract *Electricus*. But that's not what happened. He deposited the *Electricus* into her. And then she changed into something."

Nyx went very still. "Changed?"

"She became something else." Fee stared at the ceiling as though trying to pull words from the air. "Not quite a Leech, but not human anymore, either. She was something in between." He pinched the bridge of his nose. "It appeared to be some kind of experiment."

Selene wove back through their previous conversations in her head. "But don't Leeches need *Electricus* to survive? Why would they give it away? That doesn't make sense."

"I don't know," he replied. "But whatever they were trying to do, it didn't work. The Leeches demanded more specimens, and Cruz agreed to bring more Viewers to them tonight. He is scheduled to meet someone named Ji'roth at midnight near an old pier somewhere on the edge of town."

"I know where that is," said Selene. "No one ever uses it. It's too far away from the rest of the docks." Her heart shot to her throat. "But what about Jamie? You said he's a Viewer! What if they try to take him?" She started for the door, but Fee blocked her path. She tried to wrestle past him as he grabbed her wrists. "Let me go! I have to warn him!"

"Why do you think I sent him home in the first place?" he said, holding her firmly. "His puppy dog attachment to you is touching and all, but your friend needs to be as far away from this as possible. I have no doubt that Cruz and his Rogues are rounding up a fresh batch of Othersiders right now for their little rendezvous."

She stopped struggling. "So that's why you want Cruz to think I'm dead."

"The Leeches want humans with high levels of *Electricus* for whatever experiments they're running. Cruz sent Leeches after you in the marsh last night. If he thought you were alive, he'd try and include you in that group. You're a valuable commodity."

"But Cruz will find out about Selene soon enough," said Nyx.

"Not before we crash his party," Fee replied.

Selene wrenched herself out of his grasp. "I'm not staying here."

He bristled. "Yes, you are."

"You can't order me around," she said, feeling charged with adrenaline. "You said I'm a Bleeder. And maybe I don't really know what that means, but I know I can do things. I closed that Rift in the marsh. I traveled through the Barrier with you. I'm not going to hide when I can help."

"Yes, you can do things," he said tensely. "And yes, you are learning quickly. But you also require much more training. Without it, sending you outside, exposed and vulnerable, is too dangerous. We still have no idea as to the extent of your powers."

She raised her chin to meet him head-on. "Then let's find out."

***

Jamie groaned and forced his eyes open. He was lying on a hard floor. Wood creaked and splintered into his arms when he moved. Somewhere in the distance, the sound of lapping water reached his ears. He could tell that he was in a small, dimly lit room with no windows. With effort, he pushed himself up to a seated position, wincing as pain shot through his chest. His gaze fell upon a shape huddled in the corner.

"Mudge?"

The shape jerked, then uncurled and inched closer, wheezing softly. Unnerving blue eyes rolled back into a gray face that barely resembled the Mudge he knew, and he when he spoke, the voice sounded strange and far away.

"S-sorry…they…made me find you. Said…I could eat."

Jamie rubbed tenderly at his aching chest. "What did you do to me?"

"Nothing…tried…but nothing." Mudge reached for him. "Try again…"

"Whoa, back off, man." Jamie scooted out of his reach, feeling a wave of alarm.

But he couldn't take his gaze from Mudge's eyes. They burned with a life of their own, like something out of a comic book. He never would've called Mudge intimidating before—he was a below-average student who preferred making industrial music in his basement to studying—but now, as Mudge stared him down with those eerie eyes, he looked downright creepy.

"I don't get how you're going to solve being hungry by trying to strangle me."

Mudge made a weird rasping sound in the back of his throat that caused Jamie's hair to stand on end.

"Need to touch you," he hissed.

"Hey, you know I don't go for that sort of—"

His words died in his throat as a fresh burning sensation shot through his chest, just below his collarbone. Yanking up his jacket and shirt, he spotted an ugly burn, the size of a hand, seared across his skin. He remembered Mudge lunging at him before everything went dark.

"Mudge," he choked. "What happened?"

Although Mudge was shaking violently, he continued to advance, scraping and grinding his elbows into the floor for leverage, leaving a trail of blood as he slid forward.

The sight was sickening.

"T-told you," he gargled through blackened teeth. "I…h-had to…feed. You have it…inside you…"

The sinking feeling in Jamie's stomach bottomed out as he finally understood. "You mean my energy," he whispered. Snatches of Selene's story came back to him, about the creatures Fee and his crew were fighting. "You're one of those *things*?"

"Don't know," Mudge hissed back, blue eyes flashing. "But I'm…dying."

Trying to keep as much distance between them as possible, Jamie's back scraped against the splintering wall. He had no more space to maneuver in the small room, and there was nowhere to run. He fought against his twisting esophagus, forcing words out.

"Hey, come on," he said quickly. "There has to be some way to help you."

"No other…way."

As Mudge drew a terrible-sounding gasp for breath, his fingers dug into the rotting floorboards. His gaunt face seemed to stretch even thinner, and a new series of electric blue veins sizzled under the skin of his throat and cheeks.

Then he threw himself forward.

They both skidded across the floor, and the impact of their collision knocked Jamie's breath from his lungs. He balled his fist to take a swing, but Mudge was quick. And strong. He clamped his discolored hands onto Jamie's burning chest, and the fabric of his jacket sizzled away, like paper in a fire. He felt his flesh melting under those blackened fingers as something inside him tried to push itself through his ribcage, desperate to escape, and he couldn't stop it. He opened his mouth to scream, but no sound came out.

He stared into Mudge's horrible eyes—the last thing he would ever see.

A loud screech filled the room, and Mudge's body went airborne, flying across the room with his arms and legs flailing helplessly as he rolled into the wall. Clutching his burned shirt and pounding chest, Jamie scrambled painfully to his feet.

A tall figure stood in the middle of the room. He could've been the lead singer for a Goth band, with his dark leather attire covered with metal studs and long black jacket. But Jamie's blood turned icy at the sight of his face: it was something that should've been dead, with ashen skin and bulging blue veins. White strands of hair with blue tips floated around the figure's head, as though infused with static electricity, and his eyes burned like pilot lights. As his lips parted, Jamie could see the teeth, blackened and charred.

"He is not to be touched," he hissed.

Mudge's body convulsed. "You...said...I could eat."

The man—the *Leech*, Jamie's brain recalculated—wafted across the room, kneeling alongside the whimpering form of Mudge.

"No," he replied. His voice sounded metallic, like utensils rubbing together. "I said you could attempt to extract after you completed your task." The Leech pointed at Jamie with a charred, blackened finger. "At no point did I say you could have *him*."

Mudge's bright eyes flickered feverishly. "Then, who?"

As the Leech stood, he gazed down with disdain. "No one, unfortunately. You lack what I need. Your constitution is too weak; therefore, I cannot use you." He shook his head, and his white hair looked like jellyfish tentacles underwater. "A pity, too. After all our efforts, I thought we might have succeeded with you."

"Please..."

"Silence!"

The Leech kicked him to the floor, and Jamie flinched as Mudge screeched and wrapped his arms protectively around his head, curling up like a rotting leaf. Spinning swiftly, his jacket-cloak flaring behind him, the Leech fixed his eyes on Jamie.

"You, however, may prove to be more useful."

As he gripped the wall, heart crashing against his sternum and his brain racing, Jamie tried to flash a disarming grin at the Leech.

"I'm not really following, but whatever it is you think you need me for, let me assure you, I'm a bad choice. I mean, I'm lazy, I never pick up after myself, and I drink straight from the orange juice carton. Trust me, you don't want me."

"Enough!"

"And I talk too much. Ask anyone. In fact, I'm downright annoying."

"I said, *enough*!"

An arc of electricity spewed from the Leech's fingers. The impact knocked him to the floor. His head cracked against wood. The world spun, and pain flashed red across his vision. He struggled to stay conscious as the Leech approached, bolts of electricity still flickering across his hands.

A horrible cry tore through the room, and Jamie squinted through the throbbing pain to see Mudge convulsing in the middle of the room, his limbs contorting grotesquely. The network of veins under his skin burned like blue coils.

"Help me!" he screamed.

"Mudge!"

His friend wailed once, then went still, twisted face turned to the ceiling. A final breath hissed through his teeth. The blue of his eyes flickered, then went dark.

Jamie knew he was dead.

Spasms of nausea took hold of him, and he lurched, gagging, but his stomach was empty. As he clutched uselessly at the floorboards, the edges of his vision blurred, and he felt the Leech yank him up like a rag doll. He flailed in his iron grasp, but his efforts were useless as he was dragged through another room. Pushing through the blinding ache in his skull, he blinked his vision into focus.

A dozen Leeches had gathered in the room, most of them far less humanoid than his captor. As they moved aside, their twisted faces leered at him with eager eyes and wicked, elongated mouths. They hissed and drooled, like they wanted nothing more than to eat him for lunch. Electric shocks prickled his skin as he was dragged past them.

A moment later, Jamie was outside in a dark clearing, surrounded by trees and brush. He smelled saltwater; and underneath that, dead and rotting things. His stomach rolled again as the image of Mudge's dead body imprinted itself on the back of his eyelids.

"You killed him," he gasped through his nausea.

The Leech didn't answer. Marshland, dark and ominous, loomed behind them. Ahead, a dock jutted out into the waterway, its shadowy outline barely visible against the night sky. They were on the edge of town, but through his hazy vision, Jamie didn't recognize the surroundings.

"Where are we?" he choked out.

"A very special place," said the Leech.

His fingers tightened around Jamie's shirt, and he lifted him up as though he weighed no more than a sack of feathers. The sudden movement sent stars skittering through Jamie's line of sight, and his world tilted. The Leech brought his hideous face close, and his corpse lips pulled back into a nasty smile.

"A very special place, indeed."

Chapter 28

Twenty minutes later, Selene led Fee and his Trine through the back streets of St. Mary's. Thunder rumbled through the thick clouds above the water, and the threat of rain had kept most of the town's inhabitants inside for the night.

"That's the pier," she said quietly. "It hasn't been used for years."

As she looked out over the silhouette of the wooden expanse, the desolate location gave her the creeps. If Jamie had been beside her, she was certain he would have made another reference to Scooby Doo. But he wasn't by her side, and she had to compartmentalize her guilt by conjuring up images of him safe at home, playing video games and polishing off several cans of Dr. Pepper.

Fee motioned for them to stop, and they knelt behind a concrete retaining wall. The Rovers wore their dark green outfits, cloaks pulled over their heads—which made Selene feel even more raw and exposed, with nothing but her grandmother's bracelet and Fee's wrist cuff as protection. She wished she could summon a glowing blue weapon of her own.

In the distance, lightning flashed mournfully behind black clouds, but it didn't bother her—not like it used to. Compared to everything else, fear of an approaching storm just didn't rank at the top of her list anymore.

The ocean water licked the supports of the pier. All around, crickets buzzed among the cordgrass. Everything was quiet. Even Fee had been silent, and she wasn't sure if it was because he was deep in thought, or because he was still irked with her for coming along.

Nyx slid along the wall toward Titus. "Do you feel that?"

He nodded. "Leeches."

As Selene rubbed her prickling arms, she concentrated on the sensation. Her scalp felt as though it were charged with static: the same feeling she'd gotten from the blue-eyed strangers in town, as well as from the creatures that attacked her in the marsh. But the intensity level she felt here was off the charts.

"I feel it," she whispered, earning an approving look from Nyx. "How many of them?"

"Difficult to tell," said Titus. His eyes had gone milky white and out of focus. "The Barrier feels distorted here. Messing with my senses. It's like there's some kind of...I don't know...energy field... in this area." His gaze shifted to Fee. "Do you know what it is?"

"I'm not sure," he replied. "But this is obviously the place."

Shadows flickered under a pale streetlight, drawing their attention as Cruz materialized from the darkness, wearing his Rogue gear, and made his way along the docks. Five figures followed just behind. Their hands were bound, and burlap sacks covered their heads. Fee gritted his teeth as Marcelo and Paloma prodded the captives along with swords that sparked blue against the night.

Twin knives formed in Titus' hands; their amber blades hummed. "What are our orders, Phoebus?"

Fee cast the edge of his *mantellum* aside, revealing his longbow. "We will do nothing until this Ji'roth appears. I want to hear what he has to say. But we can't allow the Othersiders to be harmed, either. You and Nyx wait here. When I give the order, attack the Leeches."

"What about Cruz and his Trine?" asked Titus.

The glint in Fee's eyes was intense, even in the darkness.

"Use whatever force is necessary to stop the Rogues," he said. "But Cruz is mine."

***

Phoebus slipped through the cordgrass as Selene, at his side, copied his gait. She wasn't bad, he mused, for someone with no training. As they reached the dock, they took shelter behind one of the thick supports. Cruz and his blindly obedient Rogues were at the far end of the enormous pier—waiting, it seemed. The five Viewers sat in a huddled heap against a large tacklebox.

He tightened his grip around his bow. He would get to the bottom of this, but never at the expense of Othersider lives. A soft touch at his shoulder made him flinch. Selene pulled back, her eyes almost luminous in the dim light. Despite the determined set of her face, he could see uncertainty as well.

"How many other Bleeders have you known?" she asked.

He kept his own countenance void of emotion as he ran his hand along the length of the longbow, tracing the grooved amber designs.

"Three," he replied.

"What happened to them?"

"They didn't meet very pleasant ends."

He felt her tense. "Why?"

"They were killed."

"By who?"

Phoebus paused, hesitating longer than he wanted.

"You must understand," he said, choosing his words slowly and carefully. "I've pledged my life to protecting Threshold and the Otherside. So when something threatens the separation between our worlds, I am bound by law to act."

She didn't blink as she stared at him, but he saw the flood of thoughts behind her eyes as the truth chipped away at them, like a dam ready to break.

"You killed the other Bleeders."

He held her gaze. "Only one."

As she searched his face, looking into his eyes the same way he'd looked into hers, Phoebus felt himself in danger of giving way under the scrutiny.

"Why do you keep looking at me like that?" she asked.

He turned his focus on the bowstring, testing its tension. At his touch, the sinews sparked to life and shimmered into an electric threat.

"Why do you ask so many questions?"

"I'm insatiably curious," she replied, mimicking the tone he often used. "You said you hadn't stopped thinking about me—"

"Since the Rift," he said quickly, finishing her sentence. He studied the dark channel of water beyond the pier, feeling his emotions rippling like the waves. He set his bow aside and rubbed his temples to ease the sensation. "Yes, those were my words," he said, sensing the inner scales of his control beginning to tip. "I've tried to block it out, but no matter what I do, every time I close my eyes, I see you."

"Why do I bother you so much, Fee?"

"Because I'm a Rover. I have a job to do. I can't let my—" He stopped and clenched his jaw to the point of pain. "When I'm around you, I feel like I'm putting everything at risk."

"But you let me come with you tonight."

"Well, you *were* pretty threatening back at the inn," he replied, grasping at the momentary respite. "And, as I recall, you didn't give me any other options."

"Ah." Her smile turned sly. "I knew you were afraid of me."

His lip twitched, but he didn't say anything. Seconds passed with nothing but the sounds of water and nature, and the longer they waited in the tall cordgrass, the more aware he was of Selene's close proximity. He wanted to pull her to his chest and crush his lips to hers. Taking in a harsh breath, he fashioned an arrow between his hands and plunged it into the muddy earth.

"You have no idea how powerful you are," he said finally, breaking the silence.

"Oh yeah," she said, rubbing her arms. "All cell phones of the world, beware."

Reaching out, he took her hand in his. Her skin felt like silk compared to his calloused palms. "I sensed it the moment you peered through the Rift. I felt it when you spoke to me in that hospital room. I knew it to be true when I saw what you did in the marsh. And now, I am certain that you have a purpose in this conflict."

"A purpose," she repeated.

He leaned closer. "You have an untapped well inside you, Selene."

Tears pricked the corners of her eyes, shining in the dim light as she looked up at him. "So why does it feel like a curse?"

Fee wrapped his fingers tighter around hers. "Because you've never seen it as anything else. Before you can go further down this path, you must stop believing your connection to the *Electricus* is a flaw. It is a weapon, and one of great power, when wielded correctly."

"How can I be powerful if I don't even *know* what it is I can do?"

"Manipulating the Barrier takes skill and practice," he replied. "Rovers train for years to hone this ability, and even then, only a select few achieve it. For that brief instant in the marsh, you tapped into that well." His fingers slid over her wrist and touched her bracelet. "I believe someone else knew you'd have this power—the person who gave you this talisman."

"My grandmother," she said, her voice heavy with emotion. "But how?"

"When this is over, we'll figure that out." He let go and turned his attention to the pier. "First, we need to stop Cruz and these Leeches before anyone else gets hurt. The element of surprise is in our favor. Once their meeting is underway, we can move in on their position."

"What can I do to help?"

"I'm not putting you in harm's way. Bleeder or not, you are still an Othersider, and a target."

"How do you know all the Leeches will be at this meeting? What if some are hiding, expecting an attack? If the three of you run out there, you could be surrounded." At his expression, she shrugged. "I watch a lot of movies."

Fee tilted his head to the side, bewildered. "Meaning?"

"Meaning you need me," she continued, and her eyes lit up. "I can be the bait. If I take off my bracelet and your talisman, the Leeches will zero in on my signature, right?"

"Absolutely not. I won't allow—"

"You know I'm right," she said, extending her hand to touch his, and he felt the buzz of electricity between them. "Let me be the bait. I can draw them out into the open, and then you can pick them off."

Kneeling there in the grass, in the dim glow of distant lights, she looked as fierce and confident as any Rover. A slow, measured smile touched his lips.

"I have to admit," he said, shouldering his bow. "I like the way you think."

Chapter 29

As the Leech pushed through the mud, Jamie noticed how each step he took sunk into the spongy earth, and brown water pooled around his boots. He'd given up struggling. The Leech's grip was the equivalent of steel, leaving him nothing to do but stare at the ground while hoisted like a sack of potatoes, waiting to see where he ended up.

Despite his killer headache and the burning in his chest, he felt a measure of calm relief. At least Selene was safe. If he'd demanded she go home with him instead of staying with those Rovers, she'd have been captured, too.

The Leech suddenly heaved him from his shoulder, dumping him into the grass. A shadow fell across him, and he looked up. A large man, his face hidden against the sky by a deep, tan-colored hood, was studying him. He seemed annoyed.

"What is this, Ka'nar?" he demanded. "This Viewer is weak."

"He was an easy capture," hissed the Leech.

"I can barely read the energy levels off of him. He'd be a waste of time."

"Just put him with the group."

The large man grunted. "Fine."

"Hey, what's—" Jamie started, but a burlap bag was thrown over his head and the pungent stench gagged his words from him.

His arms were yanked back, pinching his shoulder blades, and rope wrapped around his wrists, cutting into his skin. Then he was hauled roughly to his feet. The bag allowed enough space for him to see his feet, but not much else.

"What's going on?" he shouted, though his voice was muffled through the burlap. "Where are you taking me?"

A strong hand pressed into his shoulder.

"Doesn't matter," said the man. "You won't remember any of this when it's over, anyway."

As they walked, he became aware that there were other people with them. He couldn't tell how many, but a pair of white sneakers came into his limited view, belonging to someone in a procession in front of him. After a few minutes, they left the grass and marched on concrete—then onto the rotting slats of a pier. He heard water lapping below him. Thunder rumbled in the far distance, and a hot breeze pressed the burlap against his sweaty face.

He was shoved down, and his back rammed against a wooden box. A woman was crying near him, and a man cursed under his breath. Jamie felt fear rush through him—thick, palpable, and contagious. Two sets of black boots with heavy silver buckles passed his thin line of vision.

"Only five," he heard one of the captors say. It was the strange, hissing voice of the Leech who'd carried him from the cabin—Ka'nar. "This is a puny offering for Ji'roth."

"We have to be careful," the man replied. "I'll have enough on my hands, dealing with the woman you killed and the boy who escaped."

"The boy returned to us," said Ka'nar. "It was he who brought me this one."

A steel-toed boot kicked Jamie roughly in the side. He grunted as the air left his lungs, but he kept his mouth shut. Talking wasn't going to get him out of this one, and he had to figure out what was going on so he could escape and warn Selene.

"A lot of good he'll do us," said the man, hovering over him.

"We'll see about that," the Leech replied.

***

Lightning slashed a jagged line across the sky, and Phoebus rose from his crouch. It was time to move. He pulled himself onto the shallow end of the pier and offered his hand to Selene. She took it, her grip strong and certain, and he hoisted her over the side.

Several yards away, Titus and Nyx melted into the shadows of a small guardhouse. Creeping forward, he motioned Selene behind him. His Trinemates settled behind a few dilapidated crates, and he gestured for them to stay put. He moved closer with Selene following at his back. Halting behind a storage trailer, he knelt, and she did the same.

Cruz stood, talking to a humanoid Leech, while another paced the railing of the pier, his black coat fluttering in the wind—the two from the cabin, Phoebus noted. Marcelo and Paloma, in their Rogue uniforms, were positioned on either side of the Othersider captives, acting as guards, weapons drawn.

The atmosphere rippled across the pier.

With a crack of thunder, the air sliced open in a Rift, and Phoebus drew a sharp breath as more than a dozen spindly Leeches shimmered through the light. Each creature was a grotesque abomination—distorted and disproportionate, with faces gaunt and gaping.

His skin crawled at the sight of so many Leeches in one place.

With metallic hisses, the Leeches spread around the pier, clawing at the wooden planks as they eyed the captured Viewers with eager hunger. The Rift rippled again, and two human-shaped figures stepped through, joining Cruz on the pier.

The first was of average height and build, concealed by heavy black robes. The second, attired in similar garb, was slighter and hovered behind the first as though wanting to keep out of sight.

The light quivered, and the Barrier closed.

Cruz stepped forward, nodding a stiff greeting to the first figure. "Ji'roth."

The one in black gestured to the small group of prisoners.

"Is this all you've brought me?" The figure's voice grated on Phoebus' ears.

"This is a small town, Ji'roth," said Cruz. "People are easily missed. The experiments Ka'nar has been performing have cost two lives already. I draw the line at this batch."

Ji'roth's robes trailed over the pier as he studied the group. As he passed, Phoebus noticed how the other Leeches shied away. Even Marcelo and Paloma lowered their weapons—but whether out of fear or respect, he couldn't tell. The *Electricus* readings from the figure were unbelievably strong.

Whoever this Ji'roth was, he commanded a presence worthy of an Elder.

"Then these Viewers will have to do," said Ji'roth, his voice dripping with disdain. "But for your sake, Cruz, I hope they prove to be successful." His head dipped toward the Leech standing next to Cruz. "Give me your report, Ka'nar."

As the Leech bowed, his corpse-white hair framed his face like rotting weeds. "For months, we have searched for Viewers strong enough to receive our energy, but our efforts have proved futile. Although some have been able to endure the transference, they could not extract from other living creatures."

"That is a problem," said Ji'roth. "If these Viewers are to serve as hosts for our brethren, they must be able to extract. Otherwise, both will die."

Sitting back on his heels, Phoebus exchanged a glance with Selene. Her drawn face mirrored his own. This was the second time he'd heard talk of hosting. But the word still meant nothing to him.

And who were these brethren the Leech referred to?

He was sick of questions without clear answers. Narrowing his eyes, he strained to see within the deep hood of this mysterious Ji'roth. Although he saw nothing but shadows, but he couldn't shake a sense of familiarity—something about his walk, his mannerisms, even his voice…

"What makes you think this will work at all?" asked Cruz.

"It has to work," hissed Ji'roth, his body bristling. "We have waited long enough. The time has come for my brethren to rise again. Too long we have cowered under the law of Threshold, bound by the Elders and their egotistical laws."

The Leeches raked their discolored limbs against the wood, and the Othersider captives strained against their bonds. He felt their terror like ice in his veins. Even Marcelo and Paloma, though poised, shared the same look of uncertainty.

But Cruz remained unfazed as he crossed his arms across his broad chest.

"You still haven't told me what you intend to do with these Viewer hosts, once you've created them."

"Fashion an army," Ji'roth replied.

Cruz frowned. "Of Othersiders?"

"No, Rogue," Ji'roth sneered. "An army of our own kind."

Motioning to the second figure, Ji'roth drew to one side of the railing, and the two seemed to engage some kind of conference—

although they spoke too lowly for Phoebus to hear. As he studied their huddled forms, he noticed a marked difference between their attire.

He'd thought both were wearing identical black robes, but as they moved under one of the yellow pier lights, his breath caught like icy needles in his throat. The second figure was wearing a *mantellum* of deep midnight blue—the *mantellum* of a Preceptor.

"Come, Rogue," said Ji'roth as he extended gloved hands over the railing. "I will show you."

Below the pier, water rippled—as though someone had thrown a stone into the channel. Waves splashed against the pier's supports and spread along the shallow marsh, and grasses waved like thousands of bony fingers while fish darted and seaweed wafted in the swirling current.

Then a purple glow began to shine from underneath the brackish water, filtering through the murkiness and illuminating the marsh around the pier. Phoebus looked between his feet, peering through the wide, rotting cracks in the planks as the purple light filtered through them. Beneath the surface of the water lay dozens of bodies.

Leech bodies.

Selene gasped beside him. "What is—"

Clamping his hand over her mouth, he shook his head. But he couldn't wrench his eyes away from the scene. Each Leech looked like a mummy, lined side by side, encased in a large, watery tomb. But their appearance was also disturbingly humanoid—even more so than the Leeches working with Cruz. He'd never seen anything like it before…except…

The sudden realization hit Phoebus like a punch in the gut.

"The Apostates," he breathed.

Selene pulled his hand away from her lips, and her eyes demanded an answer from him, but Ji'roth was speaking again.

"There they are," said Ji'roth with reverence as he looked over the rail. "Our brethren, confined to this watery grave by the Elders of Threshold since the Rebellion. Their bodies are trapped, but their energy remains alive within them."

"That's impossible," breathed Cruz, staring around him and beneath him—greatly shaken, despite the hard expression on his face. "The Apostates were put to death for leading the Rebellion."

"That was a lie," said Ji'roth, his tone one of smug pleasure. "Our brethren were too powerful to kill, so the Elders imprisoned them here, trapped under a powerful field of *Electricus*. It has taken me a very long time to find them. The power of the Mocama Coil has shielded their presence for ages. I will take their life-energy and place it into Viewer hosts. The Apostates will be free, and under their leadership, we'll build a resistance strong enough to storm Threshold and take back what is ours."

"Why did you not tell me this?" demanded Cruz.

Ji'roth laughed, and the hood wagged against the unseen face. "Because if you knew the truth, Rogue, you might have gone back on our agreement. And I couldn't risk that. You and your Trine have provided the perfect cover for us as we searched for the Apostates, and we grew in strength with each Viewer from whom you allowed us to extract. And all this time, we have been doing it right under the Elders' noses."

"You promised us passage out of Otherside," said Cruz. "That's all that matters to me."

"And you shall have it," said Ji'roth. "After the Apostates have been released."

Leaning against the railing, Cruz gazed into the purplish water. Seaweed drifted across the unmoving Leeches like snakes.

"But you haven't figured a way around the *Electricus* field erected by the Elders," he said. "The Apostates are trapped inside it, as they have been for centuries. So what good would Viewer hosts be, even if you are successful with your experiments?"

"We *will* be successful," Jiroth corrected. He approached Cruz as the second figure drifted silently behind him. "But what we have lacked is the power of a Bleeder at our disposal. For years, I have searched. But the Rovers were always too quick—always found them first. Not this time, however—thanks in part to you. A Bleeder can do what we cannot. A Bleeder can pass through the electrical field that imprisons our brethren. She will be able to release their energy to us, and we will infuse it into the Viewers."

Phoebus felt Selene's fingers digging into his skin with so much force that he winced, but he couldn't risk looking at her.

"The Bleeder is dead," said Cruz.

Ji'roth recoiled as though he'd been slapped. One of the Viewer prisoners suddenly made a loud, wailing noise and lunched forward, but he was met with a sharp kick from Ka'nar. The Viewer slumped over, motionless.

"Dead," hissed Ji'roth, his body shaking with wrath. "Explain."

"It was the Rover. Phoebus. I hadn't expected him to go through with it, but he told me himself that he killed her tonight."

"You knew," whispered Selene.

He silenced her with a look. He had to think. Phoebus knew Ji'roth from somewhere, he was sure of it. But what about the other figure? There was something familiar in its movements as well. How did it have a Preceptor *mantellum* in its possession? No Leech could enter Threshold. No Leech, unless—

Ji'roth screeched in fury, cutting into Phoebus' thoughts.

"I have not come this far, only to have a dead Bleeder stand in my way." Ji'roth tore off his gloves, revealing hands like charred flesh. "And I will not allow your failure to jeopardize everything I've worked for. I will breech the field myself!"

"No Leech has that power," sneered Cruz.

Ji'roth paused at this, and his sharp laugh filled the night sky. He rotated, moving like a predator. "In that, you are correct, Rogue." The figure grasped his hood and pulled it free. "But I am a citizen of Threshold as well."

It was Jareth—the sickly, milky-faced leader of the Regents.

The sight of him hit Phoebus like an arrow in his brain.

Jareth was the traitor.

"You can't be a Leech," breathed Cruz, stepping back. "You're a Regent—"

"There are more of our kind in Threshold than your precious Elders know," said Jareth—*Ji'roth*—with a low, hissing laugh. "We escaped after the Rebellion and hid ourselves among them, even obtaining positions of power over the long years as we waited for the opportunity for revenge."

"But how—"

"With the abundance of *Electricus* that Threshold provides, those of us who managed to elude your people were able to feed as never before. The purity of the energy replenished our ravaged organs, and it gave us new strength and abilities—even the ability to maintain a human appearance."

"Impossible," Cruz snarled.

"You see the proof with your own eyes, Rogue," said Ji'roth. "And after we raise the Apostates, we will take over Threshold, and then all of our kind will be healed from this disease that mutilates our bodies. We will be unstoppable. No world will be safe from our rule."

"If you're truly this powerful," said Cruz, "then why did you want a Bleeder?"

"Because using my energy to tear through the prison will kill me," growled Ji'roth, his face flushed and sweating. "But I will sacrifice my life to free my brethren, and I shall die with the satisfaction of knowing that once they rise, Threshold will fall!"

A glowing mace electrified into Cruz's palm, and he rushed forward. But the second figure intercepted him with a crackling sword, blocking Cruz's blow with Rover-worthy skill that matched any Phoebus had ever witnessed.

Stumbling back, Cruz was quick to catch his footing, but Leeches surrounded him, flashing their claw-like appendages. The second figure motioned to the remaining creatures, and they scrambled closer to Marcelo and Paloma, cutting them off from the scene.

"It's too late for a change of heart, Rogue," said Ji'roth, spreading his arms. "Too late for anything, now."

Electricus sparked from the Regent's fingers, streaking into the murkiness below. With a crack like thunder, the energy ignited the water, turning it iridescent green, and the air sizzled. Phoebus caught Selene around the waist as the pier shook, knocking them off-balance and he stared in horror at the water below.

The electrical field that imprisoned the Apostates was weakening.

Bulging veins spread through Ji'roth's skin, eating away the pasty color of his flesh, sucking life from his lips and extremities as he released the whole of his *Electricus* into the water. His hair turned white, and his eyes flickered from deep within his sockets. His Thresholder appearance melted away like flesh in a burning fire, revealing the Regent's true Leech form.

"Stay here," Phoebus whispered sharply.

Selene glared at him as though he'd just asked her to go buy ice cream.

"No," she snapped. "I'm coming with you."

Gathering his feet under him, he felt a charge of adrenaline rush through his blood. He knew his Trine's eyes were on him from their hiding place, awaiting his orders, and Selene's breath was hot against his neck, insistent, though laced with fear.

"We have one shot at stopping this," he whispered. "And it has to count." As he looked into her defiant eyes, his heart swelled, threatening to crush his ribs. "Selene, listen to me. I am expendable. You are not. Please, for the love of everything on both our worlds, wait here."

The light in her eyes dimmed as she finally gave a short, reluctant half-nod.

"For now," she said.

It was good enough for him.

Maneuvering around the boxes, Phoebus adjusted his longbow on his shoulder. He wouldn't act yet. There were too many variables, and everything was at stake.

With a last revolting screech, Ji'roth pitched forward, catching himself with his charred fingers before he could fall into the water. So that was why the Regent had looked so pale and sickly all those years, Phoebus realized. He'd been disguising himself.

Phoebus smelled the Regent's burning flesh as he shuffled his grotesque form toward the captive Viewers, who were still guarded by Ka'nar and the Rogues. As if sensing his approach, the Othersiders huddled closer together on the floor of the pier, their burlap-covered heads twisting in terrified confusion.

"Quickly," rasped Ji'roth. "The prison is weakening. We need a host. Bring me the strongest of the lot."

Ka'nar stepped between the Regent and the captives.

"With respect, Ji'roth, I believe we've been going about this the wrong way."

The Regent hissed. "Speak quickly. My time is short."

"We've assumed the Viewer had to be strong to endure the transference," he replied, studying the cluster of Othersiders. "But perhaps we were wrong. A Viewer whose organs are filled with *Electricus* wouldn't have room for ours. But a Viewer that is weak—"

"Would be an empty vessel," finished Ji'roth, His face twisted with pleasure. "Very well. Select the weakest among these to be our first host."

Ka'nar approached the Viewer that Phoebus had heard cry out just a few minutes before. Yanking the prisoner roughly to his feet, the Leech flashed a wicked smile. He ripped the burlap sack from the Viewer's head, exposing a familiar shock of red hair, and hoisted the prisoner into the air.

"This one."

Chapter 30

Hot tears streaked Jamie's face as the Leech lifted him like he was made of paper. He should've been terrified, but all he could think about was Selene.

She was dead. She was *dead.*

His brain kept screaming her name, but his throat seized up. The sack was ripped from his head, and the Leech's electric eyes bored into his. Black lips pulled away from rotting teeth.

"This one," said the Leech.

Ka'nar's discolored hand spread over Jamie's chest. The wound he'd received from Mudge sizzled, and his sternum felt like it was cracking open. A scream welled in his throat.

"Drop him, parasite!" shouted a voice.

Managing to twist in the Leech's grasp, Jamie spotted Fee striding across the dock with a glowing bow and arrow in hand.

"Rover," Ka'nar hissed.

"Yeah, that's me," said Fee coldly. "Now, release him like a good little suck-worm, and I promise to make your death a quick one."

Jamie nearly wrenched free as hot rage—more scalding than his pain—overtook him. "You said you were going to protect her!" he yelled at Fee. "You killed her!"

Fee ignored him. He pulled the string to his cheek. "Drop the boy."

The Leech laughed. "Make me."

The arrow sank into the Leech's neck like a lightning bolt. He screeched. Jamie landed hard on his knees, clutching his chest, and rolled out of the way as the creature sprawled over the wood planks. Fee notched another arrow. Several things seemed to happen at once as Jamie laid there, gasping for breath and blinking away the tears that blurred his vision.

Titus and Nyx bolted from the darkness, weapons shining; dodging as the wounded Leech shot electricity from its fingertips. Titus' eyes turned freakishly white as he pointed to an empty space, and Nyx slashed at the air with her needle-sword. A brilliant light opened up. Fee took another shot. There was an explosion of electricity.

The Leech was sucked into the light, screaming in agony.

***

Phoebus trained his arrow on the other humanoid Leech, who was advancing with impressive speed, and pierced the creature through the neck. Wasting no time, he finished him off with another shot, and Titus and Nyx sent the body careening into the Rift, sparks flying as the Leech's energy was ripped apart.

"Who's next?" said Phoebus, readying another shot.

The spidery creatures hovered uncertainly, radiating bloodlust and fear, but they didn't move. He sensed they were waiting for their orders as well.

The Regent was panting heavily on the floor of the pier, his body quivering with spasms. The second figure stood over him, protecting him, wielding its blue sword as its Preceptor cloak whipped around its concealed body in the ocean breeze.

"I don't think we've met," said Phoebus.

At his words, the figure swung at him, and he used his bow to deflect the blow, his arrow clattering to the ground. With incredible speed, the hooded figure attacked again, and though Phoebus met hit for hit, he was evenly matched.

"I'm trying," he said, ducking, "to have a conversation."

The air above him sizzled as the sword narrowly missed his head. Suddenly, the point of his arrow burst through the figure's shoulder from behind. The amber tip was coated in bluish blood as it pierced through the fabric of the *mantellum* and then ripped back through again, leaving a gaping wound.

The figure stumbled in pain, clutching its bleeding shoulder.

Phoebus shot to his feet, but before he could act, light sliced open through the nothingness of air between them. The figure dove through it, vanishing into the Rift it had created.

The light closed, revealing Cruz in the place where the figure had been, holding Phoebus' arrow like a spear.

"Well, that was rude," said Phoebus, brushing off his leather breeches.

"You're welcome," Cruz replied, tossing him the arrow.

He caught it and glanced warily at the remaining Leeches on the pier. He'd have to worry about the escaped figure later. The dying Regent at his feet, and the collection of creatures surrounding them, took precedence.

"I'm rather offended that you didn't invite me to your party," Phoebus said.

"Since when have you ever needed an invitation?" Cruz dipped his head toward Ji'roth, who was crumpled and white-faced. "What do you think of my guest list?"

"Impressive. Although your taste is questionable, obviously."

"And you heard everything, I suppose."

"I had to put a few pieces together," Phoebus replied. "Your little undercover act had even me going for a while. But I've always been clever. It's one of my admirable qualities."

Out of the corner of his eye, he saw his Trine taking positions around the creatures. Between the ones keeping watch on Cruz and the others near the prisoners, Phoebus counted twenty—not including Ji'roth and his mysterious bodyguard, of course.

It wasn't the best of odds, but it wasn't the worst, either.

He aimed the amber arrowhead at the Regent's heart, feeling the familiar charge of electricity building inside him—eager to be channeled through the weapon toward its target. Ji'roth turned his flickering blue eyes up to him, drawing in a jagged breath.

"You could kill me, Rover. But as you can see, I've already taken care of that."

"I'll try not to let it ruin my night."

"And though I die," rasped the Regent, "the Apostates will rise."

Below them, the water churned, and Phoebus felt the electrical field of the prison collapsing with each minute that passed. He jammed his arrow right under the Regent's jaw, pressing its sharp point into the hollow of his neck until Ji'roth squirmed and choked.

"Close the Elder's prison," Phoebus growled. "Now."

Bluish liquid pooled in the Regent's mouth, but his wicked smile remained intact.

"Impossible, Rover. Once the field has been opened, only an Elder may seal it."

Phoebus brandished a wicked smile of his own.

"Or a Bleeder."

"Ah ha," said Cruz. He twirled his *Electricus*-infused mace. "I suspected as much, but you are the most unpredictable Rover I've ever known, so I couldn't be sure."

Ji'roth's darkening eyes widened with understanding. His breath gurgled in his throat. Standing, Phoebus pressed his boot against the Leech's chest and pinned him to the ground.

"I'm sorry about that," he spat. "Did we just ruin your plans?"

The Regent's mouth gaped open, and an unearthly cry burst from his lips. As if being awakened from their lethargy, the remaining Leeches on the pier threw back their heads and hissed in response.

With his last breath, Ji'roth screamed, "Keep the energy field open!"

Chapter 31

His chest was on fire. Jamie dragged himself to his knees. Beneath the opening of the hand-shaped hole in his t-shirt, his skin resembled a burned crater, as though someone had taken a gigantic cigarette and held it to the center of his chest. He smelled the stench of his own charred flesh, and he nearly heaved. Taking a deep breath, he forced his gag reflex down.

As bad as it hurt, the wound was nothing compared to the grief that surged through him, taking the strength from his arms as he tried to push himself up. *Selene was dead.* His heartbeat pounded like drums in his ears, and he gulped in large, sobbing breaths of air; he felt as though he were drowning.

Light blasted from the center of the pier. He blinked and saw Cruz and Fee, surrounding by Leeches. Then, as though someone had pressed play on some epic video game, a battle exploded in front of him. The creatures were attacking, and the Rovers were fighting back.

The two human-looking Leeches who'd captured him were gone, leaving only the two Rogues—the brother and sister—guarding the prisoners. The brother exchanged a swift look with the sister and then went running into the fray, brandishing a curved blade.

Taking his opportunity, Jamie scrambled to the other captives, yanking off the burlap sacks as fast as he could. Four pairs of stunned and frightened eyes stared back at him—two men he'd seen before on the docks, a lady who worked at the diner, and a girl in he recognized from school.

"Listen," he panted. "You have to get out of here!"

"Stop!" ordered the sister, grabbing his shoulder.

He coughed and pressed a hand to his chest, wincing at the fresh ripping pain. "It's Paloma, right?" he said, ignoring his throbbing sternum. "You've gotta let these people go. You heard what that psychopath Leech person said. You can't let them die!"

"That's not my—"

"Hey, look at me," he said, thinking fast as he turned to the others. "You have to get out of here. There's an inn in town. *The Seaside Inn.* Go there. You'll be safe, I promise." He jerked back to Paloma. "They'll be safe, right? I mean, that's like, your headquarters."

"But their memories—"

"Won't matter if they're dead. You can do that thing you guys do, whatever you did with Sel—" he choked on her name— "whatever you do with Viewers later, messing with their heads, after this is over." He grabbed at her hand. "Please. This people are innocent. You know they're innocent."

Paloma studied him for a moment, her dark eyes going over every detail of his face, clearly weighing his words. Something small flashed in her free hand. A key. She tossed it to him, then slit the rope bonds of the four prisoners.

Jamie pressed the key into the Viewer girl's hands. "Go to the inn and wait there. Don't go home. You don't want to put your families in danger. Just wait at the inn and we will come and get you. Okay? Can you do that?"

Tears welled in the girl's eyes, and she nodded. "Yeah."

"Okay," he said, relief washing over him. He helped her to her feet, even though it felt as if his wound split wider as he did so. "Just run, and don't stop until you get to the inn."

They looked at each other, silently agreeing, and took off together, clambering down the steps of the pier and running toward town. Thunder rumbled over the ocean water, and a heavy breeze whipped across his arms. Jamie swallowed hard as the despairing ache returned.

"Not bad, Viewer," said Paloma. "Now, you go with them."

"No way. Not while this is going on."

She glanced at his shirt. "You're hurt."

"Yeah, well I have to do something!" he yelled, as his cavernous grief consumed him. "I can't just sit here, not when she's…gone! I have to make it count. I have to make *something* count!"

"You need to rest."

"I'm fine. It's just a burn."

As he pushed past her, his knees buckled, and he went down hard. Clutching his chest, he groaned as a wave of nausea rolled through his stomach.

"I cannot tell you what to do, Viewer," she replied. Her voice was firm, yet soft. "But I'm asking you to stay out of sight. This is not a battle for a young, inexperienced Othersider."

Before he could say anything, she turned and rushed into the chaos.

***

Selene had one thought.

Jamie.

She had to get to Jamie.

He was a few yards away from her hiding place, on his hands and knees, breathing heavily and in obvious pain—but he was alive. The four Viewers were huddled nearby, and Paloma and Marcelo stood guard.

Leaving the safety of the large crates, she inched down the railing toward the captives, keeping one eye on the center of the pier where Cruz, Fee, and the Leech called Ji'roth were talking. The remaining creatures were eerily still in hushed expectation, waiting for an order from their leader, while Titus and Nyx eased into positions on the opposite side of the pier.

Thunder rumbled overhead and lightning illuminated the rolling clouds. Everything smelled of rain, earth, and the odor of fish. As she ducked behind one of the rotting benches lining the pier, Selene heard a hideous screech, followed by Ji'roth's rattled order to defend the open energy field.

A battle unfolded.

Both Leeches and Thresholders passed in and out of Rifts of light, appearing and disappearing over the pier. Weapons clanged and electricity sparked. There were inhuman screeches and shouted commands. Explosions like thunder rocked the pier as Leeches were vanquished into the Barrier. The murky water crackled with energy, and sparks shot through the planks and missing pieces of flooring.

She shuddered at the bodies in the water—the *Apostates*. Electricity wove through their motionless forms and their sightless eyes stared upward. The hair on her arms stood on end and static buzzed through her scalp. Whatever threat they posed, it was obviously a serious one. But how could she fix this? What power could she have to do something that not even Fee or the other Rovers could do?

How could she close something she couldn't even *see*?

A new commotion at the end of the pier nearest to land caught her eye. Her heart kicked up a gear. The four Viewers were free and running away. Jamie was on the ground, clutching his chest, his face twisted with pain, and all thoughts about the Apostates vanished as she rushed toward him.

He raised his head.

"Selene!"

The way his entire face lit up when he saw her mashed all her feelings of guilt, fear, and happiness together inside her stomach. He pulled her to him in a fierce hug, even as he winced in pain.

"You're alive…you're alive," he said, pressing his cheek into her hair. "I thought, after what he said—" Jamie suddenly pulled back, and his eyes narrowed with dark fury. "Fee," he said, saying his name like a curse. "When this is over, I swear, I'm going to kill him."

Despite his fierce indignation, or maybe because of it, Selene felt a wide smile tugging at her lips. But the moment was short-lived. The sizzling hum of Paloma's blade caused her to look up sharply. The Rogue stood over them, her eyes flashing.

"Your friend isn't safe here, Selene."

Reality rushed back. She couldn't put Jamie in any more danger than she already had.

"Come on," she said, squeezing his hand. "We've got to get you out of here."

He struggled to his feet, and as he stood, she saw the nasty wound in his chest, clearly visible through his ripped shirt. Stifling a gasp, she felt her heart twist behind her ribs. Jamie leaned against her, his weight heavy as though he didn't have much strength. She wrapped her arm around his waist, heading for the stairs.

A flash of light exploded in front of them.

A hooded figure, wearing a dark blue cloak, blocked their path. It was Ji'roth's companion—the one Cruz had stabbed and who had disappeared into the Rift. Selene spotted the ripped fabric at its shoulder, and the cloak was darkened with blood. The figure tilted its head, as though contemplating something, and then it seemed to sneer from within the shadowed depths of its hood.

"Bleeder..."

The voice was smooth—otherworldly and metallic, but also feminine. The figure's glowing sword came up swiftly, and static buzzed between them, like a fuse about to blow. She felt Jamie move protectively in front of her, but suddenly, there was a sharp sizzling clang.

Paloma was between them, her sword parrying the deathblow.

"Back away, Rogue," said the figure.

Swinging its blade around, using the movement to part their weapons, the figure blasted a surge of electricity from its blade. The impact hurled Paloma backwards, and she slammed against the railing, and then fell into a lifeless clump on the planks.

Selene tried to scream, but the sound was choked off as she went airborne. Her head cracked against a bench, and stars burst through her vision. Sharp, pounding pain radiated through her skull. With a groan, she pushed herself up, checking the back of her head. There was no blood, but she felt a lump forming on her scalp.

Blinking away the fuzzy edges of her vision, she saw the hooded figure dragging Jamie across the pier by his legs. He wrenched one leg free and kicked hard, catching it in the stomach with the heel of his shoe. The figure lunged, taking Jamie by the neck and shoving him against the top of the railing, bending his body backwards and exposing his chest.

"Let him go!" Selene screamed.

Her fingertips felt hot, like she was holding a pot of boiling water. A current of heat, hotter than lava, burst through her insides. Electricity shot from her palms; the force of the energy sent her reeling backward. Her breath left her lungs as she hit the ground.

The electricity hit the figure squarely in the back. It jerked forward, its blue sword dissipating, and its entire cloaked body shuddered violently. Then, it didn't move. Selene got to her feet, her breaths rattling in her ears. Her body buzzed.

As the figure turned, its unseen face seemed to stare straight through her. It hesitated on the edge of the pier, clutching Jamie tightly with one gloved hand. And then, two things happened simultaneously—as though in slow motion.

The figure vanished into a Rift of light.

Jamie plunged over the railing.

It was like watching a car accident happening in another lane on the highway—close enough to witness, but too quickly and too far away to do anything about it. She heard him splash before her aching legs carried her to the rail. Below, she saw him flailing in the green water. Electricity surged around him, passing through him, the bolts of blue-white light jabbing at him like viscous piranhas. He was screaming.

"Fee!" she cried. "Help!"

From across the pier, Phoebus spun at the sound of her voice as though he'd been shot. He sidestepped a Leech's slashing claws, and his eyes locked on hers, assimilating the information in an instant. And then he was gone, bursting into a wall of light.

Before she could remember to breathe, Fee was back—the sliver of white light opened in front of her, and he stepped onto the solid flooring, soaking wet, and with Jamie in his arms.

As soon as they both appeared, Jamie crumpled forward, choking and spewing dirty water from his mouth. Selene rushed to him, gasping against a sob, but Fee was there, blocking her path. His face was bloody, his wet hair matted to his cheeks, and his coppery eyes burned with fierce determination.

"Close the electrical field, Selene," he commanded.

She tried to push past him. "Jamie—"

"Close it now or he's dead. We all are."

Hot tears wet her face. "I don't know how!"

"Yes, you do," he said, looking deep into her eyes. "That's what I've been telling you from the beginning. Stop holding yourself back. It's time to trust your instincts, Selene. Trust them, now!"

Fee leapt in front of a charging Leech, plunging an arrow through the creature's guts and kicking its flailing body over the side. Another Leech scrambled toward them, and Fee ran to meet it head-on—diverting it from their spot, taking it back into the thick of the battle.

"Just do it, Selene!" he yelled as he disappeared into the fray.

Around the pier, Rovers and Rogues were fighting for the survival of her world. An acidic taste filled her mouth, stinging her throat. She'd seen enough of the Leeches to know what they'd do if they ever took control of Threshold. She couldn't let that happen.

She dropped to her knees as Jamie coughed up muddy water. He reached out to her, clasping her hand with fingers that felt feverishly hot to the touch. He was shaking all over. His face had lost all color, and his normally fiery hair was matted brown with marsh.

"You have...to close it," he said, gasping for breath. "I know... you can do it."

As Jamie's pain-drenched eyes met hers, and he nodded once, then passed out. Putting her hands over her mouth, Selene stared at his unconscious form, her heart beating so hard against her ribs that it felt as though they were cracking.

She'd close the field, even if it killed her.

Approaching the railing, she started into the electricity-charged prison of the Apostates. The water Jamie had occupied just moments before Fee plucked him from death was now churning like a boiling pot, as though Jamie's body had somehow collapsed the last of the field. She blinked back the horrible image of him suffering in the water, tucking it away inside a dark corner of her mind.

She had to focus.

Everything seemed to fade around her as her vision tunneled. In some region of her brain, she was aware of something foreign that didn't belong; something getting in the way—Fee's arm cuff. And her bracelet. They'd kept her safe. But that time was over now. She didn't need them anymore. And suddenly, the metal felt stifling against her skin. The lead and amber talismans were holding her back.

Ripping them off, she let both drop with dull clangs to the slats at her feet, and a rush of power surged through her. Faintly, she registered a myriad of Leech screams as they picked up on her Bleeder signature. She sensed Fee somewhere behind her, fighting them off, buying her time.

But for her, time stopped.

She held out her arms. She closed her eyes. And she let the *Electricus* take her.

Chapter 32

It was as though she'd separated from her body. A part of her was aware of sensations—the feeling of her shoes against the pier, the harsh breeze smacking her face. On her tongue was the taste of salty air, and she smelled rotting things and the metallic scent of electricity.

But everything else was consumed by buzzing heat. She felt it spread from deep inside her, through her blood and bones and into her skin. Instinct propelled her, and she spread her fingers over the railing. Below, within the swirling green water, the Apostates stared with eyes fully open.

Electricus bolted from her fingers and pierced the surface like knives, charging the expanse of the prison. The Leeches shuddered in their mummified bodies, and their screams of rage were peals of thunder. She felt them fighting to move, to rise through the water.

Crying out with every fiber of her being, she pushed forward with her power. Flashes of memories seared through her brain. She saw everything: her childhood, her parents, her grandmother, Jamie, and Fee. Everything swirled within her.

And then, lighting struck the water.

The green lights morphed into purple, the water rocked with a shockwave that shook the pier, and she felt the electrical field seal shut. As the lights beneath the surface winked out, the swirling current calmed, and the ocean waters lapped against the supports of the pier as though nothing had ever happened.

The Apostates were trapped in their dark, invisible prison once more.

She sank to her knees, her body warm and humming with voltage. A charged exhaustion swept over her. She watched little sparks of electricity dance along her fingers, and then vanish.

"Selene!" A voice called to her—Fee's voice—from behind her. "Are you okay?"

"I did it," she heard herself say.

Fee laughed—a terrifyingly wonderful sound.

"Did you hear that, suck-worm?" he said to the Leech he'd impaled with his arrow. "Your little rebellion is over."

The Leech wailed as its body became electrical particles, vanishing into the Rift Nyx had opened beside them. As Selene wiped her hand across her eyes, she saw Fee's hand reaching down for hers, his fingers strong and steady.

Cruz and Titus were finishing off the last two Leeches near the far edge of the pier. Nyx's *nadala* shimmered in and out of the air as she repaired the Rifts that had been opened during the battle. Marcelo tended to Paloma, who had a nasty gash on her thigh, but seemed to be okay.

"It's really over?" Selene asked as Fee helped her to her feet.

"You sealed the prison," Fee replied, his smirk still intact. "Wouldn't you say so, Titus?"

Turning over her shoulder, she saw the others approaching—fairly beaten up, but amazingly fine, despite what she'd just seen. Titus, who looked at tired as she felt, nodded, and his eyes shifted into their freaky white mode.

"The field is secure," he agreed. "No weaknesses whatsoever."

"You see?" said Fee, as though it should've been obvious. "That was all you."

Selene lifted her face and inhaled deeply. The smell of rain and saltwater cleared her senses. "You guys did the hard part."

A deep crease appeared between Titus' brows. "But there's something else here." His head swiveled as his white eyes stared into nothingness. "I sense something new...a very concentrated signature, and it's very close."

The smile vanished from Fee's lips, and his eyes glinted like copper flecks. He slipped his bow from his shoulder, his posture like a tiger about to spring. "Where?"

A cold shock hit Selene with the force of a physical blow.

"Wait, where's Jamie?" She spun to find an empty space where he'd been, just minutes ago, before she'd gone to the railing. "He was right here!"

Panic seized her, wrenching air from her chest, and the warmth she'd felt crackled and froze in her veins. She felt Fee's firm touch on her arm, and his expression scared her. His jaw was tight, his eyes like glass, and deep lines marred his forehead.

"By the Grove," he muttered.

Selene followed Fee's gaze, and there, under the shadowy lights, she could just make out the crumpled form of her best friend, sprawled lifelessly across the wooden planks.

From somewhere dark and far away, she heard herself scream.

Careening and stumbling, she rushed down the pier, scraping her hands as she pitched forward, feeling the sting of splinters in her palms. She kept going, Fee right behind her, and the others behind him. But she didn't care about anyone but Jamie. Guilt stabbed behind her eyeballs, sending tears gushing down her cheeks, and cold terror pinched her airway closed, choking off her prayers that he was still alive.

She saw his chest heave, and she nearly puked with relief. He wasn't dead. He wasn't dead! Falling beside her best friend, ignoring the shooting pain that jarred her kneecaps, she reached for his hand, and then stopped in her tracks.

Jamie was awake, but his eyes were squeezed shut, and his teeth chattered between lips that were way too blue—like someone half-frozen. His face was stripped of its pinkish color, and he had turned so pale that she could see veins bulging in his neck, his forehead, and along his temples.

"Jamie?"

His lips moved, but only a strange, garbled sound came out. Pulling herself together, she grasped his hand. His skin was hot—feverishly hot—but his fingers had turned a gruesome purple, as though he were suffering from frostbite. He coughed and shuddered with violent spasms.

"Fee, what's happening to him?"

He knelt beside her, his expression unreadable as he studied Jamie's ashen face and the hideous burn taking up the center of his chest, which was visible beneath his ripped t-shirt.

"Titus," he said, in a voice that matched his countenance.

Without hesitation, Titus knelt on Jamie's opposite side and held his hands, palms down, over the wound. "His body is saturated with *Electricus*," he replied.

Pinching the bridge of his nose, Fee sighed, and the sound was heavy. "The Apostates," he said, glancing toward the railing. "The prison had nearly collapsed when he fell into the water. He must have absorbed some of their energy before I got him out."

A sickening feeling crawled through Selene's spine.

"But how is this possible?" asked Nyx, easing closer.

"I don't know," said Titus, "but he can't handle this amount of energy. Without organs like ours, there's no way for him to control it." Letting his hands drop, Titus turned solemn eyes to Selene. "The *Electricus* is eating through him."

Jamie coughed up blood and curled into himself with a gut-wrenching moan. His veins bulged and pulsed in his cheeks as he craned his neck, as though searching for something Selene couldn't see. She clutched his hand tighter.

"Jamie, it's me. I'm here. Open your eyes."

"Can't," he sputtered as his head wrenched. "It burns..."

As she held onto his hand, she screamed inside. Never had she felt so utterly helpless. The others lingered close, but kept a respectful distance, like people around hospital beds when someone was dying. Like her own family had done when her grandmother died. A sob burned in her chest.

"What do we do, Phoebus?" asked Nyx.

Jamie's blue lips were stained with blood. He pushed himself over, his eyes shut tight. "Kill me."

"No," cried Selene, throwing her arms over him. "Absolutely not. No way!"

Another form knelt beside her on the pier. Blinking back tears, she met the dark, serious gaze of Cruz. He looked at her for a moment, then at Jamie's writhing form, and then finally, he focused on Fee.

"Fee, I've watched Ji'roth's experiments with the other Viewers," he said in a flat voice. "And I've seen what happens. This boy will either be burned alive from the inside out or, if he survives that, he'll be *Electricus*-starved, and incapable of feeding. Either way, his death will be very slow, and very painful."

Selene pressed her hand to Jamie's cheek; it felt like fire underneath her fingers. "No. I don't accept either of those options, and especially not from any of you. There has to be something to help him. Something *I* can do. He's not going to die."

"It's okay," said Jamie. His voice was weak, his breaths labored, but his words came steadier now. "You heard the guy. I'm dead anyway."

"No, you—"

"Selene. You're s-stepping on my moment here."

His eyes opened, and tears leaked from his pale lashes as he stared up at her and smiled. Then a wave of pain crashed over his features, and he gritted his teeth against his blue lips. His gaze shifted to Fee.

"Just m-make it quick," he whispered. "Please."

Jamie went horribly still.

Fee's expression set into that impenetrable stone mask she'd come to know so well. Without a word, he stood, and in an instant, he had his bowstring pulled taut. As Selene stared at the tip of the voltage-laden arrow, a cold terror like nothing she'd ever known smashed into her, followed by a blazing fury.

"Don't you dare!"

Surging to her feet, she punched Fee in the face as hard as she could. Every emotion she'd felt over the last few days was crammed into that blow.

He stumbled back. The arrow vanished.

"I don't care about your laws or your stupid regulations!" she yelled. Her body shook with rage and her hand throbbed. "I won't let you kill my best friend. I won't!"

Her panting breaths were deafening in her ears, but everything else had grown silent. She braced herself, pleading for that power to come from inside her that had sealed the prison, but there was nothing —nothing except her anger and her fear.

Fee shouldered his bow and rubbed his thumb along the edge of his jaw, which had turned a slight shade of red. Although his countenance remained like marble, the look in his coppery eyes was pained and vulnerable—and even, she thought, hurt.

"As you wish," he said, sounding oddly formal and distant.

As Fee glanced at the sky, Selene prayed for anything to grasp onto, searching for any hope that might save Jamie. She'd never be able to live with herself if he died. How could she? Her anger at Fee fizzled out like the extinguishing of a candle.

The only person she could truly blame was herself.

Fee walked to the edge of the railing, and he leaned down, scooping something into his hands. As he approached, she saw him fasten a metal cuff around his wrist—the one he'd given her to wear. But something else dangled from his fingers. She touched her naked wrist where her bracelet had been. She'd discarded it before closing the energy field.

"It's a long shot," he said, holding out the bracelet. "But I have an idea."

"I'll do anything," she whispered.

"The amber resin within our talismans acts as magnet, allowing us to manipulate and control the *Electricus* in the atmosphere." Fee's coppery gaze fixed on the bracelet. "Your bracelet has proven to function in a similar way."

"How will that help?"

"The boy's body is overflowing with *Electricus*," he replied. "But if there were a way to control it, there is a chance he could be spared."

"I don't understand," she said, watching the metal flash coldly between Fee's long fingers. She glanced back at Jamie, whose breaths seemed shallower with each passing moment. "You said these things don't work with Othersiders."

Although his mask didn't falter, she heard a catch in Fee's voice. "Selene, ever since I met you, every belief I've held true has been tested." He placed the bracelet in her palm and closed her fingers over it. "I don't have the answers, but I do know this: you are the exception to every rule I've ever known."

He stepped away, moving with an agile grace that made her heart hurt. She held the bracelet against her chest, and the metal buzzed and tingled against her fingers. "What do I do?"

"You refused a quick death for your friend," he said, his voice neither cold nor consoling. "Now, as I see it, you have only two options. You can stand here and watch his life ebb painfully away, or you can take the chance that your talisman will work. Either way, Selene, the choice is yours."

The weight of all their stares felt suffocating. But it was nothing compared to the thought of losing the one person who had always been there for her. Her fingers felt numb as she slowly turned and went to her knees before her best friend.

Jamie's lips trembled with frantic movements, and she leaned closer. He was pleading for death, though his voice was barely discernible over the gurgling in his throat. His ashen face was turned to the sky, and his eyes were closed again. Tears forged trails of blood and dirt across his pale cheeks. Unleashed sobs wedged between Selene's ribs, squeezing her lungs until she felt like she'd never breathe again. She pressed her lips to his feverish temple.

"You have to stay with me," she whispered. "I can't lose you."

Taking the deepest breath she could manage, she felt her body grow resolute. Before her brain could rationalize anything else, she took her bracelet and fastened it around his wrist.

A blast of light surged from the metal, and she ducked as it burst into the night air. Jamie's body convulsed like he'd been shocked with the paddles of a defibrillator, his back arched sharply for several excruciating moments, and then fell back against wooden planks with a dull thud. His chest stopped heaving. His mouth dropped open, and every bit of him went quiet and still.

Selene couldn't see through her tears. The others stood in silence.

Seconds passed.

Then minutes.

The stabbing cry she'd been holding back burst from her throat, echoing in her ears. He was gone, her brain screamed at her. *He was gone.* She clung to him as the ground tipped beneath her, and her heart tore her insides like a wild animal. She felt hands on her shoulders and arms, pulling her away. She could feel herself fighting them off, screaming and clawing like a lunatic, but her thoughts were frozen in ice. She was trapped in grief.

Jamie gasped for air.

Wrenching free from Fee's grip, she covered her sobs with her hands as she saw his chest rise and fall again. He was breathing. She was reaching for him when Fee took her in his arms again, his hold more gentle, but twice as firm.

"Wait," he said, speaking into her ear.

As they watched, the veins beneath Jamie's discolored skin began to throb, as though someone were pouring antifreeze into his bloodstream. She could see every artery, every capillary; the entire network of his circulatory system as currents of blue *Elec-*

tricus pulsed through them like blood. The volts sizzled under the visible portions of skin, running like tiny electric snakes to Jamie's extremities.

Slowly, color returned to his lips and fingers. His corpse-like flesh brightened into a healthy pink, and the blue currents under his skin reversed direction, like waves retreating from the shore. They slid across his chest, swirling within the Leech wound, and the skin healed and scabbed over. With each beat of his heart, the electricity seemed to grow fainter; his veins shrank smoothed out under his skin, and the current disappeared completely. The bracelet glimmered against his wrist and went dull once more.

He took a deep breath, sat up, and rubbed his eyes.

"Ouch."

"Jamie!" She pulled him into a fierce, bone-crushing hug, and she heard him grunt against her embrace. "Jamie…I thought you were…are you okay?"

"I feel like I just stuck my finger in a light socket," he replied, his voice muffled against her shoulder. "But yeah, I'm okay."

She buried her face in his jacket. He smelled like Jamie—that comforting, familiar mixture of sports deodorant and clean shampoo—but his clothes held the slight stench of burned fabric and the scent of a smoking electrical outlet.

"You scared me to death!" she breathed. "Don't you ever, ever do that to me again, do you hear me?"

Jamie tried to laugh, but she felt him wince. "I thought it was very dramatic. Consider it payback for making me think *you* were dead."

"Jamie, I'm so sor—"

"Forget it," he replied, hugging her closer. "You're alive. That's all that matters."

As she released him, he unwound his arms from around her and sat back with a tired smile. He wiped a bit of blood from his cheek and ran a hand through his thick red hair. But when he glanced up and their eyes met, Selene flinched. The eyes staring back at her were not Jamie's signature green.

The irises were a strikingly bright blue.

He caught her look and frowned. "What is it?"

Before she could answer, Nyx was between them, holding Jamie's arm up to the light, her attention shifting from his face to the bracelet fastened to his wrist. He froze at her touch, and looked at Selene, confused. She tried to smile back, but it took everything in her just to hold his strange, blue-eyed gaze.

"I can't believe it," said Nyx. "The talisman worked."

"What worked?" Jamie asked, staring at the bracelet, clearly seeing it for the first time on his wrist. "Selene, why am I wearing your old lady jewelry?"

Titus joined their party, kneeling beside Nyx to study the bracelet. Jamie kept looking at her, his expression demanding answers, but she wasn't the one to give them. Swallowing hard, she rubbed the scar on her wrist, exposed without the jewelry she'd worn for the last several years.

Titus held his hand out over Jamie, like he was testing the heat from a fire. "The talisman is somehow regulating the *Electricus* inside his body," he said, looking impressed. "And keeping it from consuming his organs."

Jamie's jaw dropped open.

"From doing *what* to my organs?"

Wrenching his arm from Nyx's fingers, he scooted backwards on the pier, his bright eyes taking in everyone, lingering on Fee long enough to glare, and then finally, returning to Selene. As she forced herself to look at him, she noticed that a few of the veins along his temples and neck were still visible, like little blue cobwebs. Jamie placed his hand on his chest and stared in horrified wonder at the scabbed-over wound.

"Please," he said, his voice cracking. "Please tell me what's going on."

It was Fee who answered.

"She saved your life, boy." His voice was even. Controlled. "She saved us all. If Selene hadn't closed the prison, we wouldn't be having this conversation right now."

"Worse," said Cruz. "The Apostates would've taken over the Viewers' bodies and gone free."

With a panicked expression, Jamie lurched to his feet, swaying precariously. Out of instinct, Selene jumped up as well, her hands reaching out to steady him, but he waved her off.

"Is that what's happened to me?" he demanded, his face ashen.

"Of course not," she said quickly.

Jamie blinked several times, and the weight of his strange stare pressed into her. She knew he wanted to believe her, and she didn't blame him that he didn't. After all, she'd started this whole thing by lying to him.

She looked to Fee, and he read her expression with little difficulty. Turning his face to the sky, he studied the low-lying clouds, and the flashes of lightning reflected in his coppery eyes.

"You heard Titus and Nyx," he said finally, sliding his gaze back to Jamie. "You have an overabundance of *Electricus* in your system, and the bracelet saved your life. If you'd been taken over by one of the most powerful Leech rulers of the Rebellion, who are capable of devastating entire worlds, I think I'd know it. Besides, an Apostate would never look at me the way you're looking at me now, like some helpless rat caught in a cage."

To Selene's surprise, Jamie didn't fire back a response. He didn't even look pissed. If anything, he seemed resigned, and she could almost swear there was gratitude in his eyes—although their new color made it more difficult to read his emotions, like she was so used to doing. Choosing to ignore that disconcerting thought, she brushed her damp hair out of her face and nodded back at him.

"You're okay," she said, barely managing her voice.

Jamie zipped up his jacket, hiding his burned t-shirt. He didn't reply.

Titus, who'd taken up residence on the edge of a large tacklebox, rose lightly to his feet and approached the railing while Selene glanced between the cracks of the pier. The dark water splashed lazily against the wooden supports, as though nothing had ever happened.

"So all this time," said Titus, "The Mocama Coil has been hiding the bodies of the Apostates. All these centuries, trapped here…and in a few moments, they nearly escaped."

"That about sums it up," said Cruz, crossing his large arms over his chest. "But your Bleeder here, she took care of that."

Fee cut a sharp look in Cruz' direction, a tempest brewing behind it. "Yes, she did. But that doesn't change the fact that you and I have a lot of talking to do."

Cruz frowned. "Phoebus—"

Fee's hand shot up, like a stop sign. "I didn't say we were going to talk here, Rogue. I'm tired, I'm hungry, and I'm not in the best

of moods. Besides, in case you haven't noticed, it's going to storm."
His eyes glittered like metal in the light. "And I hate getting wet."

Chapter 33

The walk across town was a slow one.

"Is this a pity-walk?" asked Jamie as they crossed the street into town.

Selene shrugged. "It's more like a I-want-to-hang-with-my-best-friend-who-almost-died kind of walk, actually."

She'd hoped for a smile in return, but he only dug his hands deeper into his pockets. "I'm fine, Selene. Honestly. You can stop looking at me like that."

"I'm not looking at you."

"Okay, well stop that, too."

They walked quietly for a few minutes, until they'd turned the corner lined with shops and eateries. Nothing was open, save for one small bar, nestled between a pottery studio and an antiques store. Fee was in the lead by several yards, and the rest of the group lagged behind, keeping her and Jamie squarely in the middle.

Jamie sucked in a breath, breaking the silence. "I just feel a little…different, that's all."

She cringed. "Different, how?"

"I don't know how to explain it," he replied, making a face. "Just a little charged, I guess. Like I've had one too many espressos." He glanced sideways at her. "Surely you can understand that feeling."

She tried not to stare at the little blue capillaries, visible against his temple. "Yeah."

"Anyway, it's probably just the near-death experience adrenaline. So, you can go and talk to him now."

"What?" Selene felt her cheeks grow hot. "Why would I do that?"

The edge of Jamie's lip turned up. It wasn't a smile or a grimace, but something in between.

"Because you want to," he said. "And I'm not going to let

your overactive sense of guilt keep you here." He glanced over his shoulder. "Besides, I think the tall dude is really itching to ask me some questions. He's been staring at me like I'm a science experiment since we left the pier."

Selene hugged her arms to her chest until her ribs ached. "I'm staying with you."

"No, you're not," he replied. "Go and talk to Psychopathic Robin Hood before he blows something up, or kills that Cruz guy. Or shoots me. I'd say everything's pretty much a lottery with him right now."

"Jamie—"

"We'll talk when you're done. I just...I just need a little time, okay?"

"Okay."

She reached for his hand, but he flinched away. Pushing down her guilt, she jogged ahead before she could change her mind, unsure whether what she was about to encounter would be better or worse.

Fee hadn't so much as blinked in her direction since they'd left the pier, and he didn't acknowledge her presence beside him now. His face was blank, his gaze preoccupied with something unseen ahead. A red welt had formed just above his jaw from her punch, which made her feel satisfied and horrible at the same time. Why was this all so freaking confusing?

"Is Jamie really okay?" she asked finally.

"You tell me," Fee replied, his tone crisp. No smug, crooked smile or easy swagger. He was coiled like a spring. "Contrary to everyone's popular—and generally accurate—beliefs, I don't know everything."

Taking a guarded look backward, she saw that Titus and Nyx had come up on either side of Jamie, matching his pace. He looked so out of place, with his dirty jeans and singed jacket, next to the two uniformed Rovers. She hadn't noticed it before, but she realized he was limping slightly, and his shoulders were bowed.

You refused a quick death for your friend.

Fee's words floated through her mind like an unwanted ghost, haunting her thoughts.

"Why didn't you kill him?" she asked. "It's not like I could've stopped you."

There was a tense pause.

"Because you didn't want me to," he replied.

Anger flared through her, unbidden and fierce.

"I see," she snapped, curling her fists. "So all your talk about duty and laws and rules, after almost murdering me in the marsh for the same reasons, you just suddenly change your mind, because I *asked* you not to do it—like that's supposed to be some noble sacrifice on your part?"

Under the streetlights, Fee's countenance took on a spectral glow.

"Don't you get it, Selene? It's you. You've messed me up in ways I can't even begin to figure out right now. I may not be overly fond of rat-boy back there, but you love him. If I'd gone through with it, you never would have forgiven me. I couldn't live with that." His jaw clenched so tightly his face twitched. "Think what you want of me, Selene, but I am not heartless."

"So your laws—"

"The law has been my mistress from the time I became a Rover. I'd spill my life's blood for the Tenets and to keep my world safe. Nothing else has mattered, until…"

He looked away, into the darkened windows of the shops.

His confession, incomplete and fragile as glass, hung awkwardly between them. The wind whipped through the streets, blowing in harshly from the water. Fee turned them off the main street, toward the inn, following the direction of a one-lane road untouched by streetlamps. Rain began to fall—first in small droplets, then growing into a steady drizzle.

Unclasping his *mantellum*, Fee draped it over her shoulders and tugged up the hood. A part of her—the part that was still raw, angry, and confused—wanted to refuse his gesture, but the material was warm and dry. It smelled like him—wild and earthy—and her heart beat faster, against her will. Her anger slowly melted into other emotions that weren't as easy to define.

"So what happens now?" she asked.

"To be honest," said Fee, lowering his voice. "I'm not entirely sure." His shoulder brushed against hers as they trudged through the rain. "I took a chance, trusting Cruz to lead us to the Leeches, but I had no idea of the depth of his involvement. After what I've seen tonight, I don't know what to think. Clearly, Regent Jareth was a traitor to Threshold. But what about Cruz?"

She squinted at him. "Can't you just leave him to the Elders?"

"No," he said, his voice firm. Two lines formed between his brows. "There is still much to uncover here, and I'm not sure how many are involved in this treachery back in my world."

"That other figure on the pier tonight," she said, as the image of Jamie falling over the rail flashed before her. "The one that got away..."

"Yes," he replied. The word was more of a sigh than a question or a declaration.

"It was someone from Threshold, wasn't it," she continued. "But you don't know who."

"I have my suspicions," he replied. "Although I have not, as of yet, allowed myself to fully dwell on them. But because of that, I intend to bide my time until I've uncovered the truth. Otherwise, it would be like springing a trap before the beast draws near."

"That was very poetic."

"What can I say?" he replied. "I'm a poetic soul."

Using the shelter of the hood, she was able to study him as they walked—the broad set of his shoulders, his confident stride. The style of his hair and the set of his jaw worked way more naturally with the Rover uniform than his regular clothes, and she felt as though she were truly seeing him for the first time, as he would be in his world.

Phoebus, the Rover leader, someone ages and dimensions apart from her.

"You're a lot of things, aren't you?" she said.

"All part of my charm," he replied. But the cocky, carefree smile he flashed didn't reach his caramel eyes or lighten the shadowed hollows of his features.

Taking a breath, she plunged ahead with what had been burning inside her for days. "Tell me the truth, Fee."

"What do you mean?" he asked in a voice edged with defensive barbs.

"The whole truth." She'd broached the subject, and she wasn't going to retreat. "About you."

She braced herself for another round of his sharp, biting remarks.

"It was a long time ago," he said abruptly, like he wanted to get the words out before he changed his mind. "Thresholders used to live among Othersiders. We helped them openly, using our powers at will. Many of us became legends in your world during those dark centuries."

She frowned. "What kind of—"

"It's not important anymore," he said, cutting her off. "They're just stories now." He paused, and she was afraid he was done talking. But the corners of his eyes twitched, as if he was forcing himself to continue. "I had just completed my apprenticeship and was serving as leader of my first Trine, out on assignment. There was an Other-sider girl. I loved her. But she became a threat." His eyes squeezed shut. "And she was killed."

She felt Fee's carefully designed walls falling around him, like a heavy curtain at the end of a play. The rain felt suddenly cold, hitting with the force of ice against her face.

"Because she was a Bleeder?"

He opened his eyes and nodded. The movement looked so painful that she cringed.

"I'm sorry," she whispered.

"Don't be," he replied. He drew in a breath and let it out. "It was another time. And another life." He peered through the rain. "After, I refused to have anything to do with this world. And I swore I'd never let my feelings get in the way of who I was. I'm a Rover, and I'm pledged to serve Threshold."

"And what do you feel now?"

Fee looked directly at her for the first time. His hair was wet and clung to his neck and jaw. Rain glistened against his skin, pooling under the hollows of his eyes. His crooked smile returned, though fainter than before.

"Too many things to stand here talking about now," he said in a leisurely tone. "Your Othersider rain is ruining my outfit."

"I'm sure you have dozens more in your closet," she said, running her hand across the fabric. "All lined up in perfect little rows and—"

"You did well tonight," Fee said, placing a finger against her mouth. His lips parted, revealing his teeth, bright against the dark-ness. "I must say, I had my doubts about you at first. But you're made of steel, Selene Windell."

She pulled his finger away and grinned. "A compliment from the great Phoebus himself. Must be a sign of the coming apocalypse."

As Fee leaned closer, the air felt suddenly charged. She forgot about the rain as she tilted her chin to meet his gaze. His hands slipped inside the cloak and wrapped around her waist, with a strong and comforting grip, and she stepped closer to him. She could feel his breath, warm against her wet skin. As he shook his head, flinging raindrops from his hair, his lopsided smile widened.

"You are so..."

"Yeah, I know," she replied, her lips nearly touching his. "Infuriating."

***

The rain beat against the roof of the *Seaside Inn* as Selene made her way down the stairs, toweling off her damp hair as she approached the foyer. The Rovers and Rogues were all gathered in the small living room. Green and tan *mantellums* hung over furniture, drying.

Selene noticed a large empty space above the mantel, and she realized the mirror was gone.

How long would that go unnoticed by people on the other side, she wondered.

Pausing under the entryway, she observed Fee, who lounged on the couch with an almost cat-like grace, deep in conversation with Cruz, while managing to take large sips of coffee. Despite the laziness of his posture, the tension in the room was so thick that Selene could taste it, like a sour piece of fruit.

"Just for the record," he said, glancing over his mug, "I still don't like you, and I definitely don't trust you."

Cruz smirked tightly. "Good. I wouldn't want things changing between us, just because of a little teamwork tonight."

"No worries there." Fee propped his muddy boots on the coffee table, soliciting an irritated sigh from Paloma. "And also for the record," he continued, "teamwork requires equal effort by both players. Kidnapping Viewers, allowing Leeches go on extraction binges, and then leaving me to figure it all out doesn't qualify as fair play in my book."

"Fair play," scoffed Cruz. "I hardly think Leeches care about that."

"They aren't Rovers," Fee replied icily. "You are."

Cruz settled into his chair. "Well, now that your job is done here, I'm sure Grimm will welcome you back with open arms."

"They'll throw a huge party, no doubt about that," said Fee, his tone smooth again. "Complete with all the trimmings. Too bad you won't be able to attend, being banished from Threshold and all."

"You think I care, Rover? I've made my life here, and it's a good life. Threshold and the Elders can go—"

"Careful," said Fee, holding up one finger. "You may say something you regret."

"They can't do anything to me," Cruz growled. "Their authority here is limited, at best. You and I both know that."

"I don't question their authority," said Fee.

"Of course not," said Cruz. "If you did, you might discover your high-moral loyalties are misplaced."

The Rogues and Rovers eyed each other with searing looks that Selene felt like a wave pressing against her, pushing her into the railing. Fee was the first to break the tension wall as he finished his coffee, set it aside, and leaned forward.

"You want to speak of loyalties," he said, "then, by all means, let's start with yours. On the pier, you said you'd struck a bargain with Regent Jareth...*Ji'roth*...to gain passage back to Threshold."

"I had to make them think I had motives for helping them," said Cruz, propping his arms against his knees. "We've spent years building a rapport with these Leeches, trying to discover who their leader was. I'd had my suspicions that he was from Threshold for some time. And he's obviously not the only one."

"Ah," said Fee. "But since he's dead, we have no way of knowing."

Cruz didn't blink. "But one got away, and we both know where it went."

Fee's expression was a solid mask. "Perhaps."

"You've always been a favorite among the Elders," Cruz replied, a sneer in his voice. "And you and Grimm are close. You have access to the upper echelon that few could ever boast. If there are other Leeches hiding out among the high class of Threshold, you could weed them out. You'd be a hero."

"And what, pray tell, makes you think I'd do that?"

Cruz smiled—but in a slow, deliberate fashion. "Because I know you, Phoebus. You love your glorious homeland, and the thought of anything vile within its borders is enough to turn your stomach. You have no choice but to return home and root it out."

All eyes were on Fee now, and the only sound was the soft crackle of the fire. Selene took another step inside, holding her breath, as Fee's gaze shifted around the room and then back to Cruz.

"Well, you don't know me very well," he said. "Because I'm not concerned with Threshold. It can take care of itself. Otherside is my priority right now. And after what I've seen over the course of the last few days, I've decided that I'm not very pleased with your leadership here." He placed his feet on the floor and brushed off his breeches. "Therefore, I'm taking charge of this Outpost until further notice."

Cruz bolted from of his chair. "Now wait just—"

"I could report your actions to the Assembly," Fee replied, his voice like glass. "Whatever your motives, you were conspiring with a traitor. That would earn you a punishment far worse than banishment. So I think we both agree that your fate is currently in my hands. After all, as you pointed out so eloquently just moments ago, I have a far better position among our people than you."

The tension tightened like a tourniquet.

"I could tell them that you've left the Bleeder alive," said Cruz.

"Yes, you could." Fee laced his fingers behind his head. His smile was lazy and dangerous, all at once. "However, between the two of us, whose report are the Elders going to believe?"

Cruz's eyes dulled like dying coals. "So what now, then? Where does that leave us?"

Setting into the cushions, Fee surveyed the room with a careless air, but Selene had come to recognize that he was actually calculating in his head, weighing his options. When he spoke, it seemed as though it took effort to get the words past his tongue, as if they tasted foul on his lips.

"We have knowledge of the Apostates because of the actions of your Trine," he said. "And that is information worth the restoration of your name and honor, when the time is right." Fee's copper eyes focused solely on Cruz. "For now, we need to work together, both to protect this Coil and also to uncover who is disloyal among our people."

"So, you're saying we forget the past?" Cruz crossed his arms warily, his brows lifting to his hairline. "Make a fresh start?"

"Oh, I wouldn't go that far. Let's just call it...an understanding."

Without warning, Fee turned his gaze toward the entrance, and Selene's breath stuck in her throat. She knew instantly that he'd been aware of her presence the entire time. She slung her towel over the railing and stepped inside the room.

"Am I interrupting something?"

Nyx, Titus, and Marcelo looked up from their seats, and Paloma collected the towel, offering a smile and a soft hand on her shoulder as she passed by.

Fee poured another cup of coffee. "I don't know. Is Selene interrupting something, Cruz? A disagreement of some kind?"

"Not at all," he replied, taking up his tea.

"How's weasel-rat-boy?" Fee asked, offering her the cup. "All tucked in and comfy?"

"I let *Jamie* use your bed," she answered sweetly. "Hope you don't mind."

He leaned back with a sigh. "Remind me to burn the sheets later."

She sat next to him on the couch and poured sugar into her coffee. "You know, two days ago, I would've chucked this mug in your face for insulting my best friend. But now I see it's all just an act with you."

"I disagree," he replied, his eyes sparkling in the firelight. "My disdain for your Othersider companion is no act."

"Jerk."

His lips quirked into his signature crooked smile. "It's my middle name."

"Really?" said Nyx. "I thought it was Bartholomew."

She ducked, avoiding the pillow Fee chucked at her, and sat on Selene's opposite side. There was genuine concern in her dark eyes.

"So, how's Jamie doing?" she asked.

Feeling the lump of guilt in her stomach grow heavier, Selene clutching the mug between her fingers as the heat radiated into her skin. Although Jamie had insisted he was fine, by the time they'd reached the inn, Fee and Titus had to help him up the front steps.

"He's sleeping right now," she replied. "He was really exhausted."

"Nearly being eaten alive by *Electricus* will do that to a person, I suppose," said Titus as he coaxed more flames from the fire with a brass poker. "Your bracelet saved his life."

She touched her empty wrist, where scar left from the lightning strike was evident against her skin. Taking a sideways glance at Fee, she found him staring at his hands, rubbing absently at his calloused fingers. The fire's glow illuminated his prominent nose and sharp features.

"It was really you who saved his life," she said. Fee's head lifted and she continued. "You got him out of the water, and I haven't even thanked you yet." She squeezed his hand. "Thank you."

His eyes softened into the caramel apple color she remembered seeing through the Rift. The tension melted from his jaw, and in that moment, she saw the boy in the ghost light again.

The boy whose face she'd never truly forgotten.

Fee smiled. "You're welcome."

PART FOUR

"Brief as the lightning in the collied night;
That, in a spleen, unfolds both heaven and Earth,
And ere a man hath power to say 'Behold!'
The jaws of darkness to devour it up.
So quick bright things come to confusion."

—A Midsummer Night's Dream

Chapter 34

"And does this conclude your report?"

Phoebus faced the amber mirror, which he'd replaced on the back of his bedroom door. Preceptor Moth stood on the other side, hooded and cloaked as usual, awaiting his answer.

"Yes," he replied. "The Bleeder died while closing the electrical field. The Viewers have returned safely to town, with no memory of the events, and my Trine is out with the Rogues now, making sure there are no other weaknesses near the Coil."

The hood swayed slightly. "That is good to hear." The Preceptor laced the fingers of her gloved hands together. "Regent Jareth had us all fooled. You and your Trine are to be commended for your actions."

Phoebus wanted to demand answers—about the Apostates and their prison, hidden within the Mocama Coil—but they were questions he would ask Grimm directly, not through this middle-Moth communication he was forced to endure at the moment. He was playing a delicate game with the Preceptor, and he refused to make any reckless moves.

"And what does Elder Grimm say?" he asked instead.

"He doesn't believe that was truly Jareth," said Moth with an edge to her marbled voice. "He suspects the Regent was murdered after the Rebellion and this Ji'roth took on his appearance, though I don't know how such a thing would be possible. To manipulate the *Electricus* in such a way, and for so long, is beyond anything I have experienced."

"But if he was able to do that, then—"

"There is no way of knowing how many of these Leeches may be in Threshold."

Although he'd come to the same conclusion, hearing the

Preceptor say it made his stomach turn. How could the Elders not sense their presence? Were these Leeches really that powerful, or were they getting help from somewhere—or *someone*—else? He trained his gaze on the ground to guard his thoughts. Moth was too good at reading him, even at his most guarded.

"What are my orders?" he asked.

"Grimm is meeting with Elder Ania now, and then they will take this information to the rest of the Elders. I will keep you informed as to the next course of action." She paused, regarding him intently. "As for you, Trine Leader, you will be placed on probation once you return, for disobeying orders."

Although he felt the sting, he didn't show it.

"Very well."

Unspoken words hung like a death shroud between them.

Phoebus sensed the thickness of the air on both sides of the mirror. Moth was holding something back as well, hidden within her deep hood. And neither one of them was fooling the other.

The Preceptor approached the mirror, as though it took effort. He'd never known her to lack in sleek fluidity, but the way she walked seemed to suggest something was going on. An injury, perhaps. His thoughts honed in on the memory of Ji'roth's companion.

Eerie blue eyes peered at him within the shadows of her hood.

"Say what you wish to say, Rover."

Phoebus hesitated. Once the words were out, he couldn't retrieve them.

"You were there," he said cautiously. "At the pier."

Moth's head lifted. And then, she raised her arms and slid back the hood of her *mantellum*. Phoebus worked to keep his mask in place. It never failed to take him by surprise when he saw her—perhaps now, after all that had just happened—even more than ever.

Blue veins framed the edges of her face, running in web-like patterns along her temples, cheeks, and neck, as though the *Electricus* in her body had leaked through her ashen skin. Her thick black hair was shot through with streaks of white. But her eyes disturbed him the most—they were Leech eyes, with tiny pupils and abnormally large irises; such a shocking blue that they seemed to glow from within.

"You still question my loyalties," she said, in a voice low and tinged with ice.

"The evidence speaks for itself," he replied.

Her eyes fixed on him with a penetrating gleam he found difficult to meet.

"You judge me solely on the condition from which I suffer. That is not evidence."

Phoebus paused, ordering his words. "There was a second cloaked figure on the pier who eluded us tonight. I never saw the face, but it wore the *mantellum* of a Preceptor."

Moth's unblinking eyes searched his own, and he felt like an apprentice again. But the tension between them was different now, charged and ready to ignite. When Moth spoke, her voice and her expression were as smooth as the amber of his longbow.

"Your accusation rings clearly behind your words, Rover," she said. "However, I do not answer to you, a Rover on probation." Moth pulled up the hood, and her face was hidden once more. "Think what you will of me, Phoebus, but know this: I owe my life to Threshold, and I will not see our world come to ruin."

The mirror hummed with electricity, and Preceptor Moth disappeared into the amber swirl.

Chapter 35

"So, you're saying I have to wear this thing *forever*?"

Jamie plopped down on the curb next to Selene in front of her house. He was dressed in a fresh pair of jeans and an old gray t-shirt with the retro *Atari* logo on the front, a big change from the last time she'd seen him: wet, dirty, and sporting a burn wound in the middle of his chest. He looked like Jamie again...mostly. Although he was wearing one new addition to his outfit: a pair of sunglasses.

The early evening light reflected off the metal on his wrist. As she reached for his arm, she felt him wince, but he didn't pull away. She moved her fingers over the bracelet and rubbed the smooth nameplate. It was warm to the touch and her skin tingled against the metal.

"I have no idea," she confessed. "None of the Rovers really know what to make of this. I mean, after what happened to you on the pier, their consensus is that you should be dead, or at least have some amnesia about everything, like the other Viewers."

He shrugged. "Well, I'm still breathing, and I can remember." He started to touch the metal as well, but hesitated, as though he were afraid of it. "It was fuzzy last night," he continued, his voice dropping in volume. "I just remembered bits and pieces. But after I woke up this morning, it all sort of came back to me."

Selene felt him shudder beside her.

"You saved those other people," she said. "If you and Paloma hadn't freed them—"

"They would've ended up like me."

His statement fell hard and heavy between them. It was just one more answer she didn't have for him. The image of the Apostates under the marshy water, staring up at her, ran through her mind constantly. If she hadn't closed the prison, she could've lost Jamie completely, his body gutted out and turned into a vehicle for one of those creatures.

She'd saved her best friend. But at what cost to him?

"Hey, don't get me wrong," he said, drawing his knees up to his chest and looking out toward the street. "I'm happy to still be on the planet. It's just taking some time to get used to everything."

Turning toward him, Selene studied his profile. Although his skin looked normal, there were traces of tiny veins that hadn't been visible before, along his temple and running down the edge of his jaw near his ear. Not too noticeable, but if she looked closely, the veins were more blue than the normal vein color under the skin.

"What do you mean?" she asked.

He glanced at the bracelet again. The veins on the underside of his arm were visible as well, and more pronounced around his wrist, where the bracelet was fastened. Grimacing, he wrapped his arms around his knees and shook his head.

"I can't really explain it," he replied. "Things just feel different."

She hesitated a moment, her fingers tracing her empty wrist, where her skin still bore the scar. "Well, if it helps, I feel kind of different, too."

He nodded absently, as though processing through things in his head. "So, your bracelet really is keeping me alive?"

"Yeah," she replied, trying not to cringe. "I don't understand it, but yeah."

He examined it with a critical frown. "You realize this isn't going to do much to improve my already questionable fashion sense."

"I know," she said, almost smiling. "Sorry about that."

A faint sense of hopeful relief mingled with the guilt in her chest. Jamie was taking everything incredibly well. The last time she'd seen him, the night before after walking him home, he hadn't been in nearly the same frame of mind. But now, sitting here, talking to him like everything was normal, it made her want to hug him frantically and cry like a baby, all at the same time.

But her heart wouldn't let her do either.

She was going to stay strong for him, no matter what.

"But what about you?" he asked. "I mean, it's your grandmother's. And don't you need the bracelet to help you do your Bleeder thing, whatever that is?" He scrunched his nose. "You know, that sounds really gross, saying it out loud."

"Yeah, remind me to take that up with those Elder people at some point."

Looking down the street, Selene felt a new sense of calm. After living in fear for almost three years, it was strange to feel settled in the idea that the marsh didn't bother her anymore, and the thunder and lightning she'd cowered from for so long were nothing compared to what she'd faced on the pier—and the scary but exhilarating power that had been at her disposal, even if only for a moment.

"Well?" Jamie pressed, when she didn't say anything.

"Titus thinks the bracelet kept my *Electricus* in check, and kept me hidden from Leeches all these years." She closed her eyes, concentrating on the slight buzzing current in the air. "But I don't think I'm going to need it anymore."

She sensed, rather than saw, Jamie nod beside her. After a few seconds, she opened her eyes and stole another glance in his direction. He was leaning back, enjoying the last rays of the evening sun, and his dark sunglasses—something she'd never seen him wear before today—stood out under his shock of red hair.

"Listen," she said, after a pause. "I'm sorry about Mudge."

"Yeah," he replied, rubbing his temples underneath his sunglasses. "They said they'd make it look like a drowning, since nobody can know the truth." He shuddered and sat up to face her. "He wasn't the most ambitious guy I've ever known. I mean, he lived with his cousin…bummed off him, really. And he didn't care much about anything other than gaming, to be honest." His shoulders jerked again. "But he was just a kid, you know? He didn't deserve what happened to him."

"Neither do you," she replied softly.

Jamie made a sound in the back of his throat that she couldn't quite interpret.

"I don't understand why Cruz is just getting off scot-free, like nothing happened," he said tightly, and his body visibly stiffened. "If you ask me, these Threshold people don't sound like they have anyone's best interest in mind but their own."

Selene half nodded. She didn't have an answer, because she wasn't sure how she felt, either.

"Are you sure you're okay?" he asked, in a softer voice.

"I hate it," she continued, the sour taste of helplessness on her tongue. "It's like this door that's been locked my whole life has opened up, and I don't want to close it. There's so much I want to understand, but I'm..."

"Scared?" finished Jamie.

Although she opened her mouth, she felt the bubbly words fizzle in her throat. The truth was, she wasn't scared. She was burning with excitement: the thrill of answered questions and untapped powers was mind-boggling, but the very thing she wanted to explore was the very thing that had caused him to nearly lose his life. And had left him with something she couldn't fix.

She couldn't tell him the truth.

"We can't change what's happened," she said, evading her own thoughts. "So I guess we just have to figure out what comes next."

Jamie shrugged. "School, I guess. Tomorrow *is* Monday."

"Right. I'd forgotten about that."

A shadow passed under the elm tree in her front yard. Although she couldn't see him, she knew he was there. Jamie stood and took off his sunglasses, rubbing the lenses with the edge of his shirt. She could tell by the look on his face that he also knew who was waiting for her, just a few yards away.

"It's okay, Selene." He helped her to her feet. "Go talk to him."

"Not now. I'm hanging with my best friend."

"And that's really sweet of you," he replied, with a smirk in his voice, "but I'm okay, really. There's a theatre supply shop over in Kingsland that's open 'til eight. I've gotta get some colored contacts." He tapped his temple. "My parents will be home from their trip tomorrow, and I don't think these will go unnoticed."

She forced herself to really, truly stare into his eerie blue eyes for the first time—so different from the soft green gaze she'd met nearly every day for the last three years. The pupils were smaller than normal, like they'd been permanently contracted, adding impact to the already unnatural color of the irises. An involuntary shudder went through her, despite her best efforts to stifle it.

Although Jamie caught her reaction, he managed to smile in return.

"Yeah," she said, "that's probably a good idea."

He replaced his sunglasses. "So I'll catch you later?"

She struggled to speak around the lump in her throat. "I was dragged into this whole thing because of what I am. But you didn't have to be. But you were, and now look what's happened to you." She stared at the cracked asphalt. "I know it doesn't mean much now, but for what it's worth," she whispered, "I'm so sorry."

"Hey, don't be," he replied, gently tugging a strand of her hair. The familiar gesture brought tears to her eyes. "Where you go, I go. Remember?" He took her hand in his. "This wasn't your fault, Selene. And if you hadn't done what you did, things would've been whole lot worse. I'm just sorry I couldn't help you more." His gaze flickered briefly to the tree again. "Guess I'll have to leave that up to the Rovers."

She hugged him, pressing her face into his shirt, holding him close and feeling like she was falling away at the same time.

"I love you, Jamie."

"I love you, too."

He squeezed her to his chest, kissed the top of her head, and she watched him walk away.

***

Fee was leaning against the white picket fence near the tree. His hair was loose, blowing in the autumn breeze, swirling like strands of honey around his face. Last night, he'd been in his Rover uniform, but today he was wearing a simple green shirt and dark jeans. The gleam of his lopsided grin warmed her all over.

"I was beginning to think you'd changed your mind about meeting me," he said as he pulled gracefully away from the fence.

"I was tempted, but my lack of reason won out."

Fee chuckled. His expression was easy and unguarded.

"Well, for the record, I'm glad," he replied as his fingers brushed her cheek. He looked over her shoulder. "How's the rat-boy?"

"Can we stop with the nickname?"

"Apologies," he replied, smirking. "I mean, Jamie."

"That's a loaded question," she replied, feeling her smile fade. "I wasn't expecting him to take everything so well, to be honest."

"Well, you're taking it very well, so is it really that difficult to believe he'd do the same?"

But it *was* different, and she knew it. For her, it felt like pieces of the giant puzzle of her life were finally settling into place and, as crazy as everything was, it somehow made sense. But Jamie…how did he fit into all this? He was an accident, caught in the crossfire of something he shouldn't have ever known. She wrapped her fingers around the scar on her wrist.

"Jamie doesn't deserve what happened to him," she said.

"Doesn't deserve his life being spared?" Fee questioned. He took her hand, and she felt sparks along her arm. "Because that's what's happened, Selene. And you are responsible for that. He'd be dead without you."

"I know. But that doesn't make things right."

Fee didn't answer. And there was nothing else she could say about it. She could only push down the guilt she knew would never go away. She released Fee's hand and started up the sidewalk toward her house.

He fell into step beside her.

She took a deep breath. "Are you going to erase his memory now?"

"No."

"What?" She searched his eyes. "But you said—"

"I know our protocols, thank you," he replied, his lips quirking again. Then he grew serious. "It wouldn't be fair to him. I don't know that his mind would be able to come up with a rational explanation for his current condition. So it's better that he remains as he is, for now."

Looking in the direction Jamie had left, her spine tingled uncomfortably as the image of his eerily blue eyes flashed before her.

"What *is* his current condition?"

"I wish I could tell you," Fee replied, and his tone was sincere. "What has happened to him is something new, and I am, frustratingly, as much in the dark as you are." A muscle worked in his jaw, and his hand curled into a fist. "However, I believe there is someone in Threshold that might know."

"Elder Grimm?" she asked. The name sounded strange on her tongue.

"Actually, no." His eyes carried a touch of that hard copper again. "There is…someone else. An acquaintance of mine, you might say."

As she studied his face, she attempted to read the unspoken thoughts beneath his words. His expression seemed conflicted, layered with thinly veiled anger. It was the same look she'd seen on their walk back from the pier the night before.

"Can this person help him?" she asked.

"Perhaps."

"Then, let's go," she said quickly. "Take me to Threshold and—"

"Now, wait a moment." Fee pulled up short in the middle of the sidewalk. "Just because you're a Bleeder doesn't mean you can flit about the dimensions however you please. Tapping into *Electricus* is a dangerous business. Regardless of your abilities, you are still an Othersider. It would require training."

A thrill of anticipation tickled the back of Selene's neck.

"Okay, so teach me."

He frowned. "Teach you."

"Yes," she said, feeling fresh hope fluttering inside her. "Nyx says you're the best Rover she's ever known, and you've trained apprentices for years. Surely it won't be that difficult for you."

Fee rubbed his jaw casually with his thumb, but she saw the spark of her challenge igniting slowly, burning through his doubtful expression.

"It would take time."

"Then it's good you're staying in St. Mary's for a while. Isn't that what you said last night?"

She caught sight of another trail of unnamed thoughts scrolling behind his eyes.

"Yes," he replied. "Elder Grimm thought it best, after the recent events."

"And you're staying at the inn?"

"It's a good thing, too," Fee replied, cocking his head to one side. "Have you noticed the state of the rooms and the ridiculous furniture? Someone has to bring the place up to par."

"So what, you're hanging up your bow and getting into interior decorating?"

His crooked smile returned. "Well, I was thinking more along the lines of hiring you to help manage the inn. With Leeches roaming about and your new abilities in development, I'm going to need to keep you pretty close."

"I see." She matched his smile with one of her own. "That's the *only* reason?"

"Not the only reason."

Fee's expression was amused, but his eyes were intense.

As they walked, the momentary quiet between them made Selene's heart skip a beat. Spending more time with Fee would be amazing, but the thought of tapping into that well of power inside her made her skin tingle. She would learn to control it, then she would find a way to fix her best friend.

"I'll take the job," she replied. "If you train me."

Fee fashioned a gleaming arrow in his hand and held it out. Without hesitation, she took it between her fingers. Blue electricity arced along the shaft and arrowhead, wrapping around her scarred wrist, filling her with heat and current. But it wasn't a burden. And it wasn't a curse.

It was a part of her.

Taking a deep breath, she pulled from that same place deep inside her that she'd used to close the electrical field, and the arrow vanished.

"So, what do you say?" she asked, smiling broadly up at Fee.

"A challenge I can't resist." Fee adjusted the cuffs of his shirt with an overly casual flair. "Very well. I'll train you. And I suppose providing you with employment will give you an adequate excuse to be spending so much time at the inn. Otherwise, your mother might take issue with me."

"Speaking of my mother," she said as they reached her front porch. "She's got food waiting."

His brow quirked. "Taking me home to mother, are you?"

"Don't flatter yourself. It's just dinner. My mom's idea, of course."

"Of course," he replied, taking her hand. "After all, how dangerous can that be?"

She laughed. "You don't know my mother."

They stepped inside and closed the door.

ACKNOWLEDGMENTS

Thank you God, for giving me so many opportunities to stretch my creative wings. You are my everything, and I remain humbled and grateful. Proverbs 16:3.

Thanks to my family – who remain my biggest fans. To my parents, my in-laws, to my husband (and unwavering supporter) Doug, and to my boys Justin and Liam (thank you, Liam, for your technical know-how) . . . I love you!

Thank you, Trail Mix! Not only are you an amazing and talented critique group, but you are also truly wonderful friends. Thanks for always being in my corner.

Thanks to my special circles of friends. I wouldn't be here without you. A special shout-out to Erica and Heather, for all the prayers and encouragement, as well as to my beautiful students, both past and present. You inspire me.

Lydia Craft, thank you for all the work and the enthusiasm you poured into this project. Your editing was a Godsend. Thank you Christina Lewis, for having a brilliant set of eyes and going over the copy edits with a fine-toothed comb.

And finally, thank you to all my readers from all over the world, and to those who have supported me online and across my various author, writing, and cosplay platforms. You are all fantastic. Thank you so very much!

ABOUT THE AUTHOR

Christi J. Whitney is also the author of The Romany Outcasts Series (which includes Grey, Shadow, and Midnight) She lives just outside Atlanta with her husband and two sons. When not spending time with them or taking a ridiculous number of trips to Disney World, she can be found teaching high school, directing plays, making costumes for sci-fi/fantasy conventions, obsessing over time traveling doctors or cloak-billowing potions masters, and pretending she's just a tad bit British.

You can visit her online at www.christijwhitney.com.

Or follow:

Instagram / christijwhitney
TikTok / christijwhitney
Facebook / christijwhitney
Twitter.com / christijwhitney

CPSIA information can be obtained
at www.ICGtesting.com
Printed in the USA
LVHW090724130322
713329LV00020B/289